Happy Birthday Big Dan!

TJ

TJ is a member of our Washington Arms Collectors. About 15,000 members. This is his first attempt as an author. Enjoy the book!

Gregg

SOME SORT OF STAND

of Wolves and Dogs

UBS PRESS
Seattle, Wa

My sincere thanks:

I want to offer my humble thanks to my Maker and for the time and talent (or lack of it) that I have been loaned. Hopefully I am not wasting it. And... using it on a book is being a good steward of the precious gifts.

I wanted to express my earnest appreciation to these editorial personalities for their constant presence on my drives all over the west. These people: Snow, Beck, Limbaugh, O'Reilly, Harvey, Ramsey, Levin, Gibson, Napolitano, Hannity, Miller, Medved, Savage, Liddy, Schlessinger, Boortz and Ingraham have been challenging me with their ideas, their passions and their intellects; keeping me awake on the many miles alone. Please keep up the struggle for what's right.

Much gratitude (You will never know how much) to my Family. First off, to Christina for being the greatest editor extraordinaire. You put so much time, effort and energy into making this story better and helping me corral my squirrels. Your cover help was also massively appreciated. You are a constant voice of quiet wisdom. I appreciate your efforts. I am grateful also for the time Connor, Aidan, Toby, Sarah, Uncle Bob and Kelly have given to this project. All of your corrections/ideas/suggestions were crucial and important to make this novel what it is.

To my cousin, Brecke– Go Bears! Thanks for your assistance and opinions in crafting a better novel. Your work on the book proof was welcomed.

Thank you Sophia, for all of the support you have provided me at this time in my life.

To Tammy– I appreciated the point toward self-publishing/local publishers and the encouragement to take this book to print.

Thanks a bunch to my dear friend, Jason, for being the great sounding board and giving no holds barred opinions on the mechanics and function of the story.

Jori Saeger- for the use of your great cover photo! www.JoriSaeger.com

Kevin- thanks for the invaluable input on the emergency response facets of the story. You added further realistic details that I needed to make the novel the best I could.

To Rachael- I'm grateful for all of the inside publishing help.

Michael– Thanks for helping me construct this book.

Angela- Thanks for the help with editing.

To everyone else that helped and I have forgotten- I promise to put you in the next one... that's accepting the premise that the loan hasn't been revoked!

Blessings,

– T J –

SOME SORT OF STAND
of Wolves and Dogs

A NOVEL BY

TJ SCAR

UBS PRESS
Seattle, Wa

UBS PRESS

4326 University Way NE

Seattle, Wa

www.bookstore.washington.edu/books

publish@ubookstore.com

Copyright © 2014 T. J. Scar

All rights reserved. No part of this book may be reproduced, scanned, or distributed in any printed or electronic form without permission. Please do not participate in or encourage piracy of copyrighted materials 'cause it's just not nice! Furthermore, it's a violation of the author's rights and various federal and state laws. Copyrights fuel creativity, promotes free speech and creates an atmosphere for more authors to write more books. Thank you for purchasing an authorized edition.

Library of Congress Cataloging-in-Publication Data

Scar, T.J.
Some Sort of Stand / T.J. Scar

ISBN 978-1-937358-46-4

1. Hijacking— Fiction 2. Seattle (W.A.) —Fiction

3. Terrorism—Fiction

4. International Relations—Fiction   I. Title.

Printed in the United States of America

8   6   4   2   1 - 3   5   7   9   10

BOOK DESIGN BY T.J. SCAR
Publishing Coordinators Michael Wallenfels & Josh Nollette

This is a fictional story set in a real place. Names, characters, places, and incidents are solely the product of the authors' imagination or are used fictitiously. Any resemblance to actual persons, living or dead, business, companies, events, or locales is entirely coincidental.

All rights reserved. Cover photo is the exclusive property of Jori Saeger and is used by her permission. Interior photographs are the exclusive property of TJ Scar and are used by his permission. No unauthorized reproduction or duplication of the copy or the photographs is allowed unless granted use by the respective owners.

This work of fiction is dedicated to all of those that we have lost, never to return. High on my list are: Timothy, Irene, Mr. Clancy, Mr. Crichton and Mr. L'amour. May the memory of their lives, and their presence; live forever.

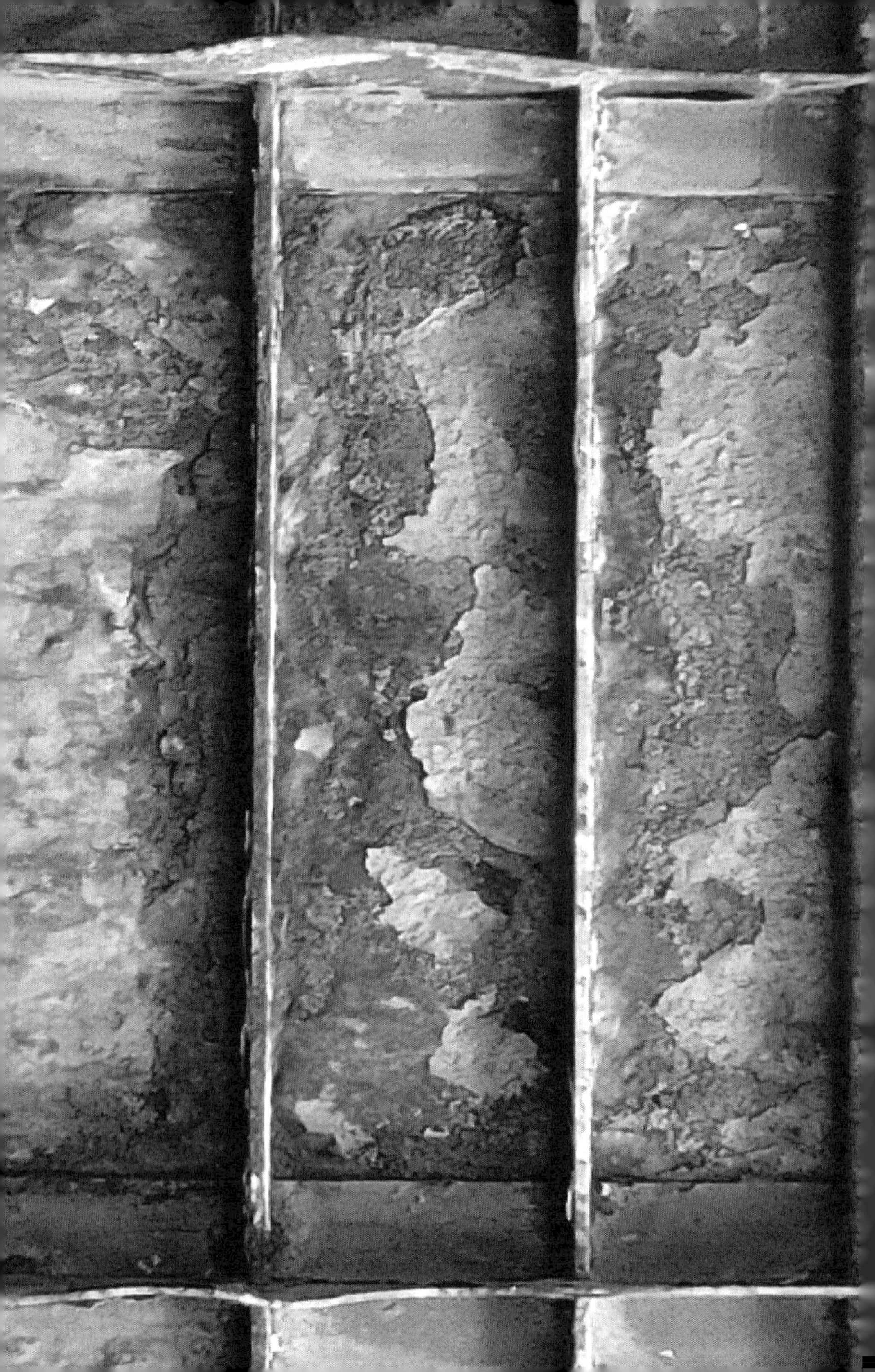

Foreword

Most people agree that in the beginning there was a void. A vast and yet empty absentness that was everything and nothing. This expanse was as infinite as it was measureless, from this side of the here, all of the way to there. An eternal maw without substance or form.

Out of that nothing, from that indefinable blankness, came forth all. Whether you believe in Creation, and God speaking it into existence; Evolution, where two random particles collided to start it all or some other universe origin belief, sooner or possibly later, humankind stepped forth.

Up and out of the varied species and numerous organisms to lay claim to terra firma, we humans were but one. What we had either been made for or had evolved to, was the big question. Pondered over the centuries by religion, science, philosophy and psychology; they all had their say. Despite often opposing beliefs, they all agreed on one thing: The humans were a flawed and weak creature.

For at the very beginning, our species was a naked, defenseless and totally ill equipped animal. We were placed in a very cruel, heartless and deadly world. Look at ourselves. Take notice as to what we were naturally equipped with to deal with the brutality. With nothing. Just like the void from which we spawned.

From birth we couldn't walk or run away until *years* later. Along with our families and maybe our tribe, it seemed we could only barricade ourselves in caves until any possible danger passed us by. Sometimes we could stay in sufficient numbers to dissuade the attacks, but that was all.

We couldn't fly like a bird to escape danger or dive unnoticed, out of the blue, for a surprise attack. We weren't armed to fight like a great Bengal Tiger, or Komodo Dragon. There were plenty of other creatures that seemed far more capable to withstand, avoid or flee from peril. When we compared ourselves to animals, we were soft and frail; without armor, wings, speed, claws, or sharp teeth.

Yet, we weren't defenseless were we? Didn't we, as a species, possess traits superior to other mammals? We have a larger brain, as a ratio to our size, compared to other animals. With this thinking brain, we were gifted or we cultivated an imagination. With that, and our intellect, we formed verbal and written languages. With our imagination and speech, we shared our ideas over distance and through time. Ideas would live on into future generations even after the originator had long passed on.

Either by divine providence or adaptation, humankind became cognizant of the ability to observe, to think critically and to invent. Ancient cultures saw the world around it and all of the creatures therein. Our ancestors began to copy and steal the greatest features from every type of animal. Those ancients used animal's natural traits for their own use.

Our ancient ancestors figured out how to build armor better than animal hide or scale. They built long blades better than tooth, tusk or claw. They developed weapons, like the arrow, that mimicked the flight of a bird in order to fight threats at a safe distance. The ancients took further cues and organized fighting men, armies, in groups to attack; like that of a wolf pack or lion pride.

Fire became a tool with our command of it. Fire lighted our way, pushing back the darkness. It became a fearsome weapon; making all threats flee or get caught up in its fury. Fire: the world's first scorched earth combat. Those early peoples survived by their cunning and by their violence, by their use of fire, by their inventiveness and their newly inspired technologies.

By wisdom, and because of their courage, our ancestors survived to live another day. Our early relatives did something else to harness animal's traits. The human began to rule over other animals; by domesticating them.

Those domesticated animals, through selective breeding, became unlike their undomesticated, wild cousins. Their cousins maintained a level of careless violence for their fellow kind that was dangerous to us. Nature was indeed a violent and harsh place, with constant grim realities. Our ancestors did their best to bred the wild out of the domesticated animals the best they could.

Yet, the more humankind tried to separate ourselves from natures law, the more we saw that the natural cycle can never be escaped. Life and death, peace and war, stronger and weaker. The age old maxim still held true: The strong will prey on the weak. But was it just the animals? Weren't some of our own kind very similar?

Out there, walking this earth on two legs, there are violent predators too. Capable only of sadistically feeding themselves; kind of like rogue lions from the Tsavo River. These violent people would rather destroy anything that comes across their path, than let it pass unmolested. There are some that would lie in wait to surprise attack an unsuspecting victim like that of a leopard or a crocodile. Some join together to form gangs in order to protect themselves, their enterprise; their territory. They even gather in groups to carry out crimes against others; just like packs of wolves.

There are others, ones that do not prey on their fellow man, but walk within a place of total apathy. They remain content to film the horrible sights before their eyes in order to quickly post it on YouTube. If these unconcerned ones don't post it, they might duck their heads and meekly hide; kind of like the cave dwellers of eons past, barricading themselves within.

These 'watchers' are either full of a total lack of concern for their neighbors or filled with such fear that they don't dare get involved. It seems that they possess a false hope that the human predators of the world will avoid them and theirs. Or maybe they are just so self-absorbed that they have lost all empathy?

What the watchers fail to realize; is that they just might be next when leaving the safety and security of their barricades; their homes. Can it be called contentment when you live to survive another day only to be fortified behind walls?

At last, there are the final few: The exceptional soul.

The person that takes a stand.

They are that rare individual that gets featured prominently in 'hero' stories from the media or in the annals of history books. It is this type of noble soul that actors pretend to be onscreen or stage. There are a selective few of us, that have had the chance to personally know some of these extraordinary men and women.

It is these extraordinary people, these rare souls, that are the ones that plant their feet down and say, "No more!" And to them we owe so much.

They have a unique type of inner character; seeing a harmful thing about to befall another and their first urge is *not to run away or watch*. On the contrary, they either throw up an alert or take direct action to *stop it*. These are the ones that continue the struggle against the proverbial lions and wolves, the crocodiles and the panthers of the world.

This last kind of person, this exceptional gift to us, will loyally serve and protect their fellow human beings, against any threat or danger. They do so out of a deep respect for life, yet totally willing to sacrifice their own lives. They *volunteer* to immerse themselves into *real danger* and the very possible shredding of their own psyches and their bodies.

They are humankind's very own sheep dogs.

Whether this rare person is highly skilled, pedigreed and professionally trained or just a common mutt. They will come to the rescue. Sometimes they come in body armor, out of the dark, and the smoke. On other occasions unprotected, just seemingly to appear out of thin air during the sounds of the sirens or screams. Sometimes, they come forth anonymously from the crowds that were only posting video. Other times, these sheep dogs, arrive purposefully out of great machines.

They use every trait that they possess, given to them by God or random chance, to pull their fellow human beings out of the maelstroms.

It is these unique personalities, these sheepdogs, that will be there to take action. Always landing in the *worst* possible places, at *exactly* the right time. They will come to lend a hand or to jump right in. Whenever they can, to do whatever they must; like guardian angels emerging out of nowhere, to provide aid, security and comfort.

Even if it's to sacrifice themselves to save a stranger.

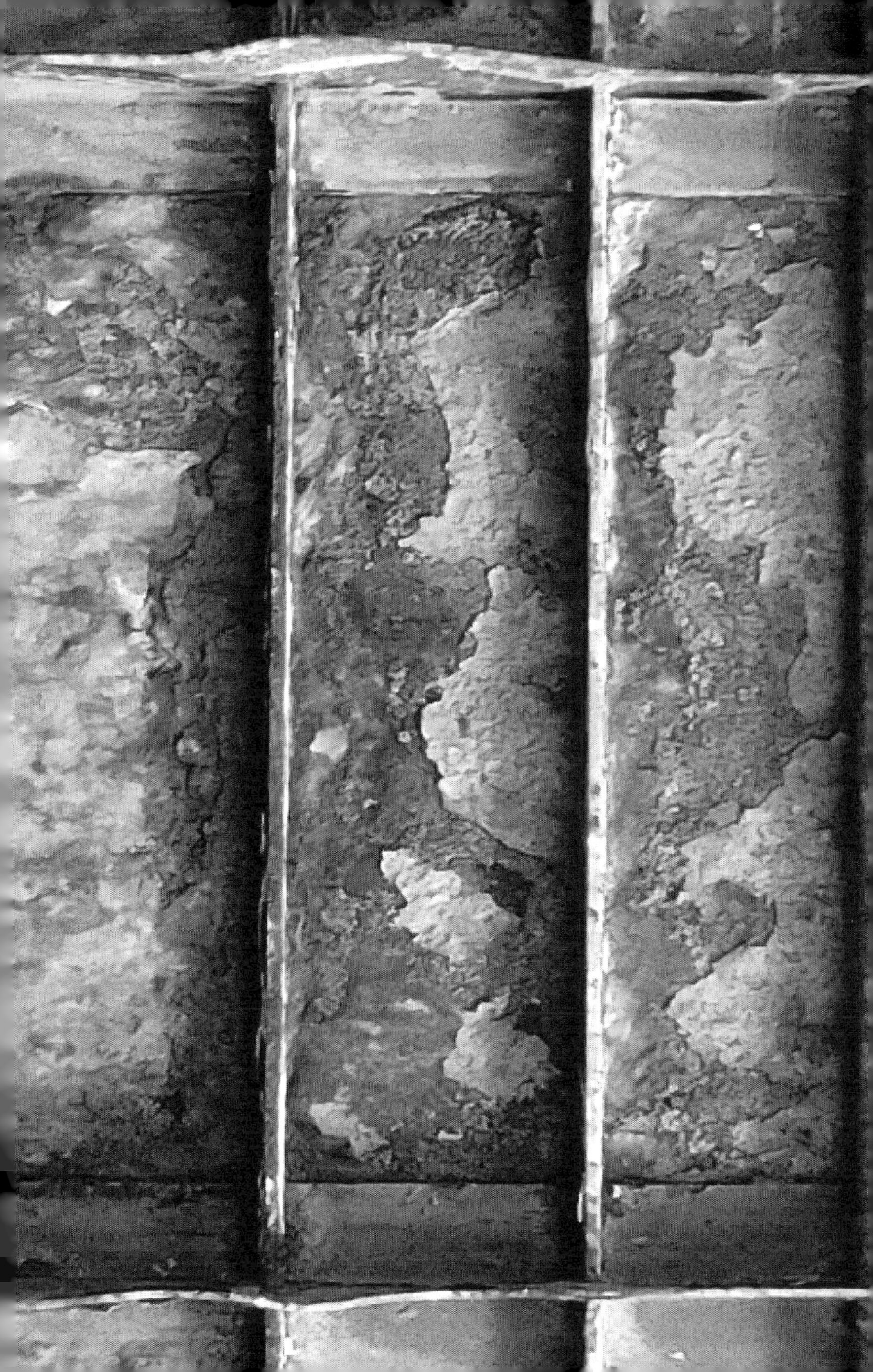

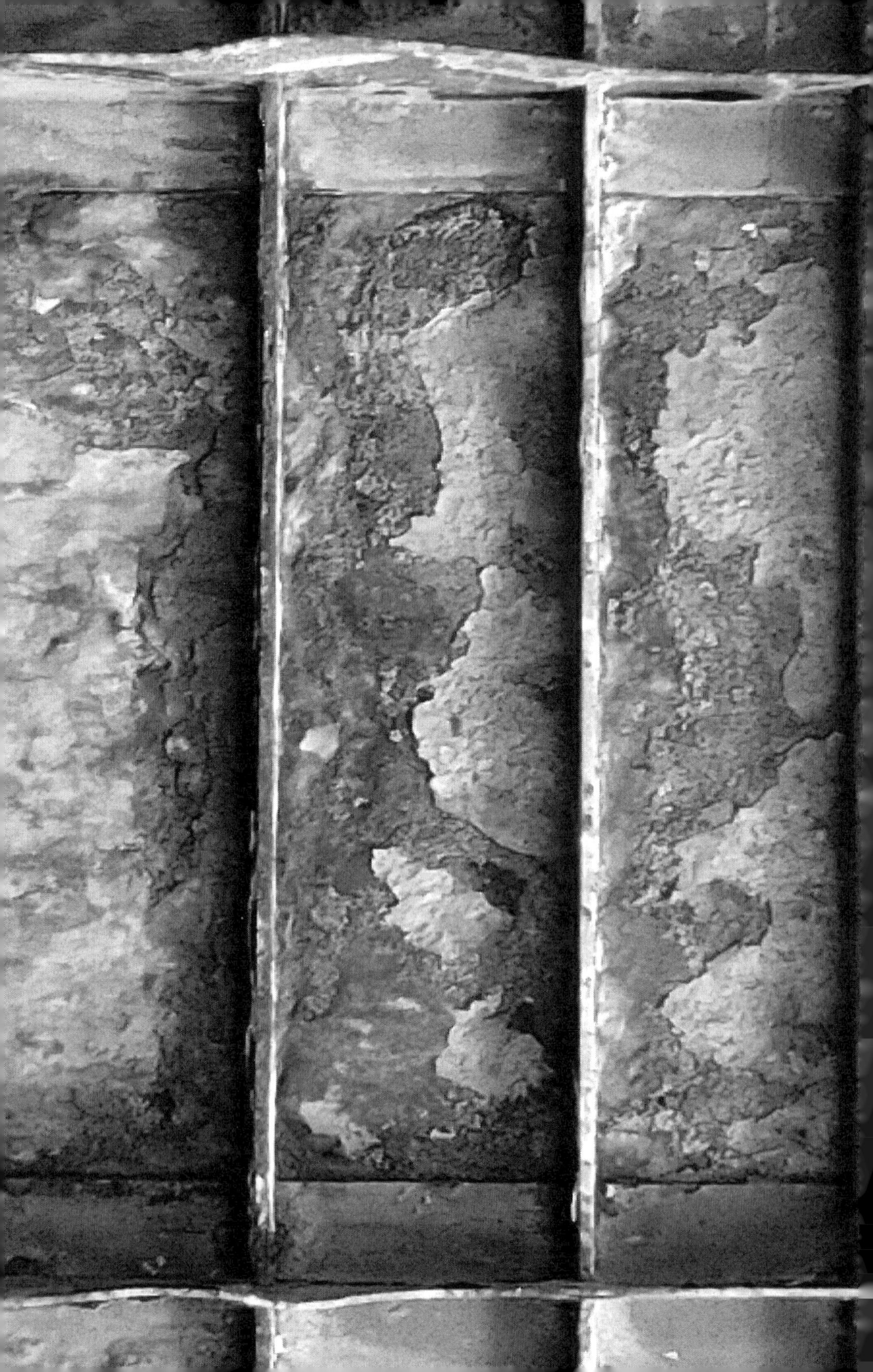

Part One

" If you have no capacity for violence, then you are a healthy productive citizen, you are a sheep. If you have a capacity for violence and no empathy for your fellow citizens, then you have defined yourself an aggressive sociopath; a wolf. But, what if you have a capacity for violence, and also a deep love for your fellow citizens? What do you have then? A sheepdog..."

-Lieutenant Colonel (Ret) Dave Grossman, Author: *On Killing: The Psychological Cost of Learning to Kill in War and Society*

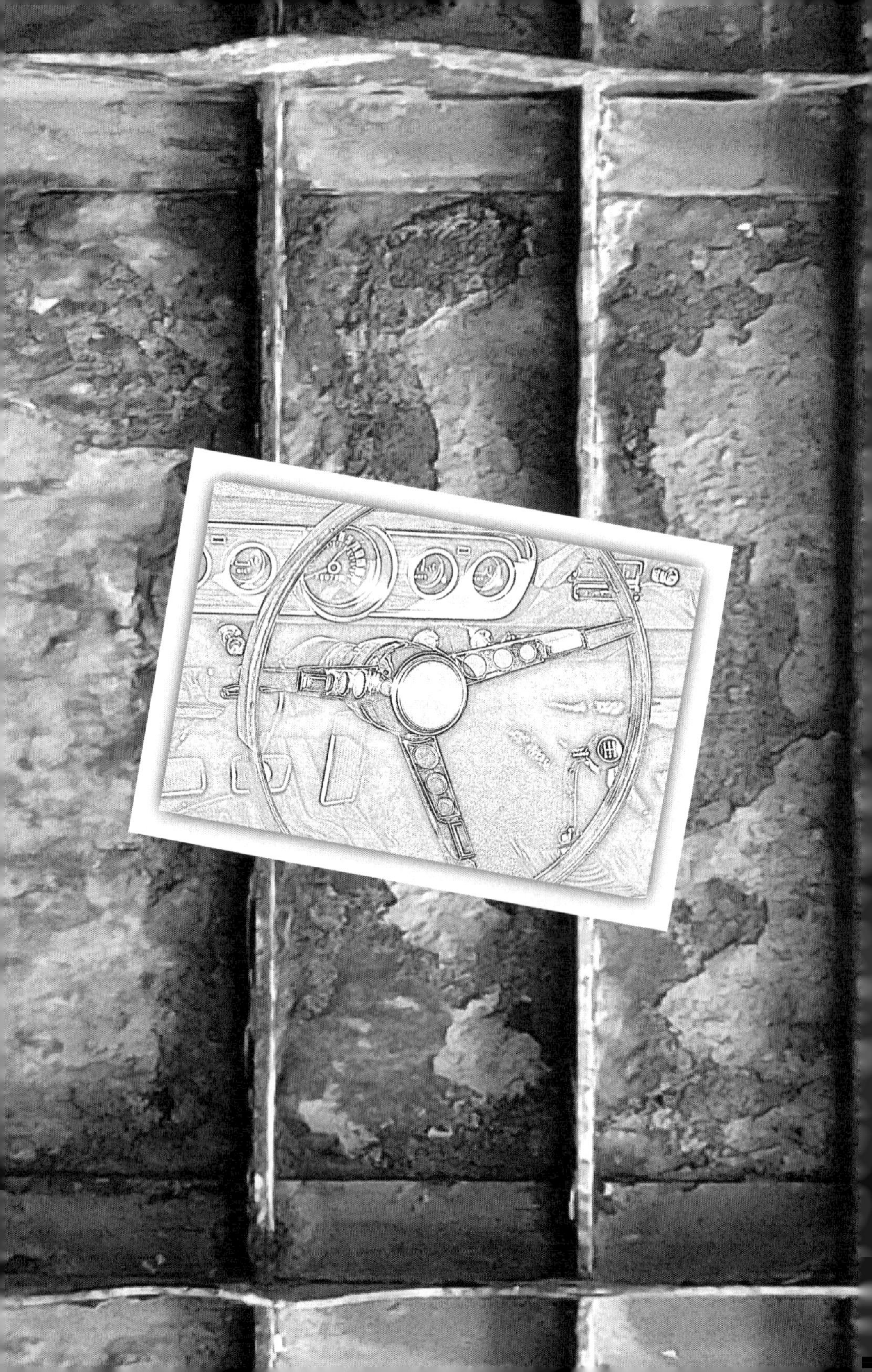

Chapter One

A Lifetime ago...

Nassir al Din had emptiness in his very being. It endured there like a hot ember that would never go out. For as long as he could remember the hollow could not be filled; ever.

There simply was neither a religion nor a relationship that could satisfy the void. Not a treasure made on earth, nor tranquil place that he visited could give him peace for long. He had seen the world and he had met lots of people. Nasir had held many valuable treasures and found all of it...plain. Oh, he still searched high, and low, for someone or something or some book that could rise to his requirement, but...he had not found it yet.

Nassir was a frequent visitor to mosque. Not because the man was religiously devout and not because an overwhelming faith beckoned him to kneel. No, it was obligation. A promise he once made to his mother. In life he found, that some promises he made, he had no intention of keeping; and he was able to rationalize them away. Some promises he had every intention of keeping, but life, time and circumstances caused him to abandon them; much to his heartbreak. And yet still, there were *other promises* that without rhyme or reason, cause or effect, *fate has allowed him* to keep them. The promise he made to his beautiful mother was one of these last ones.

May Allah keep her safe and warm...

Nassir was still in his prime. He was strong, capable, intense and quick. He kept up with the latest trends- styles of clothes, sunglasses, nuances of speech, and tech devices; without drawing too much attention to himself. For Nassir needed a little distance to hide the dark pit that existed in his soul. Yes, the man did so with an easy manner and a perpetual smile, but the hole was there nevertheless. It always was calling for more; an insatiable appetite to experience something that would finally extinguish the unquenchable need.

Nassir al Din hid a lot deep down inside, it just made it easier for him to blend in among peers and strangers alike. Life was too short to show people their own failings or shortcomings; which he tended to do once he became acquainted. *Much to my detriment...*Nassir came to find that bringing up someone else's faults for discussion or to share his own demons caused arguments and hurt feelings. *My kind of clear, straightforward logic was lost on most.*

Well, the people I had met so far...

If you were to meet Nasir al Din in the street, and you were very young, a woman or elderly; he would open the door for you. He would stand tall and strong, yet he would smile and respond a "you're welcome" to your "thank you." In that moment of passing he would have radiated to you an honest, truthful smile that came out in his words and actions.

Despite his ember of discontent, Nasir could emanate a kind of safety and comfort. It came from some part of himself that Nasir didn't fully understand. *Maybe I gave away that part of me so much that there was nothing left for when I walked into those quiet times; those time alone?* Regardless, there wasn't a single person in Nassir's life that would think he'd be involved in anything unlawful. Well, maybe just one. His best friend Dizhwar.

Nassir kept himself in shape, not for vanity, no that was far too shallow. He did so for other reasons– One, he loved antique auto racing. Managing the high-speed stress on his body and mind forced him to stay healthy for those grueling races. And the second reason was that the world's two holiest of books, the Quran and the Holy Bible, taught that the body was a temple. "But waste not by excess for God loves not the wasters." Quran 7:31 taught. 1 Corinthians 6:19 also instructed, "Do you not know that your body is a temple of the Holy Spirit, Who is in you, whom you have received from God?"

Nasir's reasoning was sound, like putting together one plus one, *just like the cars that I drove, my temple shouldn't be run down or poorly maintained. After all, you only get one life, one chance at this...and two holy books couldn't be wrong.*

Nassir was the most unusual of all of Dizhwar's recruits.

Nassir al Din had been all over the Middle East, North Africa, the Baltic's and the United States. It was all on behalf of his maternal grandfather and his grandfather's successful company. His grandfather's company, White Sands Engineering, was a long lasting and powerful family legacy. The business was started in the mid 50's by Nassir's great grandfather. After World War II, yet another of history's empires, namely the British, was failing. So with their control shrinking, the British granted national sovereignty to the country of his grandfather. White Sands started off drilling, derrick construction and later; pipeline design. They streamlined where they could, ran lean, worked hard and produced results. Later, they dove in deep into the business of making the arduous and dangerous process of refining oil cheaper and safer.

Nassir was happier and more content than he had ever been in his life. A goal, a dream, had been recently achieved when he reunited with his mother's family. Nassir, mostly a quiet man, worked at a well paying job with people that loved and respected him and he them. Yet, he still looked for the next thing, never satisfied with what he had. The darkness that no light would push away drove him to *more*. That was when Nassir became involved in what he considered to be the greatest hobby of them all: the vintage automobile racing. Mostly the American muscle cars of the 60's and 70's.

Hence his double entendre nickname of Driver. Gabriel = Nassir = Driver. Different names for distinctly different times of his life.

He was born far removed from his current wealth and privilege. Something he was just starting to become accustomed to. Nassir al Din came into this world, Gabriel Nassir Matthews, in semi-rural Yakima, Washington. Under the three hundred days of sun, and witnessing the magnificent Mt. Rainier, he grew up. His father, a Washingtonian native farm boy, met his mother when the elder Matthews was in Saudi Arabia as a military liaison, years prior to the first Gulf War.

Gabriel knew the story too well; his mother was swept off of her feet by the young and dashing American. His father had a way to charm and impress. Gabriel's parents fell in love quickly, and they would sneak out together whenever they could. Gabriel's father, John Matthews, was in the country as a "technical advisor" to the Saudi military. John supplied information, intelligence and even hands-on training in the use of the American weapons that were pouring into Saudi Arabia. For Iraq was on the rise, Saddam Hussein wanted Saudi oil for his own, and the Saudi princes could see the Saddam storm coming.

Gabriel's mother, Inayah, was a native Kuwaiti and worked for her father at one of the oil refineries there in Saudi Arabia. She had attended college in America and graduated with a Master's Degree in Chemical Engineering. Having learned the oil business from a young age from her grandfather and father. After graduation in America, she moved back with a faint hope that she could change peoples minds in her own country. But she couldn't approach and explain how she felt to her father. For Inayah's father supported the traditional customs of women being submissive to all men. So that left her as an advisor to a refinery. Everything she presented had to be funneled first through her male supervisor because this was customary. Males were in charge after all, and she could not offend any Saudi males.

Inayah bristled at the backwardness of it, but she held her tongue. Often, she knew more than her male counterparts. She sometimes even felt like screaming; being a less knowledgeable man's subordinate. She had experienced such freedom in America, yet did not want to live so far away from the homeland she dearly loved.

But the caviler American that she had met supported her breaking away from the eastern traditions. Slowly, she became strengthened by the suave American's encouragement. Yet she still couldn't bring herself to speak to her father. Traditions or freedom, the vast deserts or America; the conflict was constantly raging within her.

The pair's lives and love became intertwined and then much more. In fact, they became out-of-control complex, within eighteen months of meeting. Gabriel' mother Inayah became pregnant. The pair had known better not to get involved and then to get intimate. Yet they did, so in fear for her personal safety, Inayah left everything she knew for a new life as a woman, unmarried-pregnant, political refugee.

Inayah's embarrassment over her and her husband's behavior was still apparent on her face, years later as she related the tale to her son. Because of her choices, she was cut off of all family ties, her parents' wealth, her Muslim faith and her precious homeland.

Inayah, and John lived at the secure embassy housing, after her political asylum was accepted. They were married by a chaplain there at base housing. Later, just as the Gulf War broke out, she was sent to live with her new in-laws in Yakima. On her arrival stateside, Inayah gave birth to her first child, Gabriel, and then waited for her husband to return from war.

Gabriel's father returned home soon. When he left the military, he had served his country honorably in the Marines for one tour; as technical advisor for most of it. He rotated from the Marines to a special operator for the clandestine services after that. The hard working, salt of the earth, John Matthews, retired from all services after ten years and joined his parents at the family farm in Yakima.

Gabriel Nassir Matthews always felt like he didn't fit in. He had an unusual middle name, his mother was clearly not from central Washington *and he looked so different; almost Mexican, but not quite.* At his school, around his peers or even in the state he lived in, he and his mother always got *looks*.

On particularly bad days, when as a young boy, Gabriel would come home with a hurt spirit or a split lip or bruised face. He had been defending his Arabic lineage and , he felt, his mother's honor. It was during those times, coming home from school, that Inayah would tell him stories.

She had explained, "You are home and safe with me. Someday I will take you to a place where so much of what we will experience is belonging. So much of my life, before I met your father, showed me that. We don't realize sometimes that we have in front of us is very precious and what we flee to can be much worse." Gabriel could remember her voice, it was so vividly beautiful with a flowing accented English that the child just couldn't get enough of. "My homeland; from the sand that was ever-present in my town, to the weather, to the open air markets, to even my stern father, was welcoming me." She went on about her faith and her old life. "I just didn't know it. So, my precious Gabriel, you have it good here and someday you will probably feel better about this place like I do about where I was born."

Yet the boy was not listing to her comfort. He was listening to his mother fill his head about *what was before* she came to the United States. And the son always felt a bit responsible for taking it all away. The places she talked about and the things she did when she was young, always filled Gabriel's mind with an exotic longing for the desert. To transplant himself and his mother *back* to a better place. Despite the fact that Gabriel never lived there.

Through their talks and spending so much time with her, he had picked up her Arabic and Farsi at a young age. Sometimes he would talk to his mother in her native tongue without ever using English. Gabriel wished his mother could go back to the Middle East. Eventually she was able to reconnect to her siblings, but Inayah was never able to repair the connections with her mother or father again. Despite the entire Matthews family visiting Kuwait many times, Inayah's parents refused all attempts to make contact. Even the attempts made by her husband and son were ignored.

The life of Gabriel's father, military veteran, entrepreneur, and small business owner, was a busy one. John was able to build enough wealth to purchase his parent's farm and an additional, larger farm in Redding, California. The man was savvy and had a way with cattle, growing things and land. So the young Gabriel saw his father seldom. The son would see his father at the occasional dinner table meal, the infrequent day off or the rare family vacation. Gabriel, and later his two sisters, were raised by Inayah and his paternal grandmother.

Through Gabriel's eyes his mother was a saint. Early on in the boy's life she willingly took them to the local Christian church. It was father's will and the paternal grandparents tradition. At that time, his mother would do anything because it was his father who asked it. Occasionally, John would attend church and Gabriel could see his dad's genuine faith in God. The older man was a no-nonsense, work hard, sacrifice-everything-for-some-lofty-goal-kind-of-man. Yet, through some child-like intuition, the boy knew, his mother believed differently.

So at thirteen, right after moving into a new house in Redding California, Gabriel began to call his father John. Not dad or father, but John. At first it was just an act of teenage spiteful anger at the move. But later the ugly vice became a habit. The habit became automatic.

The son grew to distrust his father, his father's family and his father's success. It was not that John was unethical or anything, no the man lived by the Golden Rule. It just seemed like John was trying to make up for, in money, what the he had taken away from Inayah, in time and circumstance. Gabriel, and soon the girls, were all exclusively speaking Arabic at home. It became de rigueur. They would speak it among the four of them when they were not around John. When he was home they would all switch back to English. This was just another way the children grew closer to mother and more distant from John.

Years later, after Inayah was diagnosed with terminal cancer, she began to attend *salat* (formal prayer) at the local mosque and started to have regular disagreements with her evermore aloof husband. John tried everything he knew to gather the family ties back together. Yet, eventually, the father realized that his actions were meaningless and resigned himself to the course that John had only the faintest hint that his family was on.

John accepted a place of just getting along for everyone's sake. Gabriel could remember his parent's arguments, the intense whispering going long into the nights. When they argued, the couple would never shout. Gabriel couldn't ever remember his parents shouting. They would intensely whisper at each other, maybe in an effort to conceal the arguments? Who knew? What Gabriel was aware of was that the late night arguments would deny his mother the much needed restful sleep and added to her unneeded stress.

Gabriel Matthews had worked hard and saved all of his money through high school and college. He recognized he had his father's work ethic while in college. When his mother was sick all of the time, Gabriel planned for her passing. Weeks before his mother died, she tried one last time to make contact with her parents. Yet, once again, received no recompense. As Inayah's health failed, she was adamant that her son continue to take his sisters to mosque and made him promise that he would look after the girls as well. His mother also made him promise to make up with his father because, "...he has worked so hard for our family and loves all of us very much."

The first promise, the now young man, had every intention to keep. He became devoutly dedicated to his sisters and their newly shared faith. He studied the Quran and the Holy Bible earnestly and kept in daily contact with both of his sisters. The second promise, well, Gabriel planned to ignore.

His blessed mother died the year he graduated with his Bachelor's Degree in chemical engineering. He had followed in the footsteps of his mother in more ways than one. He had wanted to do something, anything to honor her life and studying what she studied and knowing what she knew seemed a fitting purpose for his path. Also, it was the only way he had left to honor her memory and her life.

The week after her passing and once everything was settled, his sisters and he moved back to their homeland. It was courtesy of his maternal uncle and aunt, and the three of them moved into a condo in Kuwait. Once Gabriel emigrated to Kuwait, he made atonement with his maternal grandparents by converting officially to his mother's faith. The young man changed his name then to Nassir al Din. He hoped the ceremony was witnessed by his mother in heaven.

Truth be known, a bit of him was still rebelling. Maybe Nassir was punishing John Matthews, maybe the young man was carrying out some secret goal of his mother's to return to the desert. When he thought about it, he just simply didn't know. He was doing what he thought was right at the moment it was happening. He felt drawn to this desert place since he could remember, and felt more comfortable in mosque than he ever did in the western Christian churches.

No matter what, Nassir al Din resolved that he would never speak to John Matthews again. The old ways had to be tossed off for the new. The old sins had to be left in the water.

When Gabriel changed his name to Nassir al Din, he began his journey of radicalization in earnest. There in the militant mosques of Kuwait, Nassir found a voice that could ignite the ember he had been nurturing. That was only two short years ago, but he was well on his way to a firm resolve that the United States was not only his nation's enemy, but his faith's enemy. Nassir kept up his outward façade, but he instinctively knew that all of the fun he had been recently experiencing would soon end.

One day he received a simple printed message in the mail.

It read "It is time." Included in the message was a mail-drop box number with a combination. In the mail box, at a not so local pack and ship store, was a package with instructions, materials and the travel reservations. Someone, calling themselves Ashan, needed the likes of him, his money, and his education. He was to embed himself in the United States and await further orders. Something was coming together and assets were needed to begin preparing. The chest pieces were beginning to move and Nassir could see that he was one of the opening moves.

Nassir let his grandfather and boss know that he had to leave on personal business to America. "I am sorry grandfather, but this isn't like racing, I need to go. I am very sorry for the short notice."

His grandfather was understanding. "The company needs someone to represent our interests in the U.S.. Lots of drilling and exploration is being done in the northern states. Why don't you go there, with pay, and start putting together an office? Maybe do some site surveys and hire a geologist?"

Nassir was grateful at the suggestion and they embraced. "That sounds good," was all

Nassir could get out, he was so overwhelmed with gratitude.

His grandfather smiled widely, "If it doesn't work out, and there are no avenues for our company in the U.S. your job will be here when you get back."

Just two weeks later, Nassir left to return to his childhood homeland. Goodbyes were given to his sisters, grandfather and his co-workers. He put his still valid U.S. citizenship to use, and was going to be moving to the Seattle area.

Nassir gave his past, up to the moment he sat down on the aircraft, one last thought. *"Despite it all, a higher order shall reign. May our paths be true and may the Prophet be glorified."* Something his mother had told him right before she passed on.

Nassir al Din closed his eyes. He pushed away all of the memories and all of the dreams that were spinning around him; they were trying to push his life over the verge of chaos.

He breathed in deeply and did his best to sleep on the long flight that headed to America.

Chapter Two

A June morning, six years ago.

The rockets screamed out from their launcher. *Vreaach! Vreeach!* The Katyusha rockets leapt out of their tubes like pyroclastics from a volcano. One after another, the unguided munitions headed skyward.

The rocket's engines bright blue flame left a trail of acrid smelling white rainbows, as the weapons soared in an arc toward their distant targets. The entire twenty rocket salvo was directed at a small mountain settlement. The settlement was a collection of mud and stone houses, just five miles over the border from this Middle Eastern country.

Something this area of the world had seen a thousand times over the centuries; one country was warring with another country. These people were willing to kill those people and unarmed citizens were paying the price. Thousands of years of human history and not much had changed. Except, of course, for the lethality of the weapons used to take human lives.

Just two hours prior, in the quiet and still pre-dawn desert, men had deployed from Russian designed vehicles. As was often the case, this *Boyevaya Mashina Pekhoty* (BMP)-3 armored personal carrier, was being used not to fight another armed combatant, but unarmed people trying to eek out a living. In the early morning dark, the armed men that came from the BMP-3 had dug primitive trenches in an arc, facing the contested border. This was in order to give themselves a little more protection from any possible enemy counterstrike. These eight fully armed troopers were hunkered down behind their make-shift perimeter. They all held their Kalashnikov rifles tight up against their shoulders, shivering in the arid landscape.

The soldier's breaths came out thick and vaporous from some of the them; yet the prepared ones, having donned micro-fleece masks had no visible breath. The masks were only a partial barrier against the cold and it made the men look particularly terrifying. The soldiers, along with their armed BMP, were there to act as the last ditch protection against their enemy across the border. In addition to protection, the soldiers were also there to help the launcher's crew in the reloading of that truck's rockets.

The soldier's looked out from their hastily made boundary. It curved around the outer edge of an area established around their recently repaired launcher: a *Boyevaya Mashina* (BM) *grad* -21 or 'combat hail vehicle.' It was a rare piece of equipment. The soldiers and vehicles were there to safeguard the precious six-wheeled rocket truck that carried the forty tube launching system. The combined truck/launcher was hard to come by in the equipment draining three-year war. It had to be protected at all costs. This BM -21 Katyusha Rocket launching truck was the last surplus unit in their country, and was being judiciously used.

Smoke just clearing the truck from its first launch, a voice barked out commands. "Move it now you turtles!" A Brigadier General screamed out over the area. His Arabic cutting through the distance and smoke. Half of the group of soldiers shouldered their weapons and leapt out of their hastily dug protection. Four men ran over to the launcher's crew and started helping in the reloading. The Brigadier, a loyal and devout servant of the one true Allah, implored his rocket artillery force to shoot and then move. He had drilled this into their training regimen.

"You have five minutes to have the next set of twenty loaded! Five minutes!!!" He shouted once more, reminding them that they were supposed to use the shoot-and-scoot tactics, firing the rockets rapidly, then moving away to avoid counter-battery fire. Yes, the Brigadier had modified the tactic that was used by the major world powers. He limited his men to stay at a location for no more than five minutes for two salvos. This was after all, a much different place than some frontline battlefield in Europe with two behemoths fighting against each other. This was the Middle East.

Training still placed value on men's lives and their equipment, acknowledging the risk for counter-battery fire. Rules of warfare stated the risks of counter-battery attacks astronomically increased every minute more they lingered. The Brigadier felt that his solution balanced the possibility of being found, backtracked, and killed with the capability to fire at a target that was already set up and dialed in on the launcher's sights. The risk had to be balanced with less waste in rockets and time.

The commanding officer for this "recon artillery" group, The Brigadier, had grown into a well trained and capable solider. He had fought his countries battles for near twenty years and had even hired himself out as a military liaison when his country was not fighting someone else. This Brigadier General had taken on this particular mission himself because these kinds of strikes were his idea, his fortè. He is sure it was why, so far, they had met with success.

Civilians would flee the remote villages that were shelled by rocket artillery, leaving ghost towns behind. After the villagers had left, his countrymen would go in, take anything of value, and flatten all of the buildings with their vehicles. A mud and stick village that surrounded a hand dug well would be reduced back to the rubble it once rose out of.

This *Sajjasa* "or cause unrest" plan, had a multipurpose goal for the Brigadier General and his country's military. It's first goal: add more refugee pressure on the centrally located towns of his enemy. This would increase the already high tensions in the refugee camps. Secondly: the result would leave little to no support structure for his enemy's military to rely on while they were fighting alone near the border. And lastly, the Brigadier designed the plan to enrich their own stores with whatever spoils the villagers left behind. Food, clothing and supplies kept his soldiers in the field longer, without costing precious funds to resupply.

Once more the battle hardened man glanced to his watch, "You should be making good progress! Five rockets should be loaded!" The General's voice was unmistakable in the clear and cold morning. Once the smoke was blown off he had almost unlimited visibility while he watched the destruction of the village, relishing in their success. He watched the accomplishments his men were having and thought back to how all of their cross-border raids had started.

"It has been awhile since you have been in the field for your country. Shouldn't you leave this *Sajjasa Operation,* as you call it, to one of your trusted colonels or majors?" The General Secretary for his country had asked him just a year ago. The Brigadier had brought this plan to the General Secretary and the Supreme Leader during a review the Supreme Leader was making of the military. All were tired of the ceasefire and their country had walked away from the UN conference. During the meeting, the Supreme Leader and the General Secretary signed off on the Brigadier's plan quickly. They called it inventive, imaginative and thrifty. Harass and fatigue their enemy while the international community dithered. Afterwards, the General Secretary pulled the Brigadier aside, needing to get in a few more questions in private.

"Yes, the duty should pass to a man with more stamina, in most cases," The Brigadier conceded. They were in the General Secretary's office. The Supreme Leader was being escorted elsewhere through the frontline military base. "But I know this operation. I have to get back out there once again. I need to know if the heartless bloodshed and dust will still appeal to this old warrior."

"Very well… old warrior," the General Secretary smiled at this. "Understand that our goals still need your talents. Soon you will need to let the younger and less experienced ones bleed for Allah. You are far too important to loose when there is so much more to do."

The Brigadier General remembered that he had bowed his head in thanks for the compliment. "I understand completely Mr. Secretary. I will start looking for a younger one to lead these missions. Thank you for your concern," now there was no better time to do it.

This was on an op that the General had imagined, planned and taught and there had been no better student than the man commanding the anti-aircraft tank. The Brigadier was going to approach his ZSU commander for promotion. Once they had finished with this foray. It was especially crucial now, since the Brigadier was going to get pulled from the field. So the creator of the border intensity plan placed his request formally with his military's higher command and got handed his last series of field missions. The General Secretary had faith in him, but he wanted to make sure he still had his combat sense and intuition.

The Brigadier General peered through his large field glasses for a minute. The glasses were screw mounted to a pole for stability. Pulling away for a second, he pushed the pole deeper into the ground to adjust its height. "Better," he whispered to them. He gazed downrange and now could clearly see the village, smoking in the distance. It appeared like their early morning attack was successful. From his powerful binoculars, figures were fleeing the village, away from the border. He glanced to his watch nervously. Doing the math in his head, the old warrior figured his men should have a quarter of the rockets loaded by now. The Brigadier peeked over his shoulder, and watched his men still unboxing crates that the Syrian made Katyushas were stored in.

"In heaven's name! Work together you fools!!!" Shouting once more, so loudly that lizards under rocks a hundred yards away heard him. He turned and gestured as he spoke to the reloading detail, "Remove one rocket, load it, then unbox the next!" His men had been unboxing four rockets, one man per box, rather than working in conjunction on one. Looking again at his watch, he knew that the next salvo was going to be outside of the five minute window.

That wasn't good for anyone.

Far above the border, a RQ-3A "Dark Star" stealth drone was patrolling the 'contested' battle space. It was totally invisible to everything except the most sophisticated and state-of-the-art search radars. Furthermore, because of its tiny size, it was easily 'lost' in the clutter of the radar return's own signal noise. The Dark Star was unarmed, its American Air Force operators deciding that loiter time, not heavy ground attack missiles, was more important than strike capability. The drone was electronically serving as an IMINT (Imagery Intelligence) and MASINT (Measurement and Signature Intelligence) asset above the contested zone without risking a pilot.

The American unmanned aircraft was part of a UN mandated coalition force trying to stop cross-border intrusions by either side of the escalating three year conflict. There *was* an established ceasefire set forth by the United Nations and agreed upon by the original aggressors in the conflict. But that was some time ago... and since talks had broken down there were violations being committed by all sides. Now, revolutionary backed rebels fought insurgents, while insurgents and local tribes on both sides fought each other *and their local governments.* All while their own governments harassed them with tear gas, bullets and the occasional shelling. To add to the upheaval, the two opposing state armies would try and beleaguer each other's support structures with cross-border raids and small scale uniformed military skirmishes.

Furthermore, each government clandestinely supported their own insurgents to fight on their behalf. It was quite the circular firing squad. Which is right where the Brigadier had placed himself.

The United Nation's had hopes to stop all three major parties from violating the month old ceasefire, but so far their efforts had proven weak. But with borders haphazardly drawn up by the British in the 1930's, it made matters hard. The UN's theory was; if the border intrusions stopped, then the conflict would subside and all parties would eventually come to the peace table. Well, the United Nations had at least good intentions.

Besides the troops and the BMP-3, the rocket artillery group was further guarded by a Czechoslovakian manufactured ZSU-23-4M4 antiaircraft system. The vehicle served as ranged defense for the launcher regardless if the threat came from land-based threats or the airborne ones.

Shaking his head in dismay, the General keyed his radio for this other support vehicle. Just a hundred yards away, the ZSU-23-4M4 waited like a silent sentinel, its radar sweeping the sky. The *Zenitnaya Samokhodnaya Ustanovka* or 'anti-aircraft self propelled mount' was another protector of the group.

The ZSU-23 Commander came back, "Go ahead for AA."

"Are you ready?" The General intoned.

"Yes, Sir!" came the enthusiastic reply. The Brigadier was a legend in their military and the antiaircraft commander counted it an honor to once again serve under him. This ZSU-23 commander was a fine leader, just like the Brigadier. Men that served his crews often bemoaned a transfer to another. The vehicle commander kept his machine and crew in excellent shape. There was regular maintenance on the equipment followed by regular exercises for the four man crew. They practiced hard at their job and it showed from the kill marks painted on the turret.

The Brigadier offered him a compliment to sooth what he was detecting as heightened nervousness. "I know you have survived many conflicts with us, particularly after last week. You did well, brother. Just keep up your diligence and I know you and your crew will come through for us."

"Thank you General, we will not let you down." The vehicle commander was honored with the compliment. With his tank's four, radar guided, 23mm autocannons and a pair of anti-aircraft missiles on each side of the turret, he possessed a deadly anti-aircraft platform. His ZSU 23-4M4, codenamed "Shilka," was also a great infantry support vehicle too.

The Brigadier queried, "Shilka! Anything show up on your radar?"

"No, sir. Nothing at all." The ZSU-23 Commander replied.

"Be observant, let me know the moment you have *anything*. Understand?"

There was not even a pause from the ZSU-23 "Completely sir!"

The Brigadier waited till he heard the customary reply and then continued, "We will be running late to our next op. The danger here will get higher by the second."

"I understand," the ZSU Commander imbued a sense of intense concern in his voice.

The Brigadier emphasized the point, "We will have to protect the launcher at all costs," and then clicked off of his radio. Letting the handset hang from his shoulder strap.

The radio headset spoke once more while it swung there, "We will. Shilka out."

The forty-tube Katyusha rocket truck had only half of its tubes functioning, the army mechanics insisted it was the sand, but it had made it through an air strike a week prior. Thankfully, the truck had been built by the Russians to withstand punishment. The Brigadier knew, from this morning's reconnaissance flights, that there wasn't enemy artillery nearby for an effective counter-battery strike. His unit shouldn't be harassed, but there were always surprises. Hiding out there, camouflaged and waiting. *I have been in this field of work for a long time; fighting and killing opponents. It was about half as long as the Katyusha had been around, but I was still doing this long enough to know better.*

The Dark Star Drone had been watching the battle space for the last two hours, waiting and watching all forces. Just forty minutes ago the Drone alerted its controller, "My God they are at it again!" An American Air Force Sergeant breathed.

He watched, via the drone he was piloting, the three combat units of the Brigadiers leave their forward operating base. The U.S. Air Force had been watching the base at the cruising altitude of 45,000 feet. The Dark Star drone made it easy keeping track of anything that they locked on to. With its massive array of sensors, cameras and systems it picked up the military units the moment they started up and generated their distinctive heat signatures. A data base for all known Russian, Chinese, American, British, German and French made equipment had been previously assembled. All of their unique heat signatures, silhouettes and various views were cataloged.

Once properly identified, the data from the drone was then sent, via a side-link transmission to a geosynchronous satellite. The information moved quickly from there down to a few different locations. Including AWACS Sentry aircraft on patrol in the Mediterranean Sea and an Air Force Sergeant's base satellite receivers in Camp Lemonnier, Djibouti City, Djibouti.

The Sergeant was quickly able to classify the vehicles as military, and possibly hostile. The Air Force Sergeant alerted his watch officer, an Air Force Colonel, while in real time he tracked the vehicles through the sand and desert. Up till the moment they stopped, just short of the contested border, everything would have been fine. For a few minutes the Sergeant and a fellow pilot sitting to his right thought that nothing was going to happen. They both leaned into the flatscreen, watching with rapt attention the actions of the ground units. The Sergeant, the other drone pilot, and now joined by their Colonel, observed the military vehicles until the combat units began to dig in.

"Looks like we are going to get busy today. Get me some coordinates just in case." The Air Force Colonel, drone watch officer, ordered his Sergeant. The drone watch Colonel pushed away from his position of leaning over the screen, "You," he said to the other pilot, "back to your task. Stop screen peeking." The Colonel walked over to the comms station grinning at his own wit.

"Yes sir." The two pilots said simultaneously, smiling at the video game reference. "On the way," the Sergeant guiding the Dark Star drone typed away at his PC, pulling down the GPS coordinates, some still pictures and the unit specifications. Using his mouse and making a few clicks, he then transferred all of the information to a data package, encrypted it, and readied it for transmission.

The other drone pilot quickly leaned over to the Dark Star operator once more, "I bet you twenty that those dudes launch."

"That would be stupid! They know the whole world is watching that border." The Sergeant thought for a moment, considered the possibilities, calculated the risks and decided. "You got me in for a Jackson."

The drone controllers, safe and sound at their base in an air-conditioned room in Camp Lemonnier; always followed procedure. Twenty-four hours a day, their combat group was tasked with using a fleet of drones to watch the movement of all units within their sphere of coverage, document them, categorize and track. And if any attack was launched by forces under their surveillance, they were to immediately alert United

States Air Force Central Command (USAFCENT) of the weapons fire.

They didn't have very long to wait. Once the possibly hostile units dug in, the Drone watched the men load and then fire their first deadly salvo. "I'll be damned! They just launched...missiles or rockets!" The Sergeant remarked to no one in particular and not very loud. He witnessed the first set of incendiary rockets fly and couldn't believe the audacity of it. He was used to calling out his observations, but his surprise at the launch and loosing a Jackson made him forget his task.

The Air Force Colonel was deep into the evidence that was being quickly accumulated, so much so that he barely turned when he heard his drone pilot. The Colonel questioned his pilot, shouting out, "Did the hostiles just commit an overt act Sergeant?!?"

"Sorry Sir!" The Sergeant shouted back this time. "Yes Sir! Looks like they are firing on a town with no visible hostiles." Apologetic that he didn't speak louder in the room full of buzzing air conditioners and other voices, the Sergeant spoke up, so his commanding officer could hear. The Sergeant scrolled the Dark Star drone's cameras over to pan onto the mud village, "We've got hostiles at four point seven to four point eight miles... ninety two degrees east...over the border. It's a clear provocation! Violation of cease fire."

Turning away from his comms desk, the Air Force Colonel grabbed a handset and called in the warning to USAFCENT. "Yes, this is Drone Control, Camp Lemonnier. Yes, that's correct. Priority message! We've got rocket artillery escorted by an armored personal carrier and an anti-air platform. Military units are committing an overt act of aggression. Targeting civilian targets in a town 4.7 miles east of the aggressor unit's locations. What's that? Hold please..."

Pulling his headset down for a moment, the Colonel barked, "Sergeant! Do you have a name for the town?"

"Negative sir! Just the coordinates. No town is identified on our maps."

The Colonel leaned back into his headset, "Negative CENT, we don't have a name. Uploading the entire data package, coordinates and my confirmation now."

USAFCENT reviewed and reconfirmed the intelligence from the Dark Star pilots. USAFCENT created a strike request and sent it over, via an encrypted satellite link, to the United Nations. The entire data pack was to go through United Nations general's staff in Germany. This was where those in charge of the North Atlantic Treaty Organization's (NATO) collation force under the UN peace accord were currently stationed. NATO command along with United Nations Military Liaisons digested the data. The request was reviewed by the UN General's staff, approved and forwarded back to the commander in USAFCENT in charge of air operations over the contested area. He proceeded to sign off on the confirmed strike request/package and passed it along through a separate set of channels.

The strike package arrived in the hands of the British airborne early warning and control aircraft (AWACS) flying in international airspace over the Eastern Mediterranean Sea. The Boeing made E-3 Sentry was the best way to remain vigilant for cross-border raids by any hostile actor within the contested area. The aircraft was derived from a commercial 707 and with a distinctive radar dome above the fuselage it had a massive radar range. With its all-weather surveillance, command, control and communications suite it could look deep into foreign airspace and still stay within international boundaries.

The AWACS E-3 Sentry was commanded by a fast-rising group captain, Alyce McMillan. She had been watching the traffic from the Dark Star, but kept out of it until she was issued a direct command. She intercepted the flash alert and strike package; quickly making her decision. After all, that is exactly what she was in her job to do. Defend people that she will never meet, against enemies that will hopefully never be able to retaliate. *Perfect strategy taught a millennia ago by Sun Tzu, in an imperfect world,* Alyce judged.

At Capt. McMillan's disposal, she had two pairs of strike-capable, multi-role, EuroFighter Typhoons. One pair was German, and was flying up with her aircraft at twenty thousand feet. The German EuroFighters were there to ostensibly guard her AWACS and a separate Dutch tanker aircraft that flew nearby. Yet, the Germans could be used for a mission. Another set of French Typhoons were at thirty thousand feet patrolling and waiting. In addition to the four EuroFighter's she had a pair of American A-10C Warthogs flying down at ten thousand feet. All six aircraft were flying combat air patrol (CAP) under her control for the express enforcement of the UN protective charter and the cease-fire agreement. Capt. McMillan decided to send her pair of Warthogs to perform the task and issued commands to her controllers for it to be carried out.

The Warthog pilots received, via the E-3 Sentry controllers and then downloaded from satellite; the entire battle space picture the American Dark Star drone was viewing. The data that was pushed to the Warthogs had additional information worked into it from USAFCENT and the AWACS Sentry. It included three possible approach vectors, recommended weapons use and status update on any other unfriendly/friendly unit(s) in the prescribed combat zone. The Warthogs, in their CAP hold position at ten thousand feet, rolled over into steep dives, placing themselves onto the azure blue waters of the Mediterranean quickly, while building up their airspeed. Flying just two hundred feet off of the highest geography they were near invisible to any enemy radar.

Just a mere four minutes after the first salvo of Katyusha Rockets fired, two war machines were inbound and bringing the pain.. A-10's were supremely capable of close air support and in turning vehicles into scrap metal.

Back at the contested border, the ZSU 23-4M4 Shilka was still on high alert. The four crewmen had checked and rechecked their weapon systems, radar, rangefinder and control systems. In a quick series of beeps, their systems had caught something on the long range threat radar. The radar operator tapped furiously on the leg of his commander as the commander sat halfway out of the top hatch, scanning the sky with binoculars. *Nothing beat eyes in the sky over electronic signals,* the Shilka commander practiced.

Sensing the tap, the vehicle commander immediately ducked down into the ZSU-23 Shilka and grabbed the radio handset, "Brigadier!! Just had contact! Scratch that. A pair!" he leaned over the radar display screen, while its operator fine tuned the reception. "Contacts! South-southwest of us!" The anti-aircraft commander called out the critical info as best as he could.

Just as rapidly as the vehicle commander called it in, the Brigadier radioed back, "What's the exact bearing?!?"

"Close to edge of range. Seventeen miles..." Then, unexplainably, the pair of dots disappeared. "Get it back!" the Vehicle Commander expressed through his clinched teeth.

The radar operator tried his best but was unsuccessful, "I can't they are gone."

Shaking his head in disappointment, the ZSU-23 Commander squeezed the transmit button. "Only had a partial glimpse. At our eight o' clock, but it's gone now. They were at a thousand feet and descending. Can't give you anything more. Positive it was not clutter!"

"Fire up your engine and be ready to move!" The Brigadier commanded. *That was all I needed to know, thank you commander,* The Brigadier acknowledged. He had the foresight to understand that something was going to be out there. *Fighting wars for far too long...it has to be either helicopters or ground attack aircraft. They must be flying low,* he knew. It was the one weakness of the ZSU-23 systems since it was put into the field. It's radar had a hard time defining and acquiring targets from the background reflections.

But from who? Was it some old Russian air machines from his enemy across the border? Those airframes were poorly maintained and piloted with meager skill. His enemy had already barely missed their recon group last week. A pair of ageing Sukhoi 25K's caused minor damage to the Katyusha truck before they were shot down by the Shilka.

The Brigadier was working out the other possibilities. There was yet a worse option. *It could be collation forces,* he told himself. *Namely British, German or American air-*

craft. Those aircraft were mostly new, unlike the former Russian ones. Furthermore, the collation forces are very deadly and the pilots are trained to a razor's edge of capability. The Brigadier feared this option the most.

We will soon see, the Brigadier considered. "We are in Allah's hands," he spoke to the all encompassing desert.

Regardless my men were here for far too long and the welcome had just worn out. "Pack it all up you fools! Everything!! Aircraft inbound!" Yelling at his soldiers to get moving, it made him feel better. At least yelling got out the Brigadier's anxiety and made him feel like he was doing something. He then radioed his launcher and armored personnel carrier the same commands. All of the vehicles immediately started up their engines, ready to flee from their positions once everyone and everything was quickly loaded.

The Brigadier General was still in his foxhole when he heard the sound of something out there in the distance. A faint echo, a low end rumble reached out to his ears and then it was gone. "The sound had to be bouncing off of the low hills, keep a sharp eye. Chiefly AA," the Brigadier radioed to all three vehicles. He glanced at his watch, mentally calculating the inbound bogies speed. The Brigadier's vehicles weren't moving yet. *Hurry, hurry, hurry, my men!* He silently urged. They were still loading up when he heard more sounds; *jet engine sounds*. He reflexively turned toward it, but out from *behind* him burst two grey ghosts spitting fire.

The Brigadier General immediately ducked down lower in his foxhole as the distinctively American Warthogs made their first attack pass. The two pilots, in a trailing formation, had each designated a target from the Dark Star's data. Flight lead, in the first A-10C, had called out the ZSU-23-4. He ordered his wingman to take out the truck launcher. Flight lead had seniority and had always wanted to tangle with one of these infamous plane killers. He had just missed the Gulf Wars and there was never any Soviet designed anti-air tanks he could tangle with during his time in Afghanistan.

The ZSU-23-4 "Shilka" mobile anti-aircraft battery didn't have a prayer against the 30mm cannon on the nose of the Warthog. The aircraft had been designed to kill armor; plain and simple. The *entire* airframe was purpose-built around its massive cannon. The lead American pilot gave the Czech made anti-aircraft tank a one second burst as he flew over it, then disappeared once more over the rolling hills. Gone as fast as it appeared.

One moment the American aircraft was there, spitting *three-quarter pound* cannon rounds and the next it vanished off to the east. The ZSU-23's armor was incapable of stopping the heavy 30mm depleted uranium cannon fire. The brief burst destroyed the anti-aircraft tank, killing the four crew members and setting its engine on fire.

The second Warthog pilot let out a longer two second burst. At the very last instant the woman saw that there were crew members reloading the Katyusha truck. In the spur of the moment, she decided to 'walk' her rounds right through them and then into the truck. It was an even deadlier fusillade than the first American ghost. Pitching her aircraft to the west, she glanced quickly over her shoulder, seeing soldiers down and the BM-21 'combat hail vehicle' explode, creating its own deadly hail.

"Flight lead, flight lead, do you copy?" Bo Peep called out. Throwing her A-10C "flying tank" back over on its central nose to tail axis, she dipped her Warthog over the next rise. The woman loved this kind of flying; *fast* and *close* to the ground. *Just like when I was a teenage girl, riding roller coasters back in Valencia, California.* Bo Peep smiled under her oxygen mask at the invincible feeling it gave her. She brought her Warthog gently up over another hill, remembering again back to Valencia, *and my first boyfriend throwing up on the Colossus.* Bo Peep giggled at the memory and began to scan the sky for her flight lead.

"Roger Bo Peep, loud and clear." Flight lead called back, acknowledging his wingman by her call sign.

"I had secondaries from launcher!" Bo Peep called out, grunting at the G's she was pushing on her A-10. "Must have hit a loaded rocket. Quite the fireworks display."

"Roger that. I had secondaries from the dash twenty three as well. Looked like a twenty-three dash four with those new missiles on its turret." The flight lead, call sign Evergreen, turned his aircraft gently for a long shallow turn. He began setting himself up for a run on the leftover BMP armored personnel vehicle. The Cal Poly educated mechanical engineer flicked off the safety on one of his six Hellfire missiles; cuing it up for launch. Evergreen didn't know if he was going to use his gun or take out the BMP with the missile, but he wanted to be ready just in case. As Evergreen did so, he called in his strike's results to the British AWACS aircraft, under Capt. McMillan's watch.

"Command, this is strike one, Evergreen. Do you copy?"

Alyce McMillan radioed back, "Copy strike one. Go ahead."

Evergreen leveled off his Warthog and keyed his mic again, "Command, we've got launcher and dash twenty-three confirmed killed. Setting up for second run on remaining APC. Confirm!"

"Roger that Evergreen. Hold!" The detached voice of the Sentry controller called back. Group Capt. Alyce McMillan promptly requested a live feed from the Dark Star drone in order to gather as much data as possible to make her after action assessment. This kind of warfare was different and unlike any other time in history. *Unlike your time Sun Tzu, I could have strike information just a few seconds after an attack.* Alyce needed to gather evidence if she was to place the lives of those airmen in danger again.

Or will I be able to tell them to come back? Capt. McMillan hoped.

Moments later, Group Capt. Alyce received a series of after action still shots from USAFCENT, owners of the drone. Following the path from drone, to satellite, to her, she got the digital stills the same time that the United Nations General of Operations received them. She called in her confirmation of their arrival and waited for a reply herself.

Back above the desert, the American planes loitered. *Hold please?* Evergreen dipped his left wing again, setting up another slow turn. *What the hell?* He watched his altimeter carefully. Evergreen kept his A-10C Warthog level during the close to ground turn. *Didn't want to cartwheel into a mountain doing all of this nap of the earth flying.*

His altimeter warning flashed and made a quick series of tones and then ceased when the hill that he flew over fell away. As every hill rose, his altimeter warning went off in regular intervals and then it would die as he once again flew past the next rise. Disconcerting to most people, but not a pilot trained in close air-support missions.

Or for that matter, Evergreen reminded himself, *be weapon's hot on the BMP if someone in command decided they wanted another pass on the launcher.* As Evergreen finished his turn, his wingman came up alongside. Per their pre-attack strategy, they had decided to exfiltrate the valley taking two different routes. Just in case one of them came under fire, both of them wouldn't have been hit by the same stream of bullets. *Furthermore,* Evergreen thought, *the maneuver added to their capability to terrify and confuse the ground threats.*

Bo Peep chimed in on their two way communications radio, "Evergreen why are we doing circles?" She pulled into a trailing right slot as they made another left hand turn together.

"We are in a hold position," Evergreen disgustedly said back. "We've been ordered to do some circles and burn some petrol. Getting a tour of the desert." Evergreen once again watched his altimeter then finished his transmission "Look for turtles and camels for PETA." He flexed his muscles against the G's of his turn and then took a serious tone with Bo-Peep, "Tune into command link for once!"

"Roger that, Evergreen."

Flying at three hundred miles an hour, the pair of A-10's did two full fifty-mile circles over empty desert. Watchful for any other threats from the ground or the air. They waited six minutes until they got instructions from AWACS control. "We have got confirmation of your destruction. Return to CAP station." Capt. McMillan commanded her aircraft. "Confirm the order, strike one."

"What!" Evergreen blurted into his mic before his professionalism kicked in. "Repeat last command?"

The detached voice of the Group Captain came back loud and clear. "Return to CAP station strike one. Confirm."

Evergreen was confused and frustrated, "Command, aggressors still on the ground! Enemy vehicle still operational. Plus troops…"

Capt. Alyce McMillan, finding this pilot's aggressiveness a normal attitude, promptly ignored his request. She did what she was commanded to do by someone else; whether it was from a general in the UN or a British one. "Roger that Evergreen. I understand. APC is no longer a threat to the border. Return to CAP for gas up and await further instructions. Copy?"

Multi-collation, United Nations, no fly zone, stupid rules of engagement! Evergreen complained loudly in his head. "I copy five by five. Evergreen out." He keyed off of the command link, "This is just nuts!!!" he yelled into his oxygen mask without transmitting anything. Cooling off, Evergreen keyed his two-way transmit to talk directly to his wingman, "Did you get that crap, Bo Peep?"

"Yes I did. Tuned in to command link per your instruction." There was a pause for effect on Bo Peep's side. She had hoped for laughter, but got silence. "Uhh, makes no sense," she stammered out trying to recover from her lighthearted humor that had just fell flat. Her aircraft punched through the sky just a few hundred yards behind and to the right of her flight leader. "We don't own em, we just drive 'em." She offered up trying to console Evergreen.

"Roger that," he radioed back as he placed all of his weapons back in safe modes. "Form up on me, let's head back to CAP station." The pair, still flying low, emerged out over the Mediterranean Sea an began climbing back to their loitering altitude.

Back on the ground, men were dead. Red stains were splattered on the desert sand where men used to be. The maimed and the burned screamed out for help. Vehicles, that moments before were fine pieces of moving parts, were now piles of slag. The injuries were numerous and horrific. Three-quarter pound bullets flying at 3500 feet per second did appalling things to men and equipment.

Once the Brigadier realized that the aircraft were not going to come back he gathered the only three uninjured men and tasked them with finding the wounded and the dead.

In thirty minutes they had most of the wounded triaged. They placed their living brothers into the BMP-3, then did their best to collect the dead. Once they were confidant they could get no one else, they sped back to their forward operating base.

The Katyusha rocket truck was a total loss along with the ZSU-23-4. Both of them were now flaming heaps of useless metal and black smoke. Moments ago the Brigadier General had almost twenty living and breathing men and now, not even half that. *It was American A-10's Warthogs enforcing the United Nations military sanctions upon his country. They were at fault for this!* The Brigadier General growled.

Despite his preparations and his willingness to act, those aircraft had made it through. *Someday that military had to be countered. All of these collation forces needed to be shut down once and for all! Those infidels needed to mind their own business and stop messing in the affairs of other sovereign nations!!*

The Brigadier silently fumed and racked his brain for an adequate response for Americans meddling in his country's affairs. *I had nightmares about this very thing and now it's come true!* The entire trip back he tended to his wounded while thinking and reasoning through matters. As he listened to his moaning men, he vowed he would do something to get revenge for all of this.

Back at their forward operating base, other soldiers descended upon the BMP with its load of wounded and dead. After ensuring that his men got the proper care, the Brigadier made his way into the command bunker irate and throwing things. He vented his rage and disappointment on a table and a tea set. Everything went crashing to the floor to announce his entrance. The three others in the bunker quickly exited the shelter; leaving him to his fury.

His mind flashed to the time when he was doing mercenary work and shifted through the conversations and the memories. The Brigadier had made many contacts, and in that moment, he decided on a different course for his life. *Some of the people I had met I thought I would never have need of. But now, among so many wasteful, dead, and wounded things; my mind has changed.*

Once back home, I will place some quiet inquiries to some of my old relationships and long term friends. These were all well placed men within various Arabic and Muslim governments and intelligence services. I will get to the bottom of my suspicions.

In his contacts and travels, The Brigadier General had caught some wisps of something new. There were rumors and hints of a new group that had been forming. An organization that functioned outside of the normal channels and had withdrawn from the main stream militant Wahhabi community.

They were doing things quietly and from behind the scenes, was what the rumor mill had been saying. *I respect their choice, the way we have been conducting our jihad against the kafir (unbeliever) needed a new strategy.* He had even heard of a select few of the really good intelligence operators up and disappearing. Not unusual for those types, specially in countries that share his faith, *but when it was with their entire families? No, men aren't assassinated with their entire families. Even Mossad or the FSB, the only two that practiced such killing anymore, could have done it to all of them.*

Something was not right and he had ignored it long enough. His instinct told him something was there and he must do his best to get to the bottom of it. The Brigadier would have to tread carefully and quietly, but he felt that he could make some discreet meetings. He'd have to ask some reasonably subtle questions and then come to some of his own conclusions.

He pulled out of his thoughts and was awash with his day's mistakes anew. *The Sajjasa was ruined!* the Brigadier cursed. His men were dead and bleeding, his reputation was damaged *and the loss of equipment,* he bemoaned.

Someday, he promised himself, *I will strike back at the Americans on their own soil.* The Americans and their allies needed to stop interjecting themselves where they didn't belong. His country will succeed. And if not his country, then his faith; will prevail. The Brigadier left his bunker with his dusty and bloody boots crunching on fine china. He headed for the surgery tent to look into anything his wounded might need.

The One True Way will always prevail. The Sajjasa Operation must spread to the states. Someday, Allah be merciful, I will be granted the chance to avenge my men.

Chapter Three

Four years prior

Dizhwar ibn Muhammad ibn Abdur Razzaq. His name meant 'Strong Slave of the Provider' is back in the United States, returning 'home' from a long working vacation.

Dizhwar had been abroad regularly for the past few years, studying and traveling. He carried dual citizenships for Indonesia and the United States, so his travel was for business and pleasure. The few years of living back and forth are behind him now. *I am home long term, and today I will have to finish cleaning out my apartment.*

A legal immigrant into the U.S. from Indonesia, it was the reason why he traveled over there so often and also the reason why he just got back. He had been visiting family and conducting business when he was notified that the purchase of his house in Washington State went through. The truth be known he wasn't in Indonesia visiting blood related family, in fact not even distant relatives; family described more of a general closeness he had to the people he had *trained* with. And his new house in Redmond, Washington was purchased in full by the group he had trained with.

Prior to his regular 'business trips' and 'vacations', Dizhwar had been living in the United States since the day before his eighteenth birthday, *and I've hated every minute, all ten years of it.*

He considered his predicament and his distaste as he packed the moving boxes. *At least I no longer have to see either of my parents, thank Allah! I thought there would never be a reason to see Indonesia again,* Dizhwar recognizes. *Yet, the ways of the most high are mysterious indeed.*

Just yesterday he celebrated his thirtieth birthday, alone in his now mostly empty apartment. His birthday celebration consisted of making his favorite meal, Nasi Goreng. Dizhwar drank two glasses of sake with his meal, and then washed, dried and put away all of the dishes. Only then did he go to bed alone.

Dizhwar obsesses about many things in his life. A clean apartment, a clean car and his clean-cut looks. He keeps a hair style that isn't military, yet has the air of authority. Dizhwar carries a bright and mischievous gaze, with eyes set close together in his narrow face. He came across to those he's come in contact with, as intense, yet observant. *But sometimes, my anger gets the best of me,* he would not so easily admit. Dizhwar continues the process of moving. Headed to a much bigger house in Redmond, Washington along with a few new roommates. As he was packing up his belongings his mind led him down the path of his past. The various turns and twists, where he has gone, and where he is going.

Dizhwar Razzaq was born to an Arabic man from Egypt and an Indonesian native. Dizhwar's mother had often talked about how his parents once shared so much together. The two met while his father was shopping for food in an open market. The lean and wiry Egyptian man practically ran over the petite Indonesian woman. He had been pushing through the tight crowds looking at vegetables when he made her spill her bag of produce all over the street.

Dizhwar had felt early on that his naive father, Muhammad, had fallen under the spell of the U.S. without considering the real facts. "…The great opportunities that the United States has…" and all of the supposed freedom that the place offered was a lie that Dizhwar tried to expose. But Muhammad was intent on selling off mostly everything their family had worked for. There was a family market, the one that his father and his mother worked years to improve on. The older Razzaq also sold the flat located above the market, which had served as the family home.

Before the family uprooted themselves, before moving to America, Dizhwar's last resort was to confide in their family's Imam about his father's horrible dreams. And even when the Imam was brought in to try to dissuade Muhammad of his intended path, the Imam was dismissed. Although the family's Imam had warned them about moving, all of them eventually left their homeland and traveled to America. None of them, especially Dizhwar, would ever be the same.

Dizhwar couldn't comprehend why his father had done such a foolish thing, but that was why Dizhwar's path was now here, cleaning out his apartment. His family had been so happy. His parents met at a market and it was their shared dream to run one together. Leaving something known, where all of them were accepted and had laid down roots made no sense to Dizhwar; at one time the ever-trusting son. Item after item Dizhwar put into boxes and all the while his disagreements with his father and the bad memories came forcefully to the present.

Once in the United States, there were soon arguments between Muhammad and Dizhwar, who was the oldest son. Long into the nights, the father tried to share with his son *the hope that was America*. Dizhwar would try to instruct Muhammad that the *so-called American dream was merely an illusion! A fantasy made up by a corrupt Hollywood machine and Muhammad was falling for it!* No matter what Dizhwar said, Muhammad would not listen to Dizhwar's common sense; the father's mind full of the promises that America held. Muhammad Razzaq felt intensely- that if all of them, together, would just give this new place a chance, their entire family would thrive.

As Dizhwar packed up his final possessions he takes a look around at his apartment's emptiness. *The same sort of nothing I felt when father up and moved all of us. From place to place, from failed dream to failed dream, again and again...*

Dizhwar's father, Muhammad, didn't anticipate the stagnant economy after 9/11 nor the anti-Muslim bigotry that the family encountered. The Razzaq family had no work, no opportunity and little acceptance in this foreign land. They moved into and out of three different cities in two years looking for the best opportunities, but found only marginal work. *Soon mother, sister and even my younger brother were forced into working just to make ends meet!* Dizhwar fumed as he made a quick trip to his car and back taking a box out of his apartment and loading it into his car. *Only more evidence our move was morally wrong.*

Dizhwar knew that his entire family would be punished by Allah for moving into the land of the Great Satan. The desperation and stress grew. The once strong family bonds dissolved. Dizhwar's mother could not take the fights between father and son anymore, so one night she pleaded with her husband, to listen to the wisdom of the son. She pleaded with son to no longer fight with his father. Yet, Muhammad was dumbfounded, and heartbroken. The older man was cut to the core at his wife's perceived betrayal, *yet the two were still together and I was the one that was kicked out...*

What cowards, both of you! Dizhwar thought about his parents. Dizhwar walked down to his car and placed more of his belongings inside of it. *My father is a worthless man, with a worthless dream, in a worthless country! Then he turns my mother and my siblings against me.* Dizhwar ruminates on the not so distant past, as the words come to mind, bitter and painful words.

He heads back upstairs and walks through the small space that he had been living in for almost ten years. He placed the last of his things in a cardboard box, and takes one last look around his room just to make sure nothing is left. Those crucial words, *a worthless country,* and thoughts about his father are seeds which Dizhwar had planted deep into his soul; again and again...

Those words, now sprouts of disgust, were exactly what Dizhwar watered with anti-capitalist books, Sharia ideology, and the attendance of any militant-led mosque that could be found. Dizhwar thought about what he might do every day. With the all of the things he learned on his four year 'vacation' he now will be finally doing *something.*

The seed had grown into a strong tree and he now lived to strike back at this aggressor. *Soon, this horrible country that so destroyed everything it touched will be made to suffer.* As he cleaned Dizhwar considered, *because of the smallest things...like what America did to my father and family. To the largest of problems like Middle East sovereignty; the United States, the Great Whore always corrupted mind, body, and soul.*

Remembering back, harboring those many slights, he recalled the hardships of paying his way through college and earning a Master's of Science in mechanical engineering. Dizhwar dredged up his search for employment and a place to live. In a twist of irony he found both, among the most different kinds of people. Dizhwar found open acceptance in the most unusual of locations; the Capital Hill neighborhood of Seattle, Washington. Dizhwar smirked at his apartments location, *among all of the sinners; the LGBT's, the communists, the unfaithful, the socialists, and the bums, and I blended right in.*

He changed his name to a more western version; Dizhwar Razzaq, purposefully removing his father's name. He wore the liberal fashions, ate their overpriced food and drank coffee in the claustrophobic corner shops. Dizhwar, on the outside, looked like a regular, liberated, metro-sexual male. Oh, but on the inside, behind his well practiced smile, he watched, boiled in rage, and waited. He remained a wolf in sheep's clothing. *Soon*, he told himself, *the path will be revealed.*

On a sunny day like today, Dizhwar realized as he was doing some spot cleaning to get his deposit back. *...And not long after I found a job, I traveled out to the Olympic Peninsula.*

He was to deliver drawings for the architectural firm where he was currently employed by, when the idea had hit him. "Blessings to Allah!" Dizhwar almost shouted aloud when the idea had washed over his consciousness. It had only taken a few months of extra-earnest *salat* and keeping his eyes open before he was presented with that extraordinary inspiration. Dizhwar took the idea, not yet a plan, to his West hating Islamist Imam. Dizhwar's Imam recoiled in shock when the idea was presented to him.

Dizhwar was ordered to forget about such nonsense," Don't you speak of this to anyone! You understand?" His Imam had said in their mosque. "You will bring down the police upon us. Or worse! There are agencies in the federal government that will come down and sweep us up in the night. And no one will ever hear from you or me again! That is for sure even in this godless country!" The words from his Imam echoed in Dizhwar's head as he stormed out of the mosque. The Imam's words had rocked him almost as much as his father's announcement to move.

Dizhwar was taken aback by the display of incredulity that he received from his blessed Imam. All of those months of learning and listening to his Imam, his spiritual counselor only to have it killed? Dizhwar was sure that his religious leader had taught about the west's excess and how it was a failing empire because of its ungodliness. There was no doubt. But what had just happened? Why the reversal? He went home to rethink everything that he thought he had learned.

"Was Imam lying the entire time?" he remembered, asking himself. "Was this sacred man corrupted by the Great Whore as well?" Dizhwar recalled that the next two weeks after approaching his Imam he never returned to his mosque or his Imam to find an answer.

Dizhwar pondered his past. He could recall that for days he was physically sick with worry and he couldn't eat. *How many pounds did I loose?* Dizhwar wondered, as he cleaned his apartment. The young man remembered all too clearly, toward the fourteenth day since sharing his idea to the Imam, the knock at his door.

The door to his apartment was wide open now but Dizhwar could see himself standing at it just a few years ago. Dizhwar remembered the man that was standing there when he opened it. It was a simply dressed, grey haired man, with a trimmed western style beard and he stood on Dizhwar's doormat with a single demand.

"Your Imam was worried, were you serious?" The grey-haired man asked in English, instead of a customary greeting.

"Who are you?" Dizhwar glared and evaluated the older man. The slightly built man standing on his doorstep, had an air of confidence and assuredness that repelled the younger.

The older man looked deep into the eyes of the younger, to see if there was the spark of rebellion that could be ignited and, once lit, then controlled. The older grey haired man liked what he saw, but was unsure if this possible recruit could keep his emotions in check. Grey Hair was reminded of himself so long ago.

Still evaluating the resident of the apartment the older man spoke, "You don't need to know who I am, or what I do. Just that your Imam sent me and that he asked that you and I have a talk. See?"

Partially ignoring that statement and filled with an arrogance, Dizhwar asked, "I have never seen you before at mosque. I ask again, who are you and am I serious about what exactly?"

The grey haired, older man looked around carefully and asked "Please, may I come in? We can introduce ourselves and discuss this privately."

Dizhwar feeling unthreatened, relented, calmed his confused anger and invited Grey Hair into his apartment.

"As-salamu alaykum," was the greeting that Grey Hair gave Dizhwar in Arabic.

"As-salamu alaykum," Dizhwar returned the greeting in Arabic with a slight bow remembering his hospitality. Dizhwar motioned to one chair and Grey Hair sat down in one of his two chairs in the small room. Grey Hair could clearly see that this room doubled as the dinning area of this small apartment.

Still, in Arabic, "Please forgive my rudeness and inhospitality." Dizhwar apologized.

Grey Hair gave a curt bow.

Dizhwar, still suspicious, but remembering his manners, politely asked "Would you like some tea?"

"Yes, please. Thank you." Grey Hair answered in fluent Arabic and smiled coyly as if he had expected the test.

Dizhwar got the water, tea and honey together in silence pondering the reason of his visitors' arrival. Was it a trap? Was this old man from the CIA, FBI or some other police agency? Who was he and why was he here? Dizhwar didn't like it, not one bit. With the water hot, Dizhwar set everything on a tray and carried it to the table where he usually ate his meals alone.

The two men prepared their tea without glancing at the other and after taking a sip, Grey Hair spoke first "How are you doing? Is everything going well?"

Caught off guard, Dizhwar answered, "Fine." Thinking better of it Dizhwar asked, "How are you? You have to excuse me, but I find it hard to engage in pleasantries when you have surprised me by coming over uninvited."

The older man smiled with a look that reminded Dizhwar of his father. Dizhwar was starting to get irritated. Further adding to Dizhwar's irritation this old man was speaking in vague terms which increased Dizhwar's discontent and further reminded the young man of his failed father. "Furthermore, inviting strangers into my house without a name is quite disconcerting."

The older man, finishing another sip of tea, spoke coolly, "Please excuse me for not giving you my real name, but I can not. For my own safety. But sometimes they call me Grey Hair. You can use that for now." There was a pause as both eyed each other warily. "Let's get to the heart of the matter, shall we?" Grey Hair asked, picking up his spoon to give the tea another couple of stirs.

Dizhwar didn't respond, trying to breathe through his growing frustration with this visitor.

"Dizhwar Abdur Razzaq, your Imam sent me out of concern for your well being." Grey Hair took another sip and then continued. "Your ideas are very dangerous and can get you into lots of trouble in this country. You can bring too much attention to your Imam and your entire Mosque. Specifically, if you talk to the wrong people about your desires. Do you understand this?"

Dizhwar nodded his head and took a sip of tea. He didn't fully trust this man sitting in front of him. Furthermore, this visitor reminded him too much of his father, all the way down to the way he drank his tea. Grey Hair's Arabic was good, but Dizhwar didn't have a good feeling about this older man. What was his purpose here? Where was he from? Dizhwar was multilingual as well. Growing up in the Indonesian community he knew Indonesian, Sudanese, Arabic and English fluently. He could speak passable Portuguese and had taught himself basic Spanish. Dizhwar felt that he could not be arrested for much of anything so far, just as long as he was careful with his words now. Any American lawyer could save him from the pitiful American justice system.

"We have known of your displeasure with this country from various sources and we now know that you have given your Imam an idea to carry out an act." Grey Hair took a sip of tea and continued, "The jihadist plan that you outlined has merit. Yet, you must understand that, if you are serious, then you can and will have help; but you must not dither or doubt with your actions."

Dizhwar wondered, *we... various sources*? and stopped at that. He shook his head in consideration, *how many ambiguities will this man speak? Is this all trustworthy?* It was leaving Dizhwar with more questions than answers. It started to make Dizhwar's head hurt.

The young man just became angrier with the added frustrations. He asked aloud, keeping the foreign language going by switching to Portuguese, "Who are you affiliated with and how do you know so much about me?"

"Dizhwar," Grey Hair started to ask in Portuguese as well, "May I call you by your first name? You no longer go by your given name. Correct?"

Dizhwar was surprised the man knew Portuguese, but he did his best to conceal it. Dizhwar nodded his agreement about his name, but was curious if this stranger was insulting him by mentioning that Dizhwar had dropped his given name? Maybe, threatening him? Did this plain dressed, fiftyish man know about Dizhwar's past too? More cryptic talk, more frustration and an even greater headache for the young man. *It was too early in the morning for all of this*, Dizhwar contemplated.

Switching back to Arabic, Grey Hair filled in a little more detail. "I am being vague on purpose, Dizhwar. I do not mince words and I have come to you on a very serious matter. I've come on behalf of some very concerned people that would like your help. Are you dedicated to your stated goal?"

Dizhwar had enough.

He leaned forward and looked Grey Hair right in the eyes, "Yes, I was serious, but it's been some weeks since I have talked with Imam. In that time, I have grown not to trust what I hear, particularly by old men that speak in riddles. If it's not you, it's my Imam, if it's not my Imam it's my..." Dizhwar almost said "father" but caught himself. Not missing a beat "It needs to be shown to me from the Book, Grey Hair. Or by evidence that I can touch or trust and I don't trust you. So, get to the point or leave." Smugly satisfied, Dizhwar sat back in his chair. He took a mouthful of hot tea, taking some irrational pleasure in the pain and then he swallowed.

Seemingly unaffected by Dizhwar's rudeness and partially ignoring his request to leave, Grey Hair pushed, "Trust me. You need to have faith in us, your leaders, and above all, trust those whom I represent. Listen to what we tell you and do exactly what we say. If you obey you will be rewarded, both here and in heaven. Choose us, make progress toward our goals, and you will have a long and lasting relationship with us. Our courage will soon be seen by all. If you do not choose us, right now, at this very moment, then you will never see me again. You will never hear from those whom I represent. Clear?"

Dizhwar was furious. The anger that simmered within him started to spill over. Dizhwar clinched his fists and released them as they sat in his lap. The young man did his best to maintain a neutral expression. *Who did this old man think he was? This aged, grey haired, pompous, and utterly weak looking man was telling him, Dizhwar Abdur Razzaq, what he was to do and then dictate to him the terms as well?* Grey Hair kept using the word understand and Dizhwar understood none of it, except for his fury and headache. *This aged man was far too secretive* and as he let that thought out, Dizhwar came up with a plan.

I will turn the table on this visitor!

Dizhwar smiled a real smile. *I will have the upper hand,* he promised himself. Because of being born and raised in Indonesia he had picked up many languages. It came natural to him. From the Indonesian he learned as the national language, the English and the Arabic from school and mosque to the Spanish and Portuguese he heard on the streets.

Dizhwar said in his best and most soothing Indonesian "I understand that you want my answer right now, but may I please have a few days to consider your offer?" seeing the doubt in Grey Hair's eyes, Dizhwar offered a final, "If not a few days then twenty four hours?"

The Grey Haired man stood up and excused himself. Dizhwar watched the man walk deeper into his apartment and proceeded to open the restroom door. Before shutting the door the Grey Haired man replied in Indonesian "You have as long as it takes for me to relieve myself…" and shut the door.

Dizhwar couldn't take it anymore.

His professional countenance left his face in a flash. He grit his teeth and rose up out of the seat, walked over to his refrigerator and removed a box that was clearly one for restaurant leftovers. Dizhwar removed the 9mm handgun that was inside it, gently slid the slide back enough to check if there was a round in the chamber and went back to his chair. *No one was going to talk to me like this in my own house! At the least, by Allah, I was going to get some answers out of this mysterious visitor.*

Dizhwar tried to look at the issue of Grey Hair from a few different angles. *This old man had to know me because this old grey sod knew the languages I knew!* Dizhwar considered, *if there were no answers forthcoming, I will kill this old fool and then go interrogate my Imam! The Imam will tell me what is going on or he will die too.*

Dizhwar was bound and determined to figure out what the hell was happening from both of these fools. He was young and full of a carelessness that one has when they have fear of nothing. He didn't fear the law, moral rules or Allah. Dizhwar resolved, *no more vagueness, no more ambiguity, I'd had plenty of that from my father and I'm not going to stand for it anymore.*

As Dizhwar sat, he pushed the front of the gun between his right thigh and the chair so that it was all but concealed. The young man smiled to himself at the pressure from the pistol, it calmed his fury somewhat. He could feel the cold steel through his pant leg. He drank another mouthful of the slightly cooled tea, content with his plan. When Dizhwar heard the toilet flush he placed his right hand on his thigh above where the 9mm pistol was and started to sip the tea with his other hand holding the cup.

Dizhwar heard the running of water and the door open. He didn't even glance at the returning stranger, so cocky was Dizhwar of his plan. The young man heard a scream fill the room.

The scream was his own.

His chair fell backwards, hard against the floor! Tea spilled all over him, and his concealed pistol went skittering under the table out of reach. The fall knocked the breath out of him as well. Out of the blue, was a man's face inches from his with a gleaming steel knife placed against the base of his eye socket. It was hard for Dizhwar to breathe, then it dawned on him that the stranger, Grey Hair, was sitting on his chest pinning Dizhwar's arms with the old man's knees.

What just happened! Dizhwar screamed inside his head. Panic started to take over his heart as he started to shake.

"You, Dizhwar, will now pay closer attention…" slithered the raspy, snakelike voice now coming out of Grey Hair in perfect English. "You, and your stupid plan with the gun! What were you going to do with that? Try to harm me? You weren't sneaky or devious, you were a child, you changed hands, you idiot! Your plan was sophomoric! Your switching of languages!"

Grey Hair patted his own chest, "You are a rabbit trying to outsmart a fox. Don't you think that if we knew you, we would know where you grew up?"

Dizhwar didn't say a word. He just lay there, pinned, dumbfounded. He was in absolute shock that this seemly weak old man had done this to him.

"Decide!!!" As Grey Hair spoke that last word the pressure from his knife increased against the base of Dizhwar's eye socket. Dizhwar started to nervously blink both of his eyes as if that might cause the blade to abate its pressure.

"On three I will have an answer." Grey Hair spoke, this time with a little less rasp; a little more like his original voice.

"One," more pressure on the knife.

"Two," a little more pressure and Dizhwar's blood started to run.

"Stop!" Dizhwar shouted in English, finally finding his voice. "I will join!"

There was a pause while Grey Hair studied Dizhwar carefully. Then, the harsh moment was all over with.

The older man got up and walked over to the apartment's front door. Grey Hair produced a small plastic sandwich bag from his pocket. Within the bag was a mobile phone. Dizhwar noticed for the first time that Grey Hair had gloves on. These were the expensive, thin, leather kind that one would expect to wear with a matching designer suit or driving a fast car.

The grey-haired man, his eyes never leaving Dizhwar's face, removed the phone, crouched at the knees, and set it on the floor. "Don't you ever betray us, don't you ever leave the house without this phone and no matter what, speak to no one about this visit." With that order, Grey Hair stood up, and let himself out the door, slamming it on the way out.

The meeting with Grey Hair was four years ago. Just a week after the visit from Grey Hair, Dizhwar got a text on the phone that Grey Hair had provided.. There was a package waiting for him at his neighborhood FedEx. When he opened the package back at home, he found typed instructions, cash, a fake passport, and a pre-loaded debit card. Dizhwar followed the instructions to the tee. He drove from the U.S. to Mexico on his real passport, as directed. Then, using the fake one provided by his new friends, took a circuitous route from Mexico to a remote village in his place of birth, Indonesia. He passed through four different international airports and way too many time zones.

The studying took years, but Dizhwar underwent specialized schooling in Indonesia.

The training camp tried to mirror the best of the western clandestine schools. There was training and education on a whole host of topics. Some of them, Dizhwar never expected; topics like armed and unarmed combat, engineering and languages. He was taught improvised explosives, sabotage and chemistry. Which household chemicals make ingredients for explosives and where the easiest places he could get much higher grade explosives.

Recipes, not for food, but for things that go bang were memorized. Dizhwar remembered one day of studying, *who would have thought you could get explosives from sugar and plaster of Paris?*

There were lessons on computers and electronics; from personal, to operational and digital security. The man took classes on lying and how to do so convincingly. Espionage tradecraft, covert surveillance, and interrogations were also covered. Most of all, there was strenuous physical training. Miles of running, hundreds of pushups, sit ups and pull ups.

Morning, noon, and night. *Get up and run, get down and do push ups then get back up and run again.* Dizhwar remembered the days well, *there was no such thing as too much physical exercise.*

In those four years he had learned so much since his agreement to join this new group, Ashan, which in Arabic literally meant "The Nest". Dizhwar was like no cadet the school, the teachers or Ashan, had ever seen. Devout, loyal, open to learn, willing to do anything. Dizhwar discovered he could easily murder and kill. He was so cold his veins bled ice. The young man had channeled all of his anger to a single pointed purpose: to excel. Dizhwar had not only passed his various fields of training, but mastered them.

This new group Ashan was lead by one man that was known to Dizhwar as the Chief Officer (C.O.). The C.O. was in turn guided by a group of selected men known as the Shura Council. These seven men were pulled in from all over the world. Some for their expertise in military matters, some for their money and influence and still others for their clandestine experience. The C.O. and the Shura had weekly reports from all of their schools and their future operators scattered around the globe.

Dizhwar was in the top 1% of the pupils. The entire command structure had taken notice of this brilliant and gifted student. If the C.O. didn't have immediate plans to field Dizhwar, this student could have been a teacher. Who knows? Maybe even someday a board member? But the need had been too great to get a few trusted men into the United States as quickly as possible, so the C.O. made a different decision. They placed Dizhwar into the field. Field assets were more necessary than another wise counselor. Yet, the C.O. was quite proud.

During the training, Ashan expressed, no drilled into Dizhwar, three vital facts:

1. No more promises of eternal glory. Glory is what can be accomplished here.

2. No more death cries of Allăhu Akbar (God is the Greatest). We will offer up our *salat* or our *dua* instead and focus on living to fight another day.

3. No more self-destructive suicide bombings. A waste of blood, people and treasure.

Ashan is to be different. Too many valuable assets of people, time and money had been forever lost since the struggle had begun. *Their intifadah (or uprising) had to start behaving like the West in order to combat it.* Dizhwar knew from his training. *This new war had to be a very different kind of shaking off; a very new way of combatting the Great Satan. Good plans must be created, approved and carried out with the minimum amount of fellow believers lost.* His Trainers at Ashan drilled that into Dizhwar's mind. *My idea has blossomed into a plan and soon things will come together to carry it out.*

This was to be a new type of militant extremism. To emphasize the point and to help Dizhwar understand his importance to the cause, he was permitted access to emails addressed to him from the head of Ashan. The emails praised his dedication and strength that Dizhwar had brought to the school. They expressed the desire, from the entire leadership team, to have Dizhwar keep up his training, he was going to be used for many a great act.

So the young man was pleased with the regard that he received at his foreign training. Dizhwar had succeeded in securing hard won stature within Ashan. He implicitly knew that his training was going to be used to spread anarchy and chaos among the *kafir*. Nothing pleased Dizhwar more. No more wasting his life pursuing the capitalist American goals, chained to their militant consumerism. A wolf trained in a Nest, no longer living like a sheep. Fit, trained and dedicated, finally unleashed to do as much damage to the Great Whore as possible.

Training that finished not so long ago, Dizhwar thoughtlessly was twirling his western-style goatee. He considered all of the factors that have led to him to this point as he now drives out to Redmond from his Capital Hill apartment. He is energized and eager to start up the next phase of the *Sajjasa*, so named by the Brigadier on the Shura Council. Dizhwar makes it out to the new house in plenty of time for his team's morning meeting.

Dizhwar comes in and sits down at the kitchen table of the place Ashan purchased in Redmond, Washington. The house is quite impressive and big enough to sleep all of them two to a room. His recruits now sit all around him, and Dizhwar listens to his people go over the plan one last time.

As he listens to his men, Dizhwar reflects, *it is quite wonderful what a little bit of money, a little time and some proper motivation can do.*

Dizhwar never came up with ill conceived plans again. His courage and that of his cell will be seen by all. His twelve conspirators in the house, his new house, would see to that eventuality.

From now on, Dizhwar promised himself after his encounter with Grey Hair, *I always drank tea my non-dominant hand. One lesson Grey Hair taught I will never forget.*

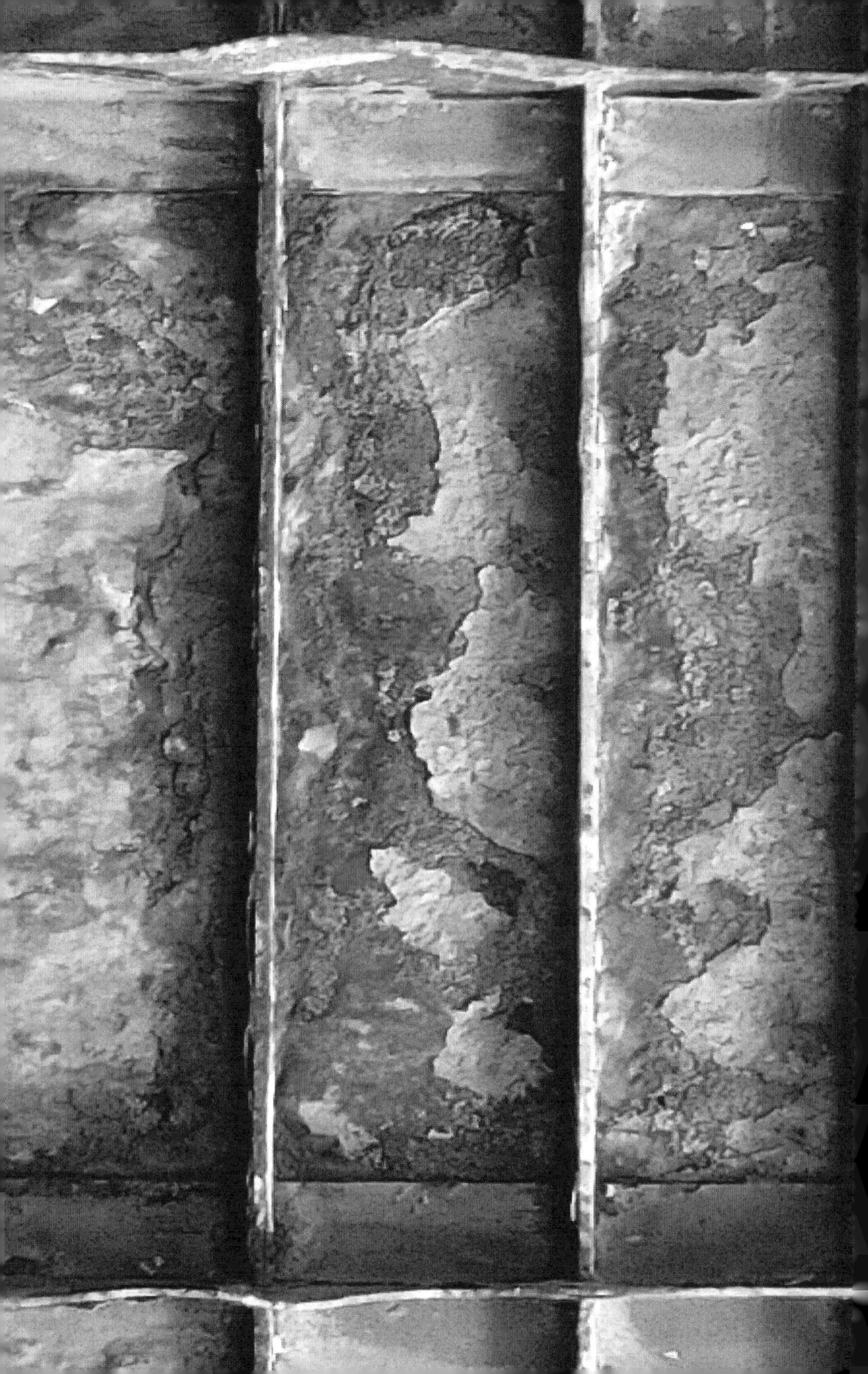

Chapter Four

Monday August 20th

The yellow fingered, smoky woman looked up to no one. She was successful, driven and completely self-reliant. Whatever she set her mind onto she would accomplish it. The goals of her life were checked off, marked by plaques, certificates and awards that dotted her office back home. Today was not any different. She busily chatted away on her mobile phone as her driver tried his hardest to get down the steep hill in ever tighter traffic.

"Mikhail I know you want this deal to go smoothly," explained in her best *understanding* voice. "That's why I flew out here, that's why I was trying to go and inspect the property first." She paused and listened to his response. Well, only half listened, because she also gazed around the head rest that was blocking her view. *What's the deal?* She wondered. *Why aren't we moving faster? I've got a deadline here!*

"Mikhail, I know you're concerned," she assured her Russian client on her mobile. "Just rely on me to take care of things. Alright?"

The Russian-accented voice on the other end remained conciliatory and trusting. Terra waits for her client to finish, grows impatient with Mikhail's longwinded goodbye, *Russians,* she bemoans. And then she proceeds to cut the conversation short.

Interrupting her real estate client, "Yes, absolutely, I've got to go now. The traffic is particularly ugly here in Seattle. I've got to find out from my driver what the hold up is."

"Kisses," and with that she terminates the phone conversation.

The moment she does so, her driver speaks up. The man had heard the entire one-sided conversation and expected to get the fifth degree from Terra. He had seen this kind of alpha type-personality before. *After all, you don't own and drive your own Lincoln Executive Service and not get intense and headstrong clients. So,* the driver figures, *I will preempt it..* "I'm sorry, Ms. Freeland. It looks like we will miss our scheduled ferry." The car's driver points to his right at the countless amount of cars that are in the ferry waiting lot. Terra's driver now has their car on First Street, driving south. It is a straight shot from first street to the ferry terminal. He looks back to his passenger, "What would you like me to do Ms?"

I hate being called Ms! It's such an archaic term! "Well, what choice do we have?" she replies.

The driver of the Lincoln town car does everything in his power not to roll his eyes. She is watching him like a hawk in the rear-view mirror. "Well, seeing as you're not from around here, let me explain," the private car driver sucks in a breath. "We can drive all of the way around. It would be I5 south through Tacoma and then back north over the Narrow's Bridge, or we could sit at the terminal and wait. Hopefully we could catch the next ferry over to the Olympic Peninsula." The driver watches his client in his rearview mirror. *She looks angrier by the minute,* the driver worries. He tries his best to lessen her anger by being truthful, "But... we might have to wait for two ferries because it looks like it's a packed terminal lot."

"You're kidding me right?!?" Terra declares, aghast at the delay.

The driver gives his best emphatic face, "No, I'm sorry…"

"Those are our only two choices to get to Port Orchard??" She blurts out. Terra checks the time on her phone and then looks to see when she has made the appointment with the realtor she was meeting with.

Her driver tired to be as caring as possible, "That's right...unless you want to take a small airplane. I can get you to Boeing Field in fifteen minutes."

Terra shakes her head, "I don't want an airplane. How long would it take for us to drive around?"

The driver pulls in a breath, and eases the car to a stoplight. "Well, depending on traffic, an hour, hour and a half. Possibly two."

The woman in the backseat silently curses to herself, *and I am going to be here for a week of this?*

Terra Freeland is staying in Seattle and looking for real estate opportunities for her client, which wasn't high on her list of things to do. *I am supposed to be on vacation too,* Terra reminds herself. *At least it was supposed to be sunny this entire week. 'Around the entire area',* the weatherman said this morning she recalls.

Terra shakes her head, dreading what her week might turn out like. Especially seeing how bad traffic is around the entire Seattle/Tacoma metropolitan area. She has to find three properties, *just three properties and then I can leave,* for her client back in New York. The houses had to be all semi-rural, fixer-uppers and close to major areas for rental income.

Oh, and Mikhail wanted them larger than ten acres. Not too hard, right? Her driver keeps looking at her in the mirror like he's silently waiting for her to make a decision. "I'm hungry," she declares. "Is there a decent restaurant close to the terminal? I'm not about to wait all cramped up in the car."

They had just come to the final stoplight in front of the ferry terminal entrance. The car that they travel in is just crawling past Ivar's and the waterfront fire station. "Well yes, there is the famous Ivar's just out our rear window and several more restu..."

"Alright, call me when we are half-an-hour from departure. I will need to find the car."

The Lincoln's driver looks up into his rearview mirror with alarm. "Find the car?"

"Thanks!" and like that Terra Freeland steps out of her slowly moving car. She slams the door and takes three steps to the sidewalk, heading toward the restaurant.

She abandons her driver to wait for two ferries, almost an hour and a half, before the car can get a spot to go to the peninsula.

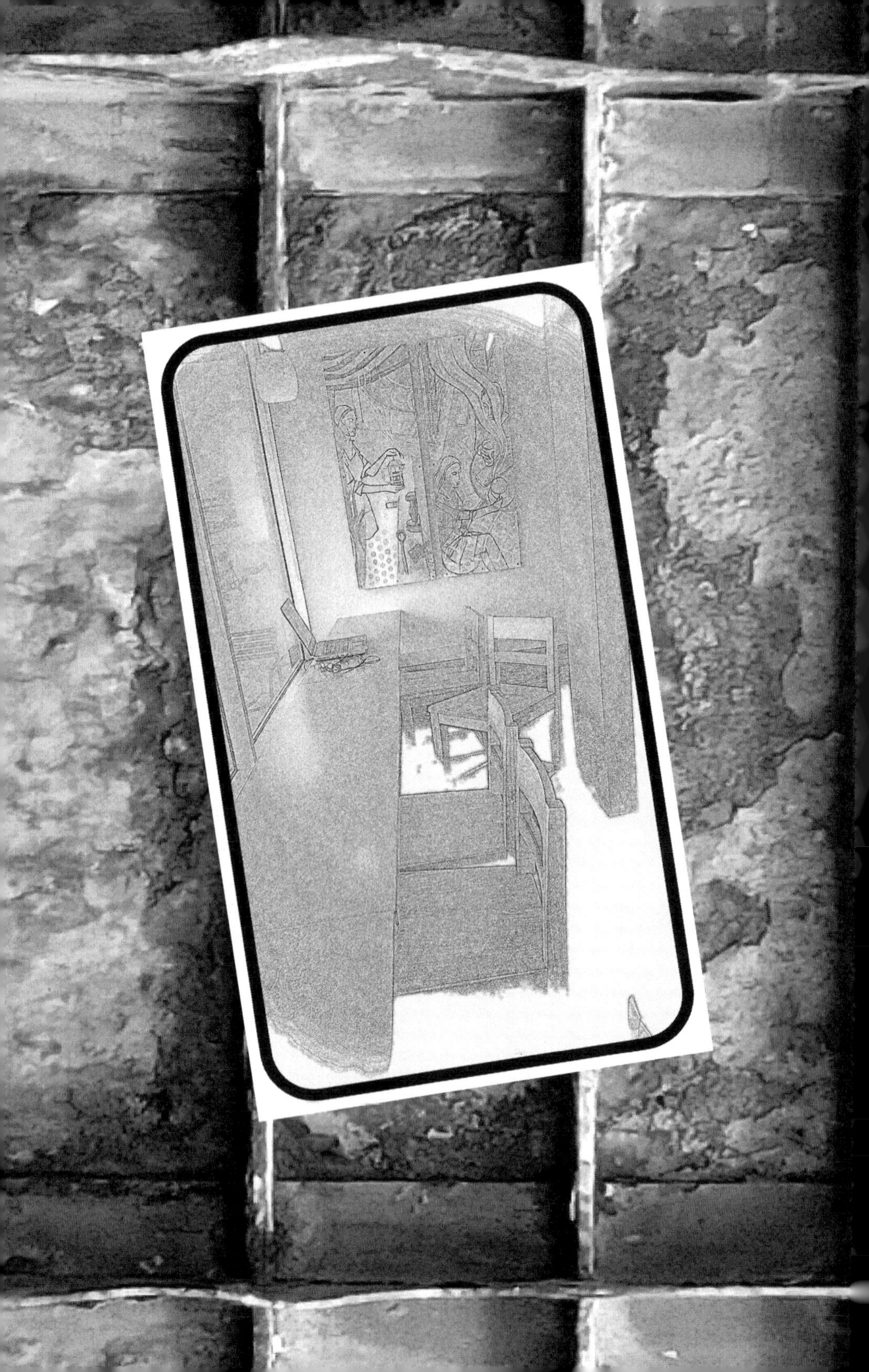

Chapter Five

Wednesday August 22nd 16:06

The name that he chose for himself was Nassir al Din. His name was a piece of the old him and a piece of the new. Nassir walks the streets of Redmond, Washington thinking, and heading for a local market.

Nassir still lives under an oath sworn to his God and...to his mother. Despite living in the states as a sleeper agent to Ashan, Nassir does his best to hold to the code that he lives by. In both his promises and his personal standards. His vows are the rock and sand that forms the basis of his concrete like being. Since being instructed to come to the U.S., Nassir strived everyday to keep himself aligned to the moral, spiritual and physical ideals that were set forth thousands of years ago.

Many faiths, many books, yet they all have the same core principals. Most importantly I had promised her, Nassir remembers. *And that means the world to me.*

The emptiness he still has in his very being is only shallowly filled by the Blessed Koran and the Holy Bible. *Yet, I read them whenever I can, for there is never enough knowledge you can gain from books.* Nassir reminds himself of that fact, as he crosses the street into a local market's parking lot. *Particularly those two books. Since leaving my grandfather's company, my learning comes from not just those precious tomes, but anything else I can get my hands on. Literature from eastern religions or western ones, monotheistic or polytheistic, it doesn't matter. Wisdom was wisdom,* Nassir knew. *No need to filter where it comes from.*

Despite his thirst for knowledge, his striving for better, he still follows his primary oath: to serve Allah (God). Nasir endeavors to be a servant in whatever way that is revealed. He swore to follow the path that The Way of Allah dictates; for as long as he has breath. Nassir does not take that lightly, so he follows The Way at the utmost of his strength and ability.

Nassir walks into the local market, orders his coffee and a croissant, pays for them and then sits at a table. *Not so heavy a burden, if you relish the weight.* Nassir smiles at the saying, as he takes a small bite of the buttery croissant.

Nassir wanders into the supermarket's deli seating area, aimlessly people watching. Yet, he has come into this neighborhood healthy market with a purpose in mind. He is following a plan and doing his best to be as inconspicuous as possible. The market, trendy in the Puget Sound area, has a coffee shop attached. *It's not a Starbucks,* he realizes. *It's a Tully's no less, but their coffee tastes better.*

In addition to doing some work, which requires using the free WI-FI, the healthy market is also a good place to people watch. People watching is a guilty pleasure of his. This happens to be one of the many free hotspots he uses for his communications. Throughout the Puget Sound area there are hundreds of free public web portals to gain access to the Web. With all of the tech giants that call the Seattle/Bellevue/Redmond area home and all of the employees that demand constant admission to their "connected lives," he is just one among hundreds of thousands.

Nassir, or his boss/friend, will occasionally check for messages to see if their Organization, Ashan, has sent them anything. Nassir is doing the sporadic check today, on behalf of his peer, friend and leader, Dizhwar. Dizhwar is tired, mainly from last night's final assessment of the operation. The final preparations went long into the morning. So Nassir volunteered to go, it was the least he could do. Besides, Nassir and Dizhwar did not have phone or internet service at their shared home in Redmond. No internet, no cable, no satellite and they only use pay-as-you-go mobile phones when they absolutely have to.

So this check for a message was a way for Nassir to go for a brisk walk and get out for a while. *Precautions, precautions, precautions,* Nassir reminds himself. *Especially now you fool.*

All of the plans, all of the logistics are finally coming to a head. Time is running short. Nassir sips at his coffee, and opens up his laptop. He logs into it and then furiously types away to log into the free portal to the Internet. Nassir is using WI-FI to double check that, being a week out, the op is still green-lighted. The Organization will be sending him a message soon and he is there at the market to receive it.

Nassir then logs into the massive online multiplayer fantasy game and his character appears in it's virtual home. The home is complete with a blazing fire and crossed long swords on the wall. He directs the avatar with mouse and keyboard out to the street that is bustling with 'people'. Every figure another avatar controlled by another human being somewhere else on the planet. After using a world map and clicking on a specific town, the Dizhwar character, now being controlled by Nassir, 'fast travels' to a new city.

A few years back Dizhwar created the online video game avatar or character. Nassir is making sure that the digital golem will be at a prescribed virtual place in real time. Lives are to hang in the balance because of this meeting in a fantasy-medieval gaming world. Nassir felt it the entire process a bit silly, but his entire team had to be careful about every bit of data they willingly give away. They were being very vigilant to remain anonymous. In the gaming world, where messages are typed, read and then vanish, this was the perfect place for Nassir and his messages to be quite unknown.

Dizhwar's video game avatar worked its way into the fake town under Nassir's direction. He found the correct virtual tavern and rest house. Nassir maneuvered his character under the sign of the White Harpy and entered. Then, Nassir al Din, the freshman gamer, directed the avatar to a seat at a table. A cup of mead appears in the characters hand like magic, while the real Nassir sits at a table drinking a caramel macchiato. The real man thoughtlessly tears away small bites of a croissant while he looks at the faces of the people that pass by. Nassir glances at the game playing on his laptop periodically, chews on the croissant, and with a perpetual smile, he looks at the people walking by. Despite his genial demeanor, the welcoming face hides many past scars.

Bury those scars, he tells himself, looking from laptop to the real people nearby. *Bury those ugly wounds where no one will ever see that which remains... or ever find them.*

It bugs him to no end, that not a single person that has walked past has looked him in the eyes. The stranger's heads are down, or stare off into the distance with a mobile phone to their ear. No one will return a simple smile. To Mr. al Din the people that move around him don't look happy or content with their lives. It appears that the throng that filter in and out of the store are just clueless sheep. These people are so caught up within themselves, so selfish, that they fail to notice the obvious around them.

Nassir observes their routine, *they fail to understand that they have no value except the value placed on them by Allah.*

Nassir is early to the scheduled meeting. He is timely because he doesn't want to let down his friend and leader, Dizhwar. Or, anyone else for that matter. He likes exceeding other people's expectations, specially when they are important ones. Nassir is prompt to meetings for this reason, so he sits and waits in the real world while his virtual character waits in the other one. Both of the men, one dressed in plate mail with swords on his hip and the other in skinny jeans and a collared shirt; are people watching.

The time for the meeting approaches, Nassir sits up in his chair and watches the screen all that more carefully. The moment comes and the flesh and blood man snaps to when he sees a virtual character approach his. This one avatar is dressed differently than the description that Dizhwar had provided him. *Maybe the people he works for are just being careful?* Nassir considers it, but he is not a video game player and doesn't know if the difference is significant or not.

Nassir utters his frustration, *I wish I understood this stupid game's purpose!*

"What in Heaven's name?" Nassir blurts out loud, as the character that he thinks is going to be his contact jumps up on the tavern table and starts dancing. Ale mugs and tin plates go flying unto the floor. A virtual crowd, within the virtual White Harpy tavern, starts to gather to watch the fool on the table dance. Mr. al Din is caught up in watching for a moment; like looking at a plane crash or train wreck or even the random drunk making a fool of himself on the street.

Then he pulls away from it, repulsed.

The well tailored and elegantly mannered Nassir, watches in sheer embarrassment as the dancing goes *on and on*. He is so embarrassed he almost shuts the screen of his used laptop. Nasir nervously looks around the café located in the supermarket, afraid of where the vulgar display might lead to. He didn't want the random child to see the display and have a complaint get passed up from parent to the stores management. The whole point was for him to not draw any attention to himself. Soon, several other online avatars are dancing on tables, *inspired by the first one, no doubt,*

"This is just gone from bad to worse…"Nassir whispers to the laptop.

He nervously folds the screen at an angle, making sure he is the only that can possibly witness the behaviors of the avatars. Male and female characters are now dancing on tables, throwing mugs and overall acting like a bunch of drunken barbarians. One pair start fondling each other and two more start sword fighting. In the midst of it all, Nassir's character is challenged to a fight as well. An in-game prompt inquires silently if he wants to join the battle or surrender.

Trying to ignore everything, Nassir al Din moves his character to the far side of the virtual White Harpy tavern. The man tries to do so, all the while trying to keep the disgust out of his real face. *Is this how these meetings always went?* He asks himself, surprised he didn't know. *I will have to ask Dizhwar when I get back to the Redmond house. Or is he in North Bend today?* Nasir silent wonders about the schedule that all of them had gone over and tries to remember where Nasir will end up.

Nassir al-Din waits another ten minutes for the contact. Enduring more debauchery on his computer screen, and even a few more 'invites' to join a tavern brawl or go on a quest. Nasir shakes his head at the display, but is careful not have his character leave the virtual tavern. He watches carefully for someone fitting the right description. In all of those minutes, there does not seem to be another video game avatar that is close to the description that he has.

Satisfied, Mr. Nassir al Din gratefully logs out of the online video game. There is not going to be a meeting today. Time is up, because Ashan never misses a meeting. As the laptop performs its shut down procedure Nassir considers. *The intifadah is a go. It seems everything that I, Dizhwar and the rest of our associates have put so much into will now come to fruition. At last we know that all of our hard work, time and energy will not be wasted.*

Closing up his second hand laptop, Nassir is glad to remove the sight from his eyes. Video games and online video gaming are something he will never get. Virtual reality was just that, virtual. Nassir stands up, putting the laptop into its bag. As the man does a cat-like stretch, first his legs and then his arms, he can't help but consider what these American games clearly showed: *These Americans are a bunch of drunken barbarians.*

En Partibus Infidelium.

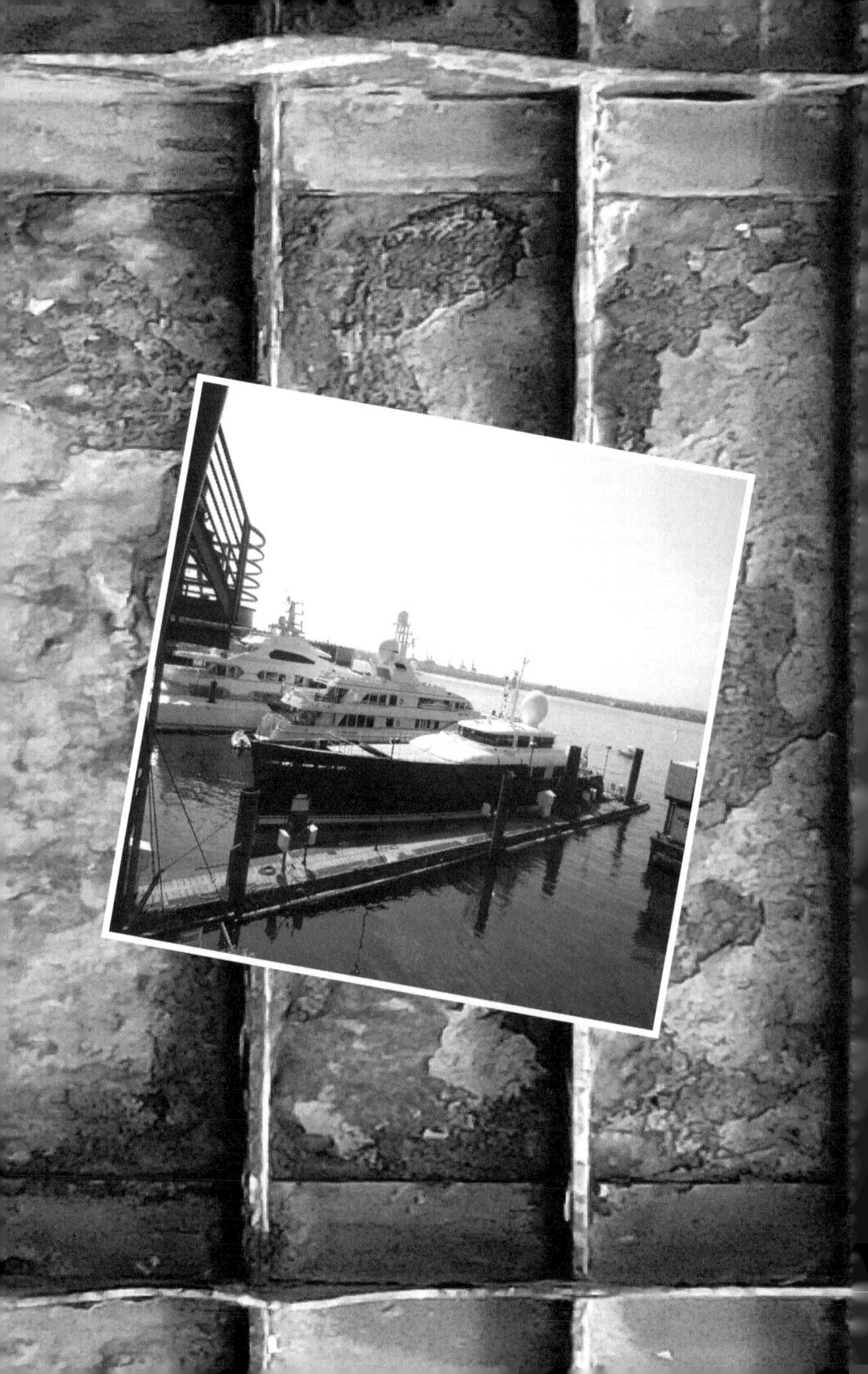

Chapter Six

Monday August 27th 10:20

"Hurry up people! What is this, a convention?" The Captain of the 150 foot pleasure yacht *Eternity* shouts up at the boat. On the foredeck is his gathered crew talking to each other. Captain Ian Sandivick is just walking up the pier from the well maintained jetty, when he notices them all loitering. *What the heck are they doing?* The rugged Captain asks himself in between each of his long strides up to the polished ship. *I go to the hardware store for half an hour and the crew goes on break?* The ship is tied up at its new berth in the exclusive North Lake Union Madison Park Docks.

Historical, well kept homes in front of manicured lawns and pathways, with close-up views of the lake and the expensive yachts. The docks are filled with these recreational ships from the privileged, wealthy, and the powerful. Halfway up the gangway Captain Ian yells, "I need you guys to finish the restocking work! Come on and get moving!" He takes off his clean white ball cap and waves it around for effect. The crew finally seem to take notice of his arrival and start to disperse. "We've got lots of work to do before final staging. We need to have this ship ready for voyage in just forty-eight hours!!"

Ian walks without even looking where he is going; he's so comfortable with his familiarity of the ship. As he walks into the main salon, he looks casually to his mobile phone to see if his ex-girlfriend has called him back. He shakes his head disgustedly seeing that Daria hasn't even had the courtesy to send him a text back. Ian Sandivick is so proud of his new job and he wanted so badly to share it with someone. Ian says to the ship, "Women can be such unfathomable oceans sometimes..." as he weaves his way up to the cockpit; bag of hardware in hand.

The expensive ship is owned by a newly wealthy pair of friends. One of the friends owns a hundred year old colonial in Madison Park, hence the docked *Eternity* close by. The other friend lives in a boathouse not far away on Lake Union. The boat house sits just five berths up from the boathouse made famous in the movie "Sleepless in Seattle."

The two friends had started up their own web based digital software delivery company just three years ago. They could take any digital code; regardless if it was raw data, images, files or an entire program, encrypt it and then break it up into small pieces. By passing it through their own proprietary software, the sender could send the data around the world with confidence. Through all of the servers, switches and nodes, and it would arrive intact and then be reassembled by the receivers computer. Their patented process can send the packets at three times the reliability, and security with twice the speed of current programs. Captain Ian was well aware of their background story and was impressed by the pair's tenacity. It reminded Ian Sandivick of qualities within himself.

Ian walks onto the polished mahogany floor of the cockpit and replaces his hat correctly on his red head. He gets back to his project of moving a pair of instrument display screens, the reason why he went to the McClendon's hardware store. Lately, he has been constantly reminding himself of how fortunate he is to have landed such an opportunity. His two bosses had done lots of hard work to get to where they were and Ian had admired them for it. *So I am trying to return their favor by demonstrating my honor at such a job,* Ian tells himself. His pair of bosses had mutual good feelings toward their new captain, so it made for relationships of respect between all three men. Ian takes one last look at his phone to see if Daria Merchant has messaged him before tossing his mobile aside and getting back to his work.

The pair of Eternity's owners were once young college kids. They had crafted software algorithms during many late night's monster energy drinks and pizza binges. The two had delusions of grandeur that they would someday be the next big tech giants. After they built the software from the complex math formulas they each developed, the two formed a company and patented their technology. Maxing out credit cards and emptying their savings. They lived in debt for twenty-eight months, seemingly an '*eternity*' for the pair, until they were able to license their new software to several smaller companies. The collection agency was a few days away from knocking on their door before they were able to start making payments on the debts.

The smaller tech firms loved the software product. The pair's company gained a reputation for its service, security and the flexibility to customize the software. Just eight months ago they hit it big, when their company was picked up by Microsoft. Once Microsoft had gotten wind of it, the two literally had Santa Claus at their door. The pair of childhood friends always promised each other that once they became millionaires they would buy houses on Lake Union and split the purchase of a yacht. Just weeks after the Microsoft money hit their accounts they were literally out looking for the ship of their dreams.

The two friends were pragmatic and still lived in the same kind of clothes they wore during their days of starvation. The pair decided on renting several different yachts first. Testing out the features, sizes and amenities. They would mostly just cruise from Portland and back on week long party cruises. Lots of acquaintances that they pretended were friends, plenty of alcohol and lots of laughter. These two wealthy entrepreneurs didn't have girlfriends, real friends or anyone to share their victory with other than each other. They had spent too much time staying up late into the early morning for lasting relationships. That was until they ran across their new captain.

It was a year ago, on their second to last trial cruise Captain Ian, then just a waiter, had befriended the pair. It was on one of the larger rental yachts. The three men had hit it off well on the voyage, joking and ribbing each other relentlessly whenever they crossed paths. There were a few prospective buyers on that trip, but none of them acted so down to earth as the pair of tycoons. The waiter described to the two how he had been on ships since he was seventeen and knew everything about what it took to run a ship like the yacht. From small Alaskan fishing boats when he was just starting off, to larger commercial trawlers as he got older. Toward his late thirties when he got the chance to work on yachts; he'd seen it all.

The waiter explained during an evening dinner party, the three were out on the deck, "Look guys, I can't get promotions on these yacht journeys. Despite my experience. Look at me. I'm Frankenstein. My hands are thrashed and too often broken mitts." The three were out enjoying the cool night air. The waiter set down his tray and turned his open palms over for the two to see.

"They look like you punched cars for a living," the taller entrepreneur commented, feeling sorry for the waiter.

Agreeing with his friend and business partner, "Definitely not normal for a maître d' on shiny yachts. Plus I couldn't help but notice the numerous scars on your arms and hands."

"Fishing was tearing me apart. The scars were mostly from hooks and barbs." The waiter agreed, introspective and worn. "If I don't keep it covered with long sleeves I become the topic of conversation, not the yacht, the yacht owner, or the party. Thankfully I've got an honest face." He admitted the part about his face only because he heard that from others. Too bad it held cold and dark eyes that had seen many storms. The waiter glanced quickly at his watch and realized how much time he was taking. "If you guys will excuse me, work calls."
The next evening the party went long and the waiter was busy. But later, in a 2 a.m.

morning game of pool, he explained to the two friends, "If someone would just give me a chance, I will prove my competence." It was the pitch of his lifetime to the two recently wealthy men. After more questions, conversations and wine, the pair bought it. That morning, the pair of entrepreneurs remembered what it was like to need a bit of luck to go your way.

The two friends pulled him aside on the deck, the last day of their test cruise. "We like your attitude Ian," one of the friends commented. He was the one that was shorter than the other. Ian was doubtful of the intentions of the impromptu meeting, but deferred his judgment.

The taller one chimed in, placing a hand on Ian's shoulder, "As you know, we are going to be buying a yacht in just a few weeks." The taller one had a flair for the melodramatic, he paused to look at his business partner before finishing. "We would like to make you Captain of her. How does that hit ya?"

Ian, the experienced seafarer asked, "Full time work?" disbelieving the two men. He didn't trust the words that the pair were speaking.

"Yep. You can even live on board." The taller one added.

"Ian, you just run it like you have told us a ship should be run. You impressed us," the shorter man grinned. "You hire the crew, we hire the cook. You run the ship the way you want with only one caveat..."

Incredulously, Ian the waiter asked, "What is that?"

"When we are on board our ship, you treat us like kings."

"Deal?" the pair asked Ian in unison.

Ian waited, not believing the moment. He felt like pinching himself. But the reality of it slowly sunk in while the pair of friends stood by each other now, all grins. "I've got nothing to loose and I want a chance. So deal." Ian extended his hand and shook both of theirs.

That was how he became Captain of the *Eternity*. It took Ian just a little bit of time to get into the swing of things. He hired the best possible crew, within the budget, that the wealthy pair had given him. His new employees had been prepping the ship since taking possession of the unnamed yacht just two weeks prior. He and his crew went through the yacht systematically, testing every function. *All faults must be discovered before the first journey,* Ian made sure of it. *There will be no surprises, no unforeseen circumstances on my first of what will hopefully be a long relationship with the two men..*

Captain Ian Sandivick and his employees took the unnamed yacht out on two trial runs on Lake Washington. They made sure all of the bugs were worked out. Ian had two 60" flat screens replaced because of intermittent flickering, *something to do with electromagnetic something or other.* Ian had one of his crew replace a door because it wouldn't close right, *after messing with the hinge alignment for three hours!* Ian mentally went through the list as he worked on the replacement of the hardware. *And a few other things just because I wanted to,* Ian smiled to himself as he worked.

After all I was Captain of a yacht capable of going half way around the world on a single tank of gas! I will use the title, but not abuse it.

The *Eternity* was christened with its name day before yesterday. It was done with public fanfare and a mention in the Seattle Times. She was the first custom yacht produced by a local builder out of Tacoma. The paper went on and on about the local jobs created and the money from taxes that were collected from the yacht's construction and sale.

Ian was officially given control of the 150 foot pleasure yacht that night at a private party. He kept having to figuratively pinch himself again and again. Ian walked around both events still reminding himself that he was no longer a waiter. *There will be no more begging for promotions on other ship jobs. All of my cold toil, smelling like fish and taking hundreds of cuts had finally paid off. Not only had I a place to live, but a ship I could call my own.*

Now, I will prove that I'm not just a scarred fishmonger. Ian felt the relief, but also the responsibility in his bones. *Yes, I had paid the price for twenty years. But now,* Ian assures himself, *just as long as I treat my employers like kings, I have worth beyond just a stupid paycheck!*

Ian lay on his back listening to his crew, busy at their jobs while he is finishing his.

"This is going to be such a nice gig," he whispers to himself.

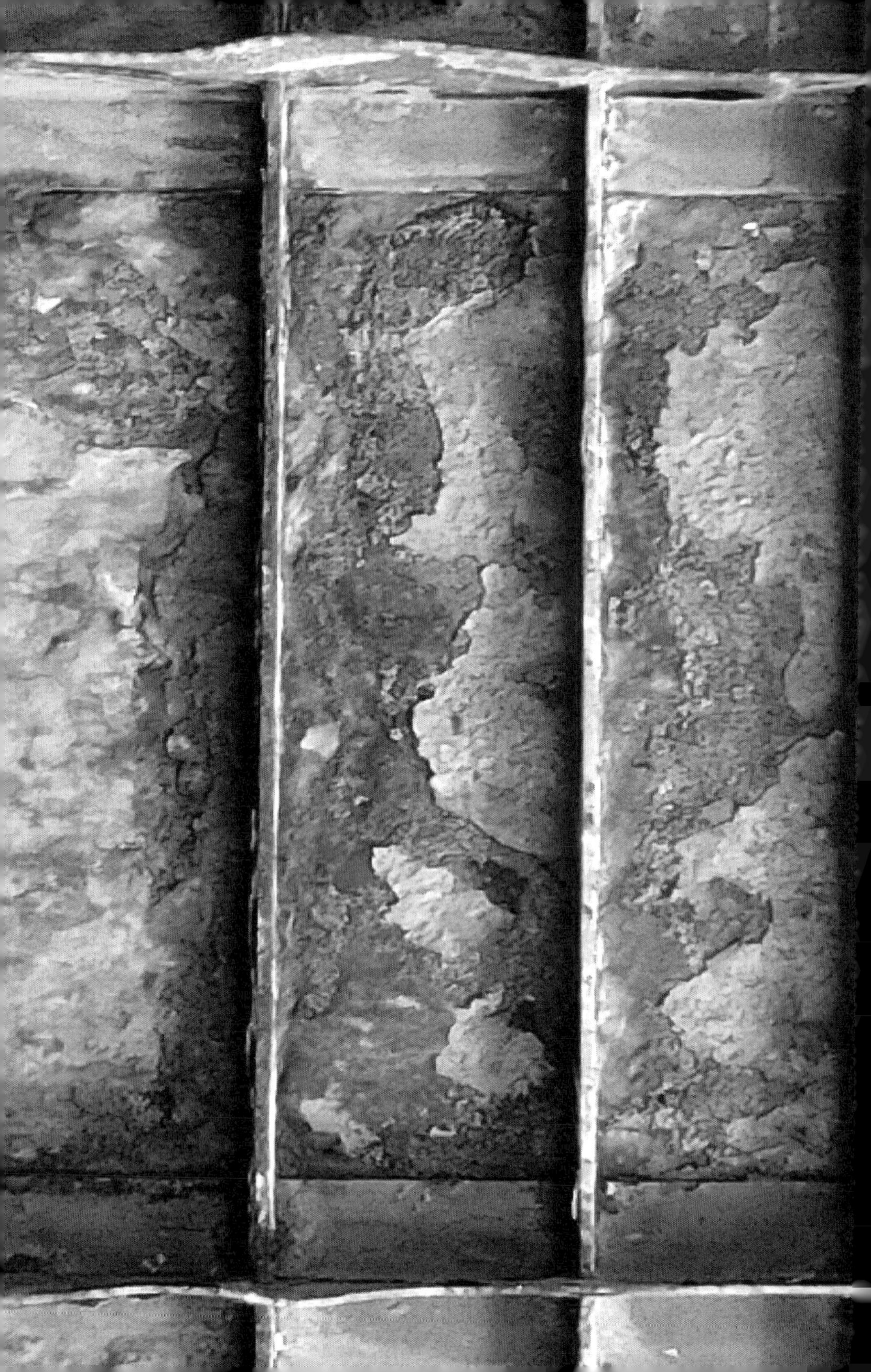

Chapter Seven

Tuesday August 28th 3:26

      The mature gentleman opens his eyes and lifts his head slightly. He raises it off of his doctor recommended, hand made, orthopedic pillow. Gazing around the room, he senses, not strangeness but familiarly in the darkness. The sounds and smells of his home give him relief that he is safe, despite his nightmare. His eyes seek out the accustomed objects and their locations within his sleeping room to confirm what he now already knows.

Everything is ok.

He breathes out a sigh of relief and relaxes a bit despite the still present images in his minds eye. He is still baring witness to his dream- a giant eagle was ripping and tearing into the flesh of one of his prized horses. All the while he was staked to the ground, forced to watch the ghastly spectacle. There were wolves in the distance pacing, waiting to tear into his critically injured horse. *And I lay there, pulling at the stakes that were pinning me to the ground. The pain was horrible, but I was still fighting against it...*

The stakes were impaling him through his arms and *legs like the prophet Jesus himself*. Despite the pain, the man continued to force himself up just to catch a glimpse of his precious Arabian horse. *As if the horrible sight would inspire my mind to come up with an idea to rescue the poor thing. Then, there were my trained falcons.* The birds of prey sat dispassionately on a fence rail. They sat close together and watched the whole scene; not doing a thing about it.

Worthless birds, the older man chastised their memory.

The gentleman pushes aside the images and lays his head back onto the softness of his pillow. He curls up around his nubile wife a little closer, gently placing his arm over her side, trying to let her assuring warmth and fragrance ease him back into sleep. Yet, sleep does not come and she doesn't even stir. He lies in bed for another hour, *envious that she can sleep so soundly*. The man stays as still as possible, not wanting to leave the comfort or disturb her sleep. Eventually he decides against it. His brain reminds him of what he already knows, *once you wake up, like you are now, you will not be able to sleep again for hours*. He faces the fact that the nightmares are connected to his stress and worry. And the anxiety that is biting at his soul is a direct result of everything that is going on lately.

As quietly as the older man is able, he eases out of the bed and into his closet. After the man puts on a robe, he grabs a bottle of water from the small refrigerator that is built into the large walk-in closet. The older gentleman unscrews the cap, takes a drink and screws it back on lightly. He watches his second wife sleep for a few minutes, then sneaks past her slender form on his way out of the room. The woman does not stir as the older man exits and heads toward his office.

The office is his default place to go whenever he has time on his hands; it is both refuge and prison cell. As the man weaves through his sprawling home, he passes a pair of doorways and a shadowed figure in a suit and tie silently starts to follow behind. The shadow that follows is a pillar of professionalism; straight back and square shoulders, with eyes that don't miss a thing. The shadow is silent, well dressed and has no shoes on.

The older gentleman finishes his water with a long pull on the bottle, not realizing he was so thirsty. Without turning around to address the man that follows with wraithlike silence, the gentleman whispers in his native Arabic, "Evening, Emre."

"Morning, sir." The fluent whisper comes back from the man in the dark business suit; the shadow had a voice and a name. Emre whispers back to his boss, "Are you having trouble sleeping again...?"

Turning the corner down one hallway and then into another, the homeowner enters into his office, "Yes, something like that." The older man, homeowner and keeper of a small security force throws away the water bottle. It bounces once into the receptacle next to the older man's desk.

The mature gentleman sits himself behind the red mahogany woodwork, looking momentarily lost behind its size. Taking in the handmade scroll work and polished surface the older man closes his eyes, and shakes his head slightly, almost imperceptibly. Taking a moment to organize his thoughts, the older man takes a deep breath. Emre had stopped nearby and was patiently waiting with hands folded in front of him; watching his boss struggle with thoughts.

"Would you please fetch me a glass of ice water and something to eat?" The older man breaks the silence. "It seems I am going to do a little work before I make another attempt to go back to sleep."

"Certainly sir.' Emre nods. "Do you have anything in mind?" The bodyguard and prime assistant waits while his employer for the past ten years turns on a pair of televisions with a remote.

Setting the remote back on the desk the older man absently asks, "What was that,

Emre?" His attention focused on the financial markets in Japan that's displayed on one of the televisions. Both large screens are now displaying video signals in bright and amazing detail on their wall mounted flat screens.

Emre responds respectfully, anticipating that he was going to get asked again, "Your food, sir."

"Ah yes, sorry, still trying to clear my head." The stations get changed until one signal stops on FOX News and the other stops on BBC America. "Some dates and some bread?"

"Olives too?" Emre wonders.

His employer smiles and looks at him for the first time this early morning. "Well yes, you know I can not refuse olives. Not too many though, the salt. Doctors and wives, you know?" Emre smiles at his employer's words. The homeowner sees his bodyguard's smile and it slightly lightens his own heart. "Dates, olives, bread and a *tall* glass of ice water if you don't mind?" The older man points at the empty bottle in his waste basket, "I seem to be thirsty…"

"You do need to stay properly hydrated…doctors and wives sir." The homeowner smiles his own smile at Emre's remark, then looks back to the two television screens. Sensing the lighthearted moment evaporate, Emre speaks up once more, in his professional voice, before leaving the room. "Kaan will watch the room while I gather your food. Is that acceptable?"

"Certainly, thank you." The older man watches Emre, his chief of security, silently disappear around the corner, only to have Kaan appear a moment later. Kaan stands just at the edge of the home office, trying to be as inconspicuous as possible. He is dressed very similar to Emre; the dark business suits and black dress shirts are the de riguer uniform for the male household staff. Shoes were not allowed in the house, so black dress socks matched the suits.

The older gentleman shifts his focus to the second flat screen. Al Jazeera is now on. The older man's gaze is one with care, that misses little, and his eyes flick back and forth between the pair. He's watching both screens, taking in all of the data and the ticker along the bottom. He is occupied by the news around the world for a few minutes while his personal computer boots up.

The computer screen is inlaid into a recessed cavity in his desk. When the slim desk top is down, it looks like a regular desk, but once lifted a 32inch touch screen is unveiled, along with a recessed place for a wireless keyboard and mouse. The homeowner adjusts the desktop of his desk to the correct viewing angle and logs on to his system. He checks his email, a file share site and pulls open an app for phone calls.

He had purchased the software from a pair of Washington State inventors/entrepreneurs. The software was tailored perfectly for his needs and that of his company. *Too bad the two men had sold out.* The mature gentleman stops his train of thought to jot down a quick note. *The rumor was they had sold to Microsoft no less and bought themselves a yacht.* The mature man finishes writing his idea down, *I would have been glad to hire them for much more money and given them a nicer ship.* The older man visually checks that the software application is fully up on his pc. He looks down in the lower tool bar to make sure that the high grade voice over internet protocol (VOIP) encryption software is ready for secured calls.

The master of the house hears quiet footsteps approach his office and looks up expecting Emre. TO his surprise the master of the house watches his first wife walk slowly, gracefully, into his office. "Can't wait to get to work?" she asks with a drowsy smirk and her usual dry sense of humor.

"Nightmares my dear." Their eyes meet and they hold each other's gaze while he asks, "Why are you roaming around at this hour? Is everything okay?"

She comes over to his desk, and kisses the top of his head. "Just thirst and a visit to the restroom," she whispers, as she pats her husband's shoulder; an assuring gesture. "I saw the light on and decided to investigate," his second wife confesses. She has a lot on her mind, but keeps her other questions to herself. Her questions were always interconnected for her, one answer leading to exponentially more trains of thought.

The woman turns away, not wanting her husband of so long to see her face. The lady begins to leave the room, but stops halfway. She knows how her husband of twenty years hates to talk early in the morning, but she reconsiders her resolution to keep it pithy. Slightly turning, and still hiding her face, "I have you for the next three nights, correct?"

The silver haired man behind the desk still can't seem to get the nightmare out of his head. He couldn't decide which was worse, *the eagle or the falcons*? He tries to think of what day it is, about to open up his calendar on his computer.

"It's Tuesday morning." His cherished first wife says, reading his mind.

"One more night, then I am yours." The older man forces a smile in her direction trying to show her some joy. Yet, he avoids eye contact.
"Very well," she whispers, not letting her sadness show. She walks past Kaan and silkily whispers, "Good morning Kaan," Kaan nods his head, keeping his eyes on the floor as she passes. He demonstrates to her and his boss, the respect she deserves.

The master of the house is left with seeing the eagle again; all diseased and gruesome somehow, diving its head into his poor horse. The eagle's head was covered in gore and despite the distractions of the televisions on the walls, he is pulled back into the visions. The wolves hover over the soon to be corpse of the horse. *My falcons, fearful of the eagle's size and power, stay back. Yet they don't even try to drive off the wolves...what gives?*

The gentleman does not need a visionary protagonist like Joseph to tell him what the dream means. *I know this is all about the operation that will take place just two days from now,* he confirms. *This new way of conducting covert action will hopefully take so many by complete surprise. So much of a shock and revelation that the nightmares will be worth it.*

The mature gentleman holds such a firm belief in his faith that, at one time he had even ostracized his oldest daughter for her unchaste behavior. *She had an illicit relationship with an American solider of all people! I was ridiculed and reproved by even by Imam for her choice.* In return, the master of the house prohibited his entire family from even helping his *fallen* daughter.

The master of the house has tried to pay penance for his daughter's apostasy. Through private and secure channels he has given funds, equipment and other support to numerous people and groups furthering the Militant Islamist cause. Recently, he even put together his own group. Uniting with others, that were like minded, in various types of business. They were now coming up on their first 'public' mission. They had done some basic snatch-n-grab and reconnaissance missions for various governments. They had charged handsomely for the OP's that they performed, but this new one was very different. He, and his associates, are about to lay it all on the line. He was even going to go so far as to include another family member for the cause.

Emre enters the office again with the food and water on a stainless steel tray. "Here is what you asked for sir. I also brought you some aspirin, in case you might have a headache."

"Thank you, Emre. That was very kind. That will be all." The homeowner pops a date into his mouth, chews, swallows and takes a long drink from the hand-cut crystal glass. Emre replaces Kaan at the door and wordlessly Kaan leaves the room to assume his previous patrol duty.

The studious man sitting behind the desk takes two aspirin out of the pill bottle and swallows them before eating anything else. *Emre is right, I do have a headache. That man is tirelessly dedicated, I owe him something more than long hours and a decent pay.* He opens his memo pad once more and types out a request for his secretary to look into what he can do for Emre. *There must be something for him or his family...his* thought trails off drawn back to his snack.

The master of the house takes a small slice of the bread, and then he reopens the secure E-VOIP application, intending to make some phone calls. His nightmare might just be a warning and he will heed it. Like the Pharaoh heeding Joseph's warning in Egypt, visions were given to men by Allah for good reasons. Pharaoh and Joseph would not ignore the message and neither would he. *Ignoring messages from Allah led to your own peril,* the master of the house promised to himself.

He starts going through the actions to personally set up a meeting to preempt the eagle from his nightmare. Every one of his trustees will be required to be there. *No excuses,* the master of the house promises himself. *Especially from the Brigadier, his pompousness can be grating and my elusive messenger Grey Hair had to be nailed down to a set time.* He fires off the encrypted email that will begin the process of bringing all of his men together.

The gentleman dials the first number from memory, their *tanazu,* their fight, was just about to begin in earnest. The Arabian horse was not dead in his vision, it was just being held down by that insufferable eagle. *It could recover from its wounds if it just had the chance.* He knew the metaphor and meaning of the message that Allah was sending. The horse was his fight against the west and the collective struggle against it. The eagle was the United States, the wolves were Britain, Israel, France and Germany. *And my falcons were all the Muslim countries that refused to join the fight.*

I promise we will all make sure everything is ready, he vowed to Allah. *And that there are no loose ends. After all I am the president of a large company, a wealthy businessman, and I sit on the boards of several other companies. Including a secret one...*

Allah has given me many gifts and I will not squander them, the older man assures.

To add to his accomplishments, he is also the C.O. of a newly formed, secret jihadist organization. Ashan was all his dream; it was all his vision. He was carefully, slowly putting the pieces together to do many valiant acts. *Soon, the timeline will be formulated and the actions steps will begin,* the C.O. smugly reminds himself. *Besides, I know how to speak to underlings.*

Waiting for the phone to be picked up, the man vows that the eagle will not feast on his faith. *It will not have myself or my brother's precious things anymore. The hawks and wolves I will have to address later.*

A male voice in proper British English interrupts his train of thought, "Good day, may I help you?"

"Transfer my call to the Amir," the master of the house returns the polite male receptionist's tone with his own demand. The CO has ties all over Europe and the Middle East, but the Amir was his closest tie back to the Muslim Brotherhood and al-Qaeda. The CO needed to make sure *amateurs don't have something planned that will throw off my own designs. I need to cover all the bases and heed the dream.*

The other end of the line remains silent for a few heartbeats, "Yes sir, but may I ask who's calling?"

"No you may not! Transfer my call, secretary... His Highness the Amir is expecting a call from me...so... Now!"

There was a moment of silence and then the click of a call getting transferred.

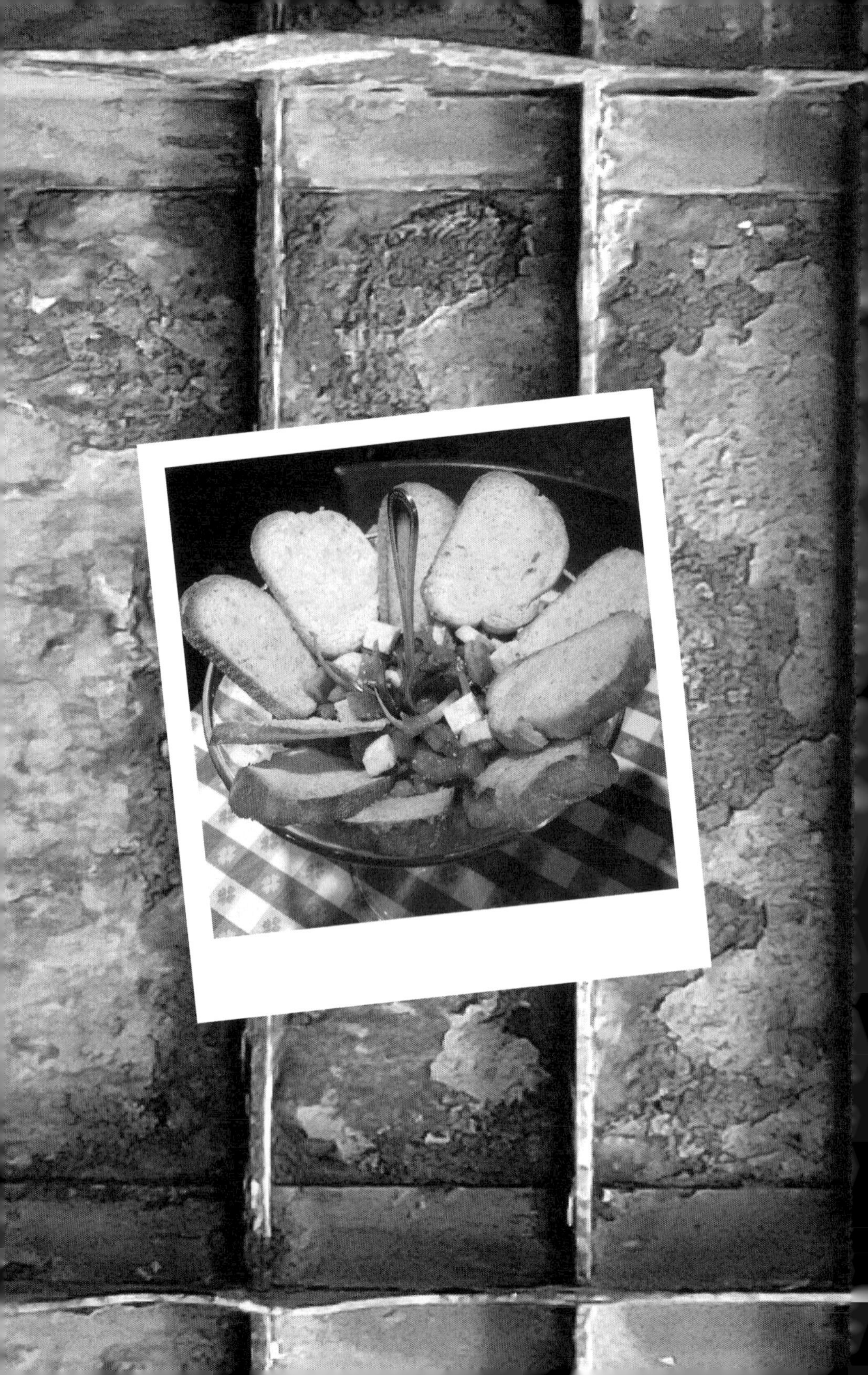

Chapter Eight

Tuesday August 28th 11:14

"Business is good. There's no doubt," Ibrahim says to his host.

Humans will always be in conflict and there will always be people needing help. That was human nature after all. Ibrahim considers as he half-listens to his dinner guest talk. *I am in the field, with some resources at hand; to help in small ways. After all that is what our meeting is about.*

Every time Ibrahim and his Organization considered that their funds will dry up, they seem to always find another revenue stream. Sometimes it's a couple of inside information stock options contracts, sometimes an office or apartment building flip, but mostly the money comes from new donors. Donors offer "contributions to the cause" in exchange for small favors.

Ibrahim Al-Duwaisan thinks about the favors that he has arranged, *everyone likes a helping hand now and again.*

"Would you like another glass of wine?" Ibrahim nods to his host's question. His host, a man of slight build, pours both of them a fresh glass from a carafe. On this trip, Ibrahim is meeting with one of his Ashan's fresh customers. This client of Ibrahim's is small and so thin that it seems a strong wind will blow him over. Yet, the man's ever present bodyguards wouldn't let that happen.

They would try to fight the wind if they were commanded to, so subservient, yet doubtless more capable than my host across the table. Ibrahim keeps the smile to himself as he takes a sip of the red wine.

Ibrahim's dinner guest is well connected within his own countries military and governmental systems. Ibrahim Al-Duwaisan watches, looking down upon him, as the man transfers a donation to Mr. Duwaisan's cause. With just a few swipes of a boney finger and a smart phone, his host ensures that Ibrahim's Organization will continue, all electronically. With that done, the pair of men resume their conversation. This time talking about a favor that this new donor desperately needs.

"Nuting big," The man explains in a horribly accented English with a sly smile. Ibrahim listens carefully as the Asian accented English was not all that great. "Just need one our dissidents tooo...disappear." Ibrahim's guest takes a long drag on an unfiltered cigarette, blows out the smoke and then takes a sip from his glass. "Maybe, it look like a drug deal or how you say, murder-suicide? There is many of them in that country. Agree?"

Ibrahim, absently nods his head still fixing his host's mistakes in pronunciation within his mind. *My host doesn't need any bad press brought down upon himself or his country. He has enough problems with all of the human rights violations. Yet, it's good that this client wants more involvement from the Organization.* Ibrahim also realizes, as he listens to his dinner guest talk some more, *that the man wants his own country's involvement kept entirely confidential. That can be easily arranged.*

Ibrahim leans in nonchalantly, grabbing a piece of the bruschetta. He savors the layered flavors and quietly asks the obvious question between bites of the tomatoes and bread. "Where?"

The client takes another sip of his wine and looks around slowly. The dinner guest looks past his body guards not even seeing them. In a melodramatic fashion, the Asian man finishes off his cigarette and stuffs it out on the floor. Crushing it beneath his expensive 5th Avenue New York shoes.

Sitting at this Italian food restaurant, just like you would on the streets of Rome seems a bit phony to Ibrahim. The irony doesn't escape him. The sidewalk dinning is one thing to create an atmosphere for the meal, but entirely another when all around you are signs in Mandarin.

Ibrahim watches his host gaze out at all of the advertising that is pasted on nearly every vertical surface nearby. The donor's gaze locks onto an ad selling a famous American Beer. The colors of the ad are red and white with a minor flourish of blue. The tagline of The Great American Lager is seen held in eagle's claws. The Asian man nods toward the beer ad and Ibrahim looks at it over his glass of wine.

Ibrahim nonchalantly takes a sip and glances back toward his dinner guest. Mr. al-Duwaisan questions discreetly, "Us?"

The slight man knowingly nods his head at the clear reference to the United States. Ibrahim nods his head as well and they are both in agreement. The bargain has been made. His host passes Ibrahim an envelope, "You will find the address and the particulars in here, thank you for the meeting. Here is to our future." The dinner guest bids farewell by polishing off his cabernet, tossing enough money on the table to cover the bill and then walks away with his guards in tow.

Business is done. For agreeing to look into the matter Ibrahim and his non-profit just garnered an additional significant donation. Ibrahim waits until his host is out of sight before opening the envelope. With a swift flick of a Damascus steel knife the envelope reveals an address, presumably for the dissident, a picture and a folded piece of paper. *The picture must be the dissident, standing underneath the Golden Gate Bridge with her family,* Ibrahim assumes.

The family in the picture is all smiles and...*will soon be dead.* Ibrahim confirms. His organization will do this favor for this new client and business will continue. *The order has been given and if the mother, the target, can't be caught alone the entire family will perish.* On the folded piece of paper are three names with a Chinese phrase at the bottom. Ibrahim searches his brain for the exact translation. *More people? Many men? More men?* He can't remember the exact meaning, *but it seems the Asian man isn't so useless after all. This must be the leads on further contributors,* Ibrahim recognizes. *I had asked politely about it toward the beginning of our conversation, but our talk never addressed it.*

An hour later, sitting in an airport, Ibrahim Al-Duwaisan boots up his company's laptop. While waiting for an answer from the airlines regarding his travel issue, he opens a secure web encryption program and supplies those new names to his superiors. The transmission is quick and encrypted up to a file share site. Ibrahim doesn't wait to download anything else; he just shuts down the laptop as fast as he brought it up.

Hopefully, The Superiors will be thankful, Ibrahim wishes. *The entirety of Ashan's funding is being put into doubt due to the poor economy. Nothing unexpected or unassailable, particularly now with some fresh blood injected into their accounts, but it is alarming nevertheless.* Ibrahim watches people pass by and considers the problem, *Hopefully these new sources of funds will be especially beneficial. When the non-profit I represent runs low on money, operations all around the world grind to a halt.*

Ibrahim felt that even with the new donors, his six Superiors will still quietly ask for more donations from their existing clientele. Those clients are expected to donate. There is no such thing as too much money. If the existing donors don't donate, there will be consequences. Thankfully though, it looks like his company can spread out the responsibility of support even further, diversifying the burden of financial assistance even more.

"Give charity without delay, for it stands in the way of calamity..." Quran 63:10. Allah wants all to be of good charity. Ibrahim recites the passage from heart despite the fact his memory isn't what it used to be. *Getting old makes it hard when faced with a requirement to meet with a reluctant giver. The meeting is never easy on the giver, but I cant do it much longer.*

Ibrahim knows the *mudharabah* (transactions derived from partnerships based on risk and profit sharing) must go on. *Wars need funds, wars need supplies, and wars need materials to carry on the conflicts.*

Ibrahim, in his Gian DeCaro business suit, gets a page over the airport terminal's speakers. He stands back in line to retrieve his three airline tickets. His grandson and stylishly dressed wife wait nearby. His Beautiful Lady is enthralling their grandson with a narration of the sights within Terminal 2 of Beijing Capital International Airport (PEK). Ibrahim is in awe of how easy his wife is able to captivate their grandson with all things; a description of an airport. Anyone else would find the subject matter utterly dry, but the tone of her voice and the choice of her words draws in the young boy. Ibrahim doesn't know who is more enthralled. His grandson, head filled with the skillful narration or himself seeing his wife in her element.

Standing in line, Ibrahim isn't impressed. He has seen too many airports. Beijing airport is huge, there is no doubt. It is filled with a host of distractions and many places to eat within the massive terminals, *but it's still just an airport,* Ibrahim thinks. *Regardless of what the vendors try to hock, from exclusive memberships, to decadent chocolates to some local bauble, it was just a building to pass through. On your way to a better place.*

The signs spread all over the airport bragged about the facts in multiple languages, Ibrahim recalls. PEK! The second busiest in the world next to Atlanta, and the second largest in square footage next to King Fahd in Saudi Arabia, *but still just an airport. And I can't wait to get out of here.*

We'll see if those airports keep their status, Ibrahim thinks to himself still standing in line. *The Chinese don't like to be second to anyone. Above all, the Americans and the Saudi's.*

"Here you go, sir. Sorry for the confusion." Ibrahim's attention snaps back to the lady in front of him. "You and your family are now all sitting in the same first class row." The female gate agent speaks with a customary smile and nod. Typical of the culture, Ibrahim smiles and nods back, but doesn't say a word. His Mandarin is just a sliver of what it should be.

The petite gate agent returns the well dressed man's grin with one of her own. She tries to keep her embarrassment at her company's failure under wraps. She smiles her best to cover for the mistake, "Sorry for any inconvenience the matter has caused." The Persian looking man dips his head to her in acknowledgement, but still doesn't say a word. She hopes that he will accept their apology and the attempt at repair.

Still feeling inconvenienced, Ibrahim just walks off with the new tickets in hand. The seating issue worked out, he sits down once again with his family and waits. One last stop on his business trip. One final, long flight. This one is going to be the worst. Nine hours to Qatar. You'd bet he fought for his family to sit together in first class. He would have taken a different airline if any of his family or himself were forced to sit in commercial. *That is way too long to sit pushed up against someone else in an uncomfortable seat,* Ibrahim confirms to himself.

Too bad they don't allow smoking, Ibrahim bemoans. *I would gladly light up one of my cigars on the flight to go with the glass of American whiskey. The pair would have been a delightful way to relax.* But he will just have to be happy with the whiskey moments after being seated. *I need one last chance to satisfy vices before I have to follow much stricter rules.*

He, his grandson, and wife are headed to Qatar for a bit of vacation and a bit of business. Very much like this trip to the Peoples Republic of China, just a lot closer to home. He is on his final leg, doing a personal favor for the people he currently works for.

The Organization that Ibrahim belonged to broke off of the Brotherhood many years ago. The Muslim Brotherhood had started to garner too much attention, their Wahhabist views weren't the problem; they were just standing too much in the spotlight. That made some Sunni Arabs nervous and they felt that more could be done with greater control on a Organization. The fewer people that knew about Ashan the lesser chance the members would get caught. You just never knew when you would be connected to someone and have an American drone drop a bomb on you. Now, this new 'company' was deeply undercover and totally autonomous.

Most messages are delivered via Ibrahim. In person-to-personal meetings, Ibrahim receives and delivers the messages. There was only the occasional encrypted data traffic or web conferences. Any kind of massive data was sent via overnight shipping, physically located on a solid state drive to the customer or contact. Never a phone call, and particularly with a mobile phone. Any World Wide Web traffic was only to supplement Ibrahim's ability to carry out his duties, never to replace them, and that traffic was always encrypted and coded. Security Protocol dictated to always be purposeful, never a spontaneous call.

Soon, Ibrahim knew, he would have to broach the idea of retirement from his beloved Ashan. His superiors in the Shura Council would not like it, but they had to face the facts. He just turned sixty-five and though still capable, he couldn't keep this up for much longer. His employer needed to begin the process of vetting a replacement for him. Ibrahim desired to spend more time with his family, chiefly his first grandson. He had fought a long time and soon it was time to enjoy peace.

Ibrahim has been very careful since being placed in charge of global field operations. Just seven years ago he was tapped by a very wealthy man to work for a cause greater than this physical world. The man, that went by the name of C.O., who bought him on, was a powerfully wealthy individual. As Ibrahim discovered, the C.O. had influence and business ties in many countries in Asia, Eastern Europe and the middle East. Ibrahim jumped at the prospect of working with the older businessman and when the C.O. had given Ibrahim a glimpse of the C.O.'s vision; Ibrahim was impressed.

Since he was a boy in Egypt, Ibrahim had always been involved in the conflict to get rid of Israel's (the little Satan) and America's (Great Satan) influence upon the world. To stop that corrupting power and to bring about the next caliphate was very important to Ibrahim. But so many of his close friends had given up their lives for that and it just didn't make sense to do so anymore. *So much waste, so many good people had died,* Ibrahim had lamented. *There had to be a better way to achieve the goal.*

When the C.O. had asked him some years ago to join, Ibrahim had a few requests before he agreed.

As Ibrahim soon discovered, the wealthy businessman had parallel concerns. That had surprised Ibrahim, but it had made it all the easier to join the Organization that started calling itself Ashan. Mr. Ibrahim Al Duwaisan and all of his co-workers in this new group were very careful. They all had created protocols that demanded computer, personal and operational security. No one wanted to end up being vaporized by a Hellfire missile fired down from a remote controlled flying toy. And Ibrahim himself, didn't get to be this old, in this line of work, without being prudently cautious.

He'd been fighting for a long time, and accepted certain risks. Yet, regardless of their continuing caution, their "coming out" was quite dangerous. The first private, international Muslim spy agency was not going to be met with open arms by many countries.

Chapter Nine

Wednesday August 29th 15:31

    Sitting and waiting. He did a lot of that. Whether it was on the phone deep inside a building or in his van, like now. *Comparatively, this wasn't so bad*, James thought.

There is a great view of some American Navy Ships just to my right. Aircraft carriers, a destroyer and some re-supply ships. The great machines loomed over the docks like silent steel golems awaiting their next dangerous deployment. Almost as if they were made by Rabbi Loew himself.

James focused toward the center of his windshield's view taking in the Puget Sound, spread out before him like a blue green mirror. *The weather could not be better for sailing, just enough wind.* There were plenty of private boats out on the water enjoying it.

The faint breeze blows through the electrician's van's open windows. James can decipher the aromas of sea water, pine trees and...*just a tinge of vehicle exhaust to add the final bit of finish.* James watches the people walk under the ferry terminal's white metal beams; a child runs in between them with her father following close behind.

James keeps his gaze moving to his left, and outside his driver's window; another splendid sight. This time it's the snow capped mountains of the Cascades.

All of these things are out there, in the distance, begging to be investigated, explored and enjoyed. Yet, I am waiting for the ferry to take me home. Straight home. Although what I am seeing is quite splendid, I cant indulge in what interests me. No, I have a deeper longing to crawl into bed and get a solid eight hours of sleep!

One thing is for sure; sitting and waiting always gets him thinking.

James Maly figures he must be going insane, delirious or maybe both. He is hungry for meals totally out of order. He's currently craving some French toast with strawberries and it's only just past fifteen hundred. He should be craving a good steak sandwich or pizza or something.

"I'll be hungry for that probably later, much later," James reflects to his van's empty cab.

And what about dinner? James asks himself, then answers, *I'll probably eat that around two in the morning.* Recently, dinner consisted of nothing more than a glass of red wine with a kalamata olive and garlic tapenade. He'd crush it all up and have enough for a couple of nights. There, in the middle of the night, he'd munch away at it on some crusty pugliese no less.

Who craves such things at 2am, James asks himself. How many people actually even eat that kind of thing, much less as much as he does? *At least I still have my health. But for how long? How much more time do I have to run like this? I certainly couldn't do it when I'm fifty. Can I do this when I'm forty? When will my body or my health begin to break down?*

Then there is the other thing that they call sleep.

He can't seem to sleep for more than a five hour stretch on his days off . Often he will take quick half hour naps on the weekends just to get him through. He could relax himself enough to fall asleep at any time, anywhere, but never for long. Furthermore, it seems his mind is always on, constantly in thought. He can't slow it down, even for a bit of blissful zoning.

It's gotta be the work schedule that's the cause for all of this, James convinces himself.

Odd hours, on call, long drives and little regularity. Raptor Electric is a good company, but the schedule is working him over.

He reflects, *Who am I kidding? I even have to look at my mobile to see what day it is.* James shakes his head and leans it against the headrest.

Lately, he even feels like a guest in his own home. Occasionally able to witness life roll on by in his house, but never there long enough to become part of it.

*But what am I going to do? The path seems so fixed in place...*His first duty is to take care of his family. Bills have to be paid, and this is the career that he is good at doing. Although the career kind of found him, James excels at it. So, the electrician works as hard as he is able.

Well, I do have all of the memories of the sights I've seen and the companies I have visited, James reminds himself.

He'd driven onto Seatac and Paine Field runways. He has been on every major freeway and highway in the state. He has had the opportunity to go into Vulcan Aerospace, the Federal Reserve Bank and numerous other secured locations; all guarded by men with guns. He'd even had impromptu behind the scene tours of the EMP and The Museum of Flight. *Work does pay for all of that. Well, at least I will have some stories to tell someone, someday.*

As James waits for the Bainbridge, Washington to Seattle ferry to arrive, he goes through what he has forgotten. He quickly pounds out a list of the things that he can *remember* that he has forgotten, on his two year old Blackberry.

He thinks about his wife and children. James wonders what they are doing and if they miss him as much as he misses them. He mentally goes through several ideas as he tries to come up with something fun for he and his family to do. It was his weekend to come up with something and trying to decide on the best weekend get-away was difficult. He always tried to come up with an original idea, with the hope it won't get a thumbs down from any of his family members.

He transfers to his work phone, going through his work calls for Thursday and Friday. Clicking through that smartphone, he sees that he has an open day tomorrow, Thursday. That means the tasks of the day will be cleaning up his work van, restocking and doing paperwork.

Good, he considers to himself. *I could use a work from home day...*

The loud ship horn blasts it's tune, a deep and resonate bellow as it pulls into it's dock. Just a few more minutes more before James can drive on.

Back to his plans, he realizes Friday is a whole different story. The call for Friday is going to involve a long drive to Eastern Washington. Probably four or five hours. Where is he going and does he have everything in his van for it? It's an ugly bummer to drive that far to a site, only to find you left a crucial piece of something sitting in the shop.

At least today, or was it tonight? He might be able to catch eight hours of sleep? Maybe with an adult beverage or two in his system it could be possible.

Even with Thursday being unscheduled, he will need to stay on this same brutal sleep pattern. Looks like he's going to wake at O' dark thirty on Friday and drive the five hours to the Tri-Cities.
"Someday," he says to himself, just over the din of the seagulls. "It will get better. I just don't know how, but there's got to be a light at the end of the tunnel." James tried to convince himself of something that he might not believe in anymore.

Turning his mind back to the present, James wonders: *Well, if I can make it home by two, and probably in bed by three or four? In the afternoon? It's such a waste of the summer sunlight, but I've got to sleep.*

The last car rolls off of the inbound ferry and onto the peninsula. A light comes to life, up on a pole fifty yards away. The light signifies it is time to guide the vehicles on board. This Washington State Ferry has a tight schedule to keep.

Maybe there'd be some leftovers? Get in some conversation with Wendi before heading off to bed?
As the worn man parks his vehicle in the main bay, he puts the van in park, kills the engine. As he slumps in his chair he watches the employees of the ferry make ready for departure.

James watches the rear gate come up in his rearview mirrors. There is a quick horn blast and then came the deep thrum from the massive engines. James feels the powerful diesel-electric engines of the ferry spool up to full power. James watches the white froth that is generated out the stern of the ship through the mirror once more. The dock drifts away and soon they are surrounded by the blue-grey water..

James promises to himself: *When I get home, I'm definitely going to take a melatonin.* Then he doses off on the ride across Elliot Bay.

Chapter Ten

Wednesday August 29th 18:00

I just want to go home, Terra Freeland begs the mirror of her hotel room. *I miss my poodle, my townhouse and my city.*

She furiously straightens her blouse and jacket; so that they sit right on her shoulders. Giving herself a slow once over from her painted red toenails, to her skirt; all of the way up to her blond hair; *it looks like everything is in the right place.*

She is shower fresh and absently smells her hair, loving the new shampoo her cousin recommended for her. Terra Freeland kills her room's television, the voice of an ESPN announcer is quickly silenced. Terra loves all things sports, especially her Falcons and Hawks and will often have the television blasting while she bathes. The man on ESPN had been talking about the ten year anniversary of Pat Tillman's death. *Very interesting stuff, what a tragedy...but I have a meeting to make.*

Over the past week, her search for good real estate deals had been met with complications. *But the second purchase was finally signed in ink yesterday,* she convinces herself. She is always trying to spin everything into a positive in her mind. Terra Freeland pulls hard on her heavy room door to make sure it latches and then makes her way to the elevator.

"One more deal, maybe tonight," she hopes out loud, alone in the elevator car. "Then home sweet Atlanta!"

She's meeting with a big property developer that has some possible land in North Bend, WA. for sale. She vaguely understands the specifics; the property's next to some private outdoors retreat and the big developer doesn't care much for the way the neighbors are improving it. *At least that's what has been said,* she tells herself. She would normally personally check into it deals before talking about it, but the jet lag and all of the driving has wrecked her sleep schedule. *I'll make sure after my little talk with the seller,* Terra promises herself. *Maybe get it for a song ink it, and then, hopefully, I can fly out tomorrow?*

She'd met bankers, title and escrow people while out in the Northwest. Terra also had the chance to talk with some home inspectors and contractors, so the trip was not a total waste. Networking was a key to her business.

She habitually taps her foot while waiting for the elevator to come to it's last stop in the high-rise hotel. *It's all about cash, and who you know in the real estate world,* she reminds herself.

If the deal doesn't work out tonight there are still two properties out on the Peninsula that are possible candidates. *Yet, I don't really want to do that trip again.*

She recalls sitting at the seafood restaurant for two hours until their turn came up, *for a stupid ferry. The food was good at the seafood restaurant, the service above par, but the wait for the ship was horrid. I will have to go back to Ivar's someday,* she promises herself.

Terra smiles a devilish smile at the thought of her driver not being too happy with her. *He had to sit in the car for over an hour and the twerp called with only a few minutes to board...hoping I wouldn't make it I assume.*

She unconsciously smooth's out any wrinkles in her blouse and gives the ferry trip one last thought. As she walks into the exclusive hotel bar, *...a petty way of getting back at me.*

Terra Freeland starts scanning the patrons looking for a female that is sitting alone. Terra also reminds herself, *her developer contact should be looking for her too.* Then, their two eyes meet and there is a brief sense of...*curious distrust?* Terra tries to change all of that by putting on her best knock 'em dead grin and then confidently strides over to her meeting.

"Hi, I'm Terra Freeland!" She's outwardly gregarious and friendly, but inside Terra is seriously confused. The woman that she reaches out to shake hands with is half her age and does not seem to radiate power or responsibility. *Must be an assistant or a intern,* Terra convinces herself.

The other woman smiles genially, "Heloo Terra. I'm Mackenzie. Mackenzie DeMets. It's veryy nice too meet you at last."

Terra recognizes the last name as the contact she is supposed to meet, but their email chain always said Mack DeMets. Terra is curious and a little thrown off, "It's nice to meet you too. After what, a week of emails?"
"Sounds about right. Please," Mackenzie motions with her arm, "...have a seat. Are you hungry or thirsty? I took the opportunity tooo order both of us waters, but if you want anything else I'm afraid we will have tooo call over a waiter."

"No thank you, this is fine for now. Business before eating I always say," Terra gives another one of her big grins and it is returned with a cool smile and a slight tilt of the head.

"Then let's talk." Mackenzie sits after Terra does. Terra can almost see something change in the woman; like a cocoon being opened up and a new creature being revealed. Terra watches as Mackenzie efficiently opens a manila envelope with a few pages in it. "I had my assistant pull up the vitals on the property plus some pictures." Her voice was measured, soft and confidant. "So that you may have a good idea what we are trying to offload from our portfolio."

"Your assistant?" Terra is even more interested and it gets the best of her. "You seem to be not a day over twenty-five and I have assistants that are the same age as you. If you don't mind me asking, what is your connection to Evergreen Wilderness and this real estate deal?"

"Well, I'm thirty-two, Ms. Freeland, but I have some very good genes. My family is in the waste disposal business. Have you ever heard of DeMets Waste Management?"

"...No..." Terra hesitates, detecting a bit of steel in the young woman's voice. There was something there from the moment they locked eyes, *like the woman was only making a token effort of selling?* Terra wonders.

"My family has made a lot from that business and we have spun off several other entities. A small logging company with cherry-picked operations, which works in symbiosis with our paper recycling and dump operations. The groups strive to make more profit than the previous year; like any good organization should. The individual groups cohesively help out their sister operations to work toward their goals as well."

Terra nods her head in agreement, "Just like me. I strive to make more profit than the year before and try to do so on a leaner budget as well."

Mackenzie coolly smiles and tilts her head just like she did before. Then continues, "...we also own two car museums. It was my grandfather's private collection." Mackenzie beams for a moment of joy, then the flash is gone, quickly covered over with her natural expression.

Terra knows body language, even took a class in it, and she realizes she has come across too strong. *I might be in trouble here...* she realizes. "A car museum? I'm sorry I didn't know your family was so successful..."

"We keep a low profile." Mackenzie interrupts with a smile. The young woman takes a sip of the ice water, swirling it in the glass. Still without saying a word, she squeezes a lemon wedge into the glass before looking into Terra's face again. "Evergreen Wilderness (EW) is a conservation and preservation project that my mother and father started with my grandfather's wealth. It is built in order to give back to the community and for long term property management. EW purchases land, we try our best to return it to it's natural state and then use the land for low impact activities." Mackenzie stares straight into Terra's eyes and it makes Terra begin to worry.

I think this deal is blown! She curses herself. *I didn't do my background or my research. I'm such an idiot!* Terra scrambles for something, anything to grasp at for a recovery.

"I run Evergreen Wilderness," the young woman states flatly. There is no smile or tilt of the head, the young lady is serious with *responsibility and power.* "I use Mack because it was my nickname since kindergarten. You see, when I set my mind on something I'm as difficult to stop as a Mack truck. Mack is my badge of honor." Mackenzie pushes over the pages with pictures on one of them. Terra sits silently, smiling and nodding her head; trying to recover from her mistake. *Think Terra, think!*

"My family and I were not too happy when this particular owner purchased this acreage next to ours. He out bid us in our attempt to grab up both of the properties simultaneously. We talked with him and his accountant, a very serious and quiet man. Quite tall and well built from my recollection." Mackenzie pauses again to sip at her lemon water and Terra keeps her lips closed, afraid she is going to make another mistake.

"The new owner, an Asian or Middle-Eastern looking man about my age, denied our generous offer. Then the man came in with a large crew and started construction. They cut down quite a few trees on the property and laid out the sawn logs to dry. In that first year they also built outdoor exercising areas and a shooting range. A shooting range no less! The summer of the next year, he had his crew build some gaudy log cabins with the dried logs. My family and I were very disappointed. But we spent some time and took a look into things. From the beginning of their process we studied their approvals, permits and such, but everything was by the book. Legal and legit according to King County and the City of North Bend, WA."

Mackenzie looks at Terra to make sure the older woman is following along. "I understand completely, please go on," Terra encourages.

"We are no longer interested in trying to improve a property when the one adjacent to it was being so... uglified."

Terra looks over the pictures and the information on the following pages. Her mind goes back to a few days ago, when she was just getting into the car to head to the ferry. Just moments before the lane in front started moving. Terra is getting the same kind of out-of-her-control-rushed-feeling.

Mackenzie sits quietly and absently takes a couple more sips of lemon-water, waiting for Terra's response. "Well this information looks really thorough. I will have to do an onsite inspection and verify all of the facts myself and then we can talk about a deal. I will let my client know what I think and then we can talk price... does that sound good?"

The flash on Mackenzie's face says it all. A moment of distain and then it's gone. Terra sees that what she just said is not what the young lady wanted to hear. "I was anticipating we could do some initial negations tonight." Mackenzie DeMets leans in, "but you don't trust my data?"

"No, its not that at all." *There it goes. I just lost the deal.* "I have to do some verification first, that's customary with people that I have never met before. Why don't we agree to..."

"Why don't you look everything over and give *my* assistant a call." Mackenzie, interrupts with a distant and detached voice. She finishes her glass of iced lemon-water and stands up, "You two probably have a lot in common. Seeing as you're both about the same age."

Mackenzie DeMets walks away with a light and smooth walk. People moved out of her way as Terra watches the young lady and then looses sight of her as she walks out onto the street.

Acrimonious, the word just falls into Terra's thoughts. Terra figures the pages in front of her don't matter much anymore, and now she will have to find a new car service too.

Because it looks like I will be heading to the peninsula again on that stupid ship...

Chapter Eleven

Wednesday August 29th 21:01

A few good looking twenty something's check into hotels along the Seattle waterfront. These four men have an air of importance without being to flashy about it. They carry themselves with a sense of wealth and confidence as they each check into separate establishments at around the same time. Their olive complexion is completely ignored, hidden by their professional demeanor.

The men stride in; engage in pleasantries, adorned with fashionable attire and pearly white smiles. They blend in perfectly with the five-star clientele that frequent Seattle's waterfront hotels.

Yet, these men are just actors. Although on the world stage, they are still carrying out a facade to distract from their real intent.

The twenty something's play the part brilliantly.

Their demeanor and attire is a diversion from their false driver's licenses, and stolen credit card numbers. This foursome of twisted hearts, just arriving into Seattle, wasn't a band, or a sports team.

No, they are there to kill people and break things.

In every war there have always been spies. These spies of sorts, are in Seattle to work their spy craft; cause mischief and mayhem. An advance team from a larger cell that has been operating in the Pacific Northwest for quite some time. These four formed the point of the spear of an even greater organized and equally motivated group of fanatics. On this Wednesday night, important tasks need to be done by these men. Many lives are about to depend on it. Not as many people will be affected, as say the fans at either a concert or football game, but give them credit, this is just their first escapade.

One pair of men are more or less glorified thugs. This first pair is less refined, less skilled, than the other set of men. But the thug-duo came across as genial enough. The first two are there to provide support and security to the second set of men. This first pair are the *protectors,* the guardians for the other two.

The second set of men, the *specialists,* are college educated, mechanically inclined and decently trained at a lot of things. A sort of renaissance, jack-of-all trades kind of men. The second set of men were well-read with many talents. These *specialist's* had specific diving skills. It is their talents as scuba divers that they will be using this evening.

All four had left their training camp in North Bend Washington earlier that afternoon. The four men, whose real names were: Jibril ibn Amirzade ibn Amir Khan, Tarriq al-Qasim, Raphael Webber and Parvez ibn Saeed ibn Abd al-Aziz Habibu-llah, took the time to make ready for their 'evening out.'

The mayhem makers reason for being in Seattle is not for tomorrow nights melody making at the concert. Nor is it the pre-season NFL football game. On the contrary, these *specialists* and *protectors* have come to prepare for what happens *after* the big events.

At the appointed late hour the *specialists*, Jibril and Parvez, dress in thick wet suits. Then they don their loose fitting and trendy clothes to cover their suits. The seven mil thick, full body wet-suits were designed to keep them warm in the frigid fifty degree water of Elliot Bay. The pair of *specialist* divers meet down on Seattle's 1st Avenue and wait for their other two colleagues.

Along with the wet suits they wear, each *specialist* also carries a backpack that is stuffed with identical gear. Within those two packs were a small single oxygen tank, goggles, fins, underwater radio, rope and explosive charges.

Soon another pair of men come walking up the street toward Jibril and Parvez. The four mayhem-makers join up once more. The *protectors* and the *specialists* exchange handshakes all around.

Appearing, from any onlooker, that friends are just meeting on the street, Parvez looks to Tarriq. "Did that woman just give you her phone number?" Parvez queries Tarriq with a smile.

Tarriq, the largest and best built of the four, is one of the *protectors*. Tarriq carries himself like a well cultured bodyguard, not a possible fanatic. Born in Las Vegas to Palestinian parents that fled the war torn Middle East. He grew up in the United States and believed in all of it once. He believed in absolute truth, justice and the righteousness of the American way.

But one day, while working as a bouncer for the wealthy and famous on the strip, Tarriq had confronted two white men for treating a lady horribly. He didn't lay a hand on either of them, Tarriq had just gotten into their personal space a bit. His intent was to intimidate and make the two men uncomfortable. Nevertheless, the pair of college aged men turned the tables quickly on the big Palestinian.

The two strangers beat Tarriq badly. To add insult to Tarriq's injury, the American justice system was not able to prosecute his assailants due to the pair's wealth and privilege. Tarriq was heartbroken and had nowhere else to turn. Tarriq was soon comforted by his family's faith of Islam, and then strengthened though his ordeal. He had never been a religious man in all of his years prior, but he had to search for answers. Tarriq needed reasons why he had been beaten and why there was no punishment for his two assailants. That beating, was the headwaters of Tarriq's drift down into his current activity in Seattle.

Tarriq returned Parvez's smile with his own impish grin, "I will not kiss and tell, friend."

Jibril, shaking his head at the suave Tarriq, turns to the other conspirators "How's your rooms you three?"

"Good," Tarriq responds quickly and then looks back and forth to the other two on his right and left.

"Fine, just fine..." Parvez's voice trails off as a Tesla Roadster passes by on the street catching his attention. Seeing this, Raphael turns away, separating himself from the rest by a few feet.

Raphael, another of the *protectors*, just nods his head in agreement. The jovial attitude of the three unnerves him. After all, this is serious business that they are about to undertake. Raphael thinks the other three are taking their assignment a little too lightly.

Raphael had been a drifter since he was fifteen and this is the first time he has had faith in something other than himself. He is very dedicated to the cause, with an unnerving fervor. *Protector* Raphael is working hard within the cell to further the progress of Militant Islam. Not stand around on the street corner and talk about women or hotel rooms or gawk at cars. He would rather go about tonight's tasks with silent efficiency, not this jocular banter.

Catching himself, *specialist* Parvez swings his attention back on the group. "Is everyone ready?" The other three men nod their heads once in near unison. "Well, let's go then," Parvez encourages as he turns onto First Street and begins his trip up to Broad Street. The other three follow close behind.

The four make a turn onto Broad and walk west, down from their hotels on First Street, to the Seattle shoreline. The shoreline, with its concrete walkway lined with closed shops and restaurants, are quiet and mostly vacant. The men pair off, one *protector* and one *specialist,* and go their separate ways.

The first group, Jibril and Tarriq, move to the north end of the waterfront walk. Jibril and Tarriq walk the mile to the commercial docks. This is the place where the cruise liners tie up to. Tonight is no different and a glaring example of a gaudy tour ship lies quietly beside the walk. The cruse terminal is the place where the precious cargo of vacationing passengers enter and exit the ship for parts like the Inside Passage, Vancouver Canada and Alaska's glacier fields.

Parvez and Raphael head to the south end of the waterfront. They walk slowly and get as close to the fireboat terminal as reasonable. The SFD fireboat terminal just so happens to be right next to the massive ferry boat terminal, so their loitering doesn't attract undue attention. In fact, the four don't raise any suspicions on the mostly empty waterfront. The men's targets for this late evening foray are the cruise liner docked at its terminal, and the three Seattle city municipal boats docked at the fireboat terminal.

All four men make sure that no one is around. On opposite ends of the waterfront the wet-suited Jibril and Parvez remove their outer clothing and secure themselves to a rope via a carabineer on their waist. Almost simultaneously, on each end of the waterfront, each *specialist* crawls over the railings and drops into the water. Also in near unison, the two *protectors* lower the divers their packs.

The guardians, Raphael and Tarriq, wish their teammates good luck with, "my Allah be praised" in a whisper. Then the two *protectors* turn away.

Left standing on the walkways, the *protectors* secure the rope to the railings. The rope will be used as much as an emergency form of communication, as a way for the divers to find their way back in the pitch black water of Elliot Bay. While floating, Jibril and Parvez attach their swim fins, affix their goggles, tanks and disappear into the obsidian colored bay.

The divers are unnoticed by anyone.

Both divers; one under the cruise ship terminal at the north end, and the other in the south end, has to get to the required boats entirely by feel. They cannot use any illumination that might give away their locations. They make their way slowly, twenty feet under water, to come up underneath each ship. Within the inky black water, they place the shaped charges.

On the two larger crafts, the explosive charges are placed next to the propeller shafts, and on the small pair of secondary ships, the charges are placed right behind the twin massive outboards. Jibril and Parvez work diligently in the cold and murky bay, placing the small, timed magnetic explosive charges with care.

As they work to the sounds of their breathing, both men can feel the cold water from

Elliot Bay slowly penetrate their suits. Their hands, feet and ears start to go numb from the cold. The frigid water works on the men further and the numbness gives way to pain.

The divers had practiced many times for this. In a unheated pool at their North Bend campus. Nevertheless, both men discover quickly that the pool water never seemed to get as cold as the salt water of Elliot Bay.

Despite their discomfort, the men focus acutely on the details. The two divers make sure the charges are firmly attached. With practiced care the divers turn on the timed detonators. A sense of expectancy fills their minds. Will the homemade electronics work? Is there enough waterproofing? Will the dangerous things accidentally go off in front of them?

The two men wait for the small green status LED's to appear, and for their concerns to be confirmed or denied.

The explosives are small by design. They were carefully created and tested at their campus as well. The homemade chemical compound that made up the explosives, the detonators and the waterproofing were put through every test. The charges were tweaked and modified until they were watertight, detonated on time and exploded with the correct yield. The explosives were not created to sink any of the ships, but to incapacitate their engines. Maybe even punch some reasonable holes in them. More crippled ships meant more people to rescue.

Just a moment passes, but everything goes right. The green LED lights come to life on the detonators and the pair of men follow their ropes back to safety. The cruise liner and the municipal ships are oblivious to the divers' presence. The guardians remain in their over-watch positions, ostensibly smoking their cigarettes. The diver's guardians have their radios ready to beep out warnings to the divers.

The task to set the explosives are crucially important.

The pair of Search, Rescue and Firefighting watercraft, on the south end of the waterfront, are pivotal to the rapid response of any emergency out on Elliot Bay. The third municipal boat in the south end is a high speed Marine Patrol craft run by Seattle Police Department. Thus, these three municipal craft are prime targets for tonight's operation. The pair of fireboats, one as large as a nice yacht, and one a small glorified Zodiac, are Seattle Fire Departments and Seattle Search and Rescue's only major way of responding to incidents on Elliot Bay. The high speed patrol craft is SPD's only quick way to respond to incidents out on the bay as well. Currently, all other SPD Harbor Patrol Craft are stationed behind Ballard Locks.

Other than these three boats, only the coast Guard is capable of responding to shipping emergencies upon Elliot Bay and within the larger Puget Sound. Although, the Seattle FD has the two boats, the larger of the two is the quicker and more capable of the pair. If either of the high speed boats were crippled, it would effectively take out the crucial ability of the closest emergency responder to act.

In the cold and black the divers make it back to the place where their ropes lead out of the water. Just under the surface, they use their underwater radios. Each diver transmits a series of clicks to their *protectors*, making sure the coast is clear on the shore. If the divers, Jibril and Parvez, receive the correct amount of clicks from the guardians up above, then no one is around and they are able to come up. If the pair of divers receive the incorrect amount, they plan on staying put.

This Wednesday night, each of the divers receives the all clear signals.

Almost simultaneously, on opposite ends of the waterfront, the divers emerge out of the icy water. The two *specialists* are eager to escape the freezing black. Raphael and Tarriq assist their teammates up by the rope around each of the diver's waists. Both Tarriq and Raphael were chosen for this task because they were the strongest out of the twelve.

The pair of *specialist* divers can barely move their fingers to grip the rope from their frigid twenty minute dips into Elliot Bay. Each *specialist* changes out of their suits right there on the sidewalk, as fast as they can.

In an act of compassion and survival the two *protectors* dry off their two charges as the once submerged men hurriedly dry themselves. The divers throw on their clothes over their damp bodies. Their *protectors* stuff the soaking wet suits into the divers packs while the *specialists* dress. The whole process, from the *specialist*s being pulled out of the water, to the removal of the suits, to redressing takes just a little over a minute.

All four men had practiced the entire process back at the North Bend pool. Their practice paid off and the four men's exposure time, for being caught doing something suspicious was cut short.

Once the costume change is over and everything is stored back away in the packs, the four men split up once more. The mayhem makers find their way separately back to their hotel rooms. The frozen divers take hot showers and then change into dry clothes. The *protectors* had the packs and worked hard at wringing out all of the water that they can from the wets suits. They do their best to get out the water.

After the shower and dressing, neither of the *specialists* are looking forward to the moment that they will have to put those suits on again. Even with the *protectors* draining out most of the sea water, without the body heat, the suits will be like putting on ice cubes.

The pair of divers, now warmed by their hot showers and dry clothes, make it back downstairs. Both of them have hot coffee in their hands and are trying their best to get some of the hot fluid down. They are each in turn picked up by a rental car driven by one of the *protectors* and with replenished backpacks.

For all four men have yet another visit to make tonight. It is just a short trip away. Just a few miles north in the northern Seattle community of Ballard lies the next target.

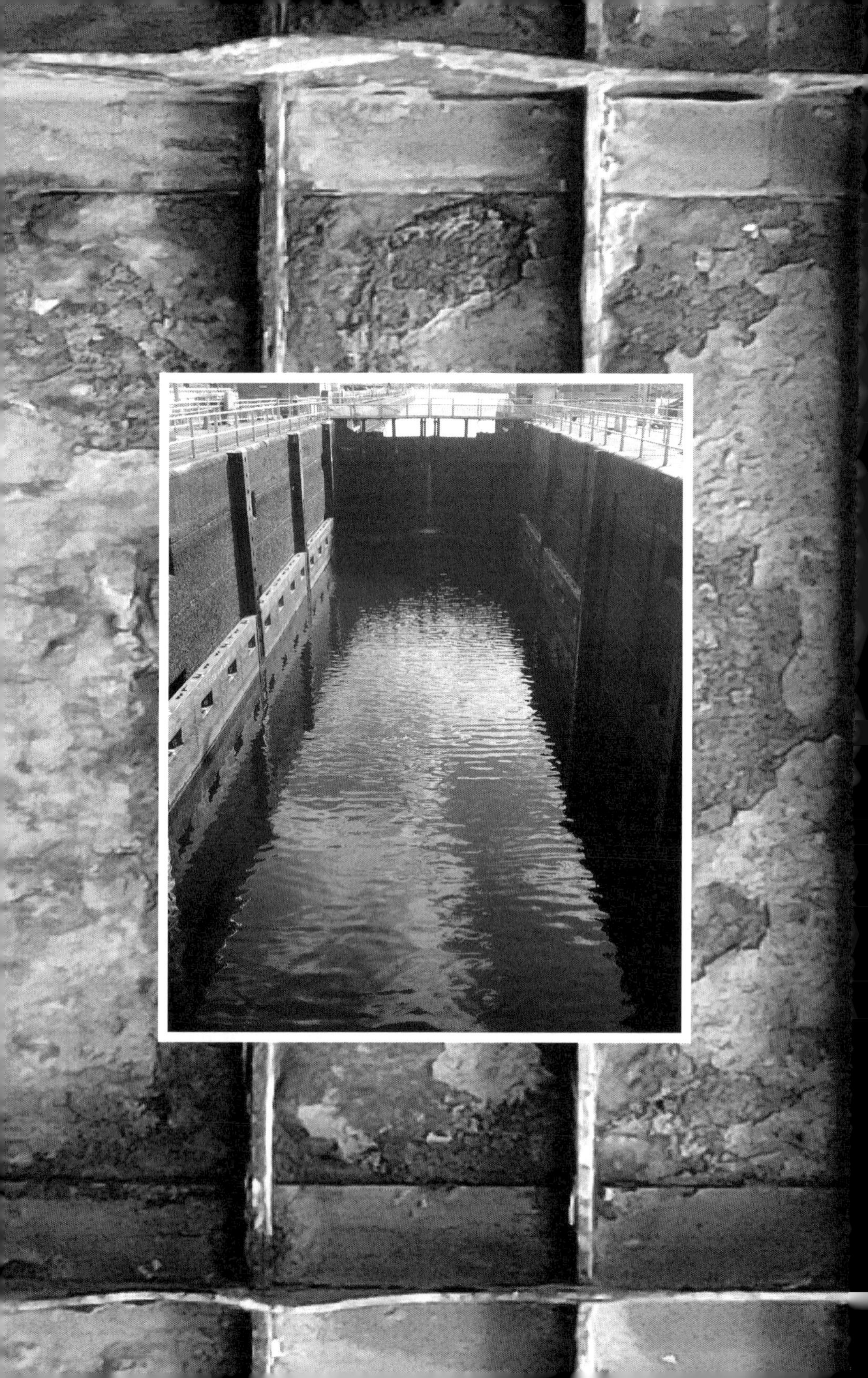

Chapter Twelve

Thursday August 30th 01:31

    The Hiram M. Chittenden Locks were named after army major Hiram Chittenden who was the lead Seattle district engineer that designed and surveyed the location for the locks. He was an accomplished engineer, inventor, industrial designer and author. Hiram worked on engineering projects in Yellowstone, Seattle and wrote a history on the early fur trade that garnered him widespread acclaim.

Hiram M. Chittenden Locks, known locally as The Ballard Locks, are the only way boats can exit the fresh water lakes of Union and Washington. These beautiful lakes touch numerous nearby communities including Seattle, Bellevue, Mercer Island and Kirkland, just to name a few. All ships, going to and from the lakes, have to pass through this narrow channel and the two pairs of gates, to get access to the salt water of Elliot Bay, the Salish Sea and the Pacific Ocean.

Needless to say the Ballard Locks perform many critical duties. First off, the locks constantly maintain the water levels of Lake Union and Lake Washington at twenty or so feet above sea level. Next, the gates stop seawater intrusion into the pair of freshwater lakes, thus keeping the ecosystems of both lakes intact. Lastly, the Ballard Locks regulate the flow of ship traffic into and out of the lakes.

There are two sets of locks, one much larger than the other, for the commercial, pleasure and military ships to pass. Each pair of locks has two doors, one set on the lake side and another pair on the seaward side. The smaller lock can accommodate ships of 30' x 150' and the other can take ships of 80' x 825' long from up and into the lake or lower them out to the sea.

The four men get there via a ZIP Car. They use the car sharing service to procure them wheels for the evening. Their team had scoped out the area around the Locks previously and had found that the Ballard Locks had seriously secure gates on the entire perimeter. But the Hiram Chittenden Locks bordered the Carl S. English Jr. Botanical Gardens... with horrible security.

"It bordered a federal installation run by the Army Corps of Engineers. And this is how you protect it..." the large man's voice trails off. Tarriq busts through the chain link fence of the gardens with a pair of bolt cutters. An easy effort for the big man. The security fence was not much of a deterrent and the Tarriq scoffs at the poor security. "What a joke," Tarriq enters first, whispering to himself as he goes. With the locks closed at 1:00am and not opening again until 4, their team figured they would be safe. The big panther like shape moves outside of the arc of the cameras. The dark clad figure of Tarriq surveys the scene before the others enter. In a bit of grace and accuracy surprising from the big man, he fries the four CCD security cameras with a modified handheld laser. Satisfied at blinding the cameras, Tarriq gives an all clear wave to his conspirators.

"Go, go, go!" Jibril urges the three of them forward. They are dressed in black as well and they pass through the fence and split up again. Jibril and Raphael pair up, heading to the smaller lock, lock one. Parvez heads toward Tarriq and lock two.

"Hey handsome, fancy meeting you here," Parvez jokes with Tarriq as he catches up to him.

Tarriq has just finished pocketing his supped-up laser pointer. "You are definitely not my type." Tarriq grins as they walk. "You are far too skinny," the big man says as he pokes Parvez's arm. "...and far too hairy." They keep up the lighthearted banter as the pair confidently stride to the set of upper doors on lock two.

"Well, since you don't want me I guess you can't peek as I change into my eveningwear." Parvez, says in his best coy voice.

Yet, Tarriq hasn't looked at Parvez since they stopped walking. He's watching for anyone that might come in from the fence that they entered. "Get in there ugly, so we can go eat. I'm hungry and cold."

"You're cold?" Parvez chatters out of his clinched teeth. "Why don't you slip into this wet suit that feels like its been in a freezer?"

"Age before beauty…" Tarriq snidely remarks as he walks a few yards away on alert.

"Eeehhh!" Parvez lets out a whispered plea as he slips further into the wetsuit. "I wonder how the other two are doing..." he asks Tarriq. Trying to get his mind on something other than the ice pack he is climbing into.

The other two are quiet. Raphael is all business all of the time and that despite Jibril's goading at dinner. The two settle into an uncomfortable silence before carrying out their tasks. Jibril, originally from the city of Kashgar in western China, was born to Arabic parents. They all immigrated to Los Angeles when he was just six. The boy quickly got caught up in the Chinese Triads Gangs at eleven. Cash deliveries, encrypted messages and warnings were his forte'. By nineteen he had accrued a criminal record and began serving two years in jail for a gang related crime.

That was when Jibril had a visit from his past. A Muslim priest, visiting the facility Jibril was jailed in; reminded him of the *former* way. The way Jibril had been raised, and the faith that he didn't know he still had within him. It was the perfect time. It's why Jibril is sympathetic to Raphael Webber and Raphael's street-smart, loner background.

So Jibril respected the silence between them as they walked. Jibril's stint in the Chinese gangs of Los Angeles gives him an appreciation to those who know how to survive.

Once at the locks edge, the pair of divers do their final zip up into their suits with a few whispered curses. They shiver and move their arms rapidly trying to warm up their icy wetsuits. After a few moments the two *specialists* drop into the water and go about their dangerous work.

The two divers place more homemade charges next to the locks recessed pair of control motors. One small demolition package gets placed on the system that controls the smaller lock's upper doors and one gets placed on the mechanics for the larger lock's upper doors. The divers secure the explosives to the concrete side walls with two quick shots of .22 cal explosive anchors.

Just like in their previous foray, they are watched over by their two now armed *protectors*.

The *protectors* remain much more alert at this location than in downtown Seattle. There is a suspicion that they could be watched by other hidden cameras. Not to mention that these locks were right under the nose of Seattle Police Departments Harbor Patrol base. Just a half-a-mile away up Lake Union.

In fact, this is the real reason why the four men were there. Bust the concrete with the explosives, water pours in and no more motors. No motors, equals jammed doors. And jammed doors mean no passage for Seattle Harbor Patrol. *Boo whoo,* one of their group had joked during the planning stage. Without Seattle Harbor Patrol, there will be more strain on the existing search and rescue craft. Chaos, confusion, and stress on the sheepdogs are always a good thing.

The two pairs of men finish their work in Ballard without any issues. The divers were in the water only ten minutes each and aren't as frozen, like in their previous dive in Elliot Bay. While there, they didn't have a visit from a law enforcement official, nor unannounced security guards. They replace the cut fence with green painted wire ties made just for this purpose. Jibril and Tarriq both smile at the thought of some half asleep Ballard Lock worker trying to figure out what in heaven's name was going on with the cameras. "You are going to smile about that all night won't you?" Jibril asks as they get back into their car.

"You know he will. That grin will not leave his face until he falls asleep." Parvez answers for Tarriq, from the cramped back seat.

Tarriq grins all the wider, "You know it ugly," directing his reply to Parvez and the two laugh at their inside joke.

On the drive back to the hotels, the divers change for the last time tonight. No sense in having someone recognize them, or for that matter; walk around in freezing wet suits as your underwear. They return their ZIP car at a stall a mile away from their nearest hotel. Parvez didn't have much to worry about because yet again the car was paid for with a stolen credit card account.

The men walk together for a few hundred yards, still bantering with each other; Raphael still quiet and somber. Once they are a few blocks from Tarriq's hotel, which is the nearest, they make plans to eat and spilt apart to head to their different hotels.

Later, the four meet up at the famous Seattle landmark, 13 Coins. Open till early in the morning, they enjoy a great late night dinner; the tradition there at the restaurant. The quartet hit on their waitress relentlessly, but she rebuffs their advances. Regardless, the four tip the young and pretty waitress with twenty percent. She did a great job, besides, it was a forged credit card too. *After all, when it's not your money, who cares?* The men make it back to their rooms by 4:00am.

Tarriq falls asleep, still smiling.

Chapter Thirteen

Thursday August 30th 7:30

"Unsustainable" by Muse is the alarm. Three minutes and forty-eight seconds of music fills the small front room with the band's colossal sound. All of the music comes from a mobile phone lying on the floor.

A young man wakes from the best dream he's had in a long time. Recalling his dream, he and his girlfriend were on a mountain side meadow, hiking up to a fully stocked and secluded log cabin.

The young man lying on the futon grins at the memory and the hope of it. *I can't wait to see the woman again*, is the first thought he has after the dream. The woman, a very alive and real lady, has the young man in knots. *The Big Question,* the young man contemplates as he lays there on the couch. The question is a problem that's been vexing him for the past two months.

When and where do I propose? He asks himself as "Unstainable" ends. *I've got to find the right time and place*! Trevor Jacobs tries to encourage himself to do it, and do it soon.

Trevor restarts "Unstainable." Muse's song progresses, the lavish orchestration, the deep lyrical themes and the complex melodies are why Muse is his favorite band. Trevor has all of their music and has seen them in concert, three times. He sits up, listening, and tries to let the music drown out his thoughts of a proposal. His girlfriend has been so distant lately, just not herself, and Trevor wonders aloud, *will the events that come treat me well?*

The young man stayed up late last night, online gaming, trying to forget his concerns. He was younger, never liked alcohol much, and since he was young had used video games to let off steam. Trevor keeps trying to convince himself that everything is going to be okay, but he still couldn't remove that one sliver of doubt. It was that doubt that he tried to drown, that ended up making him fall asleep on his futon couch.

Pushing away the negative thoughts, all 6'3" of him leaves the futon, grabbing his phone. Muse continues it's repeated tune. Trevor is built more like a greyhound than a body builder. Long sinewy muscles flex across his legs and back as the twenty-five year old strides into his apartment's sole bathroom.

He starts up the shower and while it warms, fires off a "Good morning sleepy head," text to his love.

Trevor docks his phone into the charger. Setting his phone on the back of the toilet, music still blasting, he takes a ten minute shower, and quickly shaves his face. *What did I do to land this job, especially in this economy*, he considers to the mirror. Trying to get his mind on something other than the question; the proposal.

Thinking far too much, he marches back into his bedroom and flicks on the news. Hoping it will drown out his thoughts when Muse did not, Trevor watches the television for a few minutes. Putting on his pants, he walks out of his bedroom bare chested, carrying his shirt.

In the kitchen, he pulls out his blender and his toaster from the cabinet. In the process of putting on his shirt, Trevor places into the blender tofu, fruit and orange juice; then he presses start. Into the jaws of the toaster oven goes a locally made blueberry bagel, crank it up to max; start.

The news is talking about the economy again, Trevor tells himself. *The President is trying hard to get us out of this stagnant economy, and hopefully he will soon.* Trevor tries to have high hopes as he finishes getting dressed, rubs some gel into his hair and makes it back into the kitchen just prior to the bagel's smoke.

Trevor yanks the toaster's plug out by the cord, removes the partially smoking bagel from it and shuts off the blender. Grabbing a knife, that looks clean off the counter, he spreads some butter on the two halves of the bagel. Before taking a big crunchy bite, Trevor shuts off his television. Back into his kitchen, Trevor takes a bite out of the bagel as he pours his fruit concoction in a travel mug,. Then he stuffs his mobile phone into his breast pocket, so he can still hear the music and exits his apartment.

Despite just five hours of sleep, he is out the door just twenty minutes after his alarm. Oh, the energy of youth and how it is wasted on the young.

Trevor takes a cinnamon toothpick out of a small container and mindlessly savors the hot spice. Driving into Seattle for work is his second favorite place to think. He's sure his Beautiful has received his text, read it, and has gone back to sleep already. Checking his phone for the second time, he decides to focus on the driving. The scenery is assuring as he heads south to get on Interstate 90. Rural houses and farms, many huge pine trees and a creek running beside the road. Just what you would expect here at the foothills of the Cascades.

Then, his thoughts drift back to his girl.

The energetic Mr. Trevor Jacobs doesn't expect a quick response from his girlfriend, as she works waiting tables at 13 Coins and doesn't get out till early morning. So, to say she hates getting up early is an understatement. The woman positively loathed getting up before 10am, even on her days off. She loves her sleep. If you ever had the audacity to make her wake up before 8am, you'd better have a letter from God himself. For him to send her a text just before 8 am probably has got him into some hot water. He did not care. Trevor couldn't help containing his excitement for the girl and he wants her to know it; every minute of her life. One of the things Trevor liked the most was pushing her buttons, because they were just so lovely.

Chewing on his toothpick, Trevor drives on I90. Thoughtlessly driving, his mind drifts back to her again. When he first saw her, he had to meet her. After meeting her, he had to take her out. Their first date was dinner at an Italian restaurant. Every "anniversary" he took her out to the same place, so that they might enjoy their memories. During their first dinner he made a passing suggestion that he liked a particular comedian. Their second date was her surprise at a comedy club for the comedian. At that moment she had his heart with the thoughtfulness and those tickets.

Oh, did they ever have good times. He was captivated with her from those early moments. All of their dates had been delightful and many were memorable. She would suggest something or sometimes he would. It never seemed to matter because the pair had such similar interests. Cooking, camping, hiking, long drives and mini-vacations, they lived like there was no tomorrow.

"Wow! Made it in an hour." Trevor declares, pulling into the ferry terminal. He finishes the trip from rural Carnation to Seattle in excellent time. His music kept him and his thoughts company. He always allotted two hours for the trip for traffic and now he is able to go into work earlier.

Excited at the extra time, the young man parks his car by nine, in time to catch a free ferry ride to the peninsula and back before work. *Enjoy some people watching, soak up the peace and appreciate the sights*, Trevor tells himself. He puts his toothpick behind his ear and grabs the uneaten bagel and half-finished smoothie.

On the ferry, he thinks back to his lessons on the Puget Sound. The waterway has had so many names. Now it's changed again, because of the 2010 naming convention involving Canada, the United States and numerous native tribes. It is now officially known as the Salish Sea. The Canadian and American governments had to hash out a common name with the Indian Tribes that didn't involve the name Puget. After all, that guy, Vancouver, didn't discover it, he just named it arbitrarily after his ship's lieutenant. You couldn't have wealthy old white guys naming things now, could you?

Trevor remembered that according to Oceanic Science, The Salish Sea is a maze like system of interconnected waterways and basins covering seven thousand square miles. Sometimes he imagined, while riding the ships for work, how the glacial ice during the Fraser Glaciation carved it all out. Tuning it into one of the largest inland seas in the world. It includes Washington State's Puget Sound, Elliot Bay, the Strait of Juan de Fuca and the San Juan Islands. *The San Juan's would have been massive mountains if it wasn't for all of that water.*

In addition to the United States territory, the sea encompassed British Columbia's Gulf Islands and the Strait of Georgia as well. The massive waterway reaches from Desolation Sound at the north end of the Strait of Georgia in Canada to Oakland Bay at the head of Hammersley Inlet at the south end of Puget Sound. It is massive, reaching past Vancouver, Canada down to Olympia, Washington. The inland sea is split roughly in half by the Strait of Juan de Fuca, which is the major access channel into the Pacific Ocean.

Trevor brought to mind the first time that he came down to the ferry offices for *the interview*. It was almost four years ago while getting his Bachelor's Degree in marine biology, He was nervous and unsure of himself, but the meeting turned out alright. How fortunate. He was thankful to whatever led to having scored him a decent government job.

Over time Mr. Trevor Jacobs had worked up to loadmaster, showing an uncanny ability to load the vessel in a balanced and space effective way. Trevor was seriously tempted to make this job his career. He loved Seattle, the waterfront, the Salish Sea and the job. The views were great, the pay was good and he got to meet people from all over the world. This government job was the stability he needed, no, craved in a career. To think, he had just been at the right place, at the right time.

"I am just lucky," he guesses out loud. "First the job, and now the girl."

Driving to Seattle may be his 2nd favorite place to think, but his time on the ferry is his favorite place to think. Admiring the views on his round trip before work he catches up on current events. Trevor checks the news web sites of CNN, BBC, NY Times and Drudge to see what is going on in the world.

On the ferry ride back, he walks past a sign that reads "Assaults on Washington State Employees will be prosecuted to the full extent of the law! Chapter 47.60 RCW." He smirks at the mostly pointless sign on his way out onto the front observation deck. *What will a sign do to someone who is intent on carrying out something evil? What does it matter? It will never happen on the ferry. It's like having a drug free zone around a school when mostly everywhere is a drug free zone.*

Trevor turns his mind away from the negative and back to the positive; the scenery. The city skyline, patiently draws ever closer like a far away cloud. Under the constant breeze, Trevor jumps into his Facebook app and then his email accounts just to make sure he hasn't missed anything with his friends. He likes being in the know and often engages in small talk on current events with passengers and fellow crew.

If you could see the young man walk off the ferry, you would know he is on cloud nine. From his walk, to the perpetual smile on his face he radiated a feeling of happiness. Trevor strides over to terminal control building and clocks in at 11:50 am. Ten minutes early. On his way back to the ship that he had just traveled on, his mobile phone vibrates.

His heart thumping in his chest, She writes "Morning 2 u. I will get u back ;-)"

Trevor pops the saved cinnamon toothpick into his mouth, grinning from ear to ear. He steps onto the M/V *Wenatchee* with one thought: He couldn't wait till she does; he couldn't help but think about her cute buttons.

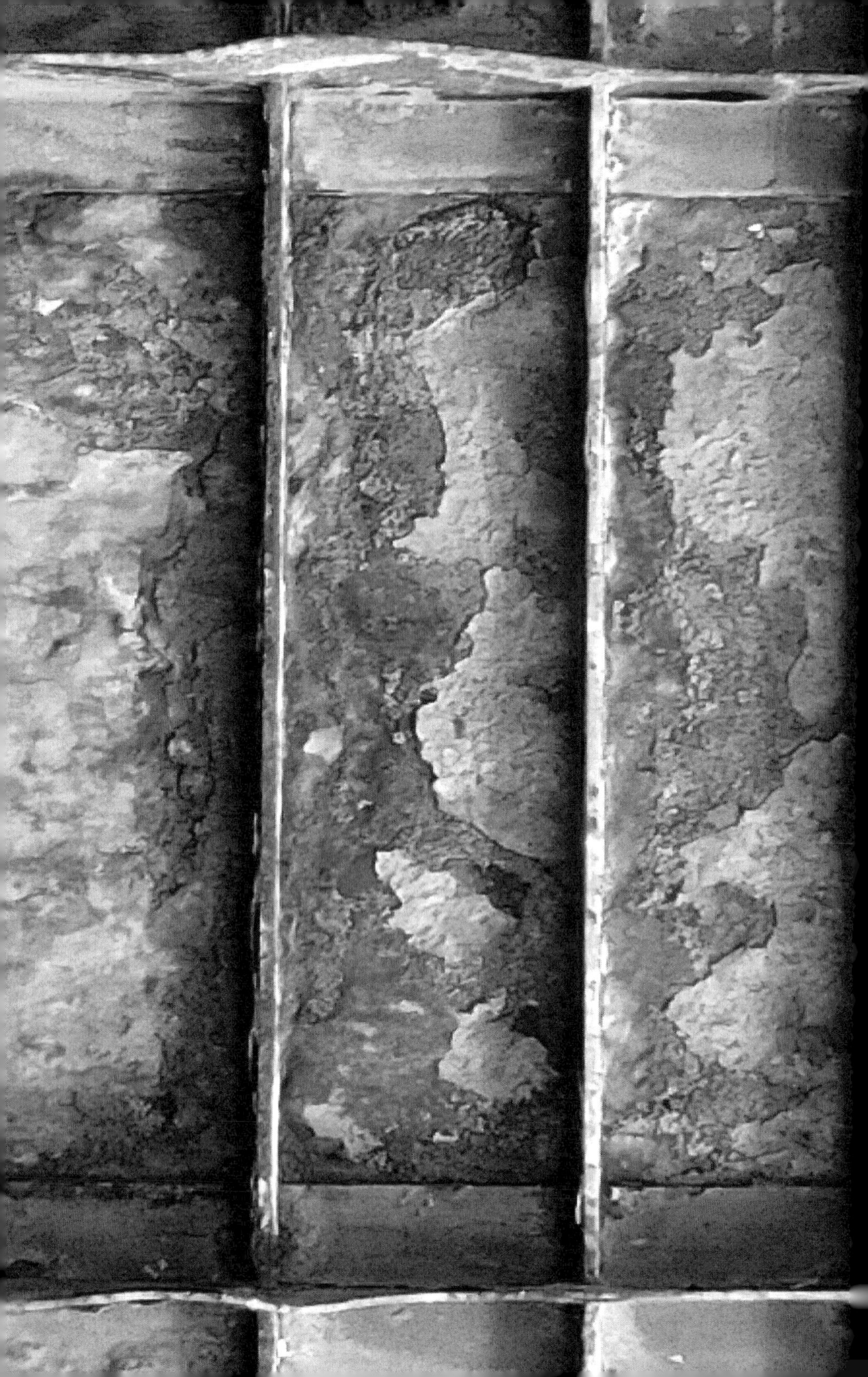

Chapter Fourteen

Thursday August 30th 12:00

In this hour people are converging upon Seattle. It's not just Trevor or James or the four mayhem makers. *Some are actually heading into the city to enjoy it.*

Many of the people are heading to town early for the concert or the game. For those events people are coming from as far away as Forks and Chehalis, Enumclaw and Snohomish. Even a few from Spokane. Others are getting up, telling their loved ones goodbye and merely just going into work. Working for the city, the county, Key Arena and Century Link Field. There was work at the Amtrak Yard that employed a fair share of hard working union steelworkers just a few blocks south of Safeco Field. Interstate 5 into downtown was busy with traffic as it passed under the jet planes landing at Boeing Field.

There were people like, Oliver Redmond, veteran of Gulf War I and II. He was heading in to Ballard for his duty as operator to run the Hiram Chittenden Locks. Oliver started his shift at 14:00. He was famous for getting there an hour early, drinking a full cup of coffee while he read *OffGrid*, *Recoil* or *Wilderness* magazines. Oliver's shift ran all of the way 'till an hour before midnight. He would be sipping coffee and reading his magazines the entire time.

Another man, thin and well mannered, was driving to Vulcan Enterprises (VE). VE was the largest privately owned hanger west of the Mississippi river. Clifton Bantell was a private pilot for the wealthy and famous. He somehow was able to navigate life, doing all of the right things, at the right time, and now he was flying those that had money and power all over the 'States and the world.

A couple were driving up from Puyallup, with their two teenage sons. They had just moved up to Seattle and were going to spend the day downtown at the Pacific Science Center and then later at the Seattle Art Museum (SAM). The Pacific Science Center, other than the butterfly exhibit for mom, was for the children, while SAM was for the adults.

Another man, this one a well seasoned Nordic oil tanker seaman, is riding the bus into Seattle for his job as a Ferry Boat Captain on the *Wenatchee*. Capt. Michael Blair had finally gotten out of the cold and the ice in Northern Europe. *Thankfully, I will no longer have to experience four months of darkness.* He landed a job to hang his hat on, here in the Northwest.

Another two of the Captain's fellow crewman, a brother and sister from Kent, Washington are driving into work in their beat up '72 Ford F-150 pickup truck. The two live just a few blocks away from each other, commute together as much as they can, and have remained close despite various curve balls life has thrown their way. The brother used to work as an IT systems engineer in Kirkland, but just couldn't take the demands of the job anymore. His sister had been working for King county parks department when she heard about the rare opening in the ferry service. She found the job had great pay, good benefits and regular hours. Plus, she got to ride on the ferry for work.

The views and being on the water made her work a pleasure. It was a big difference riding on the ferry versus her old job in the parks department. *Experiencing transients sleeping in bathrooms and cleaning up human waste on the sidewalks or riding around on a ferry answering questions to tourists? Hmm not that hard of a decision.* Now that she had the ferry job for the past three years, the worst thing had been an occasional unruly passenger. It wasn't long before another opening was announced, *brother,* she called him the moment she found out about the opportunity. *You need to apply for the job.*

Another three ferry crewman lived within biking distance to the Seattle ferry terminal. And although only one man actually rode his bike in, rain or shine, down from the trendy Capitol Hill neighborhood, the three had commutes that were mercifully short. One drove down from University Place and the other came up from nearby Burien on the sparsely used light rail.

The African-American from University Place was near retirement, just biding his time before he started living off of his healthy pension. His wife and he had raised three great kids, all in college and now, with the last one finally moved out. *I can't wait. Fly fishing is calling me and there were two many rivers to explore and not enough time left in life to do it.* Washington and Oregon had salmon, steelhead, bass and walleye that were calling him.

The young woman from Burien was just beginning her career with the ferry service. Her husband had just been shipped off to Saudi Arabia with the joint Striker Battalion out of Joint Base Lewis-McCord. She had been told, by her new husband, to focus on her school and finish her degree, but that wasn't going to happen. *Screw that,* was her sentiment. She was going to go make some good money while she had his paycheck to pay for their mortgage. They didn't have kids, and for that matter they couldn't even agree on a dog. Their one year marriage wasn't looking like it was going to last, but she would have to wait and see. *Will my man come back from his second tour any better than his first?* That was her asked-to-often-question. In the meantime she kept her wedding ring in her jewelry box. *With no debts, I will have some of my own cash in savings to fall back on.*

Also at this very hour, in an expertly designed skyscraper, overlooking the Persian Gulf; men were asking if all things were indeed ready. The C.O. had a horrendous midnight vision that had awakened him from dead sleep. Eagles and wolves and falcons and a dying Arabian horse were things you couldn't ignore. The meeting was called for. The Shura Council of Ashan went through the entire plan that was about to be carried out. After the briefing and making sure all of the Shura were aware of the changes, the C.O. opened the floor for final discussions.

"Now that the main business has been concluded does any of the Shura have anything more to add? Questions?" The Chief Officer of Ashan and principal founder of the organization started. "Let's go ahead. Who's got something?"

The Brigadier General opened, "If I may start, I have some questions. My first to the C.O., can anything be improved upon during these last minutes?"

The C.O. responded "I don't think so. You have everything before you. We have been through this plan very carefully." The C.O.'s voice was being brought in via a remote and encrypted connection. Some of the seven architects of Ashan were there physically in the high-rise office and some had remoted in. Either via an encrypted web video tool from those recent entrepreneurs or a secured landline audio connection.

"Is everything set and ready to go Grey Hair?" The Financer, one of the seven, was a wealthy banker, options trader and futures broker. He sat there in person in a fine suit. The picture of him in the suit and sitting in the handmade leather and wood chair looked like it was out of Esquire Magazine. Add in the polished cherry wood table that he sat in front of and it could have been in Forbes Magazine. The Financer wanted to make certain all of the I's were dotted and the T's were crossed.

"We have all been through the entire operation in detail," Grey Hair explained to the Brigadier and the Financer that had the questions. "Gentlemen, all of us are aware that both of you have gifts of seeing any loose ends, but this mission seems as secure as we can make it." Gray Hair was a former intelligence operator, and currently was virtually remoted in. His face displayed on a flat screen just like his boss. He was stroking his hallmark grey beard as he answered.

"I would like to know if the quote, distractions, un-quote, are going to be enough to keep the law enforcers at bay? Principally the American Coast Guard? I still think the primary team is out in the open without any support." The Brigadier posed his question to the C.O.. The Brigadier had men butchered in combat against the Americans. He did not want to repeat the same mistake.

"Everything will be fine, brothers." The Mariner interrupted. He was loud and boisterous as ever. He seemed used to the corporate shipping boardroom where he ran roughshod over all voices. A big and powerful man once, his muscle was slowly being neglected for good food and the company of admirers. After all though, he *owned* the cargo freight company and the trucking company. He declared loudly to all that would make eye contact, "Everything is going to plan! With Allah we have..."

The Programmer interrupted, "The extra support is crucial C.O.. I second the Brigadier's concern. Secondly, Breaker and I have some serious concerns about the electronic security of the mission."

"Yes, that is right," the Programmer's cousin, the Breaker, confirmed. The Programmer owned his own software company that had locations in Qatar, Ireland, Virginia and in California. He knew his stuff, and along with the Breaker, a former long-time electronic security officer in the Iranian government, he wanted confirmation. "Both of us want some assurances that the team's home made jammers will function. Last I heard the tests on them were just small scale."

"Why can't we address this by killing two birds with one stone?" The Financier asked quickly.

The Mariner jumped in, "Brothers!" Continuing right where he left off, "Everything is going to plan. Put to rest your fears! All of this arguing is just wasteful."

"If I could finish my point, Mariner." The Financier waited until all of the separate conversations had stopped. "What happened to the idea that the two couples should act as a backup team? That would provide support that the primary team needs, plus the couples could create more distractions on the spot or extract the team if they run into trouble?"

Seemingly unaffected by his Board's concerns, the C.O. spoke up, "Grey Hair, knows most of the operatives well, seeing that he recruited them, he was also last to see our team. I think he can best address everyone's concerns. Especially regarding the Coast Guard and the point of the back-up teams as well. Gentlemen, let him speak, please."

Grey Hair was typically quiet and slow to speak. He had a personal credo, *slow to speak and quick to listen.* There was silence and a bit of a delay until Grey Hair said anything. "Look," the man started, twisting his pointed beard. "I already disagreed with the idea of using the couples as emergency fire support teams. In fact I've expressed vehemently that the two couples, 'pilots' and 'fishermen' don't have the training to perform such a task. I submitted evidence to bolster my belief. Programmer, Brigadier...I thought this issue was settled months ago?"

Grey Hair gave a steely gaze through the video screen he had remoted through. Not a single man wanted to step forward and say anything to this 'grey ghost' they called a peer. Grey Hair came and went as he pleased and if he ever showed up at their door, there would be nothing but fear and concern to fill the mind.

Not hearing a response Grey Hair continued, "This is all of the resources we have at our disposal at the moment. We have worked for years in bringing together this operation. I've talked with all three teams. They *and all of their equipment*, are ready. The Coast Guard will be hamstrung and the opportune moment will arrive..." Grey Hair took a sip from a cup and the CO continued Grey Hair's points.

"The Seattle news made a big deal about taking one of the Coast Guard ships out of service. All of you remember that?" The men at the table nodded their heads, and the CO continued. "...That overhaul that is being done has a lot of people and money involved in it. In Washington's state capital, Olympia, they're trumpeting the news as a possible jolt to the local sluggish economy. You all know that the confluence of events are what drove us to this moment." The CO looked over all of the men through the large monitor. "We timed this for effect: Both the Coast Guard being down one vessel, the Navy having an aircraft carrier in port, fresh from the gulf, and the packed game/concert will ensure maximum end-product."

"Besides," Grey Hair jumped in once more buttressing his CO's points. "...If we don't want to spoil this precious moment or *confuse* our operatives, it's *too late* to try and *alter* things. Agree General?"

The Brigadier hesitated, knowing Grey Hair was using his own prior opinions against him. "I agree, with caution. It's not good to change things on people in the field, particularly these people so late in the plan." The Brigadier was quick too. He swiftly found a way to emphasize his own point *and still look like I was agreeing with that damned Grey Spy.* "But, for the sake of our men in the field, we need to be flexible in order to perform minor changes... if we see a problem...those two couples have to be ready to provide something..."

"Good." The C.O. joined back in, interrupting the Brigadier's last point. "If there are minor changes Grey Hair will be monitoring the OP in real time. All of you are also welcome to remote in as well. If there are any last minute changes then, Grey Hair and I can decide on what is best. All of us are keenly aware this is to be our group's first real strike, and it looks like everything's gone over..."

"Our first *real* strike!" The Mariner extorted. The room was plunged into icy silence. "At every turn we've met with success! We should be confidant that Allah is with us! After all we have made it this far without a single problem."

"Every single person here wants the attack to go off successfully, I understand this." The C.O. said in his calming voice. "I know we do not want any of us, or our people in the field, to get burned in the process. Let's take Grey Hair's assurances to heart and have the Mariner's faith in the cause. The plan is a good one, we have all made sure of that. May Allah pour out his blessings..."

And so time went on. Their meeting was soon adjourned and the men went about their other legitimate businesses. Twelve o'clock changed to one, one o' clock to two and people went about their preciously unique lives.

Everyone had individual wants and needs. They were all trying to work out their place in the world. There among Seattle's skyline and waterfront. There under the roofs of the twin sports stadiums; clueless sheep.

Also among the desert sands and the 110 degree heat of the Persian Gulf; wolves circling their prey.

Living and working, stressing about their busy schedules and having a little bit of fun in the process.

Sheep, wolves and maybe a few sheepdogs; pursuing life, enjoying their liberty and trying to find happiness...

Chapter Fifteen

Thursday August 30th 14:00

      The four mayhem makers, among Seattle's six-hundred thousand, wake up Thursday afternoon. They are not well rested, but they're ready for tonight's phase of the operation. After getting a bit of Seattle's world famous coffee into their veins, the lack of sleep becomes a distant ache. With the confidence they earned from their previous night's success, the group is feeling quite indestructible.

The men have a very leisurely and fulfilling morning. With still time to kill before their next op, they enjoy Pike Place Market, The Needle and The Electronic Music Project (E.M.P.). Fresh off of their fruitful evening of being underwater tourists of sorts, in their ironic sense of humor they decide to take a stroll along the waterfront. This is superficially for people watching, but the men are grinning outwardly over their previous night's clandestine actions. They end up spending most of their late afternoon hanging out along the shoreline.

The four look out on a perfectly calm bay with water colored a deep peaceful blue. A few commercial container ships are moving lazily through the water as if the beautiful summer sun was urging them to go slow. There are private yachts out on the water too, along with sailboats being pushed by the warm breeze. There's not a cloud in the sky; a beautiful afternoon in Jet City.

The mayhem makers and the citizens that they walk among find the sun is still quite high for this late hour because of the city's northern latitude. And it feels like the entire state has come into town to revel in it. There are a multitude of people downtown among the skyscrapers, window shopping in shorts and t-shirts. Crowds gather down on the waterfront among the piers, shops, and restaurants. Visitors take in the splendid mountain and ocean views and soak up the great weather as well.

A brilliant August sun shines late into the evening over Elliot Bay. The city is practically busting at the seams with roaring crowds gathered at Seattle's Key Arena and across town at Century Link Field. Plus there's the tourists taking in the late summer evenings in Seattle. The locals know of the fantastic summers up in the Northwest and try to keep it a secret from the rest of the United States.

"Let them think that it rains here all the time," was the mantra, "After all, locals need to have some sun without the tourist crowds, before the long, grey, wet winter comes."

On this warm Thursday night, Key Arena, the Seattle Center concert staple, is hosting

The Red Hot Chili Peppers in grand style. The band is well into their second set of funk, alt, hard and punk rock melodies. If the sound of the crowd is any indication, they are doing it exceptionally well. With their punctuated rhythms, high intensity stage personalities and out of the ordinary song styles, they have the packed arena delighted. As the lyrics roll out about sex and music, love and friendship, drugs and alcohol; the crowd sings along in surprisingly good harmony. Showing their love for the band with the memorized Peppers lyrics.

At Century Link Field, formerly Qwest Field, the mood wasn't all that different. At the same time of the Chili Peppers concert, the assembly of sports fans are happily supporting their NFC team with its fight against the Oakland Raiders. This is the last of the pre-season games. The people, from all over Washington, cheer on their team which is well on its way to a win against the Raiders.

Called the 12th Man by their team, they are a loyal bunch, braving inclement weather and long distances to see the Seahawks play. There are plenty of number 12's in the sea of fans, the number that was given to them by the Seahawks in thanks for being such great supporters. These are the same fans after all, that made the old Kingdome the loudest stadium in the NFL. This was also the same group of devoted fans that watched, to their surprise, the 2010 NFL season. That season, the Seahawks made history by making it into the playoffs despite having a 7-9 record. The fans didn't care how they did it, they didn't care that the Seahawks had the best record in the worst division at the time, the fans devoutly wore their 12's.

..And the thoughts were similar elsewhere.

Well, kind of.

The four that consider these crowded streets and packed stadiums good reasons for joy and celebration. However, they are filled with a twisted joy to cause mayhem. These undercover agents feel this is a target rich environment. But, their visit isn't about just randomly killing people, to these group of men that kind of thing is child's play. Give anyone a legal semi-auto rifle, a pipe bomb or for that matter a simple knife and even the untrained can cause great harm.

Consider that even without modern weapons, there is still the capability to cause chaos. In Genesis 4:18, a description of possibly the world's first weapon, the rock, was used to murder. Even in our technologically advanced and educated world, a simple thing can be used to kill. Someone truly deranged and well motivated with a knife could injure dozens before being stopped by law enforcement, a brave citizen or their own cowardice.

No, the mayhem makers know that there is so much more that can be accomplished by all of the bloodshed. Much more than just simple mass-murder. These four can make a statement, small or big, or even try and change the political course of a city, a county or a state. The logic went, the higher the death toll, the greater the possibility of even changing national political policy. Some presidents capitulate. When pressed some men are just cowards. They were going to shock the system hard enough to make the strongest retreat into their homes. Just wait and see, this attack is only the beginning of a larger wave of aggression that will soon wash up on the shores of the United States.

Yeah, that's what the conspirators really want. Force a nation to alter its behavior by causing heinous acts of violence, get the populace up in arms, and then the American politicians will bend to a new course; remarkably it's often the wrong one.

The four men take particular pleasure in watching the people from the peninsula come in on the state ferries; presumably for either the Chili Peppers Concert or the Seahawks game. The mayhem makers have a great view of the ferries, as they come and go. They requested to be seated next to a window of another Seattle seafood staple; Ivar's. From their restaurant table, they can clearly see the Washington State ferries rolling in and out, just opposite of the soon to be doomed municipal boats. Like the throngs of people at the concert and the football game this evening, the quartet also enjoys the warm late afternoon sun.

"Too bad we can't get our meals out on the nice deck," Tarriq says aloud, to no one in particular. He pulls off a piece of the sourdough roll, butters it and pops it whole into his mouth.

"Yeah, we can get bombed by all of those seagulls," complains Jibril.

With a grin on his face Parvez interrupts, "Out of all of us, it would be Raphael that gets hit with droppings first."

They all laugh, and look at Raphael, who is caught up eating his clam chowder. Looking up from his bowl, he gives the three others a serious face and continues eating. The three ignore Raphael's stern look and carry on a healthy banter throughout the meal. There are only rare comments from Raphael who still is immersed in the seriousness of their operation.

The four settle into silence as the meal nears its end. The weight of tonight's assignment settles heavier on all of their minds. They each quietly enjoy a dessert, then Jibril pays the bill with another stolen credit card giving the waitress a fifty dollar tip.

"What the heck!" was his attitude. It wasn't his money. The waitress had kept up a very good demeanor, despite being slammed with customers. Jibril was all about spreading the wealth around, he was sure the credit card company would eat the charges anyway.

Besides, Jibril had the notion that he just might come back here afterwards. The girl at 13 Coins was cold, but professional, but not this one. She seemed to be smiling a bit too much. Maybe the tip will get her to say yes when he asks her out?

20:00. An alarm goes off on Tarriq's phone. He pulls it out, terminates the alarm and looks into the faces of his cell members. He doesn't even need to say a word. It is all understood. The time has drawn near for the next step. The end of the meal's silence carries on as they leave the seafood restaurant.

They disperse from each other once they exit the restaurant. Tarriq stands alone looking like he is checking out the skyscrapers that loom over the waterfront. Raphael keeps his eyes on the sidewalk in front of him and walks slowly toward the walk on entrance for the ferry. Parvez loiters at the Old Curiosity Shop, while Jibril picks up a conversation with a Native American street vendor selling hand-made totems.

Yet, with backpacks or man purses over their shoulders, concealed weapons in shoulder holsters and the bags, they each walk into the ferry terminal for the next phase. The ferry terminal's white iron structure providing architectural inspiration. During their walk on board, the operatives have an almost universal thought: How were the foolish ferry passengers going to know that tonight was going to be a chaotic trip home?

Chapter Sixteen

Thursday Aug 23rd & Thursday Aug 30th

This twenty-five year old woman had received the order. *She was "Pilot" and finally it was green lighted!* Jennifer had exclaimed when she got the video game message. She deciphered it and was instructed to pickup an envelope at her local pack and ship store, via coded text. *I have been chosen to do something! After all of this time I was being activated!* Within the package were ten thousand US dollars, a USB stick, a forged credit card and fake Canadian Operators Licenses. The licenses were for both automobile and aircraft.

Jennifer read the information contained on the USB stick, committing every detail to memory. Then, she walked out to her husband's garage and smashed the small piece of plastic and circuit board with his favorite framing hammer. She held the large tool two-handed.

When the she arrived at the airfield the next day, Jennifer was nervous and excited at the same time. A light airplane, fueled and ready, was waiting for her at Vancouver Field in Canada's British Columbia. The rental aircraft operator took a look at her fake ID and forged signature. They matched the reservation. The credit card, with an account belonging to someone totally unaware, was swiped and she walked to her aircraft with one bag over her shoulder and larger ones in each hand.

The light airplane, a Cessna, was pre-reserved by one company, connected to a web of shell companies that led back to her benefactor. The rental was purchased under her recently arrived fraudulent credit card by the benefactor whom set up all of this. She got in, went through the procedures that she knew so well and then pulled her Cessna into the sky with plenty of runway to spare.

She flew the light aircraft to Everett, Washington for a week of sightseeing, shopping and getting away from her duties as a young mother. Jennifer was blown away that when she landed in Everett, parked her aircraft, and made it all of the way to car rental; she did so without ever being approached by customs. *What a country!*

It was her "big vacation," and she couldn't decide if it was memorable because it was the first time she'd been without her husband for a week or because she was so looking forward to the trip home.

And now, this Canadian national, without an American Passport, is heading back.

The sound of Jennifer's single-engined, light airplane is heard over the Salish Sea. The Cessna 182 is on a flight from Everett, Washington to Vancouver BC. It's passage takes it up the inland sea, over scenic Whidbey, Camano, and Fildago Islands. The pilot has a panoramic view of the Olympic mountains far off to her left, the Cascades off to her right and the San Juan Islands, below.

Yet, she pays them little attention. Despite the long sunset creating purple mountains to her east and lighting up the Olympics to her west, she has other things on her mind. Jennifer is a skilled pilot and this flight will put her skills to good use. She has held her license for five years and possesses a sharp intellect and an intense personality. As she goes through her final preparations, *this will help with the unemployment situation. I won't be so hard pressed trying to find another veterinary job 'cause this 'side job' has come along!*

The cute woman, known by her friends as having a bubbly personality, left Everett Field happy and focused. She took off at the precise time and the exact day to put her over the middle of the Strait of Juan de Fuca by 20:30 on Thursday Aug 30th. The plane was on autopilot most of the way. It gave Jennifer time to change her clothes and braid her long black hair tightly, before securing it with multiple hair-bands. After her costume change, she slid the pillow back underneath her rump to give her the height she needed to properly fly the airplane. She holds meticulously to her flight plan. Right up to the minute before she calls Air Traffic Control (ATC) with emergency engine trouble.

Jennifer flicks off autopilot, and keys her mic, "ATC Vancouver this is Cessna nine zero one beta five out of Everett, en route to Vancouver." Jennifer waits a moment and then her radio crackles to life.

"This is ATC Vancouver. Go Ahead, Cessna niner, oh, one, bravo, five." The professional and calm voice of ATC Vancouver gives her another smile. She can't help it, this whole process was bringing her...joy.

You're in for a surprise, she tells ATC in her head. "ATC, I seem to be having some throttle issues. Plane's slowing down by itself. I can correct the problem by pulling back on the throttle and then returning it to it's former position." As if to demonstrate her problem she pulls back on the throttle and up on the stick causing her aircraft to climb and then stall. It pitches over controllably, into a gentle dive and slowly regains enough airflow under its wings to once again fly. Much like a roller coaster getting to the top of a rise and slowing, right before going over the other side and gaining speed.

"Niner, oh, one, bravo, five, Do you need a redirect to alternate landing?"

"Negative, ATC," she smiles a particular impish grin, "the issue seems to be gone now."

"Roger that Cessna niner, oh, one, bravo, five; issue is gone? Please advise: What's your destination? How many passengers?

"This is Cessna niner, zero, one, beta, five. We are inbound to Vancouver B.C. Four on board including pilot."

"Copy that Cessna niner, oh, one, bravo, five; advise the moment your condition changes. Roger?"

"Roger that ATC, Cessna's out." Yet, she isn't worried, not in the least.

The Cessna 182 is an inherently stable aircraft. It is well engineered and designed and, in fact, there is nothing wrong with the airplane. Not only that, but she is the only one on board. She holds the plane level for two more minutes while she checks her GPS location and then puts the plane back into a stall condition, as long as she has altitude she can glide this particular airframe with ease. High wing monoplanes, such as this Cessna, are well-built and easily flown machines. *And this one in particular was steady and incredibly forgiving. Such a shame...but it is the best type of airplane to crash in*, she thinks with an impish grin. Jennifer regains control of the 182, pushes up the power and does her practiced maneuver two more times. Knowing she is being watched on the Canadian radar out of Vancouver, B.C. and possibly Everett Field's tower in the U.S..

Moments pass and Jennifer receives a radio call from ATC Vancouver. She places the aircraft level as the call comes in, "This is ATC Vancouver. Niner, oh, one, bravo, five, what's your status? Are you in distress?" She doesn't say a word, but hums a Lady Gaga tune, waiting.

Jennifer's radio barks into life once more, "Cessna niner... oh... one... bravo... five...out...of...Everett! This is ATC Vancouver! Please respond!!"

The woman ignores the request and maintains silence for ten more minutes. She receives several more calls from ATC Vancouver British Columbia. Jennifer uses that time to pass far north of the San Juan's and out into the open Strait of Juan de Fuca. She gets hailed by Everett Field out of Washington State but ignores that call too.

A few moments later, she determines the time is right. *Now for the real show,* she grins at her remark and keeps it pasted on her face. The young lady skillfully performs a few more erratic stalls, bleeding off more air speed for altitude until she is just five hundred feet off the water.

Still purposefully on the American side of the Strait of Juan de Fuca, just two miles south east of Point Roberts, Jennifer makes one more call. "Mayday, Mayday. This is Cessna nine, zero, one, beta, five out of Everett. Engine failure! I repeat engine failure..."

Jennifer's petite hand kills the radio, rips the headphones from her head, and tosses them to the passenger chair. The headphones hit the chair and then the right side door with a clunk! Their momentum causes them to roll off of the seat and onto her small scuba tank, mask, fins, buoyancy compensator (BC), and floatable dive bag. They stop moving on the floor, next to a small grey cylinder that looks like a miniature torpedo. Now, below a hundred feet, the aircraft is out of the line of sight from both the American and Canadian radars. It is quickly and simply hidden in plain sight. Just like so many aircraft that go missing every year, Jennifer's Cessna is now among them.

She giggles at how truly easy everything is. The lady skillfully lets the 182 glide at a hundred feet for a few hundred yards, aiming slightly north. The aircraft gains a bit more lift because of the water's ground effect. It allows Jennifer to strap on her gear without much concern for flying. The plane gently stalls out the last time, kissing the water. She has five minutes, plenty of time to allow her to strap on the scuba gear before the plane submerges completely.

Activating the purposefully cracked Emergency Position Indicating Radio Beacon (EPIRB) at 20:30, she slithers gracefully out of the partially submerged Cessna. She ties a lanyard from her waste belt to her floating dive bag and heads for the Canadian coastal town of White Rock.

Satisfied with her work, she powers up the gray cylinder, a seascooter. Essentially, a sealed rechargeable battery, in an aerodynamic tube, attached to a small high-speed propeller. In the dark and cold Puget Sound, Jennifer remains out of sight of any rescue craft for as long as she wants. With the help of the seascooter and the scuba tank, the woman glides a good fifteen feet underwater, for over a mile. With her neutrally buoyant dive bag following along behind like a reluctant puppy she passes through the murky water. The cold black ocean hides her as easily as if she was buried alive.

Jennifer is successful at everything. She had prepared meticulously and had run exactly what she was going to do through her head a hundred times. She even purchased a flight simulator to make sure her timing, heading and expected stall speed would be within the water's ground effect.

Piloting the seascooter by a digital compass and map display on her wrist Jennifer makes it to the Canadian shore without being discovered. The woman slips out of the dive equipment and momentarily shows her entire lithe and fit body to anyone that is looking into the copse of trees she is using for her changing area. Jennifer is quickly into her street clothes pulled from her dive bag. All of her dive equipment goes back into the bag and she nonchalantly walks out of the trees toward Marine Drive Park. She calls up her ride on a throw away mobile to make sure he is close, and continues her walk for 30 minutes until she sees her ride. The man is sitting on his hood innocently watching the sunset with a cup of coffee in his hand.

Approaching the car she tosses the phone into the bushes without its battery. Jennifer, ecstatic with her success, places all of her gear in the rear and gets into the passenger side of the waiting vehicle. The man comes into the drivers side and hands her the still hot cup of coffee. She leans over, gives her husband a quick peck and whispers, "Our way is true."

Her husband whispers it back to her, as he places the van in drive and points it northward, back toward home.

The two Canadian Nationals had once toured the Mediterranean during their college years abroad. Many years ago when they were young, open to new ideas and free from any conventional western ones. They were recruited by a Grey Haired man while the two of them were attending graduate college in Spain.

At one of their last meetings with the older man, the couple didn't need much convincing to join up with him. They had been long term followers of the Way. Muslims already and slowly drifting toward some of the more militant ideas. The couple attended various militant mosques in their travels in Europe and the Mediterranean.

So it was no surprise to have been approached to help a group, "...that needed a little help now and again for their Islamist cause," The Grey haired man smoothly explained. He took a sip of sparkling water and provided more details. "Nothing dangerous you understand. I don't want to jeopardize your future plans. And of course nothing you won't be paid handsomely for."

They liked what the interesting man had said. The two didn't need the money at first, just liked the sense that they were needed. That they could do something great and more important than themselves was an honor. But since immigrating to Canada, which is what they were directed to do, the couple have started up a family. And now, the money will be put to good use.

As the husband guides the family mini-van back onto the freeway, his face is lit up with pride at his wife's success. As the two head back north, Jennifer sees the look on her husband's face, squeezes his hand lovingly and takes a long drink of the coffee. She glances back to her two sleeping children, and her heart is about to burst at her sense of accomplishment.

The two small kids are snug and asleep in their car seats. They were lulled into their slumber by a time honored undulation of the car's tires on the freeway.

The children are completely unaware that mommy and daddy are up to something.

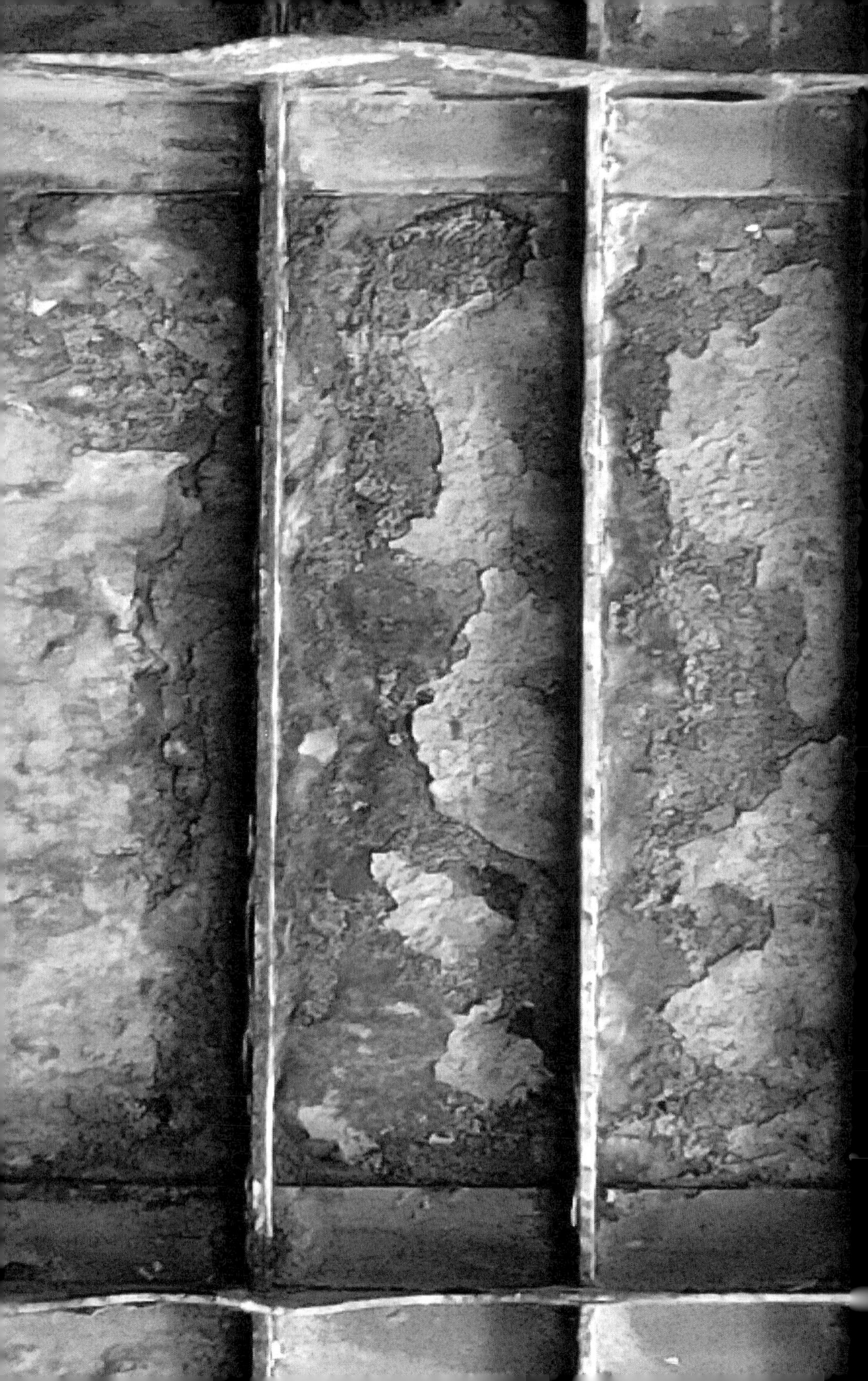

Chapter Seventeen

Thursday August 30th 19:30

The United States Coast Guard (USCG) within the Salish Sea cover a massive seven thousand square mile area of water. It is roughly the size of the state of New Jersey. There are almost a dozen cutters, the term USCG used for their commissioned vessels, that call Puget Sound home. Needless to say, there are never enough ships or men to adequately cover that kind of area.

A third of the Coast Guard's fleet are the deep water, medium and heavy endurance cutters, that travel mostly *out* of the Salish Sea. These larger cutters patrol all the way north to Alaska and south to Northern California. The deep water cutters have to patrol the Pacific Ocean from the Aleutians to Hawaii.

The other two-thirds are smaller, coastal patrol cutters, that are stationed permanently at various ports along The Strait of Juan De Fuca, Elliot Bay and the Puget Sound. They are clustered mostly in the American north, due to the Strait being the major artery for shipping to the northern United States and all of western Canada. Unfortunately, or fortunately, depending on who you are, there is a weakness in the Straight that can be exploited.

The smaller Coast Guard patrol ships out of the towns of Port Townsend, Bellingham and Orcas Island make it to the airplane crash in all due haste and remain on search grids, along with Canadian rescue craft out of Vancouver BC. Later, they are joined by a helicopter out of Port Townsend, which was delayed by an intermittent turbine starter. The helicopter works in conjunction with the water craft laying out an exhaustive search. After two hours, the aircrew, running low on fuel, is forced to return to base before the patrol ships. The Coastal Patrol Cutters stay on site until midnight. They continue to chase the intermittent signal of the EPIRB even after an hour after the Cessna's damaged EPIRB dies out from water intrusion.

The searchers in the north, never find the missing plane or the supposed bodies.

The final two remaining Coast Guard vessels stayed in the south Sound, not investigating the plane crash. They are to cover the central and south Sound and are stationed near Seattle, Washington and farther yet, in Olympia. In fact, the patrol ship stationed near Seattle, is currently at Bremerton Naval Shipyard, down with a week of engine repairs. This now leaves the entire central and south Sound covered by only one Coast Guard patrol craft.

The men in Ashan have been watching carefully and the confluence of all these events played directly into their hands. Ashan had done their homework well.

At approximately the same time as Jennifer, the Canadian pilot, leaves Everett, two other people leave Horse Head Bay in their 1976 Silverton Sportfish. The 27-foot convertible Silverton isn't much to look at, being built in '76, and is due for some major surface refinishing. The paint and the fiberglass is flaking, the epoxy deck coat is yellowing and the windshield is cracked. Yet, that doesn't matter much to the two fishermen.

When Jaroslav and Anastasiya bought the craft, Jaroslav cared about one thing, "Does the boat run well?" Jaroslav asked the old owner.

Anastasiya finished her husband's thought, "...and does it float?"

The two, with Anastasiya at the wheel, work their boat expertly out of Horse Head Bay, through an inlet and into the South Sound. The fishermen have all they need on board their boat. They have their fuel tanks filled to the cap, extra fuel in a pair of small red fuel containers and two bags of gear for a long night out of fishing. The Silverton has tires draped all around the edge of the craft to keep it away from pylons just in case they have to dock up against a pier or another boat.

The young couple were recruited by Ashan only a year and a half ago in the Ukrainian town of Kerch, on the sands of the Black Sea. The pair were already loyal followers and incredibly concerned about the repugnant influence of the American Society on their country. The Russian influence was bad, the American capitalists were far more dangerous.

The couple were approached and befriended by a charming grey-haired man who listened much and talked little. He had approached them with news that their Imam was a friend of his and the Imam had asked for Grey Hair to talk with the two. After only a few weeks of gaining the couple's trust and loyalty, he met them at a cafe and gave them the pitch. Grey Hair asked "You two are young. You should have money so you can see the world for a while."

"Well, we are trying as hard as we can, but this area doesn't have the best employment situation." The Jaroslav explained in his native tongue, leaning into Grey Hair for emphasis.

"Leave this town for something better." The older man replied. Grey Hair had a way of finding just what was in his recruit's hearts and exploited it. "Both of you are youthful and full of passion. You have nothing tying you here and it's poor economy and hopeless outlook. The Russians have annexed this peninsula and its not going to get any better. Go make some money, travel, and do some needed work for the people that I represent." Grey Hair suggested in the best way he could. He never demanded, just offered his opinion.

The older man had done his research and knew of their desperate circumstance. Grey Hair will take advantage of whatever he could to recruit. Regardless if it was the couple's naivety or their gullibility. *It was so easy when the pair were susceptible to the most minor encouragement,* Grey Hair rationalized. And although he could see they were reluctant to leave their homeland, because of their rundown apartment and jobless future, this would be quite an opportunity. *They will realize this. All they had to do is make a deal with me and they will have plenty of money and a chance for a little service to Allah.*

Jaroslav and Anastasiya did not have the legal means to immigrate to the United States. Both of them were poor and neither one had a marketable talent that would get them a good work visa. Yet, Grey Hair knew right where the weaknesses were in the American passport and Immigration system. He got them both enrolled in Washington State University in a foreign exchange student program and had their temporary student visas Fed Ex'd to them in a week.

The two could not believe that it had been so easy to travel into the United States, when they found it so difficult just to get secure a passport. Eager to get out of their deplorable circumstances they said good bye to homeland and made the trip to the U.S..

Now, driving the Silverton, they both can't wait to get out. For they were '*the fishermen*'. The stress is really starting to get to Anastasiya. The nervous pair are anxious about their first "real" mission despite their exhaustive planning. Plus, Anastasiya is in constant fear of getting a knock on the door because of their student visas being six months expired. So much for Grey Hair's words that everything would be okay. *Nothing is okay,* Anastasiya screams in her head. *We are both doing everything in our power not to have the stress affect our relationship...and there's no telling when that will end...*

Anastasiya consoles herself as she drives the small fishing craft, *we have a rental car waiting for us at Tiltlow Park. It is just south of the bridge, on the mainland side of the Sound. We dropped it off there this morning and no one knocked on our door. If only the car could whisk us away from everything instead of just back to our apartment out on the peninsula.* Anastasiya's stomach was in constant turmoil and she was talking to herself to try and make it better. *It wasn't working though, because I haven't been able to eat anything for the past two days.*

Anastasiya looked forward to tomorrow. *Tomorrow, we will finish packing and move to the next station, somewhere over in the Midwest and get this whole business behind us.* She had been trying to talk her Jaro into taking the money and just disappearing. But, she knew the type of people they dealt with. *It would be a fools errand to try and do such a thing.* The boat bounced up and down on the waves, a fine spray hitting her face and she just tried to compartmentalize it all.

As Anastasiya drives the Silverton fishing boat, Jaroslav keeps an eye out for any other ship traffic. There are a few boats out on the water fishing and catching the evening sunset, but no one too close. Seeing the boats on the water Jaroslav remarks to his love without looking away from the other boats, "Hopefully, the boats will thin out once we get closer to the bridge."

Anastasiya glances to her partner, smiles nervously and refocuses on her navigating. *I am not liking this one bit,* she tells herself. *Regardless of the money, their faith or the cause.*

The both of them had been practicing this moment for several months and the upside down stomach feeling had *never* hit her. Not once during that entire time of training. Now she couldn't help the guilty feeling she kept having. She tried to stuff it down, box it up, but the thought that what she was doing was wrong in every way kept nagging at her soul.

Her partner, husband for the past five years and her best friend since grammar school knows her well. Jaroslav sees her unease and tries to encourage his best friend in their home language. "We timed our departure perfectly Annie. The GPS says we will be there in just fifty minutes."

Anastasiya absently nods her head, still not breaking away her focus from the water. She doesn't want to look her partner in the eyes. *Not right now my love,* she silently tells him. To have him see the fear and uncertainty in her face would only make her feel worse.

"Look, we have been through this entire plan," he continues in Ukrainian, "You know we can do this." She still ignores him. He forgets about talking anymore. Resolving instead to keep watch, and lifts the binoculars from his chest.

Still gazing intently toward her destination, Anastasiya finally breaks her silence in her first language of Ukrainian, "Jaro, I want to spend a lifetime making my own decisions, not in a figurative or literal jail. My handsome, I can't help the feeling that this is all wrong, regardless of what the Americans have done."

He lets his binoculars hang and stands beside his best friend. Jaroslav rubs her shoulder reassuringly, partially ignoring her concern. "We won't get caught. Ashan has helped us plan for everything." Seeing her body language Jaroslav knows he isn't getting through.

In his most assuring voice he continues, "My sweet angel, we have a duty to perform and we will be rewarded for it. Here on Earth and in Heaven. Remember, just a few of these missions and then we will head back home. Wealthier than we imagined." He pulls one of her hands away from the wheel, holds it in his. "Then we can start a business... and a family together... remember?"

Calmed by his words Anastasiya whispers in English, "I remember. Okay."

"Do you need me to drive?" He questions back in his non-native tongue.

"No, I can do it. Besides," she lets out a small grin, "I'm a better driver than you."

Jaroslav grins at her English, and her accent, then moves about the boat making it ready.

Their small fishing boat makes it's way up the channel and around a small bend. From that point, they can see the massive bridges that connect the Kitsap Peninsula with the city of Tacoma and the mainland. The pair of twin spans and four towers is now clearly visible. The original Narrows Bridge was finished in 1940 and dramatically collapsed the same year. Nicknamed Galloping Gertie, the mid-span failed in a violent twisting caused by high winds resonating the bridge at its natural structural frequency. A second bridge was finished in the 1950's and a third was built in parallel to the second in 2007.

The pair arrive on site, under the older bridge at 20:45. They park right next to one of the westbound bridge's concrete pylons that hold one of the massive support towers. Seeing that they are behind schedule they hurry into their dive equipment. He helps her into hers before putting on his. He places their clothes into the dry sack, while she anchors the boat. The pair are careful while they walk around the deck that's also covered in old tires. He tests his air tank, giving her the thumbs up and she does the same. They each take a spare gasoline can and empty the contents all over the craft. After dumping the gas, she looks back at her best friend, "Our way is true."

Jaroslav gazes intently into the eyes of the only woman he's ever loved, for a moment, before saying it back. The man watches his lover sit on the gunwale with their dry sack, Anastasiya waves, and falls backwards into the water. Satisfied that everything is ready, he opens up emergency channel 18 on his short range VHF marine radio. "Mayday, mayday, mayday! Engine fire on board, westbound Narrows Bridge, far pylon. Please hurry!"

"This is the United States Coast Guard. Please state your name and vessel." The voice of the operator is a practiced drone.

Jaroslav, the fisherman, just smiles. He waits a minute by his watch, listening as the radio crackles to life again.

"Repeat your emergency. I say again, repeat. This is the United States Coast Guard!"

"Fire on board, Silverton Sportfish, Narrows Bridge, we're abandoning ship!"
Leaving the radio on, he makes his way to the gunwale and steps over it into the Sound. He swims the ten feet to his wife and she hands him the marine flare gun, loaded and ready. Grinning at being able to have the honor, he pulls the trigger. His flare makes a beautiful arc and then the Sportfish goes... Fooush in a firestorm!!

The worn Silverton goes from functional, yet ragged boat, into raging inferno in less than a minute. The tires catch fire after a few minutes, spitting out a thick, acrid black smoke. The two gaze at each other for a second, smiling wildly, before putting in their mouthpieces kicking on their seascooters, and disappearing under the waves.

In less than five minutes, there are numerous mobile phone calls into 911 for a boat on fire under the Narrows Bridge. A rescue helicopter from Bremerton Navy Base is the first to arrive on scene to aid, but with the boat still burning obscuring black smoke, the helicopter is reduced to shining it's searchlight around the area. They did their best to loiter and try to find anyone in the water.

Tacoma police and fire arrive and Gig Harbor fire and rescue are on the scene seven minutes later. Both bridges are awash in red and blue lights as both directions of the bridges are closed as a precaution. Within ten minutes of the initial 911 calls the Tacoma Fire and Gig Harbor Fire pour water on the boat despite it being underneath the northbound bridge. Their application of the water is only slightly effective.

The last remaining Coast Guard Cutter, out of Olympia, responds with all due haste and arrives on-site to a still burning hulk. They use their onboard fire suppression gear and along with support from on top of the bridge, have the fire out in a grueling twenty minutes. Another Coast Guard boat surprisingly arrives out of Tacoma. This small Piranha type boat is a fast, rigid-hulled twenty five footer that was finishing a homeland security mission before hearing the mayday. They are stationed out of Bainbridge Island, but instead of returning home their duty called. As the Piranha arrives, the search and rescue helicopter leaves for refueling.

The Coast Guard Piranha joins the search of the smoking hulk. They are curious as to the long burn time of the vessel and inspect it closer. The firefighters have a sixth sense about infernos and they are curious as to why it was such a hot burn. Some of the Coast Guard senior officers are immediately suspicious. They didn't know that there were tires anchored to the craft, but the thick black smoke has them guessing. They also were unaware that the insides of the tires were laced with homemade thermite to insure a hot burn and melting of the tires.

Not immediately seeing obvious human remains on board, they throw out buoys tied to lines to contain any possible fuel or oil leak. They leave three of their number in a smaller craft to continue the inspection. The men in the dingy will be on site to find the reason for the black smoke, and look for the remains. While their fellow responders are inspecting the wreck, the two larger craft follow the tide south. The Cutter and the Piranha search the general area for the survivor that called in the mayday.

The current is strong in the Narrows due to its funnel like shape. Depending on the tides, a person or a body can be swept up toward Seattle or downward toward Olympia quite quickly. The larger pair of ships expand their search, gradually moving farther south while the small launch dingy ties off on the concrete bridge pylon. The Cutter and Piranha call for additional helicopter support while they motor farther and farther away from Seattle.

The Coast Guards' search grids begin to grow. Because of this, the distance between them and Tiltlow Park increases as well. The first rescue chopper arrives back on scene to assist and proceeds to work in conjunction with the two Coast Guard boats. They all remain on station searching, investigating and performing hull recovery until the helicopter leaves first and then just past 23:00 hours the ships call off the rescue.

The fishermen emerge from the sea just as the pair of Coast Guard ships round a bend. With the way open, the couple hurries for the trees in Tiltlow Park. They change quickly, just like their co-conspirator Jennifer does in Canada and, like Jennifer, the couple walk calmly to their waiting car. They decide to head to one of the numerous Irish pubs in Tacoma for dinner, since getting across the bridges tonight is going to be a nightmare.

They sit close, holding hands constantly and kissing often. They try to enjoy the ambiance of the restaurant and attempt to keep up their smiles. The two Ukrainians eat, drink and do there best to forget about what just transpired. Anastasiya puts the Harp Lager away especially hard, trying to keep away her doubts about what she has done this evening. But her inner demons keep coming back again and again. She can't help but realize that she is on the wrong side of things. She orders another beer and seeing this Jaroslav stops drinking. It looks like he will be their driver home.

Jaroslav and Anastasiya are ten thousand dollars richer and one step closer to moving back to their homeland of Ukraine. Maybe, just maybe, they will be able to have a nice life together.

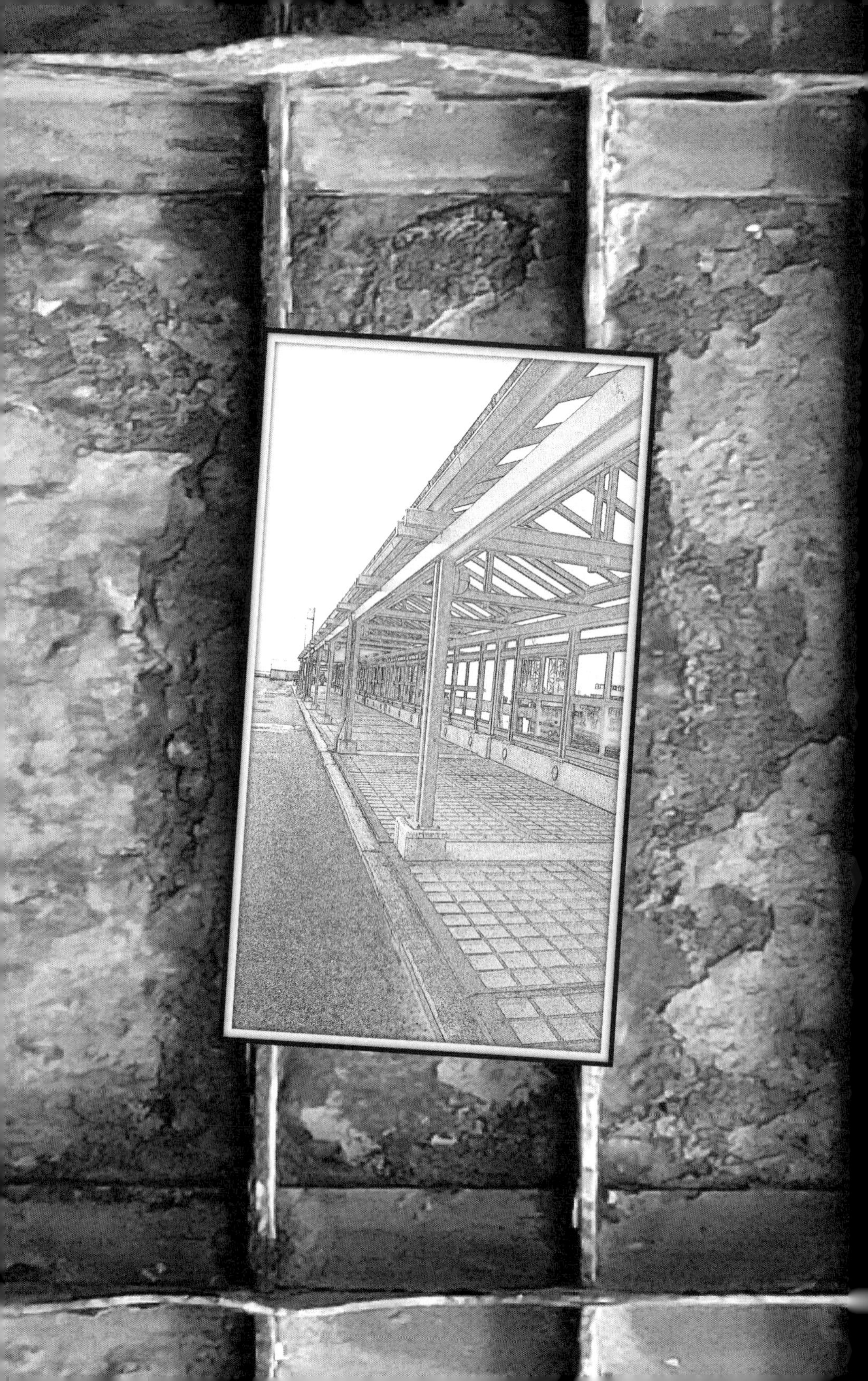

Chapter Eighteen

Thursday August 30th 19:35

      Buzzzz, buzzzz, the charging mobile phone vibrates on the bookshelf next to the bed.

The overworked electrician is right in the middle of a peaceful dream. Everything that is within him says that the call is also just part of the same dream.

"Let it go," his dream-self begs, "Fall back to sleep. You don't need to wake for a long time."

Buzz, buzz, buzz the vibrations come quicker now and the ring tone starts softly. James Maly finds himself in the place right in-between reality and slow wave sleep. The melatonin he took to help him sleep still has hold of him. "The Rain Song" by Led Zeppelin begins to play in addition to the buzz of the vibrations. In a state of low consciousness, Mr. Maly pushes himself up from his stomach, and out of bed. He grabs the phone so quick, that his action yanks the charger clear out of the wall socket.

James pushes the green answer button and harshly whispers "What!" Blinking, stumbling and groggy, he walks into the bathroom. The charger is trailing him like some primitive tail. Gently closing the door, he slides his back down the vanity. James winches as his legs touch the cold tile as he proceeds to sit on the tile floor.

This was his custom when he got phone calls late at night. On autopilot he would grab the phone while in its vibration stage, so that it wouldn't wake his sleeping wife. He would step into the master bathroom, closing the door, before answering a phone call.

"Jimmy? What gives? Were you sleeping already?"

"Yeah, I was..." James's emphasis on 'was' causes it to be a stretched out plea.

"Couldn't find anything to do on a Thursday night?" The voice snickers on the other end. "Jimmy, don't you have the day unscheduled today? Did you work hard doing something else? Like cleanin' your van?" His boss for the company he worked, Raptor

Electric, always called him Jimmy when he was in a teasing mood. And James couldn't stand it.

James still has his eyes closed and is still cringing from the cold tile floor touching his skin. James lets his boss, Flynn, drone on. Finally seeing an opportunity to cut in James explains to his boss, in a return stream of connected thought. "I've got a four hour drive to a 6am call in the Tri-Cities for the morning, I've got to get up early Flynn so I went to bed early, and don't call me Jimmy. Please???"

James pauses, does not hear a witty response, so he continues, "Why are you ringing me, I'm not on call this week, Right?"

"No, no you're not, but I can't get a hold of Nick who's supposed to be the on-call tech," (ignoring all of the other things that James had said). "It's a call for a downed network circuit over on the Bremerton Naval Base and you know how they are…" The boss's voice trails off before finishing.

"Yeah," James says in an exhaled whisper. He hesitates, his eyes wanting sleep. James continues, "Well I bet Nick is out with his woman or at home playing video games. So that means I would have to go out to the peninsula now, go fix whatever, and try to make my four hour drive for Friday?" James questions, a little concern in his voice.

The smiling Flynn on the other end of the mobile phone of course knew all of the call information before he woke up James. Yet, James's boss still liked riling people. Flynn was always trying to outdo himself. It was probably why he couldn't ever stay married for long.

"I'll make you a deal," Flynn continues. "You go out to the peninsula right now and fix up the Navy real good and then, when you finish, you can call it a day. We have the call scoped for six hours, then you can forget about the long drive in the morning. I'll get someone else to grab your Tri-Cities call. That way, when you get finished with the Navy call you can head home and get an early start to your weekend."

"Deal. Send me the call." James hits the red button and hangs up on Flynn. He looks at the clock on his phone, 19:37. He'd been asleep for almost two whole hours.

"Suck," he curses to himself under his breath and walks out of his bathroom into the master bedroom. The bed is completely empty. The light is still coming in from under the door, which leads out into the hallway. James figures out only then, that everyone must still be awake.

The joy of working for a living, he thinks to himself and considers that for a moment. *Sleep odd hours, work unusual schedules, and constantly away from the family. It didn't seem to be worth the money sometimes.* James pauses to rub the tired from his face and eyes with both hands.

I am going to change this soon, is his final reflection, *talk it over with Wendi, maybe a different employer. Maybe move to Idaho and start a farm?* He disconnects the chargers from the phones, throwing both of them onto the bed and flicks on the bedroom light.

James has permanently tussled hair and a mustached face that still looked boyish under the facial hair. Lately, he carries a perpetual neutral look that leaves even those that know him uncertain if he is angry or happy. Still fit from younger days, he does his best to maintain it. James does some push-ups and some sit-ups and then heads into the bathroom.

He quickly runs his head under the faucet and fixes his hair in the mirror. He stretches his tired body repeatedly while getting dressed in the clothes that he set out for the early morning. He doesn't even bother a shower or a shave. James grabs his two Blackberries, Bluetooth headset, belt, pistol and knife, then heads out of his bedroom. The electrician, father and husband walks downstairs, balancing himself heavily on the railing because of his still groggy state.

"Hello, you three," he speaks to his kids as he passes. The kids are playing Xbox in the family room and now he slows his stride listening for their reply. As he does so, James adjusts his unbuckled belt and pistol holster because the holster always has a way of digging into his side.

"Hey Dad," is the reply in three part zombie-like harmony. Shaking his head with wonder if his kids aren't becoming the creatures that they pursue in the game, James walks around the corner to the dinning room where he will likely find his wife.

His wife, Wendi Maly, is there in the dining room, working.

What a beautiful lady. James exhales in a heart felt sigh. He stops for a moment to watch his wife work and feels so lucky to have her in his life. His constant presence of stability. Looking at her, she brings a smile to his face. He is so proud of what she has accomplished. In addition to running her small business, she keeps the house in order and she makes sure they all stay healthy and happy.

Wendi does weights with their children at the local 24 hour fitness. The kids mostly socialize and swim while she works out. She is conscious of what she eats and does her best to make sure it's the nutritious stuff *for all of them.* So much so, that James and the kids sneak in the occasional hamburger when she isn't in their company. James *just noticed* she had recently dyed her hair with multiple highlights. Looks like her shoulder length hair was just cut in a current style. *Well,* James felt, *the haircut complemented her natural shape and beauty.*

Probably like every middle class family in the United States, the dining room table is prime real estate. It not only serves as the central meeting place for meals (excluding the breakfast nook table), but it's the place where homework is checked, school projects are built, bills are paid, guns are cleaned and work is accomplished.

Wendi has laid down a thick work tarp that's stored in the nearby coat closet across the dinning table. She is currently using the table as her decorating center. She has her laptop, mobile high-res scanner, printer, various swatches of cloth, color chits, magazines and a variety of other items gathered on the table. Watching her, James has the notion that she must be putting together a proposal for a new client. Wendi would visit a customer's house, evaluate their clothing styles, closet space and color choices. Then, her small business service, would perform a complete clothing and closet overhaul. Complete with new wardrobe, closet, shelves, paint and lighting. She loved her work very much and really loved making the extra money to supplement her husband's income.

As James comes into the dining room, Wendi has concern written all over her face. Her husband is supposed to be sound asleep until o' dark thirty tomorrow. "Is everything ok? Did the kids wake you up? What's wrong?"

Her questions come in a machine gun like fashion, everything all interconnected. James reflects as he answers. "It's nothing, beautiful. Kids are ok, just got called into work." He reasons that just about hit all of his wife's points. He holds her head gently in his hands, gives her a good kiss and then another on her forehead for good measure. He continues past her, finishing buckling his belt as he makes his way into the kitchen.

Wendi watches him pass by with concern in her heart. She felt that his answer was quite short, almost rude, but decides to just let it go. She loves him dearly and is thankful for his work efforts. Wendi knows that her mate is pushing his limits, but they need the income. She consoles herself with chalking up his demeanor to being half asleep and overworked. She tries not to take his attitude personally. Setting it aside without another thought, Wendi goes back to her business.

Back to a hope that someday her husband will not have to work so hard.

James makes himself a couple of peanut butter and jelly sandwiches, fills a large Thermos with milk, grabs an apple and a mini-bag of Fritos. *Got to prepared because there is no telling how long the call is going to take or when I'm going to be hungry. With my circadian rhythm messed up...tonight making it worse.* He tosses all of his food, and a few bottles of water in a lunch box. Sitting himself down on his handmade bench, the place where the whole family takes off their shoes, he puts on his work boots. The bench was purpose built by him to fit in an alcove that leads into the garage.

James places his Israeli Arms pistol, which he has a concealed license for, in it's paddle holster. He makes the habit of always carrying it; so many hours alone, so many miles with no one around. Sitting still for a moment, he holds onto the smells and sounds of his house. Not looking forward to leaving. Pushing himself up he heads out through the garage. Stepping out he yells, "Goodbye, love ya…" and closes the door without waiting for a response. Life is wearing him thin and this schedule isn't helping.

James fires up his big van and is thankful he had time earlier in the day to clean and organize it. *God knows when I will have the chance to do that again.* He considers the organized work van as he also mulls over his two route choices to get to the Olympic Peninsula. Coming from Black Diamond, in the foothills of the Cascades, he can drive down and around through Tacoma and over the bridge to the Peninsula or drive into Seattle and take the ferry.

"Ferry…" he says to himself. Sleep is still gnawing at his mind like some greedy addiction and tonight driving all of the way around didn't seem like a good idea. He considers the chance he might catch a couple of minutes of sleep waiting in line at the terminal and definitely will catch an hour nap once on the ferry. He leaves his home in Black Diamond, drives the fifteen minutes to Highway 18 and then east twenty minutes to Interstate 5. He gets on I-5 with another thirty minutes to the ferry terminal.

James checks the ferry schedule on his mobile smartphone and sees that the ferry leaves at 21:05. He is pushing it in order to catch that ferry, but he can probably make it. Within a few minutes behind the wheel, the man is almost comatose. He's so tired. He tries to stay alert by shaking his head, stretching his back and legs, then realizes the radio is off.

"What was it," he asks himself out loud, "does it take half an hour to realize the radio's off?" James flicks it on to catch the latest talk radio news and traffic. He needed something to engage his mind before he turned into a driving zombie. Or maybe he already was and it was too late?

He half listens to the radio and the broadcaster talk about the ever shrinking middle class. James settles again into a comfortable silence with the evening talk radio as his trusted companion. He navigates his van in behind a semi-truck with trailer, the logo of 'Knight Transportation' emblazoned on the back. The electrician allows his vehicle to drift into a significant gap until there is a large following distance and sets the cruise control. James figures nobody will jump in front of him if he's following a slow semi, and that would allow a little space for phone work.

He pulls out his work Blackberry from the car charger and glances at the display. For the next few miles, James glances back and forth from the call data on his blackberry to the semi-truck ahead. Yes, he was reading his phone and driving at the same time; nanny state beware.

"... and the traffic around Seattle tonight has been brutal," the traffic reporter let's his audience know. "The football game ending now in downtown. I5 south and northbound from the stadiums is just starting to get heavy. Plus, there's a concert at Key Arena ending in a few minutes. We are starting to see some early traffic from that." There was a pregnant pause for effect, "Warning drivers, avoid downtown if you can!"

"Crap! Suck! Piss!" He cusses to himself, a little more awake now. More of a formed complaint fires through his synapses "Jeeze, its going to be a madhouse down there at the terminal."

"Oh well," James says, talking to the windshield, "I am already too close to Seattle to turn around and head to Tacoma."

His attention back to his smartphone, something doesn't make sense about the information he's reading. He re-reads over the call description listed on the phone and grimaces. James grinds his teeth, exhales forcefully, and tosses the phone on the dashboard. His boss had suckered him! The call wasn't for the Navy! No, instead it's for a contractor that built equipment for the Navy. James' company had spent two weeks of twelve hour days upgrading that site.

James's electrical company is constantly hamstrung by the IT manager of the defense contractor, because the man would never leave things alone. The information manager was only into his thirties, but his weight, anxiety and constant need for micromanagement was going to lead him to an early grave. The IT manager was constantly tweaking with settings, panels, wire runs and the like. "...carefully managing his companies' assets," the heavy-set man would say. James drives the remaining minutes thinking about where he is headed and what the IT manager could have possibly messed with.

"Pish and twaddle," James remarks, as he pulls into the busy ferry terminal. *The IT manager is going to kill himself from stress or one of his vendors might just kill him from the stress he gives them.* James waits in line to pass through the ticket booth with work singularly on his mind. Since finishing the defense contractor job three months ago, James or one of his co-workers was at that company site about once a week for "warranty work" related to the install. A quote from Han Solo comes to mind as James pulls up to the ticket kiosk, *I have a bad feeling about this.*

"Where are you heading?" The attendant asks without even looking at him.

"Bremerton, please. Round trip. Is there any room left on the 21:05?"

The look of confusion that James gets back is telling. "Twenty-one-oh five?" The teller asks.

"The nine-oh five ferry." James shakes his head at the attendant's confusion.

"Oh got it. Yeah," the attendant laughs nervously at her mistake. "We have just a few spots left. The next ferry will fill fast too, busy night." She hands James his ticket, "Thank you very much, here's your receipt. Lane fourteen." The attendant drones her well practiced ending to the transaction.

After paying the ferry toll, James stows the receipt in the ash tray, drives into the correct lane and parks his E-150 van. *Only ten minutes until the ferry arrives, definitely not enough time for a nap.* James confirms. *Not unless I want to wake up to a symphony of horns from all of the drivers behind me.* James speaks from the knowledge of witnessing the scene himself. The owner of an unmoving car was either asleep or off getting a "quick" bite to eat that causes multiple horns to ring out upon that unmoving car. The driver of the car will face dirty looks from other drivers and the sheer derision from the ferry crews. Sometimes, as punishment, the ferry crew will hold the driver for the *next* ferry.

Oh no, not me, James promises himself.

Smelling all of the aromas from the restaurants on the waterfront, James starts to feel hungry. He won't have time to hit any of those places, but there is a McDonalds right here at the terminal. *I could just grab something out of my lunch box?* He tries to convince himself, *you did pack the food for this very reason.* But his taste buds tempted him with the thought of an ice cream cone.

"Yep!" James says pounding his steering wheel. And in that spur of the moment, James takes off. He weaves around through the cars, watching a Seattle police officer perform exterior vehicle inspections. James steers clear of him and his partner, a bomb sniffing dog. *Don't want to be too close, especially with a .45 on my hip,* James tells himself as he picks up his pace. He's able to make it to the fast food restaurant and back in good time; the arriving ferry just letting off its load of cars from the peninsula.

James is halfway through the cream, the sweetness and cold of the delicious cone. He talks to himself between bites, "the perfect end to a warm August day and a tasty way to start my own." *It's my reward for only getting a few hours of sleep before coming back to work.* He takes a bite of the ice cream and deems, *the cone helps to calm frustrations of getting a repair order for this evening!*

As James works on the ice cream he watches people in and around their cars. There is a family next to James. A wife is sitting in the front seat reading a Michael Crichton novel and the father is standing next to the car holding his son on his shoulders. The father is pointing at the sights as his son asks questions. James then looks over to a blond lady in the lane to his right sitting in the back seat of a Lincoln Town car. The driver of the car is busily talking, while the woman is chatting on her mobile phone and touching up her make-up.

James finishes the cone, starts up the motor to the van and waits for the ferry worker to motion him forward. It takes only two minutes of sitting at the head of line fourteen, engine running, before James gets the nod and he drives the van onto the ferry. He's directed by a young loadmaster, toothpick in mouth, into the center "garage section" of the main auto deck. James drives into the ferry's main parking area, over onto the far right side.

James parks, cuts the motor, shuts off the lights, and cracks the windows. He sits there a moment enjoying the different smells than are so different from his house. Smells of the ocean and the large ferry. Oil, diesel fuel, rusting metal and car exhaust mingle with the aroma of the salt water.

Just out the window of his van a sign on the ship's bulkhead implores you to "Stop your motor, set hand brake, do not release brakes until ferry docks. Do not start motor until directed by crew."

James smiles at the demands and finds the sign quite unnecessary. It was so funny because the sign was just common sense. He leans his head back on the headrest as the movement of the waves, the ocean and the mechanical smells all soothe him even more than the ice cream.

Sighing out loud, James locks up the two front doors from the inside. He stoops through the divider door into the back of his E150 and locks the big slider door on the side of his work-van as well. The window in the back is tinted, so it makes the back of his van a nice dark place to catch a nap. Rather than reclining the drivers seat, he lays down the self-inflatable bed roll and sleeping bag he keeps for just such occasions. Both are normally used for his infrequent backpacking trips, but have found more use in his work van.

James would occasionally take naps in the back of his Econoline van. Sometimes it was nice to be able to catch an hour nap, than get anything to eat or push himself so hard that he falls asleep at the wheel. If he ever got tired on long road trips he would pull into a Wal-Mart, supermarket or the rare rest stop. Occasionally, he would even use the roll and bag on twenty-four hour installs. The self-inflating bed roll and bag provided a much needed break.

James lies down on top of the sleeping bag and roll and looks for some soothing music on his mobile phone. Finding Natalie Merchant, he clicks on the Ophelia album, jacks in his ear buds and sets his phone alarm. He pulls his heavy canvas jacket over his chest, gives in to the melatonin still in his system and is soothed asleep by Natalie's angelic voice.

Five minutes later his mind checks out of reality and back into deep sleep. Right where his mind wanted to be a little over an hour ago.

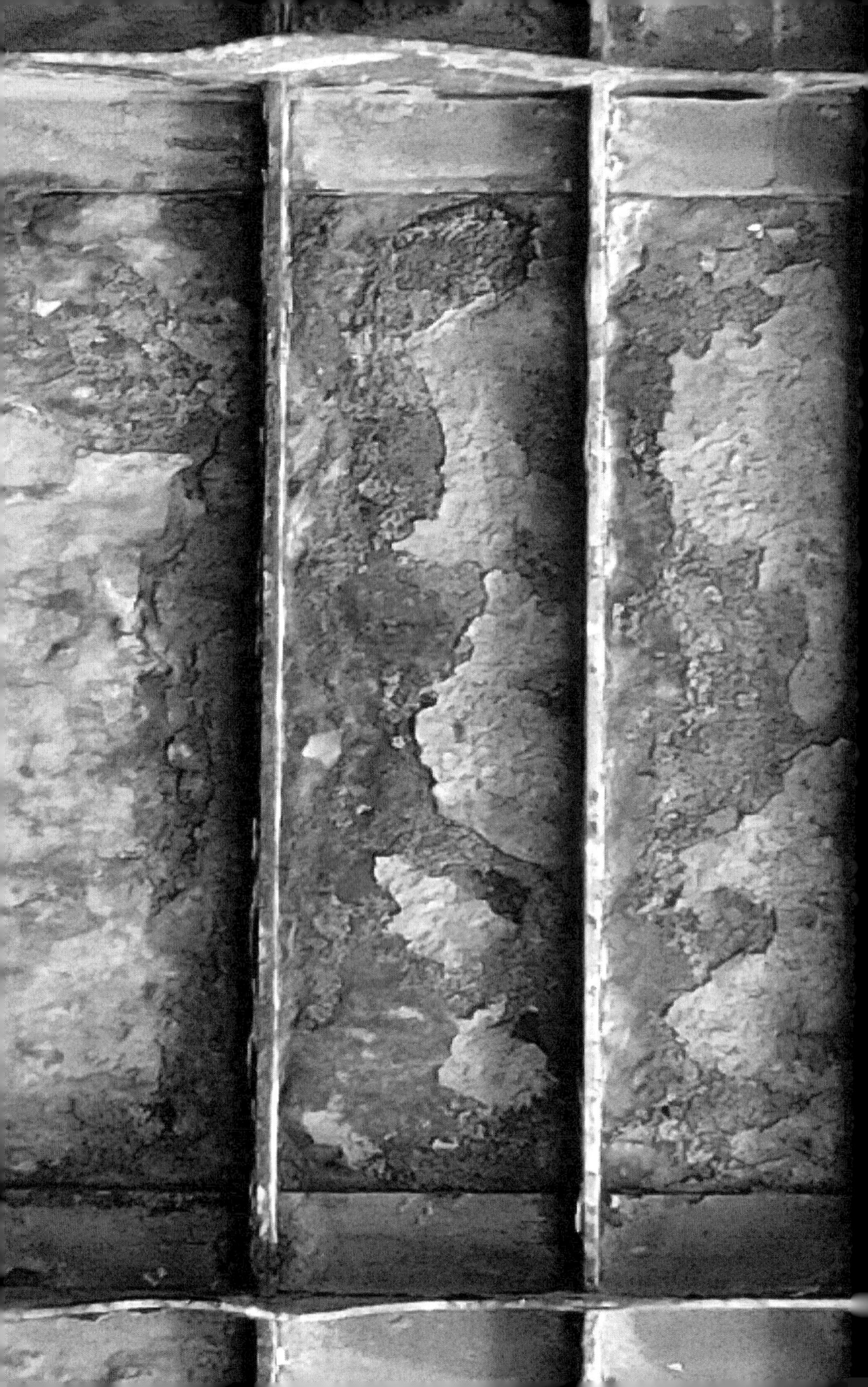

Chapter Nineteen

Thursday, August 30th 20:00

Dizhwar Abdur Razzaq is ecstatic and nervous. Today; his day, his plan, the idea given to him by Allah on some errand, is finally going to be carried out. There is no stopping it now. The remainder of his team are en route to their area of operations (A.O.). At the same time Dizhwar and his driver are leaving North Bend, a set of his men are arriving from the peninsula, while the other cell members are finishing their seafood in Seattle.

All that previous weekend in the woods, Dizhwar had practiced relentlessly with his 9mm pistol and his AR-10. His efforts were to practice some shooting skills, as much as work out the nervous jitters that the day was bringing him. He could still smell the aroma of burnt gunpowder and evergreen sap that permeated his light jacket. The aroma of the two scents made him grin as he rode in the car with his driver.

The acreage that Dizhwar had practiced at was used by his team regularly. It had been purchased a little over three years ago by one shell company, held within another shell company and held by still another. All of them were owned covertly by Ashan, his patron. The fifteen acre camp up in the mountains above North Bend was private, secluded and a place that afforded a tremendous opportunity to become something great for the group.

Not long after the property was officially theirs, the entire team went to work on a ten foot high fence and secure gate. The twelve emissaries from Ashan built the structures, shooting range berm and other improvements, making the entire place look like an outdoorsman's getaway. The road leading to the camp had regular traffic on it year around and his people always came up in cars by the twos or threes. After the mission, hopefully, the wooded refuge will still be here. And with any luck, Dizhwar will be able to come back to it. As the car travels, he thinks long and hard about everything that his team has accomplished.

His group of young operators, were intensely motivated, encouraged and highly trained. The gathering of this cell was the result of months of careful questions, and long processes of making sure that these recruits were, most of all, loyal. They were pulled in from all over the western United States and had been given a safe house to live in Redmond, WA. Through Dizhwar's careful indoctrination, hard training and major efforts in gaining their trust, he radicalized this group into militant Wahhabists and trained warriors.

If only they follow their training, Dizhwar reflects as he stares out the car window. He silently encourages his men, *remember training and trust each other...*

At the end of their eighteen months of education in Redmond, Washington and the rural property outside of North Bend, Washington, his group was ready to do what was needed of them. Dizhwar made sure, per his hard schooling overseas, these recruits know how to follow a plan, follow orders, shoot, defend each other and rush an enemy inside a building. Two of his recruits had previous explosives experience, another already knew electronics, and yet another had been piloting large fishing vessels in Maine before moving to the Northwest. All of these skills will be used to the utmost and Dizhwar is thankful for all the help he has received from Ashan, "the home office," and his teachers back at the Indonesian school.

"Is there anything that was overlooked?" Dizhwar asks his driver and fellow saboteur. "Did we miss anything obvious in planning? Could it really be this simple, this easy to carry out attacks on American soil, on it's citizens?" The questions kept rolling out of Dizhwar's mind.

The driver of their vehicle knows better than to answer directly when Dizhwar is clearly in a questioning mood and just lets his team leader speak aloud. His driver keeps his attention focused forward, carefully obeying all of the traffic rules.

"Yes, it is. Like lambs to the slaughter! We are Allah's Holy Knights..." Dizhwar speaks out once more to no one and then falls silent, again within his thoughts.

Mostly everything had been provided by the C.O. and Ashan's contacts. If there was something Dizhwar simply couldn't get his hands on, he would log on to an online game web site, look for a specific character within the game and post the questions to that virtual character. That which was needed would arrive in a cardboard box within a few days. If the items didn't arrive, an envelope of American cash would arrive with a USB stick. On the stick would be a name and number to contact to purchase the needed item or items.

Dizhwar had met his fair share of black marketers, drug dealers, thieves and had paid out wads of cash for the things that were needed. In this way, Dizhwar purchased otherwise legal semi-auto guns without paperwork, raw ingredients for explosives without questions, and the occasional chemical or compound without the usual government oversight. Dizhwar's superiors assured him that America was the land of plenty. As long as you had money, you had plenty.

Just the day before, "Thank Allah, and may he be greatly magnified by our actions." Was how Dizhwar had ended his blessing to the gathered group. The enigmatic leader blessed them, Wednesday morning, before they split apart for the mission. The rest of the team wouldn't be in route till now, this Thursday evening, but he'd wanted to offer his blessings to them as a whole before reuniting with them again.

All of them had spread out to carry on their tasks, and although everyone will arrive at the Seattle ferry terminal at different times, they will all board the same 21:05 ferry to Bremerton. Once onboard and parked, the twelve will each separate into the ship, heading to assigned locations. All of the group, including Driver and Dizhwar will have just a little time to loiter, and to catch the evening sunset over the Puget Sound. *Maybe even say a silent dua to Allah for safety?* Dizhwar wondered.

Today, they will strike a blow against the world's enemy and get away with it. The U.S. had been all over the world in the guise of peace and left too many men, women, and children bloody and dead. The greed must stop! The Greatest Whore the world has seen will taste the same pain she has inflicted all over the world. The Higher Muslim Order shall reign supreme. The American military was especially at fault. The Americans worked hand in hand with the Jews in Israel to usurp true and righteous organizations. Groups that strived for an independent Muslim state. Their way, the caliphate's way, was true. The American Defense Department, the American military and the American government will pay a price for its support of Israel.

Thus, Dizhwar's team chose the greatest nearby target. They will strike a blow at Puget Sound Naval Shipyard, an old symbol of power and naval strength since World War II. Dizhwar weighed up, *...and as we strike at the base, it will also be one against the United States. The start of something bigger, we don't know exactly but more conflict is coming.* Dizhwar confirmed, *The Way is clear. A quick punch in the face before the body blows come. Blows that will have a lasting and powerful effect. Only one way was true; May Allah be praised and may His Prophet be glorified.*

Dizhwar has followed the plan meticulously. Now it was his turn to take part. On their drive to the ferry, he calls in the bomb threat to the cruise liner. A simple affair and he felt quite calm doing so. 20:30 is what the phone reads as he yanks out the phone's battery. Dizhwar tosses the pay-as-you-go phone and its battery out the window. Dizhwar watches both smash into pieces on Interstate 90.

A few minutes later they get off of I-90 and head into downtown Seattle, making their way to the waterfront. The driver of Dizhwar's automobile pulls up to the entrance gate of the ferry terminal, engages the attendant in some small talk, pays the fee and heads into the correct staging lane.

They are the second vehicle to pull into lane fourteen as they were directed by the gate attendant. Dizhwar's driver parks right behind a big white contractor's van with an eagle holding electrical sparks emblazoned on the side. Dizhwar asks his driver "You've got your lines down good enough to start working at the ferry gate. Have you been practicing?"

Smirking, Driver, a.k.a Nasir al Din, responds. "I have been practicing. I am very nervous and I didn't want to mess it up and raise any suspicions."

Dizhwar, happy with his compatriot's answer, doesn't respond, just smiles to Driver as the man kills the engine. They both sit in silence, absently people watching. In little less than a minute, the pair watch the owner of a big van in front of them, get out and head for McDonalds. He weaves around a police officer with a dog and then strides quickly into the restaurant.

"Do you think he is a regular partaker of that fast food poison?" Driver asks Dizhwar. Driver is a devout reader of Holy Books. He's probably the most educated on the Islamic and Christian faiths out of the twelve. The man also prefers to be called Driver by the entire team, rather than his taken name of Nasir. He felt it gives him a distinct connection to Dizhwar and stops the number two phrases with him being second in command of the team.

Driver believes in all of Islam's tenets and tries his best to follow them like they were divine laws. Due to the fact that his mother died of cancer, Driver held to the strict habits of good fitness and diet. *She will always be my inspiration,* he promised. Driver ate really healthy. Mostly vegetarian, with the occasional Ḥalāl allowed meat. Essentially, only Ḥalāl foods were permitted and then only in moderation of portions.

"I don't think so," Dizhwar finally comments. "Maybe he just had to go take a leak."

Five minutes later, they watch the owner of the van, a hard worker by the worn looks of his clothes, and boots, come back with an ice cream cone. Driver smirks at Dizhwar's incorrect guess and they both sit there again in silence, waiting patiently for the ferry to begin boarding. They get passed over by the dog, but they have nothing to fear. They have nothing attached to the exterior of the car

The pair follow the electrician's van onto the ferry, but since their vehicle is a car and not an oversized van, they are motioned by a youthful loadmaster with the name Jacobs stenciled onto his bright orange safety vest. Chewing on a toothpick, Jacobs points their late model Japanese car to take an upper berth along the ferry's port side auto deck. The berths, along both sides of the ferry, have upper and lower levels for all of the regular size cars.

Driver parks and kills the engine.

The two men walk upstairs to look around the ferry. They'd been on the Wenatchee at least ten times in the past few months, memorizing every turn, doorway and feature. All of their people had been on the ferry at least twice in the past week making sure that they were familiar with it. A few months ago, Jibril and Parvez had even paced off all of the distances on the ship on one of their own rides and had constructed a 1/50th mock up for all of them to become familiar with.

Biding their time, Dizhwar gets a coffee and a muffin while Driver gets an orange juice and a banana. "Why don't you get something else? Like a soda pop or coffee or even a tea?" Dizhwar asks his friend.

"Why break our tenets, our propriety, when it is not required?" Driver asks back as they head to the cashier to pay.

"Religious tenets? Driver! I'm just saying you can live a little. No one on this ship cares and after a while probably will have other, more pressing considerations."

Driver gives his leader a look and then pays for their food. They loiter about their AO, waiting among the picture takers and the tourists for just the right moment to carry out Allah's inspired plan.

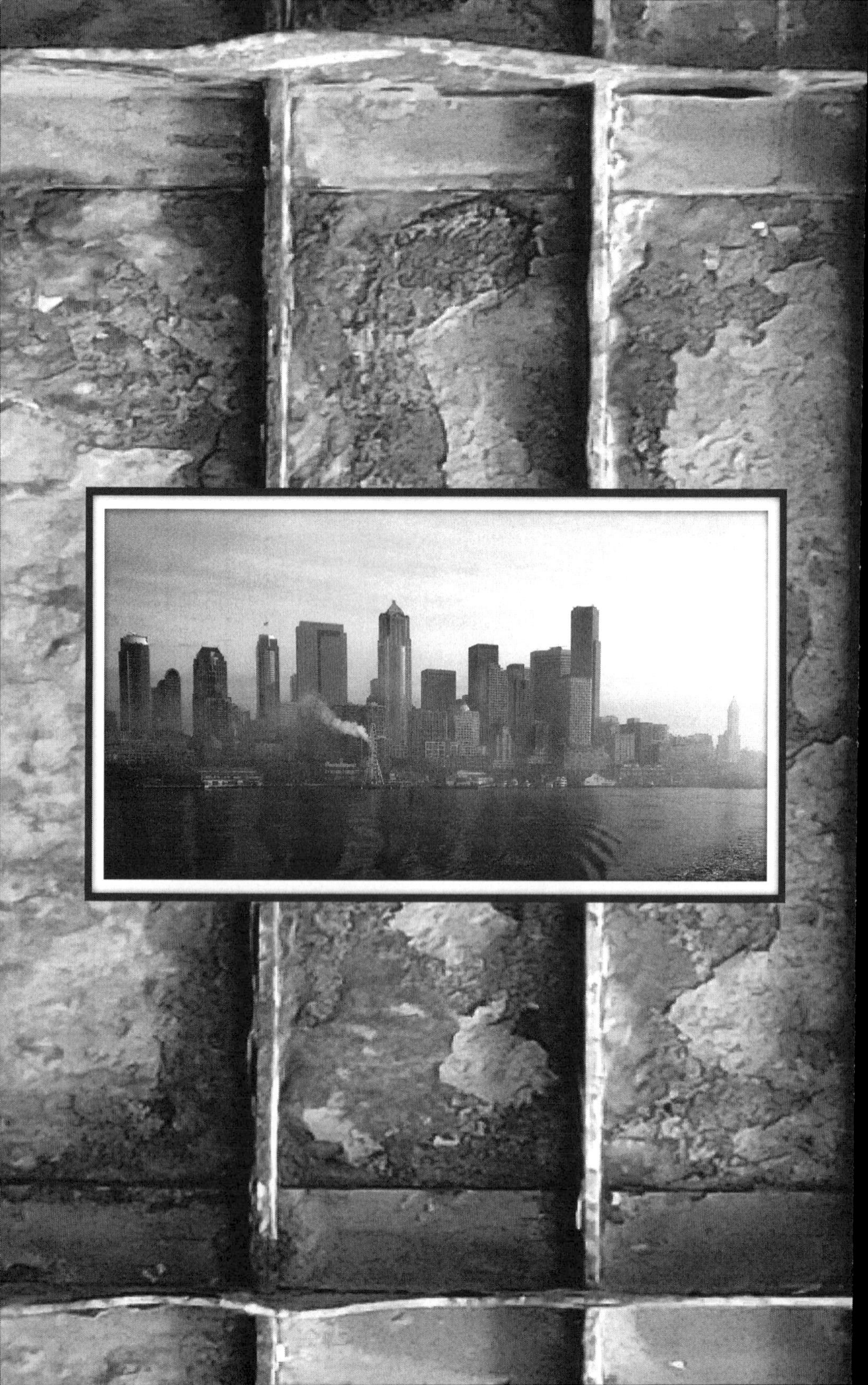

Chapter Twenty

Thursday, August 30th 20:50

You could say that Latisha Reynolds boards the M/V *Wenatchee* with more of a weary looking shuffle than a full speed walk.

Latisha is one of the numerous passengers that walk onto the *Wenatchee* rather than drive their personal vehicles on. It is significantly cheaper to park your personal car at the park-and-ride and walk onto the ferry from the peninsula. Even if you have to get a bus ride to your final destination, twenty dollars a day for a round trip ferry ride turns into a hundred dollars fast. That is why Latisha is walking and that is also why she missed the previous ferry by only a few minutes. *All because of a metro bus and a red light,* she bemoans the waiting it cost her.

Another hour. One red light! Latisha curses to herself, as she sets foot on the metal pedestrian arch that swings in to connect the land based terminal to the ship.

Latisha is clearly taking her time up the gangway. Other passengers flow around the slower moving woman, grumbling under their breath. She is bone tired. Her feet are killing her. She did everything one can do to look for a job today and she is returning home empty handed.

Now, Latisha clearly doesn't give a rip about *anything.*

Latisha isn't concerned about the fact that she's holding up the foot traffic around her. The bone tired woman doesn't care about the sun, about the views or the aromas from the restaurants. *Nothing has appeal,* the forty-eight year old woman talks to herself again, *just eager to get home, take off my shoes and have this day end. Eat some chocolate and drink some tea...*

Latisha had hustled today. She had flat out worked her feet to blisters with countless stops at various companies downtown. It seemed it was an endless procession of up the elevator and wait. Walk down the street and wait. Dropping off resumes, filling out applications and waiting. Latisha had two interviews scheduled for today, in addition to the visits for resume submittal. Yet, nothing seemed to work out as planned. Lately life was feeding her lemons and she didn't have the energy or time to make lemonade. "What a stupid saying," she says to the back of a gen X'er with headphones the size of cinnamon rolls on his ears. He couldn't hear anything anyway with his hip-hop so loud Latisha can make out the musician and the song clearly *from five feet away.*

Things had turned sour right at the beginning of her job search.

I should of just turned around and called it a day then, she ran the thought past her mind. Her day turned bad right at the first interview. On entering the offices of the first company, she got a smile from the dolled up receptionist and was told that the interviews would be given on a separate floor; off Latisha went even higher into the Columbia Tower.

Inside the second set of offices, she got the polite smile from another too beautiful and too young receptionist. You know that kind of smile. The "I'm smiling to hide my thought that you shouldn't be here" kind of grin. After Latisha gave the perfect face, perfect hair, perfect teeth receptionist her name, the receptionist gave her another sugar smile.

"I'm, sorry," another grin "the position has already been filled. Sorry, have a nice day."

"Ugh!" Latisha exclaimed and felt like giving the blond girl behind the desk an earful. But, she didn't. What was the point? Dejected, Latisha left before she reconsidered saying or doing something to the first employee she ran across. That one incident would sum up the rest of her day.

Concerned that she wouldn't make it to her next interview, Latisha took a quick look at her phone to confirm the time. She noticed there was a voice mail. Checking it, she received a cancellation for her next interview. She was desperate to find something soon before her and her husband, Malcolm, were upside down on not only the house, but everything else as well.

It seemed that bad luck followed her and her family wherever they went. First, they left the crime ridden city of Chicago in 2000 for Mississippi.

Leaving "The Windy City" was bittersweet. She and her husband both attended college at the University of Chicago and had met there as well. She and Malcolm had started a family late, but too quickly were parents of four kids. She gave birth to all of their children in Chicago and had just about raised all of them in a house that had become their home.
The entire family was sad to go, but there had to be a better place for their family. Schools weren't great, crime was bad, shootings happened daily and the value of their house wasn't even half of what it used to be. The year they left, there were 633 murders in that city. Both of them were tired of fighting against everything at once.

What the heck, was the universal family opinion, *it couldn't get any worse. Let's try the Gulf South for a change? It would be nice to live someplace warmer.* Just when life seemed to stabilize in the Gulf Coast of Mississippi, there was this thing called a hurricane.

Katrina. On Monday august 29th 2005, that pretty much said it all.

The Reynolds family lost nearly everything in the storm. Whatever wasn't in their safe, that had been securely bolted to the concrete foundation, was gone. It was odd to come back to a house that they had just started feeling was their home only to find a single solitary safe.

The horrible fact settled in; house, belongings, and keepsakes were either water damaged by the tidal surge, lost to the winds or smashed to little pieces. They bittersweetly picked up the bits that were still left and the safe, then moved the heck out of there.

Thank you very much, Mississippi. But your surprise on the five year anniversary of moving into their home was too much to bear. Someplace with no tornadoes, hurricanes, blizzards, heat waves, or earthquakes was now on the list. The selection of states that fit that criteria were very few. But the idea of the northwest held a romantic notion within Malcolm's heart, their decision was made.

Washington soon became a blessing, there was no doubt. It had opened it's arms and welcomed them without question. The people were nice, the real estate prices weren't bad and jobs seemed plentiful. If you could hold on past the grey weather, you were rewarded with spectacular scenery and a great environment for the outdoors. Malcolm continued his career in law enforcement and she resumed her full-time mother duties. Well, with the occasional culinary job just to break up her homemaker monotony.

Four years before retirement, her husband was off duty and hunting with a coworker. The two men were traveling on a wet and foggy mountain road high up in the Cascades. The forest service road lead them to their secret hunting spot.

In a twist of who's after whom; a twelve hundred pound bull elk decided, since it was hunting season, it would like to take out a hunter or two. The wreck was horrific. Upon arrival, emergency responders couldn't even tell what had been hit or who was in the car. The incident had been called in by a nearby homeowner when the man had heard a collision.

Both men were severely injured by the impact. The elk was running across their path from passenger side to driver side at its full speed of almost thirty five miles and hour. The speed of the truck was fifteen miles and hour on the dirt road, so the final impact speed was close to fifty. When the truck hit the elk it was a slight angle to broadside and the impact caused the truck to serve off the road into an embankment.

Malcolm's coworker, was driving and his skull was crushed by the impact of the elks fourteen inch long, eight inch wide, shoulder blade. Malcolm's coworker didn't survive the trip to the hospital. Malcolm was permanently disabled. His numerous broken bones and moderate brain injury was from taking the mass of the elk's body as it rolled up the hood and into the windshield. The four year old bull elk was killed; but it did get *two* hunters.

From there the Reynolds downward financial spiral began. The kids were left with the obligation to put themselves through college. All of their parent's payments for college stopped, literally in it's tracks. Accounts were depleted and budgets were cut. But insurance that didn't cover everything and the bills that were left was the worries of the day. Soon, there ensued a constant shell game with bills. Latisha was now taking care of everything– the care of her husband, house maintenance, automobiles, and finances, was all on her shoulders.

I had so many hopes pinned to today and now, all of the pins have been yanked out. She dwells on this thought while she walks up a set of stairs to the main passenger area of the ferry. She passes by the man with the headphones, who is already in a window booth. Latisha searches for a place that she can have some personal space.

As Mrs. Latisha Reynolds makes her way to the front, she starts carefully weaving in and out of people; rushing to find a good chair to sit in. Latisha squeezes past a blonde woman that is dressed nice, but smells like cigarettes. The smoky woman is standing in line of the small café that is on-board the ship. The smoky woman is in line behind two middle-eastern men; one with coffee and the other with orange juice. *Not me,* Latisha tells herself. *The budget is already tight and I'm not going to pay some overpriced amount for bad food...*

"It was all Chicago's fault," she whispers, smiling at something her husband used to say in his ironic sense of humor. The woman makes her way to the front row of seats with a great view of the far away peninsula. Latisha sits down heavily, picking a seat as far away from anyone as she can.

"Welcome to Washington's State Ferry system," the voice from the overhead P.A. system says soothingly. Narrated by some local news personality, it continues on with it's *about to leave* announcement.

"Please remember, once the loading has begun, the Captain's permission is required to disembark the vessel. Please if I may have a bit of your time, for a moment. I want to direct your attention to the emergency zodiacs, life rafts, and the life preservers..."

As the man droned on about the escape plan, emergency equipment and more, Latisha tried to zone it out. The locally famous newscaster talked more about security and maintaining control of your bags. Latisha slouches down into the vinyl seat and makes herself comfortable. Her focus is back out over the bow of the ship all of the way across The Sound.

There, like a distant emerald green island, was the peninsula. At the park and ride, out there on the peninsula, was her car and her way home. She had only a fifteen minute drive from the terminal park and ride to her home. Her kids would all be gone and her husband would have a caretaker there until she arrived. *One red light late!*

Latisha fires off a text to her husband's caretaker. She lets the caretaker know that she will be a little late and then sets her phone into her lap. Latisha considers her life, *always things to do! Out in town or round the house and the list never seems to get any smaller.* She tries to push that thought out of her mind for now and concentrates on just getting home.

She encourages herself, *once I'm home I will prioritize the tasks as best as I can. After all I am just one woman and it is a big house.*

How am I going to break this news to Malcolm? Latisha mindlessly twirls her finger in her hair, absently going through her tiger-print cell phone as it sits on her lap. No one has called, no one has emailed, no one has texted. She tosses it back into her purse that sits between her feet.

What did I have the stupid thing for in the first place? I am so connected to the world and no one is talking to me. She pulls at the lock of her hair just over her right ear. *No use complaining, I probably won't be able to afford the stupid phone soon anyway.*

Latisha lets out an audible sigh as she relaxes in the chair. Without a care, or looks that others shoot her, Latisha takes off her shoes. Yet, because of the looks from others, she places her shoes between her feet and sets her purse on top of them.

Latisha escapes in that moment, the feeling of her sore feet being free, and she closes her eyes for some peace. *I wish I had a set of those cinnamon roll headphones...I'm sure they would do wonders at drowning out all of this noise.*

At least I can get an almost hour break, Latisha consoles herself, then her head rests against the back of the chair and she nods off.

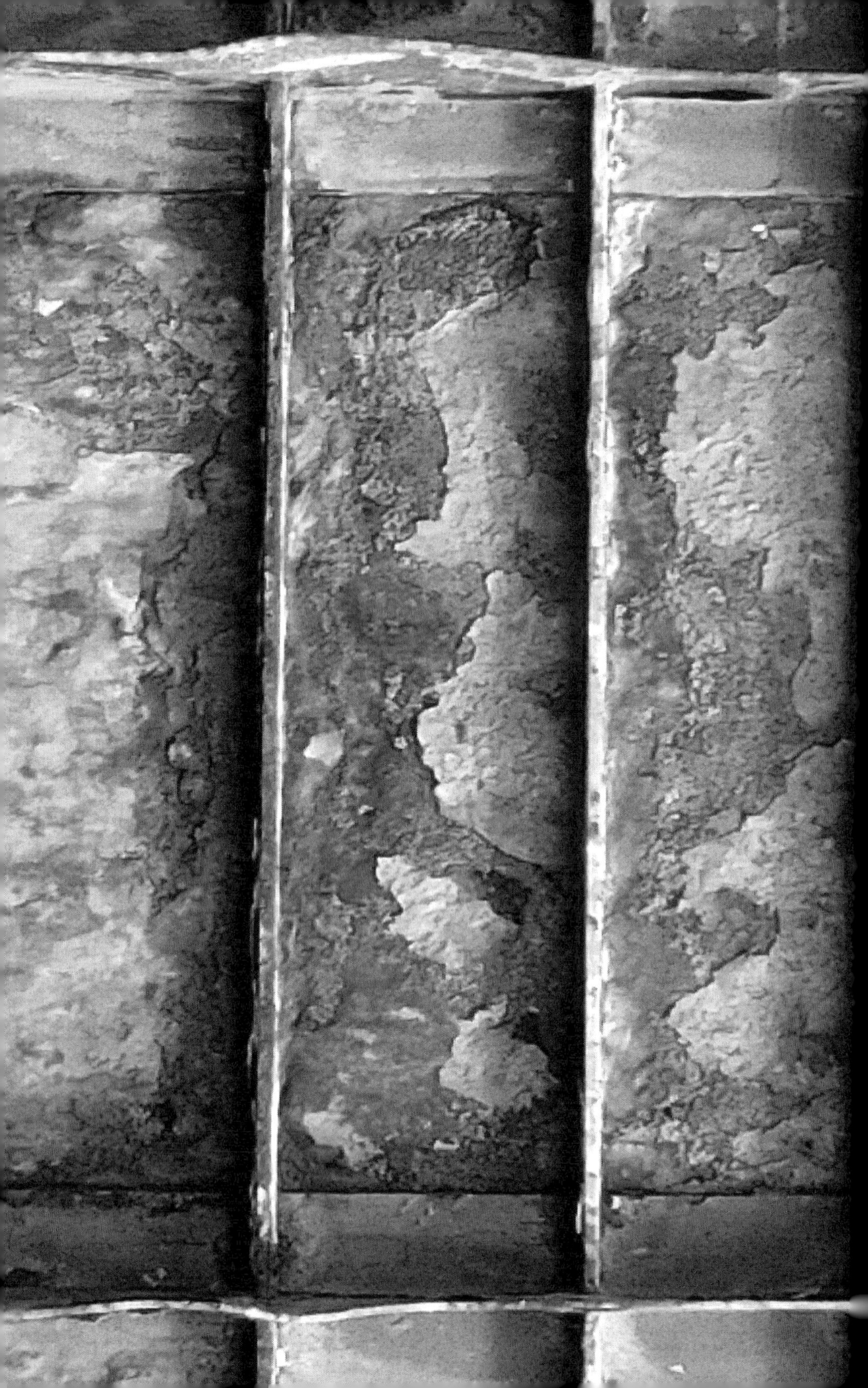

Chapter Twenty One

Thursday, August 30th 20:50

"So, as I was saying, it was just too much for me everyday. Going to the same place driving the same road and dealing with the wolves and weasels of the world... So I got out of it, bought this *slightly stretched* Lincoln and started driving around people such as yourself." Brad looked up in his rearview mirror to see if his client had dosed off or was paying attention.

Terra gave one of her knock 'em dead grins, "Sorry, had to make a phone call, but I was still listening," she lied.

"Well," Brad said, continuing his story. "I have been doing the executive transport now for six months and it's going along nicely. I'm really glad to get out of the courts and kind of take life by the horns. You know, live by my own means and motivations."

"What a pile of.." Terra punctuates the end of her sentence with punching the end button on her phone and throwing it against the overstuffed chair next to her. *Well at least I know that the bridge is burned,* Terra told herself. *The stupid little know-it-all garbage hauler granddaughter wouldn't even return my phone calls!*

Brad sees the episode and realizes he had been talking to no one for the past bit. He turned around and silently fumed, *how much of my life story have I divulged and she wasn't really paying attention?*

Terra Freeland hadn't really been listening to her driver. She was just placating him. *He talked more than my last driver,* so as soon as he started with his recent exhortation she dialed Ms. DeMets phone number.

Terra wanted to squeeze in one last attempt to call little Ms. Mackenzie DeMets before subjecting herself to a ferry ride, drivers that wouldn't shut up and staying at some dumpy three star hotel on the peninsula. *And now that chance is gone...*

"So are we a go? The lane next to us is going." Terra's new driver, nervously chatted on. "I need to know if we are going to bow out before our lane starts moving."

"No it's fine," Terra breathes out her words as she is shaking her head and rubbing her neck.

"What!" The driver exclaims a bit to loud and looks back over his shoulder to gaze into the face of his passenger. Their lane starts moving.

"Just go!" Terra motions with her arm, in a gesture of *turn around and stop looking at me, as much as get on the ferry.*

Their car is directed onto the ship by a young man with a toothpick in his mouth. Brad follows the man with "Jacobs" stenciled on the Chicago-Bear-orange vest. Obeying the guidance, Brad heads to the left side of the ship. Terra and Brad are then directed by another with a similar west that points them up the upper berth ramp. Brad drives slowly, watching for the possibility of a foolish passenger stepping out into the narrow driveway. He has a vision of smacking a passenger with his right sideview mirror.

Terra watches her new driver, Brad, *who is bigger than a house*, skillfully navigate the narrow distance. The Lincoln negotiates the gap between the wall of the ship and the other lane of recently parked vehicles.

Terra wonders, *how could Brad actually be in law enforcement when he was that fat?* Another ferry worker stands just behind the car in front of them urging with her hand to come closer.

Terra does a double take. She is immediately curious, *this ferry worker looks a lot like the one that pointed for them to go up the second level car ramp. Brother and sister working on the same ship?*

The female ferry worker, adorned like the rest, packs in the cars as close as possible. She does this in order to allow as many cars to get on the ferry as it can possibly hold.

The moment the car is put in park Terra is out the door. Momentarily, she leans in and lets Brad know what she is doing. A small courtesy, "Look this trip is about forty-five minutes across. I'm not sitting in the car the entire time. Do what you want, but I'm going to grab a coffee and some Advil."

Brad just sits there in stunned silence. Although he is just her driver and not her friend the lack of respect still hurts. *First the woman lies to me about listening to what I was saying and now she ditches me the moment the car is in park?*

And with that Terra Freeland leaves another one of her drivers by himself. She is going to try and find something on the big boat to make her happy.

Terra wonders, *maybe this ship has a restaurant on board like the Needle...one that revolves or something?* This is only the second time she's ever been on a ferry. Terra doesn't know anything about the large car haulers which is why she looks around aimlessly for a minute trying to find the stairs up. She asks herself more mundane questions as she finds the stairs. Terra is really needing to go get her coffee.

Chapter Twenty Two

Thursday August 30th 21:05

Trevor Jacobs, loadmaster, gets the last vehicle loaded onto the packed ferry. It is a busy night with the football game, the Chili Peppers concert and the tourists. *And it will stay that way until late tonight,* Trevor foresees. *Lines are already forming to get onto the ferry for our next trip to the peninsula!*

Over his radio, Trevor orders the lot docent to stop anymore incoming cars. There is room for a few more vehicles onboard, but the young man is worried that they might have been maxed out on their carry weight. Trevor the Loadmaster has been roughly adding up the numbers in his head and knows he is close. Trevor doesn't want the boat to sink because it's overloaded, *which probably won't ever happen,* he assures himself. *From what I know of ships, they are normally designed to carry over and above their rated weight. But excess weight does not do good things to the ferry's big diesel engines or our passage time.*

It is Trevor's job to manage both the incoming vehicles on the pick-up and the outgoing vehicles during the drop-off. *I've got to do my best and forget about the four extra spots. The spots would only have a combined extra 10,000 pounds of estimated weight, which wouldn't have been so bad...if we didn't have three semi-trailers!* Trevor confirms with his knowledge and training and feels comfortable with his decision to cut off the last of the incoming cars.

The young man is a watchman of sorts. The job of the Loadmaster is to watch for size, weight and height of the vehicles as they roll up and onto *his* ship. Trevor is an efficient loadmaster. You might even say he has a talent or gift for it. The first thing that any driver of a vehicle will see, as they pull onboard, is Trevor with his stenciled name of 'Jacobs' on a bright orange reflective vest.

Chewing on a toothpick, Trevor makes last minute decisions where to place the vehicles onto one of the world's largest ferries. Trevor gestures with his hands and arms, directing the arriving vehicles all the while computing in his head. Other ferry employees take his cues and distribute the vehicles according to his direction. Trevor must not locate too much of the load on the port or the starboard side, nor too much of it fore or aft. He feels the responsibility intently and cares deeply for his *Wenatchee*, the crew and her passengers.

It is my ship, he feels, more so than any of the crew besides the Captain.

Trevor makes sure the last vehicle has the red colored chocks, a wedge to prevent forward or reward movement, under the rear tires. After checking, Trevor transmits an, "We are all clear," to the ship's pilot and walks over to the rear rope gate. He gives a quick nod to a coworker and in unison, the pair heft the heavy braided rope gate into place. They jointly clip the ends of the gate into eyelets that secure it to the stern of the boat.

Trevor throws a nonchalant wave to the lot docent, signaling to raise the dock ramp, while he and his co-worker check that the flexigate is locked into place.

This flexible gate is lowered during unloading and loading. The procession of cars drive over it as they arrive onto the ferry. The bottom of flexi-gate is permanently tied to the deck, but not the sides. Procedure dictated that it has to be raised and locked into place before departure. The gate isn't tall or rigid, so it won't stop someone with the motivation to jump. You couldn't lean on it, since it was made with cross linked rope in a checker pattern, but it is strong enough to stop a vehicle from going over the front or back of the boat.

I guess a car is worth more than a person? Trevor wonders that every time he raises the gate into place. Why someone would not come up with something better is beyond him.

The louvered steel dock ramp rises up into the air. Hydraulics whine and metal pings as it flexes, as the incredibly heavy bridge between the mainland and the ship rises higher and higher. The ship's engines come up from idle.

As Trevor walks away from the flexi-gate, he checks in once more with the pilot, "Confirming stern gate is in place, shoreline ramp is up and all is clear for passage."

The Captain, Michael Blair, radios back, "Thanks Trevor, good job."

Trevor can feel the massive diesel engines spool up faster and faster beneath his feet. Huge engines begin to spin propeller blades faster and faster on steel shafts. Trevor looks out over the stern and watches the white froth rise up out of the rear of the ship. The propeller blades send a fine white spray of saltwater out of the stern and toward the dock. The breeze shifts, and Trevor is momentarily awash in the mist and enjoys the moment like a child under a summer sprinkler. Then the moment is gone as the huge ferry pulls away from land.

Trevor and his coworker begin working their way forward; making sure the ship is ready for passage, staying aware of anything out of the ordinary. No loose wires, ropes or chains. All doors and hatches secure, nothing in the way to cause accidental injury to anyone.

Out of the eight crew on board, both of these men are to be the safety officers for the night. During this evening's trips back and forth from the peninsula, they have been tasked with roving the ferry. Because it is their rotation, they will have to cut out a lot of the visiting with passengers and instead focus on the safety of the ship. The two will still point out bathrooms, cafeteria, stairways and the elevator. They still politely answer the geographic and landmark questions too, but the pair of men will more or less have to act like stewards, tour guides and safety officers all in one.

As he ascends the stern stairs, Trevor just shakes his head, grinning. *What an awesome job.*

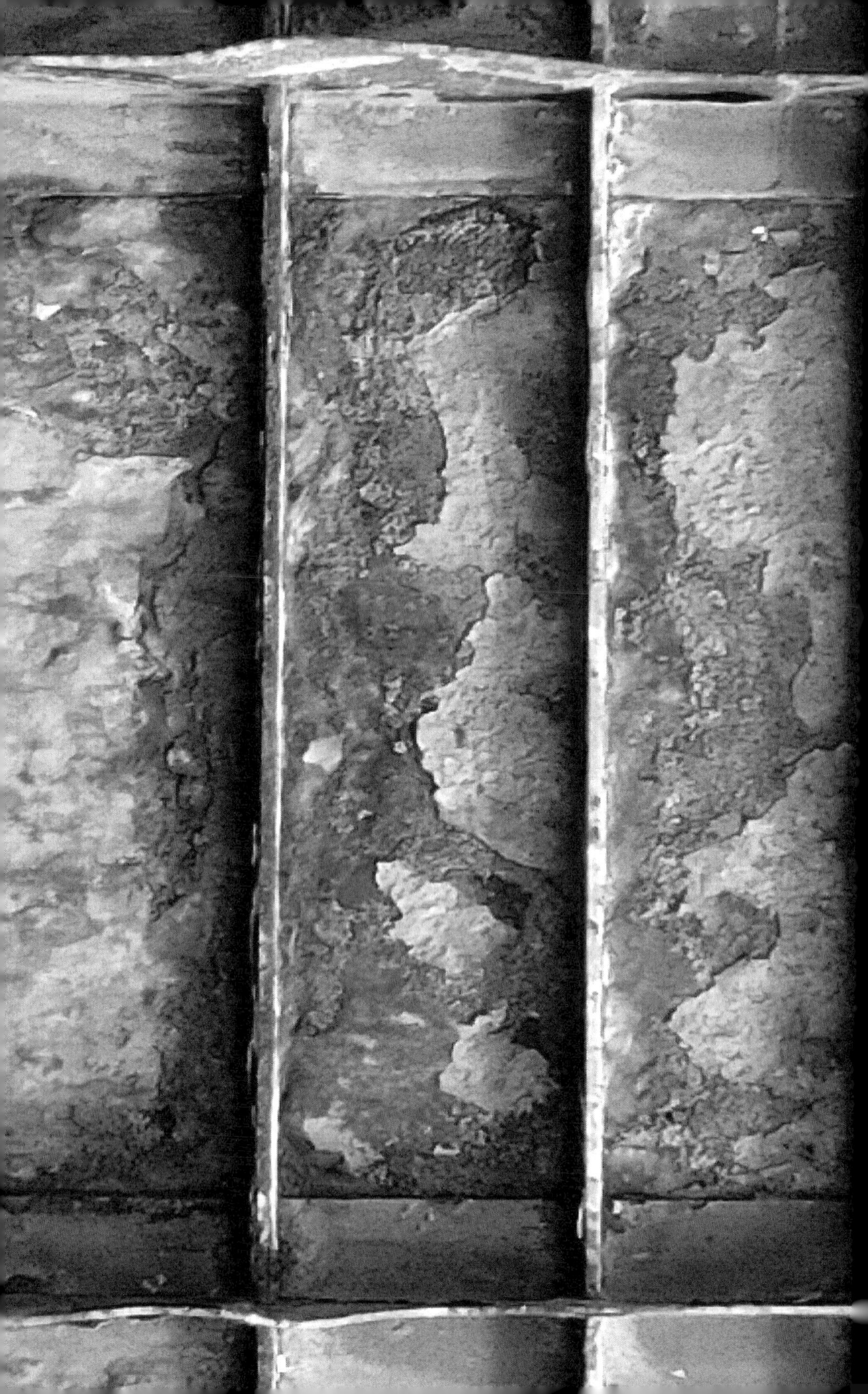

Chapter Twenty Three

Thursday August 30th 21:05

The motor vessel *Wenatchee* is one of the largest in the Puget Sound fleet of ferries. She, along with her two sister ships, the *Puyallup* and the *Tacoma*, are the second largest double-ended ferries in the world.

The entire fleet is named after cities in Washington State and the *Wenatchee* is no different. These Jumbo Mark II class ferries have sixteen thousand horsepower diesel engines and can carry over two hundred vehicles, all while pushing eighteen knots. The M/V *Wenatchee* was launched in 1998 at the cost of eighty million dollars to the taxpayers of Washington. The ferries travel back and forth, day and night over the flooded glacial valleys of the Salish Sea.

That entire Thursday, the M/V *Wenatchee* is pulling unusual duty on the Bremerton route, because her junior ship, the *Kitsap*, is down with steering and rudder work. The *Wenatchee* normally runs the Bainbridge Island route, but due to the mechanical failure of the *Kitsap* and the heavy traffic, she's needed to run a non-stop Bremerton and back route. Another ship, the *Kittitas* has been pulled out of its normal route to cover for the *Wenatchee*, while its Mukilteo to Clinton route has to suffer with just two small ships.

The distractions of the plane crash in the north and the boat fire in the south have drawn away the majority of the waterborne emergency responders. Those remaining to cover the Elliot Bay have surprises attached to their hulls. The operation to distract and overload the emergency system is working well.

The four ship charges are set to go off 10 minutes after the *Wenatchee*'s departure of 21:05. The charges at the Ballard Locks are set to go off once they are closed *anytime* after 21:00. A cruise liner, the pair of fireboats, harbor patrol and the locks will be crippled at the same time the conspirators have full control of the ferry. This will add the last stroke, en cauda venenum, to the first responder network.

"Make the enemy look where you are not," Sun Tzu writes in the Art of War. Ashan's plans hamper the capability of the emergency responders to respond effectively, so that the real attack will have a greater possibility of success. Helicopters run low on fuel and have to return to their airfield. Ships will be in the wrong place when they are desperately needed elsewhere. Fake attacks will have the greatest amount of noise with no one to rescue. All the while, the real attacks come in silently, with little response for the true victims. The smoke screens will be lit, thick and numerous, disguising the scope and nature of all of the attacks. The smoke screens will demand investigation in order to find out what's a real fire or just a facade. While the real attack will be quiet, a surprise and in the dark.

From the back of the ferry, Dizhwar and Driver gaze out over the water. Like a pair of tourists, they stand at the rear observation deck railing. The men had finished their refreshments and now watch the Seattle shoreline slip away. "Have you heard if the fisherman and pilot were successful?" Driver quietly asks his boss.

Dizhwar grins. Only himself, Driver and Ashan know about the airplane and fishing boat distractions. Those that contributed to the airplane and fishing boat attacks were separated from the main cell. In case of capture, Dizhwar didn't need the authorities tracing those four people back to his more important goal.

Leading the Coast Guard on a wild goose chase was truly brilliant, Dizhwar reflects. "Yes, the mobile contact number has this message." Dizhwar plays it for Driver, "Angel is home, octopus has returned to the garden." They both smile at the meanings and know that their chance of success has increased a hundredfold with the Coast Guard out of the way. All cell members send a yes text to the same phone, assuring Dizhwar that they are all on board the M/V *Wenatchee* in plenty of time.

Five minutes roll past into the ship's journey and the pair watch the Seattle shoreline move further and further away. Looking like a Jori Saeger picture; the sea turns into a white froth behind the ship, as the wake points right into downtown. Satisfied with the distance, Dizhwar pulls out an encrypted radio. He looks over at Driver and the two make eye contact. Driver turns from facing Seattle, and faces the pilothouse. Unbeknownst to the car ferry, it is now out in Puget Sound all alone. Driver inhales in once, savoring the last peaceful moment and then he nods his head. Dizhwar, concurring his friend's silent message, begins the mission by sending out to his entire team a three click radio burst.

The twelve radicalized operators initialize into simultaneous action.

On every parking level, the team brandish firearms and start yelling. The crew members are the first to be pacified. Six gunman take up their rifles stored in vehicles and methodically clear the car decks of all passengers. Shouting orders as they move in coordinated fashion, they hurriedly check for passengers still in their cars, forcibly removing the people from their vehicles. Through shoving, cursing and veiled threats the passengers are corralled up the stairs and into the fore passenger deck. The hijackers do their best to refrain from indiscriminate gunfire within the heart of the ship, worrying that their bullets might cause some sort of catastrophic damage.

While clearing the main car deck, Jibril takes control of the situation. "Abia," he shouts over the cries of passengers and the other conspirator's shouts.

"What!" Abia Al-Tikriti retorts back, not even looking at Jibril.

"Sweep the car deck once again! Check the bigger vehicles!! If you find any passengers, radio."

"Now wait a minute..." Abia shoots back, throwing up her unoccupied arm.

"We've got these people and your duty is patrol. So go patrol!" As she turns around, disgusted, Jibril adds "...and take Khoury!!"

Frustrated, and out of earshot from Jibril, Abia adds "We've done this search once already."

Abia shoves her way past Khoury, moving back to the front of the ship. Abia turns to speak and finds Khoury several yards back.

Abia gestures to Khoury "Will you keep up," and proceeds to again distance herself from the younger man.

At 21:12, while the first six are capturing the car deck, Hakim Ali and Raphael Webber are standing right next to two crew on the lounge deck. With their rifle's stocks folded and concealed in large backpacks no one knew. These two focus on the crew members first as well. Hakim and Raphael take control of the lounge decks, both fore and aft. The pair move all of those passengers and the two crewmembers in to the forward lounge area. Without firing a shot, their simple act of brandishing firearms and shouting threats gain them complete control.

Once Hakim and Raphael meet Jibril's group of four they start zip tying passengers to chairs. A few of their numbers stand guard. Then, the six men search their captives for any cell phones or firearms and remove them from their owners. Batteries come out of the phones and then the phones all end up in a heaping pile on a table. Any pistol that was found concealed on one of the passengers goes right into the gunman who found it waist band. After all, there are some people in the state of Washington that did have concealed pistols permits.

Back on the car deck, Abia makes it to the fore part of the ship and lights up a cigarette. Scoffing at the sign just a few feet away warning, "Open flame and smoking is prohibited on the car deck."

Abia Al-Tikriti is the second youngest saboteur in the group, but she doesn't look it or act like it. She was born in Iraq, but grew up in New Jersey. Just two years ago, she moved out to Bend, Oregon to follow her boyfriend west. *Yet, the sucker dumped me and left me without a place to live for months.* Forced to live in a halfway house until joining, she has a hard time respecting people, *particularly ones that remind me of my lousy ex.*

Abia waits next to the giant opening, staring at Khoury until it seems *the mousey little boy is paying attention.* "Remember vehicle searches?" Abia grills Khoury.

Khoury Dhakâ nods his head in agreement, hesitant to say a word and deciding that it's best not to. To him, Abia was the worst to be teamed up with. She was rude to him and everyone else, seemingly without any reason. At least Khoury couldn't ever figure out why.

"You do those two far lanes and I will do these two." Abia searches in the windows of the nearest truck, looking over to Khoury to make sure he is doing it right. Satisfied, she heads to the next vehicle and Khoury follows her example. At first, the pair perform their duty well, looking into the windows of every big vehicle. They climb up on bumpers, tires, and hoods to finish their inspections.

The pair move from fore to aft, double checking the oversized vehicles in that main cavernous space. Toward the middle of the dual rows of vehicles, Abia, frustration clear in her body language, begins to slack off. She starts cutting corners. She is getting impatient, only performing a quick check of a big moving truck, ignoring the box on the back. She stands on the front tire of a contractor's van to peer into the front and sees that the seats are empty. Quickly, she tries once to open the side door, it seems locked and Abia figures that the van's owner is upstairs already.

She looks over a concrete mixing truck and a landscaping truck as well, just glancing into their cabs. Satisfied, Abia lights another cigarette and waits for Khoury to finish his checks. Once Khoury meets up with Abia, acknowledging his area is clear, Abia and Khoury join their fellow brothers in arms up on the passenger lounge deck.

At the same time as the passengers are rounded up, 21:12, Driver along with Monifa, move to take control of the fore pilot house.

Also at the same moment of 21:12, Dizhwar leaves Driver, and meets up with Abdul. Abdul left his car just moments before, and once joining up with his leader, they head upstairs to the aft pilot house.

The secure command areas of the boat are always locked. On opposite ends of the ship, Dizhwar's group and Driver's group destroy the pair of locks that are part of the green rubber-covered security gates. The gates enclose the two pilothouses on both ends of the ship.

The gate's locks surrender to more small homemade charges. Both pairs of gunmen take the fore and aft pilot houses during the explosion's aftermath and confusion. Abdul and Dizhwar quickly zip tie the pair of crew in the aft pilothouse. Driver and Monifa capture crewmembers in the fore pilothouse. Trying to sort out the confusion, the Captain surrenders to Driver as Monifa pushes past and secures more crew. Driver mostly ignores the Captain and moves past him to the ship control panel. Driver pulls the throttles back to half power and waits.

Looking over the length of the boat, and seeing his men in control of the fore pilothouse, Dizhwar radios out to Driver, "All secure?"

"Secure." Driver's deep and self-assured voice comes back. "Waiting for your arrival."

Dizhwar pages out to all radio channels "Radio check. Radio check." A signal that the two control rooms have been taken. His men are to radio back individually, confirming that the entire group has complete control of the ship. They do just that in measured order and Dizhwar clicks out another three radio beeps, a signal to the team to begin their next objectives.

"Take these two crew to the fore pilot house and Driver," Dizhwar instructs Abdul. "I am going to check on everyone while you do that. Once you've delivered the crew head back here with Monifa."

Abdul agrees, "No problem," with a smile and heads off with the two crew. He pushes and shoves them along to meet up with his friend Monifa.

Monifa and Abdul have been in an on again, off again relationship, but in the weeks leading up to the mission they kept to only smiles when no one was looking. Only Monifa got his jokes and she was the only one among the twelve that he implicitly trusted. Abdul was the tactful comedian of the group, always trying to keep things positive and lighthearted, despite their grim plans. He gets along great with everyone except for Raphael.

Walking with confidence and authority, Dizhwar heads downstairs one level. The Group Leader passes through the passenger area checking quickly on all of his men before continuing back up to the ferries fore control room. Dizhwar once again meets up with Driver in the fore pilothouse. Dizhwar looks with a smug confidence on all of the captured ferry crew that is forcibly seated and zip-tied before him.

During the initial hostage taking, two crewmembers escaped detection. These particular crewman had hidden away in a chain storage locker after seeing the passengers get moved upstairs by people with guns. After the capture of the ship, the two quietly discuss what was the best thing to do.

Trevor insisted he will run up to warn the pilothouse crew and his co-worker will go below decks. For the co-worker points out that the ship is nothing without its engines. Once the highjackers are out of sight, Trevor and his co-worker split up. It was decided between Trevor and his co-worker that one would call out the warning to the Captain while the other would do their best to shut down and lock out all of the engines. Both of them had called out furiously on the radios, but no one had answered. They each hoped that their errands would be met with success and gave each other a resolute grimace before splitting off to their duties.

The secondary set of goals for the hijackers is to maintain complete control of the ship and to begin preparation for their final tasks. Two of the hijackers, Abdul and Monifa, remain in the rear pilot house for caution's sake. Two more operators, Abia and Khoury start up constant patrol throughout the ship. While four men, Faaiq, Raphael, Tarriq and Hakim retain control of the passengers in the lounge deck. The final two men, Jibril and Parvez, head downstairs into the engine room to complete their assigned tasks.

The pair of gunman, heading to the engine room are once again called on to do the dangerous work. Making their way back downstairs to the engine room access door, the pair are moving quickly. Just ahead they hear a door shut and glance at each other with alarm. "It seems somebody has been missed by the initial search," Jibril says to Parvez. Jibril and Parvez quickly rush the door and someone fights them from opening the latch on the other side. The door is clearly marked with "Restricted area! Authorized Personnel Only!" in yellow and red. The watertight door has its dogs partially engaged so a single man can't forcefully open it.

"Together," Jibril acknowledges to his teammate.

Parvez nods, "On your count."

"One, two, three!" They both yank simultaneously on the arm latch and it comes free with a clang. They trip over each other getting the door opened and are barely able to catch a glimpse of a man just below them. He has a luminescent bright orange vest on and has just made it to the bottom of the stairs. They are sure it is a crew member, the pair of conspirators can see the safety vest the man has failed to take off. The crewman glances back quickly and disappears once again out of sight. Jibril and Parvez run downstairs, raise their weapons, and encounter another door in the process of latching.

The pair work much faster this time, and have the door opened with little struggle.

Before plunging in Parvez glances over to Jibril, "Take us to glory."

"Allah, take us to glory," Jibril responds, nodding his head in agreement.

They find a single man, wearing crew member clothes, attempting to do something foolish with the secondary engine controls. Without saying a word, the pair raise their rifles, and each fire a round into the crewman; careful with their aim.

The crewmember collapses, his lungs and liver punctured by the pair of 5.45x39 bullets. Wracked with the pain of his injuries, the wounded man curls up into a heap on the floor; his body is wrenched with agony. After everything he attempted, and all of the effort he has put into it, his shot to be brave has proven fruitless.

His two assailants watch the man spasm on the deck from his pain and do nothing when he calls out for help. The pair of gunman drag him away from the engine control panel, and stuff the dying man into a maintenance closet. Locking the man into the darkness to die alone.

Parvez clicks his radio and waits for a response.

"Go ahead for Dizhwar." Dizhwar responds.

"Engine room secure. One crew member down."

Dizhwar is filled with pride at this. The last goal has been accomplished. His cell will not be oppressed. All of his men performed admirably. "May Allah be praised and may his Prophet be glorified!" Dizhwar radio's back to Parvez.

The ship is under complete control in a little more than fifteen minutes. As far as they know, no radio distress calls have been sent, and now nothing more will be sent. His pilot house guards are deploying jammers. The team's homemade jammers are set to foul up all radio communications except the frequency that Dizhwar and his team's radios are operating on. No more cell phones, no more ship-to-shore, no more unauthorized transmissions, period.

The evening's events have been carried out with cunning and precision. The stillness from the ship is deafening. The silence is entirely chilling. Everywhere on the ferry, the only thing that can be heard is the voices of fanatics. Ten of them going about their tasks with brutal efficiency. Led by two leaders, Dizhwar and Driver; opposites, yet united.

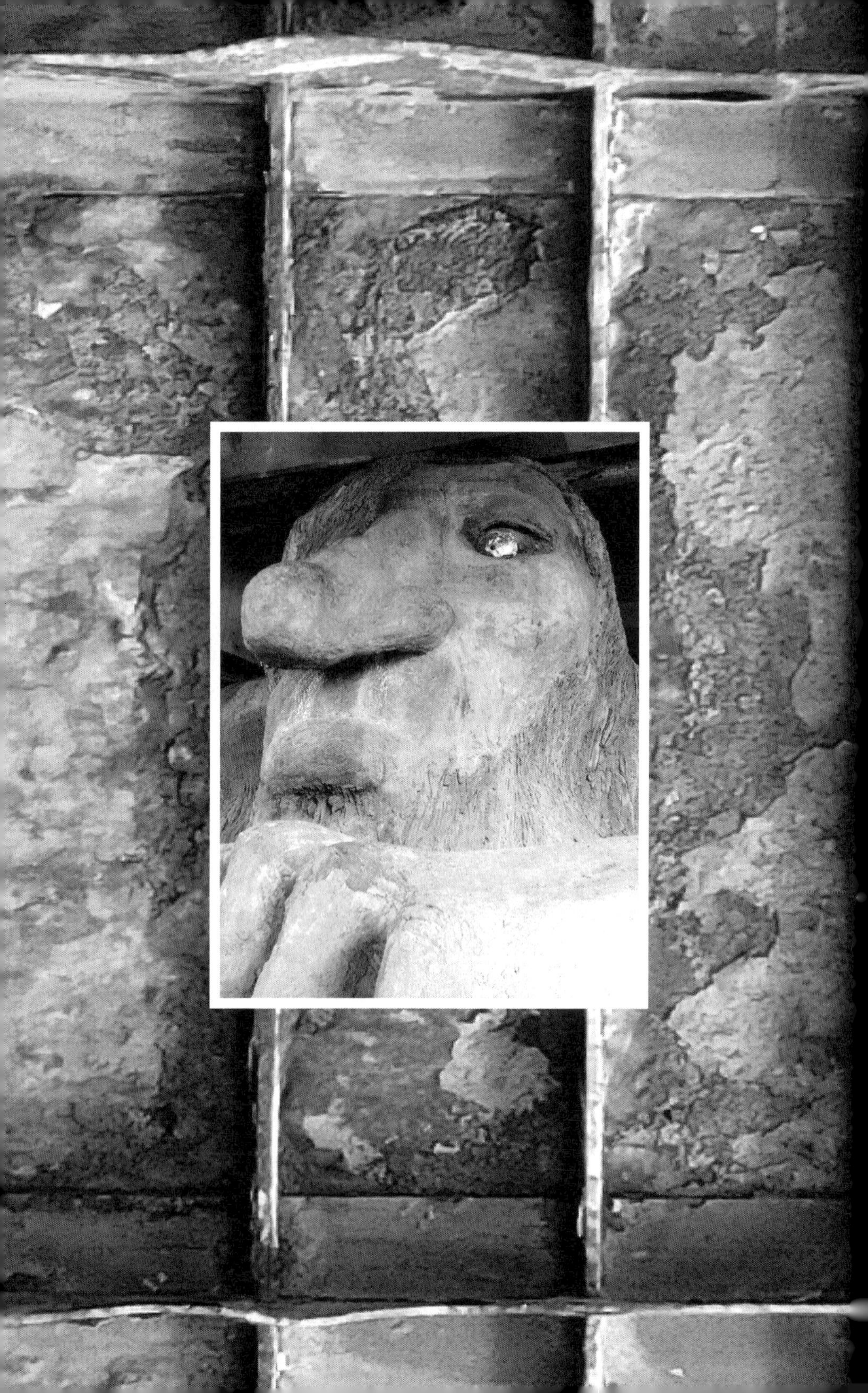

Chapter Twenty Four

Thursday August 30th 21:15

At the Ballard Locks something horrible has just happened. The lock operator, Oliver Redmond, had just made sure he had a green light on the lake side doors of the larger lock, Lock One. The light indicated that those upper lakeside doors were fully closed. It was just after the light came on, in its green hue, when the Oliver saw a brief geyser of water shoot up by the recessed door motors. A moment later, Oliver sets down his coffee and calls into the pleasure yacht, *Eternity*. "Have you guys seen or heard anything odd?"

"I felt and heard something, control house, but I didn't see a thing." The pilot of the *Eternity* calls back. "We were all looking forward to the next door. What was it?" The pilot of *Eternity* responds

"I don't know *Eternity*," Oliver looks past his magazines that had been on the controls that are now lying on the floor. "Water just shot out of the channel ten feet from your ship. Are all of your systems functional?"

They better be, thought *Eternity's* Captain Ian Sandivick, sitting on the chair behind the pilot. Ian pushes the pilot out of the way and quickly clicks through all of the ships systems on the touch screen monitor. All systems are reporting back nominal and his expensive yacht has no problems. Ian grabs the radio, "Lock Operator, everything is green; I've got nothing here." Ian looks to the lock control house and speaks once more into the microphone, "I'm going to get my crew to tie off the ship. They will give it a quick inspection before the tying. Why don't you check your systems before you open the lower gate?"

Captain Ian is concerned. This century old lock might just have damaged his multimillion dollar floating palace. His state of the art yacht was the personal property of two wealthy software engineers and they were going to be taking this ship out on its first trip. *It better not harm this ship,* he fretted. Ian and his crew of six just got the *Eternity* cleaned, updated and stocked for the long trip to Australia via Hawaii, the Marshalls, Fiji and New Caledonia.

Agreeing with the point Oliver radio's, "All right, *Eternity*. Tie off and while your doing that I will run a systems check." The Oliver Redmond runs through the system board, rocking the test switches back and forth under each of the twenty four channels. Each channel controlled or monitored a function of the entire four door, dual lock system.

Oliver would rock the switch to test, wait for a green light, switch it back to its normal mode and then move to the next channel on the board. This system was state of the art back in the eighties, when it was last upgraded, and was not without it's quirks. *But a geyser? A possible explosion? Were my eyes playing tricks on me?*

After getting only one red light on Lock One's upper door motor, Oliver figures something must have just shorted out. *Ignoring what he thought he saw*, still not believing he witnessed an explosion, the Oliver continues through his checklist.

I was almost off of my shift! Oliver Redmond grumbles. He looks out the windows and sees the yacht's crewmen scrambling to secure the ship. They had to tie off the ship in the middle of the lock and have their tie ropes let out slowly so the ship stayed in the center of the channel while the water was let out. *...And now the stupid upper lake doors on Lock One refuse to open. I couldn't have seen an explosion could I?* Oliver keeps doubting what his eyes and ears were reminding him. Oliver glances out the window to see that the gleaming yacht is almost ready to be lowered to sea level.

Oliver runs a quick test on lock two. The test comes back all green. *No surprise,* he tells himself while he considers the facts. The smaller lock two is already filled with fresh water waiting for a scheduled sail boat to pass through in an hour. Oliver gets a green light on his door circuit panel, which meant the Upper Lock doors for Lock Two are now in the process of opening.

Satisfied with the continuing test, he flicks the door switch off and when the large metal doors cease their opening travel, Oliver flicks another switch to close them.

"*Eternity*, I've got a problem with the upper doors on your lock, but that doesn't effect you at all. I've tested all of the other systems and the doors are secure and in place. I just can't seem to open your Lock One upper doors anymore."

"Well, does that matter Sir?" Ian asks. "We are already in the lock. So, what does that mean?" Ian confrontationally radios back.

"Did you guys hit them on your way in? See any damage on them?"

Ian shook his head at this operators incompetence. "No control, we didn't hit them or see any damage." Captain Ian had just about enough of this; *like I would inspect lock doors when I was busy watching my guy pilot the ship?* It was clear to him the operator was grasping at straws to try and explain the malfunction. *Maybe it was as simple as: the lock was just too friggin old?* Ian shakes his head, but breaking Ian's train of thought, the radio comes to life again.

"Are you guys secure and tied off?"

"Affirmative, Control. We are just about secured now." Ian looks out over his crew and waits for each one to give him a wave of completion. "I need you to let us out of here as soon as possible." Ian's reply back is terse and short. He is doing his best to not get angry. *But one of these times,* Ian begins to tell himself, *I need to talk to the owners about docking this ship someplace else. Someplace other than Lake Union. Somewhere on the other side of these old locks.*

The operator flicks the switch that opens a valve on the side of Lock One. This allows the fresh water from One to spill out into the lower channel that leads to the sea; which gradually lowers the yacht to sea level. The ship begins to sink slowly down into Lock One as planned.

While that happens, Oliver multitasks, and as he maintains control of the work that's going on in lock one, he gets a green closed light on Lock Two's Upper doors. The moment he watches his test complete a green light come to life. Vooush!!! Another geyser of water erupts from Lock Two!

Oliver had been watching the control panel and out the window at the same time. So, he was looking directly in the direction of the column of water. It sprays down upon the gangway and the fantail of the *Eternity.*

While any ship is in his 'pens', watching the yacht is Oliver's responsibility, "Holy Crap!" He yells out loud in the tiny control room. Oliver hurriedly clicks transmit on his radio "Tell me you saw that, *Eternity!*"

"What the frig! What's going on in there?" The surprise is clearly coming through Ian's voice. All sense of anger and frustration had momentarily evaporated.

Oliver quickly responds, "Hold, *Eternity,* I'm stopping your passage."

"Your doing what?!?" comes the plea from Ian.

Oliver Redmond ignores the yacht Captain's request. He systematically shuts down all of the Lock's functions. Oliver kills the power to pumps and motors. He electronically shuts the valves allowing water into the Sound and places both of the Ballard Locks into a safety lockout position.

Oliver's last act is to kill all of the electrical systems except for the outdoor lights. He still doesn't know what is going on, but he isn't going to be fired for damaging the hundred year old system any further. "Oh no, not on my watch," Oliver mumbles to himself as he flicks the last of the switches.

"Operator!" Ian calls out on the radio. Ian Sandivick waits a moment and then tries again, "Lock Operator please respond!"

The radio next to Oliver Redmond bursts to life for a third time. Lock Operator Oliver looks at the radio like it's stinky garbage. "You've got to let us out of here," the radio pleads. "Don't hold us! *Eternity*'s owners are going to be pissed off if this yacht isn't at the Seattle pier by tomorrow morning!!"

Oliver doesn't even bother to respond, "I don't care about your boss," he says to himself in his otherwise empty control room. *So what if they miss a day or two on a vacation to Hawaii or Cabo San Lucas or wherever that gaudy thing is going.*

Oliver takes a gulp of his coffee and pulls out his rarely used Federal Emergency Management Checklist (FEMC). He starts following the FEMC procedure for Hydraulic/Electrical Lock emergency. Oliver's first step of shutting the entire lock down has already been accomplished.

"Check," he confirms to himself. Now, with that part of the list completed, he picks up the phone for a call to the United States Army Corps of Engineer's Emergency Desk, which is step two. After all, that is what the checklist says to do.

The Operator's radio comes to life once more, "For the love of sanity's sake!!! Lock Operator!! At least throw over a boarding bridge so I can get myself and my crew off!"

Ian, sitting stranded on his *Eternity*, is getting the distinct feeling that this yacht captain gig might not be all that he thought it would be.

Chapter Twenty Five

Thursday August 30th 21:25

      Something is nagging at his sleeping mind. James isn't even dreaming this time. There is just this dark, lurid, abyssal sleep. James wants badly to stay there in that place of escape, but he can't avoid the nagging feeling that something is just not right. It has an authority over his desire to take a nap. It compels him out of his slumber. Feeling forcefully resurrected once more today, James lays there with his eyes open.

"This must be how Lazarus felt?" James wonders aloud. At least he is partially restored by his nap. Something has caused him to awake. A small and quiet voice that's warned him all is not well. His senses are heightened and they try to reveal something to him that he can't rationally work out. *Curse his groggy head!* He feels it in his gut, not in his still cloudy and sleepy mind. James sits up, moves back into the driver's seat, and takes a look around. He sees from the dashboard radio clock he'd been asleep around twenty minutes.

Looking out the window, everything seems totally normal. The ferry, the cars, the water, the view. Mentally pushing away the cobwebs of sleepiness he stares out the window a bit more. The people? There it is! The people seem to be gone. And, everything is quiet. The usual deep thrum from the engines is missing too. The sound from the diesels seem quiet, almost like they were at idle. The view is barely changing, which confirms his thoughts about the engines. As if the ship is in slow motion, which is wrong. Where are the people? People are always milling about, looking at the Seattle skyline or the late summer sunset; enjoying the ocean breeze. *What the heck is going on?* James seriously starts to feel like a character on the Twilight Zone. From the clock on his dashboard he knows he couldn't have been asleep for long.

He gets out of his van and barely closes the door. Unsettled, he walks around his van heading toward the stairs leading to the passenger deck. The smell of the ocean mingles with the smell of the boat, and the warm smells of car engines. The engine from the last car he passes is still making the faint tick, tick, sound that aluminum makes when cooling. As if trying to confirm it, James randomly places his hands on the hoods of three different cars as he walks. They are all still warm. The electrician makes his way around the final car, and thinks he captured a glimpse of someone's back, walking just out of the stairs and away from James. Curious, James picks up his pace toward where he saw the mysterious figure.

This could be the first person I've seen since waking up, James thinks as he follows far behind. James walks through the stairway passage that leads from the main oversize car area to the lower car berth and comes around the corner to observe the profile of a man carrying a rifle. The Twilight Zone comparison hits his mind, anew.

Standing just six feet away is a someone standing sideways to James. James thinks for just a moment: *Security? No, it's all wrong.* Then he realizes the figure is not a man but a woman. *A woman in plain clothes, and a black vest. The vest possibly body armor? The figure is carrying a rifle?*

And as she turns toward him, James notices that she's carrying an AK-74 Kalashnikov. James knows it's a newer version of the venerable AK-47, invented over half a century ago. James knows, *no security in the U.S. would ever carry such a weapon.* Due to its importance in the Cold War and the Middle East the weapon bears a profound stigma in the West.

Oh this isn't good, James tells himself, a sinking feeling adds to his confusion. He hesitates, and the gunman finishes her turn, stopping to stare right into James's eyes. There's immediate surprise in her eyes. The figure's face reflects as much shock in seeing James, as James's at seeing her.

The adrenalin hits his system. James nervously spits out, "Excuse me, is uh, something wrong?" as he mentally goes through so much in that brief moment.

Use of force and self-defense training are what feeds through James's mind first. In a millisecond his mind flashes all of the statistics that were shared in class about crimes using dissimilar weapons. He remembers that the percentages are in his favor when you're this close, even unarmed against a gun. The armed one is just too close to engage the target effectively with a firearm. Time and distance is needed to react, which you didn't have when one is this close; unless the shooter's in the correct shooting stance: Barrel pointed in the direction of your vision, firearm held slightly away ready to be used.

Ms. AK. has not taken any of these actions. She has her rifle slung over her shoulder and she stares at James with a look like *what are you doing here?*

The pair are only three to four yards apart, her rifle is carried in an across the shoulder position; barrel pointing skyward. Maybe realizing her mistake, Ms. AK starts to bring the rifle around, but there's not enough time for that. Almost like an Epi-pen to the heart, James springs into action. James rushes forward, right palm facing upward, fingers bent into a fist. As he does, James wonders at the choice that's being forced upon him, but wills himself to his defense. There is going to be a strong chance for death, and James is determined that he's not going to be the receiver of that fate.

The rifle comes around too slowly, strap just now clearing Ms. AK's elbow. James deflects the barrel away from his own body with his left hand and lunges with his outstretched right fist at the throat of Ms. AK. The intention is to hit her hard in the throat for an immediate and incapacitating blow.

But, James's aim is off and he's unnerved by having to fight against a woman. His fist glances off of the side of AK woman's neck with little effect. Now they're both toe to toe.

Heart racing, James's second blow is aimed for her midsection and again his aim is off, it hits high. James gets a reaction, but not to the effect that he needs.

Ms. AK swings out with her leg trying to trip him up, to get him away so that she can bring her rifle around. She kicks with all of her might, but her attack is aimed right behind his knee and she hits his calf with little effect. The pair start grappling with each other, the intensity of their fight building.

The woman tries to use her legs as much as possible, making knee jabs to her assailant's stomach and groin. Only occasionally using her left fist.

James struggles, keeps up a reasonable defense, blocking her blows with his forearms. He has the reach over her and James throws more relentless blows. Forcing himself to fight hard. He hits, he hits, and he hits.

Ms. AK tries to deflect James's fists by ducking and weaving, but her arm is still in the sling of the dangling rifle. She throws a punch to James's face, makes good contact and tries to use the moment to discard her rifle.

James is fazed by the blow, but again, he viciously hits at the vital area of her midsection, then switches back at her throat. The woman is feeling the punches and is slowing, but is still able to send a few more blows against his side.

Ms. AK steps in close now, and tries to hit James in the groin with her knee, but James dodges her leg by twisting aside.

After moving away from her knee, James changes up and hits to the side of her body. As he does so, he takes a half-step backwards to use his longer reach to his advantage. He wills his opponent to fall as he changes again and hits at her face. Both of them fight viciously, in a dance of intermingled fists, dodges and blocks until they are both winded.

They both start dragging now, their wounds and the fierceness of the fight is depleting their energy. In a pause, the woman sucks in a breath, about to yell for help. James senses this, and aims his fist at her throat once more.

Before she can shout, Ms. AK receives the blow full force, unable to dodge it. Her cry now extinguished, Ms. AK starts gagging and coughing from the impact to the front of her neck. As the moments pass, she's provides an ever lessening defense.

From the beginning, the gunman's dominant arm was caught up in the rifle's sling. *I was so stupid to have slung the rifle over my shoulder!* She curses herself for the mistake. Abia can't keep up this kind of half-guard for long and she is finally able to discard the rifle.

She is still coughing and hacking from the blow to her throat and can barely catch her breath through her partially collapsed windpipe. She resorts to standing hunched over. More hard blows land on her and she tucks up even more, guarding her core. Abia uses her left and right arm, to protect her face. She stands there wincing from the blows, trying to think of a way out of the fight.

But I don't even have the time for that, Abia knows. *If I lower my defense to call on the radio my assailant will lay me out.*

With the woman hunching over, James resorts to using his knees on Ms. AK just like she used on him. James only takes a few lunges with his knees before his opponent goes down in a moaning heap.

The fight now over, both of them are separated from each other by an arm's length. There is a pause, a few seconds as James catches his breath. James steps slowly and kicks away the AK-74 from the fallen woman.

He goes down to his knees trying to calm his racing heart.

Between heavy breaths, "Who the heck are you?" James shouts at the fighter. There's no response. "Who are you and what is going on here?" he continues, but to no avail. The AK woman seems to be unconscious.

"Nuts!!!" James exclaims. He still has the adrenalin in his veins, affecting his patience and his mood. He kicks her hard to make sure she stays down, then he walks over to the woman's AK-74 and picks it up before heading back over to his opponent.

James leans in close, and pokes her with the barrel of the rifle. Asking again to the prostrate woman, "Who are you?" Still nothing.

Frustration growing, James gives his prisoner another swift kick into her side and gets a moan for the reaction. James tries to figure out just what to do in the moment. *I should drag her back to my van and try to get some answers there. It's got to be safer there than being out here in the open.* James thinks hard, *I don't dare go any farther into the ferry if there's more people like this on the ship. It is just too risky. Plus, if this is some sort of police exercise, anti-terrorist training, or God knows something else, I need to find out. I don't want to make any more possible mistakes.*

Slinging her rifle over his back, James grabs Ms. AK's feet and begins pulling backwards. In just a few minutes, James isn't impressed with his progress, even over the smooth steel of the ship. James turns around, so his back is to her, places one of Ms. AK's feet under each armpit and pulls. *There it is, a bit faster and not as hard to navigate.* James makes it to his van and drops his prisoners legs. Watching his captive, James opens up the van's sliding side door, moves his bag and mat out of the way and judges the space within his van.

Would it be big enough for the both of us? Might as well try, so with tremendous effort, James places the limp woman inside his van, crawls in after her, and closes the sliding door.

James searches AK's vest and pockets, removing the few found items. There are four spare magazines for the AK-74, a body armor vest with the magazine pouches, a knife, a mobile phone, a radio, and twenty or so loops of thin, greenish rope. It pretty much confirms to James that this woman is no cop.

No ID. No badge. Nothing in the form of personal identification. James proceeds to tie up the woman with zip ties that he has for bundling cable.

"If it walks like a duck and talks like a duck…" James says to no one in particular. Reminding himself that what he is possibly in could be very bad. He struggles with what to do next.

James's brain is running at ninety miles-an-hour. He tries to sort it out as quickly as he can. *If I take action, then I need to get some more facts. I'm not going to carry out some sort of vigilante act blindly. Furthermore, this prisoner is, so far, the only source of facts!* James sits next to the tied up woman, *if I'm to do nothing, just sit in my van and wait, then I can just leave this poor soul alone and tied up.*

"What am I going to do with you?" James asks her. "Leave you alone? Beat you even more??"

He shuts his mouth, but the questions come fast in his head, *What's the right thing to do? What's the responsible thing to do?*

The electrician dropped out of Krav Maga training after only completing the first full session. He couldn't afford them anymore. He's just a working class guy with too much going out and not enough coming in. He did have a concealed pistol license, and practiced with it once a month, but it was out of a desire to protect himself and his family. *I'm no cop, nor ex-military,* James warns himself. *Any special training I've had has been randomly picked up along the way.*

James is faced with too many uncertainties. He tries to shake it all off and finally decides on an action, though small. James gets up and grabs his bottle of water out of his lunch box. The AK woman's hands are tied behind her back and via another set of linked ties her feet are tied as well. James figures he must wake her. The least he can do is try and negotiate with her. James wonders, *maybe just ask nicely will work?*

James pours out a thimbleful of water onto the woman's face and waits, nothing. The electrician doubles the amount and gets a reaction. Sputtering and head shaking goes on for a few seconds before Ms. AK looks around her environment, and then locks eyes with James.

"Good morning, sleepy head!" For now, James figures the light hearted route will be the best tact.

Ms. AK's response is to struggle against the constraints for a few moments and then to relax again.

"You are not going to get out of those cable ties. They are industrial strength." With that James demonstrates the strength by nervously holding up a container in Vanna White style to the highjacker. "See," James points to the words 'industrial strength' on the container.

He does not get a grin from the woman. He looks at her honestly, "Answer a few of my questions first, then you will be free." James speaks, lightheartedly, setting down the water bottle and the zip tie cylinder.

"Go to hell!" Ms. AK snaps back rather rudely, renewing her struggle against her bonds.

James isn't taken aback by the declaration; he figures this woman is not a police officer but, so rude? "Look, friend, I'll cut you out of those if you just answer some of my questions. What's your name? Why are you carrying around the AK and the body armor?"

James waits, when he gets no response he asks the question he'd been really pondering "How many others kidnappers or saboteurs or whatever you call yourselves, are there on this ship?"

The woman's eyes light up. Then, in a flash, the light was quickly extinguished.

That got a reaction. James thinks, but he still gets nothing out of the gunman except for silence. James figures that he'll go through the saboteur's stuff in front of her. The electrician picks up the gunman's phone. While doing so, watching his guests' face. The Droid touchscreen phone is screen locked, so it seems pretty useless and he throws it aside.

He goes through her bullet proof vest, checking to see if it has anything other than full magazines in the pockets. A radio! James hadn't heard a thing from it. He inspects it and realizes it was off. James rotates the knob that doubled as a power on, and volume. It clicks on, squeaks for a second and then goes quiet. James knows he shouldn't try to transmit, so he sets it down next to the phone and tries the nice guy routine again.

"What's going on with you? And this ship?" James tries to use his nicest voice. This time, there is no reaction out of his prisoner. James sighs deeply and then leans back against the side of the van. Ms. AK pulls in a breath, lets out a quick scream and then is silenced by James's pistol to her forehead. He sets his pistol opposite of his prisoner and moves the AK into his lap. James removes the magazine, and pulls back on the bolt to see if a round was chambered. Much to James's surprise, an un-shot round ejects from the chamber.

"What in God's green earth are you doing with this?" motioning to the rifle. Still no answer, the woman has completely clammed up, yet Ms. AK watches James carefully. James explores the unloaded rifle until he figures out how it works and its safety. James pulls back and releases the bolt on the empty gun, points it in a safe direction, and then pulls the trigger.

Click! The firing pin smashes home.

James re-tests it repeatedly with the safety on and then off, making sure he knows how the gun works.

Click! Satisfied with his familiarity with the rifle he reloads the magazine, jacking a round into the chamber with the safety on.

Again out of ideas, James puts on the body armor over his shirt, not planning anything in particular, just out of a lack of not knowing what to do. With fear and uncertainty James is bewildered, *I don't know what the procedure is for this kind of thing.*

And if I did, maybe I don't even want to do it?

The overworked electrician sits there a moment to think and is watched by his prisoner.

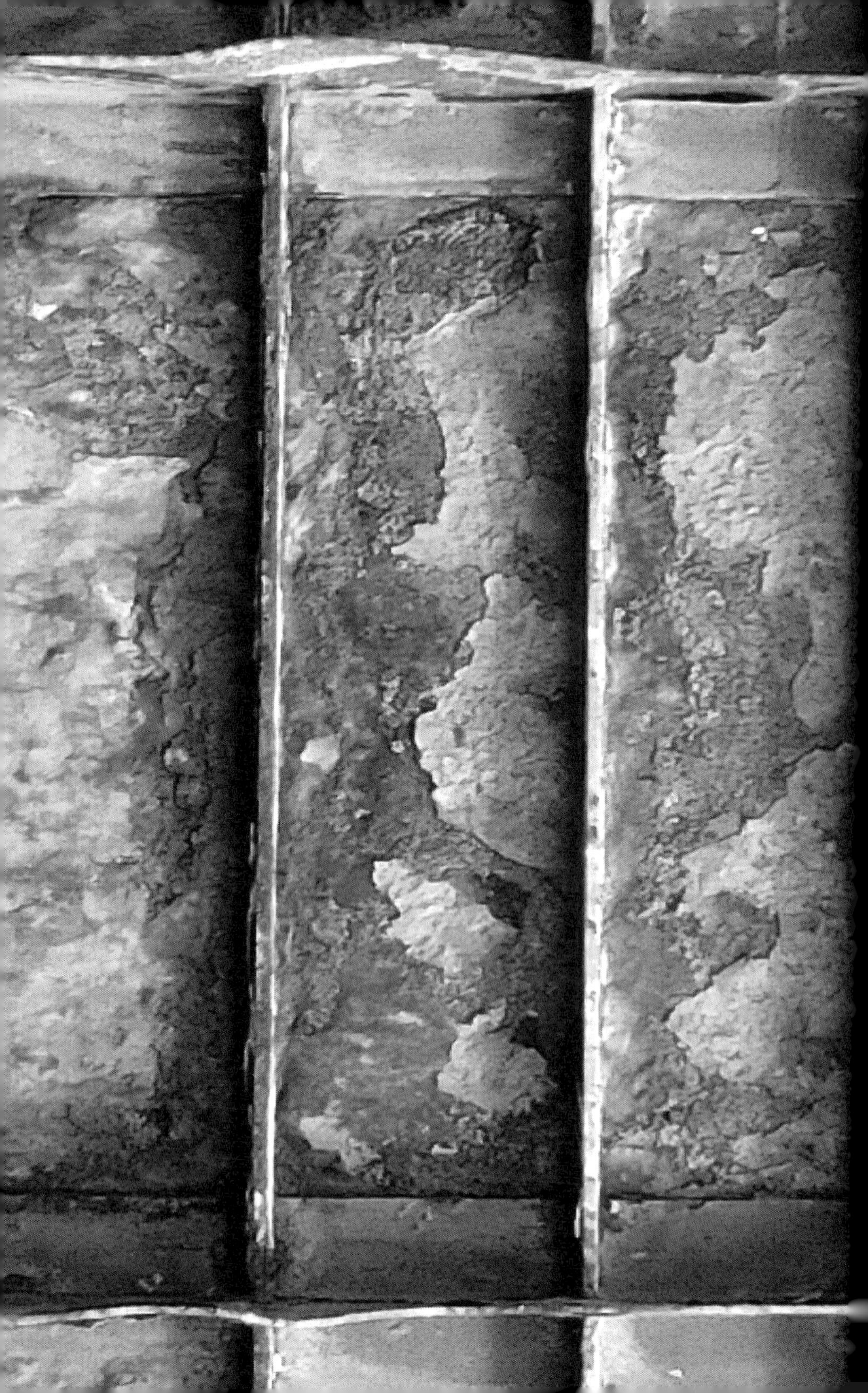

Chapter Twenty Six

Thursday August 30th 21:25

Click! Click! Clack!

"Just what do you think you're doing?" the woman asks the only other occupant of the rear pilot house.

Clack, click, click...The man deftly unfolds and folds a butterfly knife. "What does it look like? I'm bored and I'm going to clean my nails."

"Shouldn't you be watching for any problems behind us, like we are supposed to?"

Click! Click! Clack! "Take it easy Monifa, look around you," the man gestures with his arm behind and to his side. An elegant seven inch blade in his hand. "There is nothing around."

He is right. There is not a single boat close to the large ferry. Partly because it is such a large vessel and other ships give it a wide berth and also because of the late hour.

"Well stop that thing you do with the knife, *Craig Edward Argens*. It's dangerous and you're going to jam that thing up your finger or something worse. Like drop it on something important..."

Monifa watched him flinch when she mentioned his former name and it gave her a *bit of satisfaction*. She knew the buttons to push only the way a woman could. *I have to do something to him for not putting that dangerous butterfly knife away.*

Clack! Click! Click! "Why don't you just step outside and go bug someone else *Cleopatra?*" Abdul didn't like to be called Craig, that was his former Christian name. But, Monifa hated being called Cleopatra even worse.

Monifa Bashandi el-Shazli was born in Egypt and has the olive skin, high cheekbones and the long black hair of a native Egyptian. She had gotten teased relentlessly when a letter from her father and fallen into the hands of her fellow American Army buddies. Her father had called her "his Cleopatra" in the letter and the mostly male platoon had not let her forget about her childhood nickname. Then, in a late night of drinking, Abdul had heard the reference brought out. He witnessed Monifa's explosion of anger on a former solider and Abdul had remembered the name for future use.

Abdul smiles as he watches her grit her teeth and stuff down the flash of furry. Abdul continues to witness her struggle with some biting rejoinder, but she cant. With nothing witty to say back to him, she just grabs a pair of binoculars and starts to look out the rear pilothouse window.

Astonished at her composure, Abdul folds the knife in a quick flourish of his hand. Click! Click! Clack! Clack! Click! Click! He doesn't even look at the knife but instead watches Monifa's face as the knife flies away; barely under control in his hand. She flinches with the sound of the blade, but that was it. "What?!? You're not going to go off on me? Had enough already?"

"I'm not going to dignify your rudeness with a comment." She states it plainly, not even pulling her eyes away from the binoculars. "Besides, I'm not like that kind of violent person anymore."

Abdul scoffs at her comment. He walks up to stand beside her and brushes a few strands of her raven black hair from her face. "What gives?" He says sweetly.

She scoots away a little farther from him. Once out of his reach she lets the binoculars hang from their strap and she ties back the few strands that escaped her previous attempt at tying them back.

"I particularly enjoy our verbal sparring, even a little fist fight. It's one of the things that I assumed would make this trip go by a little faster. You know, you and me in a confined space with nothing to do...fall into some old habits?"

"The mission is what gives! You dope..." Monifa was still searching for something to get a rise out of her partner. Then it dawns on her, "I didn't think hicks from Idaho are that clueless? You might be witty and sometimes funny, but *it isn't appropriate.*" Monifa waved her hand around his head, "That all needs to be boxed up until this is all over. You need to take this seriously!" Abdul just gives her a coy grin and Monifa tries to reinforce her point, "All of it, Abdul!"

Abdul doesn't even flinch at her attempted comeback. "Monifa, there is nothing going on. What we are doing back here isn't too serious! We guard a pilothouse from no one in particular, we already have control of the entire ferry! We got stuck back here 'cause we are the better shots with rifles and that's about all we can do. Besides, all of the rescue boats can't get to us..."

"They can't get to us uhh..." She interrupts his thoughts and hands him her binoculars. "Look for yourself, genius."

He looks out over the waterfront, taking his time in locating the Emergency Boat terminal. As he looks over it, he sees that all of the ships are still intact. Clueless, he asks, "...so what of it?"

"Those very ships that you are staring at were meant to blow a few minutes ago. Remember the schedule?" She waits for his answer and not receiving one continues, "I guess not."

He shrugs his shoulders, admitting nothing and looks back through the window. "So what are you suggesting?" He questions while handing the pair of binoculars back to her.

"Well it looks like we might have a visitor or two if those ships don't get taken out. How about you watch them closely?"

He half-faces her and half-faces the wind coming in through the pilothouse's open door. "And what my queen are you going to do?"

"I don't know," she tries to keep her mocking tone tuned down despite his continued ribbing. "What do you think I should do? Maybe call Dizhwar?"

"Look, this isn't the Army. Everything doesn't go down according to the time schedule." He looks out at the ships and back into her dark eyes.

Silence is her response, because she *knows* it bugs him.

"Well then why don't we give it a few minutes and watch what happens?"

She is silent once more. Abdul knows, *that could only mean one thing. That she disagrees with me.*

"I will wrestle you for it?" He jokes, trying to get her to lighten up.

"Yeah right you're twice my weight *and* strength." She snips back, still considering his idea. "Plus your reach is a third longer than mine."

Abdul holds the knife once more in his hand about to unhinge the catch on the bottom of the handle. She shoots him a dirty look, "About calling, well, I guess your idea sounds alright to me, Dizhwar is more than likely busy with all kinds of other stuff. Besides if it keeps you from playing with that stupid knife once more, it's worth it."

"But you haven't seen me catch the knife in my teeth yet," he smiles as he speaks, trying to relieve the tension of the moment. "I can do all kinds of tricks with it. Did you ever see the sci-fi movie 'Alien'?"

Monifa gives Abdul a blank stare.

"Oh, yea," Abdul laments, "you don't watch sci-fi."

"I don't know what's worse about you Abdul. The fact that your family are all Idaho potato farmers or you are just clueless when it comes to appropriate behavior."

"You are just jealous that I can shoot better than you!" He jabs her side innocently with the butt of the knife. "...after you were in the Army *eight years!*"

Monifa shakes her head and turns away from him. She brings the binoculars to her eyes to look out over the stern of the ship. Abdul looks at his knife, about to flourish it again and then pockets it.

The two settle into a few more jibes, a few more insults. But both of them now watch for approaching ships.

Knowing that her point was finally listened to; Monifa grins.

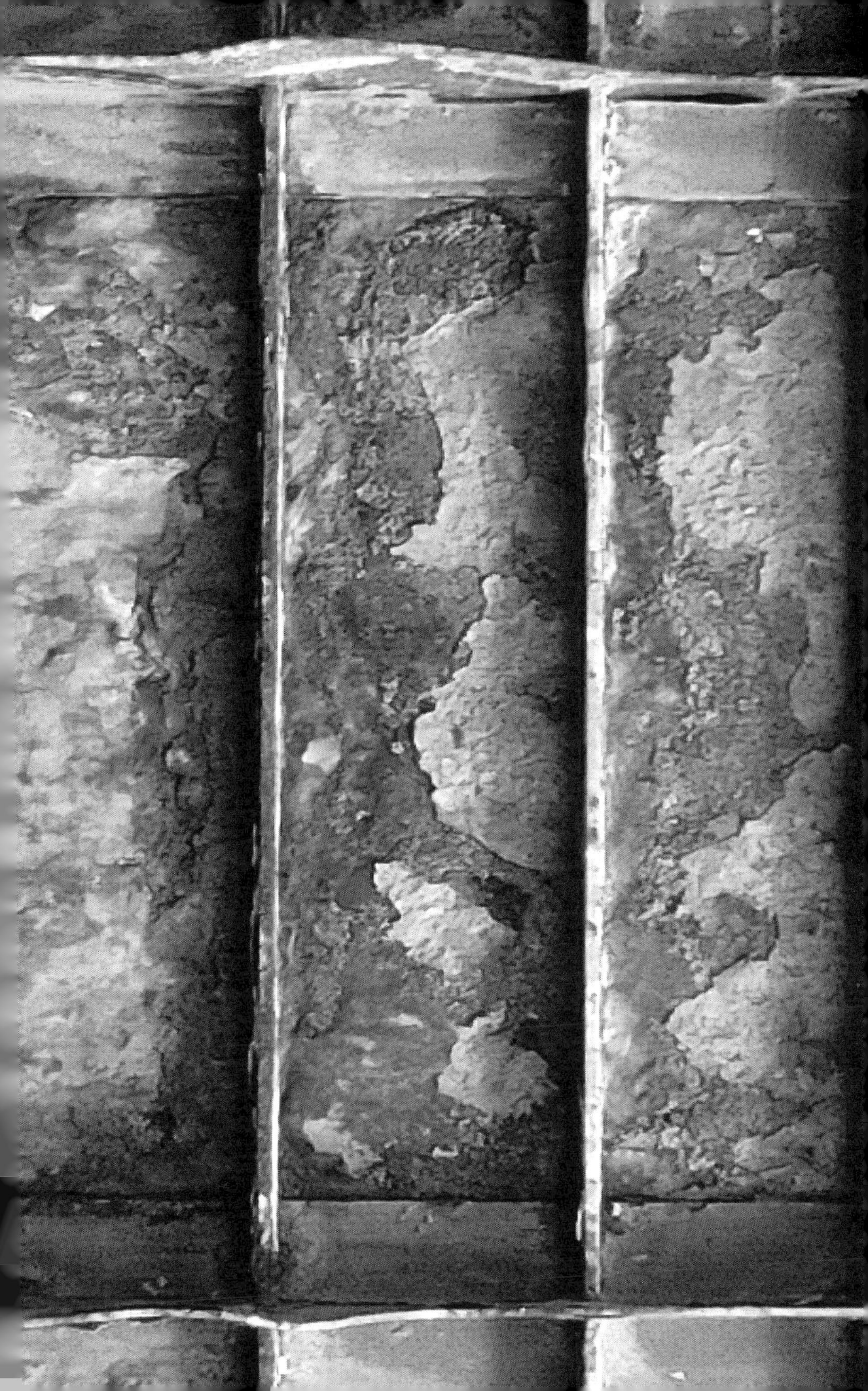

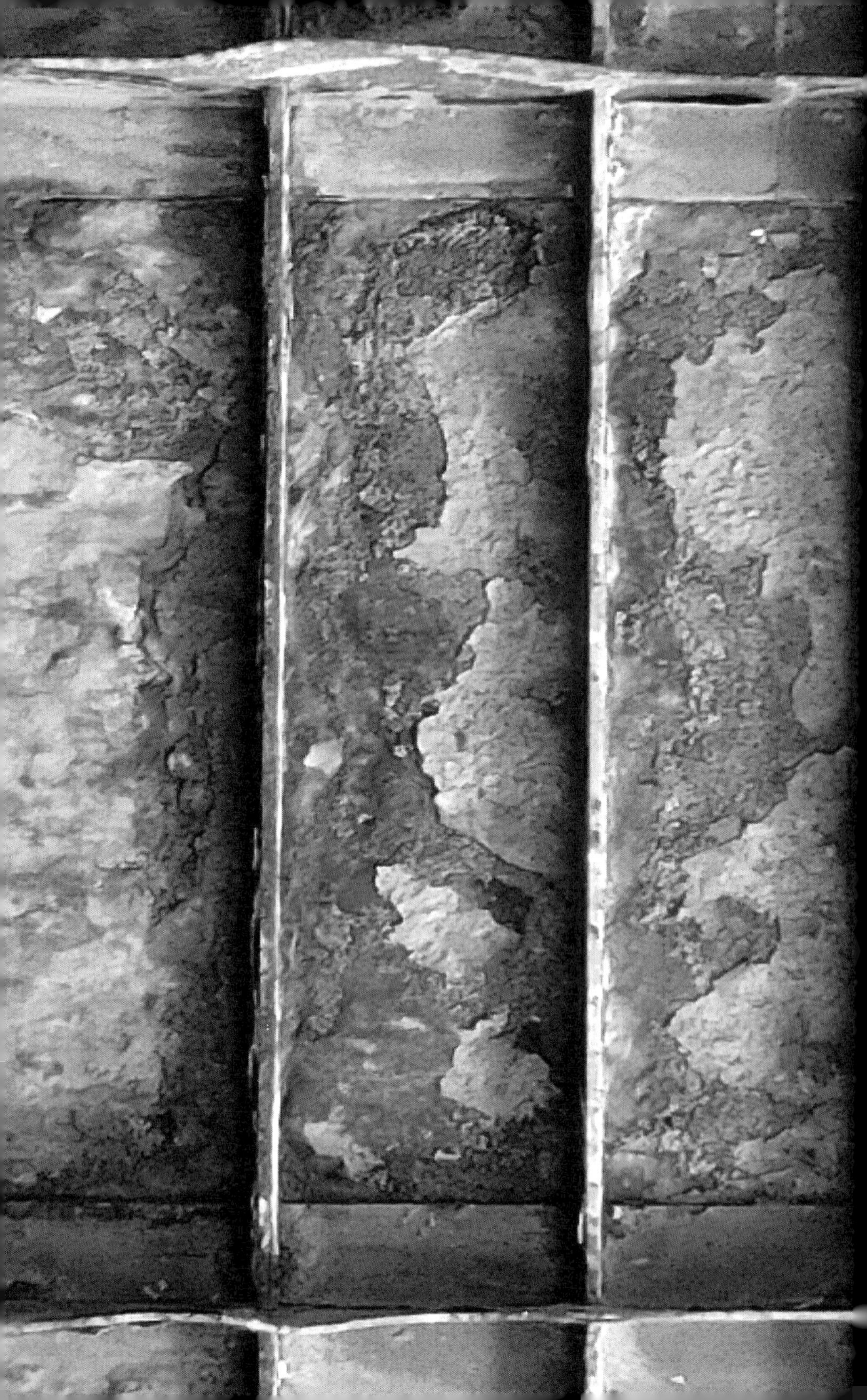

Part Two

" There are three types of people in this world: those who make things happen, those who watch things happen and those who wonder what happened."

-Mary Kay Ash, Founder of Mary Kay Cosmetics

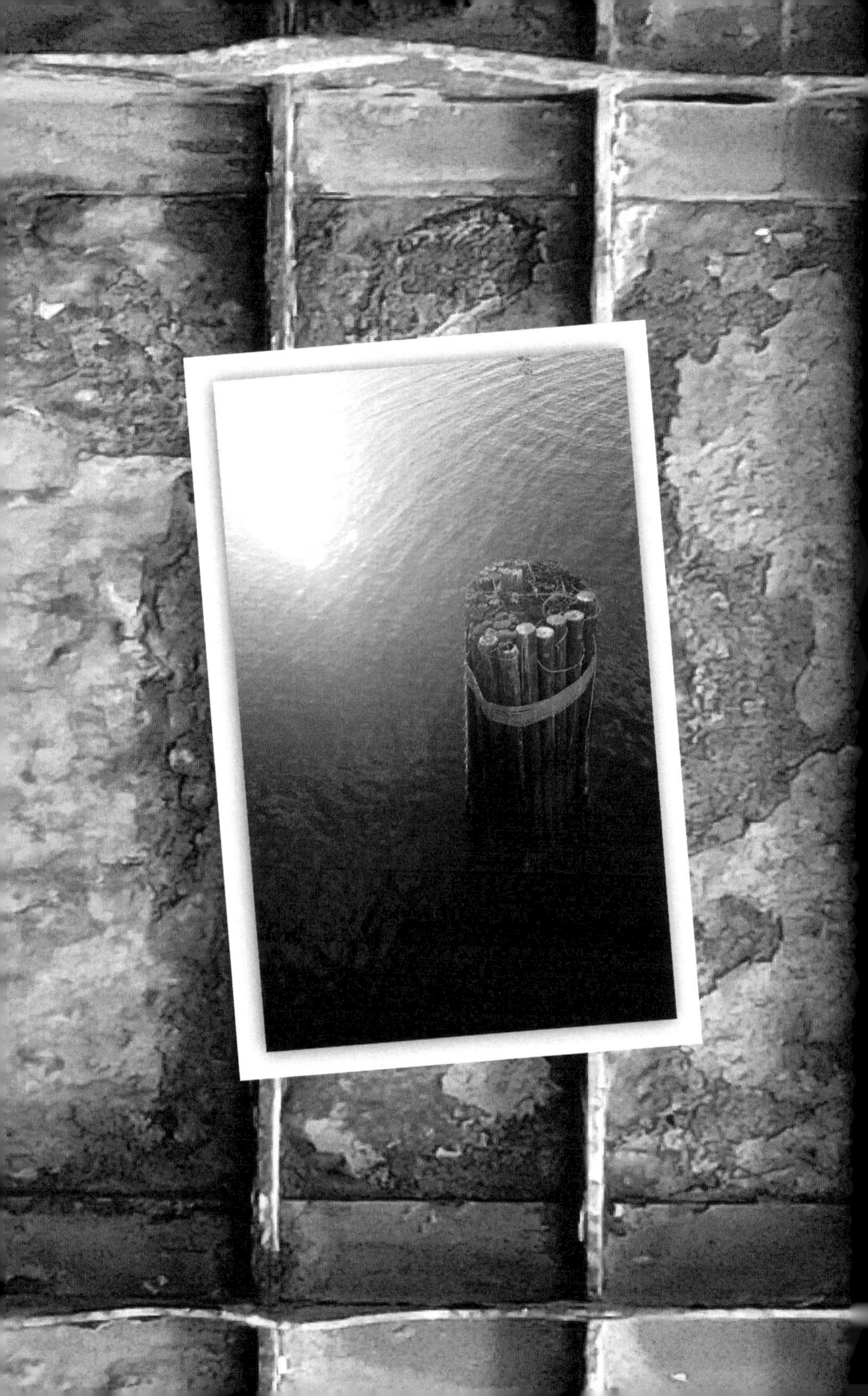

Chapter Twenty Seven

Whichever side that you choose, less government or more; boogie men, both real and imagined, have been used by governments throughout the centuries as harbingers of change. Sometimes those dangers materialize and other times they do not. For very good reasons and sometimes for reasons that *seem* good, these regimes want change for their own goals. Existent and nonexistent dangers allow governments to encroach on individual liberties for national safety. After all, why 'let a good crisis go to waste?'

Power can be more centralized, more authority is granted to the administrations and less oversight results; all good reasons for governments to make light of national dangers, whether they exist or not. There are those that argue that the erosion of liberty for security is justified. Others believe that if there is an erosion of liberty for security, we will have neither. Since the reprehensible attacks on 9/11, terrorism, and the perceived threat of it, has been at least good for one thing: the expansion of the federal government.

Both in size and scope, in reach and capability, various branches of the government have grown. The reason that is given, "...to be more capable to ferret out terrorists, foreign and domestic," seems like something all of us could get behind. Yet, we find the agencies that are trying to perform such a task simply become ever more expansive since 9/11 and the mass murder of our citizens. Doesn't it bear to question; are those organizations more lethal, more capable? Or just more bureaucratic? And just what exactly are these expanding branches of government more capable of?

It comes across to a few, that those same government institutions that failed at protecting us on 9/11 have been rewarded, not dissolved, reduced or streamlined. They have not become leaner or meaner or more capable of striking fear into the hearts of our enemies. On the contrary, they have been gifted with budgets that grow exponentially. Along with the expanding budgets, they have been delegated power to create more programs to keep us "safe" when that power is not given by our Constitution.

There are currently a total of 16 different government agencies that are looking for evil men intent on destruction. Men such as the mayhem makers in Seattle and many, many more.

Yet, Dizhwar and his group's judicious use of technology has kept the United States and its numerous security agencies blinded. Geospatial Intelligence (GEOINT), Imagery Intelligence (IMINT), Open Source Intelligence (OSINT), Signals Intelligence (SIGINT) Measurement and Signature Intelligence (MASINT) and Cyber Intelligence (CYBINT) assets are actively searching the vast amounts of content that is out there in the world.

Internet usage, filtered from volunteered data from Google, Microsoft, Facebook and other Tech Valley powerhouses, to metadata patterns pulled from mobile phone calls; is all being peered into. From software spiders trolling the net for keyword flags to multi-level diverted path transfers; the taking of private email on its way to its destination and passing it through filtering without the two parties ever knowing.

These capabilities, and so many more that we the people don't know about, are all greater abilities that 16 government agencies use to watch, track and store information on *everything*.

Without congressional oversight, satellites are in the air watching suspicious persons or places. OSINT scours open public databases like school, marriage, census and voting records without a search warrant. IMINT makes images and maps of both domestic and foreign neighborhoods from satellites, aircraft and drones without any regard to the Posse Comitatus Laws. Drones, designed for military usage, have even started flying over American cities and border areas. All of this creeping erosion of liberty; an ever expanding effort to search the crowded mass of three hundred and fourteen million free citizens.

All for just a few rotten ones.

"If you give up your liberty for your safety, you will end up with neither." Benjamin Franklin knew this over two hundred years ago and so does Ashan with murderous intent. Ashan constantly shifted their usages, methods and devices. They kept their liberty because they valued it and that ensured their own security. This was instrumental in keeping their entire twelve member team and the all important mission out of the American intelligence searchlights.

In the instance of the high-jacking of the *Wenatchee*, the NSA, America's largest spy agency, is blind. That's because, unlike their fellow American citizens, all of the terrorists practiced physical, digital and operational security. Any sliver of those metadata patterns could have been tip-offs to the 16 alphabet agencies that hunted them. So these men simply kept no pattern. The terrorist cell used public terminals or bought used laptops from the pawn shops or hole in the wall PC retailers. They would use the personal computers, whether desktop or laptop, for only a few months, remove the hard drives and toss the machines. Tuning around and buying themselves another used one due to MAC address tracking.

Mobile phone use, by these 'Servants of the Most High', was kept to a minimum. If they had to make a call, then these men made calls only with pay as you go phones (PAYG). Only a few of the team made calls regularly and they would do so from different locations with one phone, tossing it and picking up another PAYG phone. Never establishing a pattern, just like with their laptops.

The "intelligence agents" in Washington State and back at Ashan's headquarters simply didn't generate the useable data that could be linked to anyone or anything specific. These agents stayed away from web sites and activities that had anything to due with the big Silicon Valley tech companies. They used encrypted software on their machines, spoofed Mac addresses when they couldn't change devices and they paid for web portals that hid or masked their searches.

The cell relied on the solid security of moving data through overnight shipping, not the World Wide Web. The Washington cell and Ashan took their security seriously and did a good job of keeping it their business. Analysts at the various agencies poured over all of the alphabet groups intelligence, but could not gain digital clues, link analysis, or anything solid to this specific group of actors. No sleep patterns data, no religion based communications or locations nor any social position data.

Despite all of the government's hard work, despite all of the freedom and liberties that had been given up, there were still no threads. Not a single strand lead back to the spiders in North Bend or their puppet masters in Ashan.

Dizhwar, his team, and the Shura Council at Ashan were confidant that they had snuck past the various intelligence agencies searchlights.

What they didn't know was the extent of their success.

Ashan's wolves knew too well about the rampant political correctness in American society. They knew that the average citizen was no longer engaged in the political process. They knew about Washington D.C. and its group-think. They had watched the news and saw a total lack of enforced borders. The cumulative effect of these things made the terrorist's tasks all that much easier. So, the capture of the M/V *Wenatchee* went off with total surprise. No resistance came from the sheep dogs at the local, state or federal law enforcement agencies.

There was no alphabet bureau warning, with a smoking gun in hand.

Thousand year old warfare, typical Sun Tzu strategy. Ashan was extremely subtle, even to the point of formlessness. They were extremely mysterious, even to the point of soundlessness.

Thereby, Ashan was to be the director of *their opponent's* fate.

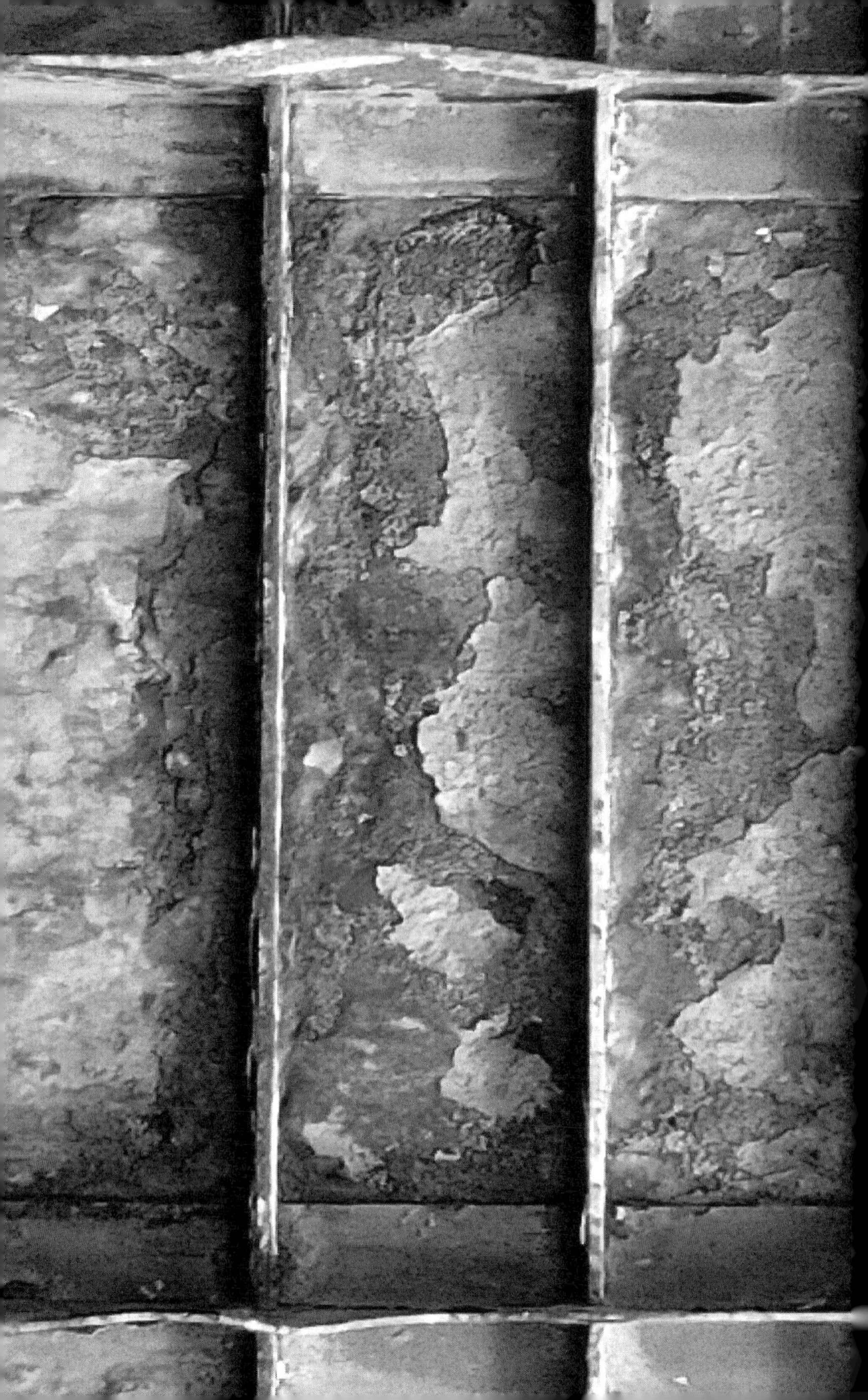

Chapter Twenty Eight

Thursday August 30th 21:30

Now, for Dizhwar, something has changed. His joy and excitement is quickly fading. He is pulled out of his good mood, half an hour or so into the ferries much slower trip across the Sound. The terrorist leader feels a premonition pass lightly over his conscience. Within the pilot house, Dizhwar pauses to meditate for a moment, trying to let the ghostly thought provide more information, but nothing further comes. Dizhwar goes over all of the gauges and asks aloud in Arabic, "Driver, does everything look ok to you?"

It takes his trusted right-hand man less than a minute of looking at the gauges before responding back in Arabic, "Yes, everything looks in order, why?"

Dizhwar explains his concern and Driver listens but does not offer any comment. Dizhwar waits a bit longer for the premonition to grant him anything more, but when nothing comes he answers Driver with a laconic, "It's nothing, keep watching the crew." *Silence, without distraction is what you might need,* he wonders, so Dizhwar exits the pilothouse.

Dizhwar puzzles over his concern. *My team has a good plan; we worked through it during numerous times at the North Bend mock-ups. In those training sessions, everything was asked. Flaws that were discovered in the plan were immediately corrected.* Dizhwar tried to build trust and unity within his team of twelve. They were all trained, devout, well equipped, and motivated for the goal. *So why am I feeling like this?*

They all new each other's strengths and weaknesses and in the eighteen months since becoming a team, had developed a strong camaraderie. *Then why my apprehension? Why the premonition?* Dizhwar asks himself again.

"Slow the ship down, Driver," Dizhwar shouts through the open door. "As slow as possible, but remember we need to maintain steerage." Driver does as he is told, slowing the speed of the ferry to just a few knots. Dizhwar asks of this in order to give the men in the engine room time to set up *and to give me time to work this out.* The pair in the engine room, at the bottom of the ship, need as much calm as possible to finish their task *and I need to figure out why the shadow passed over my thoughts.*

Dizhwar hopes that the ship's slowing will look to everyone on the outside that the ferry is running a little late; from the state agency that monitors the ships, to any emergency radar operator. Furthermore, it gives the terrorist leader more time to think about *why I have this feeling.*

Something is off, he tells himself. He goes through a mental checklist, comparing his watch to the itinerary for the night and then it hits him, "The underwater charges!" he almost shouts it out, *thankfully I'm still thinking in Arabic.*

"Is something wrong with the charges?" Driver asks back in Arabic from inside the pilothouse, hearing his boss's declaration.

Dizhwar leans in through the open door, "Yes. The Cruise liner and rescue boats. They should have gone off by now." Realizing this, Dizhwar calls Abdul and asks him to shut of the jammers temporarily. Dizhwar shuts off the jammer just outside the pilothouse he is in and waits to hear back from Abdul.

Dizhwar's radio chirps. Dizhwar looks and sees it's Abdul. "Go, for Dizhwar." The leader says quickly, as he begins dialing the first number for the first cellular-detonated explosive.

"It's off, Dizhwar."

Dizhwar calls the explosive's mobile phone numbers, to see if the cell antennas are still active. *I will try to blow them remotely,* he tells himself. He calls the numbers one after another while looking off into the distance, waiting for the telltale sounds of explosions. Nothing! Dizhwar quickly makes encrypted radio calls to every one of his men. Just a few seconds a piece. First just to check on all of them and then to ask questions of his divers. He keeps coming up with one of his team missing, Abia.

Dizhwar thumbs the page button on the radio, just after setting the dial for Jibril's channel. In addition to being encrypted, all of the team's radios have an individual designator assigned to them. Whenever anyone transmits they have the ability to transmit to an individual, to a group, or to the entire team, but regardless, the radio always transmitted its designator code to the receiving unit(s).

"Go… ahead… for… Jibril!" a bit of shouting over the almost idling engines.

"Jibril, the charges, last night haven't gone off. You sure you set them correctly?"
A pause. Dizhwar is sure Jibril is conferring with Parvez.

"Yes. Attached… and… set." Verifying that the charges were placed correctly by Jibril and Parvez, Dizhwar once again checks on Abia.

He clicks Abia's channel once and then twice, with no response. "Abia! Do you copy?"

Abia is one of the two patrol guards. She is also one of the trained Zodiac drivers and the only backup explosives team member for the men in the engine room. From the beginning, she was always a bit antisocial yet remained deftly competent. *She might have even had a problem with not leading the mission herself,* Dizhwar felt, *but...she never refused to answer her radio.*

Yet, no matter how many times Dizhwar tries, he can't get a response. If Abia has run across someone they have missed in the primary sweep, there could be a fight going on right now. She could be in danger or even be dead. Dizhwar has been instructed by his backers, Ashan, not to needlessly sacrifice any of his men. Regardless of his militancy Dizhwar is not careless or reckless with his people. They are all supposed to exit this mission together. They are all to escape and fight other battles. There is to be no self-sacrifices, no martyrdom, no hundred virgins in paradise. Allah, His Name be Praised, has other plans in store for every one of his team members.

So, convincing himself the woman is just lost, and not wanting to alarm the others, Dizhwar radio's to Khoury.

Khoury Dhakâ is on patrol duty. Young and inexperienced, he barely made it onto the team, the job of patrolling fell to him. "Go ahead for Khoury," he offers the official greeting as his radio comes to life.

It's his commanding officer, Dizhwar. "Where are you?"

Khoury responds in his best official voice. "Upper deck, patrolling." Khoury tries to come across with authority.

"Have you seen Abia?" Khoury's radio questions.

"Negative, Dizhwar."

"When was the last time you saw her?"
Rattled a bit by the inquiry Khoury pauses a moment, "We... finished our search of the cars, headed to the passenger deck to check in with Jibril. Afterwards, we split off. I think she was heading to the lower car deck."

"Head down there and see what she's doing. Abia is not answering her radio."

"Certainly. I am breaking away from perimeter patrol. I will find Abia," the young man finishes, then gives clicks off.

Dizhwar shakes his head at the thought of Khoury. Driver, seeing this just raises his eyebrows.

"I know what your thinking, Driver." Dizhwar comments, seeing the man's expressions.

Still concerned for Abia, "I just hope Khoury remembers what to do. That he finds Abia and both of them resume patrolling."

Driver nods, keeping quiet at first, but then changes his mind and decides to say something. "That Serbian has been through more than you or I ever have. Bad parents, country and luck, but his attitude is still honest despite his life. He is always willing to do whatever we ask of him. He will remember what he's learned. Give him a chance to succeed like you have done once already."

Dizhwar half-raised a hand in surrender to Driver's points, "I will." He focused his mind on things of greater concern. Dizhwar steps out of the pilot house to glance back at the still receding Seattle shoreline before he calls Jibril and Parvez again. He asks if they could step out of the engine room for a minute this time. After Dizhwar gets a call from the pair in a quieter environment, he asks "What could have gone wrong with the charges?"

"Not sure, boss," Parvez is the first to answer. "Both of us are sure that the charges are armed." Parvez should know. He was an avid diver growing up in Hawaii when his parents emigrated there from Pakistan. Just four years ago he ended up finding a job with an underwater construction/mining outfit out of Seattle. He is one of the two demolition experts on the mission.

"Maybe the timers are off?" Dizhwar could clearly see the firehouse and the cruise liner terminals and neither looked like they were under any distress.

"Possibly, Dizhwar. When I left my charge I had a green light and the timer was counting down." Jibril replies.

Parvez radios in the moment Jibril's has ended. "I am sure my timers were functional as well. It's possible they got water in them. We had problems in manufacturing the first few sets. Still though, cell call should have blown 'em."

"I just tried that, they didn't blow."

"They must have gotten water logged. There's no other reason. Backup switches should blow the charges in a bit," Jibril adds.

The backup switches were two spring loaded contacts held apart by a piece of twisted paper. It was primitive, but it worked. In the case of the electrical timers malfunctioning due to moisture, the backup switches would take over. The paper would absorb the water, its tensile strength would weaken and eventually break. The timer contacts would snap together, and short out; igniting the charges.

"They better…" Dizhwar responds to the pair and terminates his transmission. *What about the bomb threat?* He had called that in himself. *What happened with that? Shouldn't Seattle police department have responded to the cruise liner by now?* Dizhwar runs through more of his questions. *Where were the emergency cars multicolored lights? Just parked out of sight? What about the Ballard lock charges? Did they blow?*

As if some omnipotent being had heard his questions; There! Right then and there was a distinctive noise coming to him from across the bay.

"Binoculars!" Dizhwar shouts to Driver. Driver obeys, and takes out a low-light pair from his bag and tosses them to Dizhwar. Dizhwar hurriedly braces his elbows on the railing and glances first at the fireboat terminal and then scans the cruise liner.

Neither one looks like it's damaged, Dizhwar observes, *but there's lots of activity around the cruise liner.* He can see people starting to gather at the ocean side railing of the waterfront walkway. *Gawkers looking at what though?* The cell leader wonders. Some were pointing toward the cruise ship, other's were looking down the coastline toward the municipal docks. *Well, it was possible that the cruise ship charge went off, but what about the other three?*

Dizhwar waits at the ship railing, glancing back and forth from the fireboat to the cruise ship. Yes, there seems to be activity at both, but the fireboats and the Harbor Patrol craft look like they are being made ready for departure. The cruise ship is beginning to list to starboard.

Another pair of sounds comes drifting in across the bay.

A deep Voouum!

Dizhwar looks back and forth reflexively to the two ship terminals and sees that the smaller of the two fireboats has disappeared in a white spray. The second, larger fireboat is underway. The Harbor Patrol craft is tilting stern heavy into the water. *Three explosions have occurred, not four,* Dizhwar confirms.

"That wasn't supposed to happen," Dizhwar says aloud, grinning. The charges for the two fireboats must have gotten swapped in the blacked out dive conditions. The charges weren't built to sink either of the boats *if they were put on the correct ones.* The explosives were there to just knock them out of service.

Well, Dizhwar tells himself, *it didn't go exactly to plan, but, if those noises are the explosions and the large fireboat heads to respond to the cruise liner, then the goal is achieved.*

Blessings to Allah.

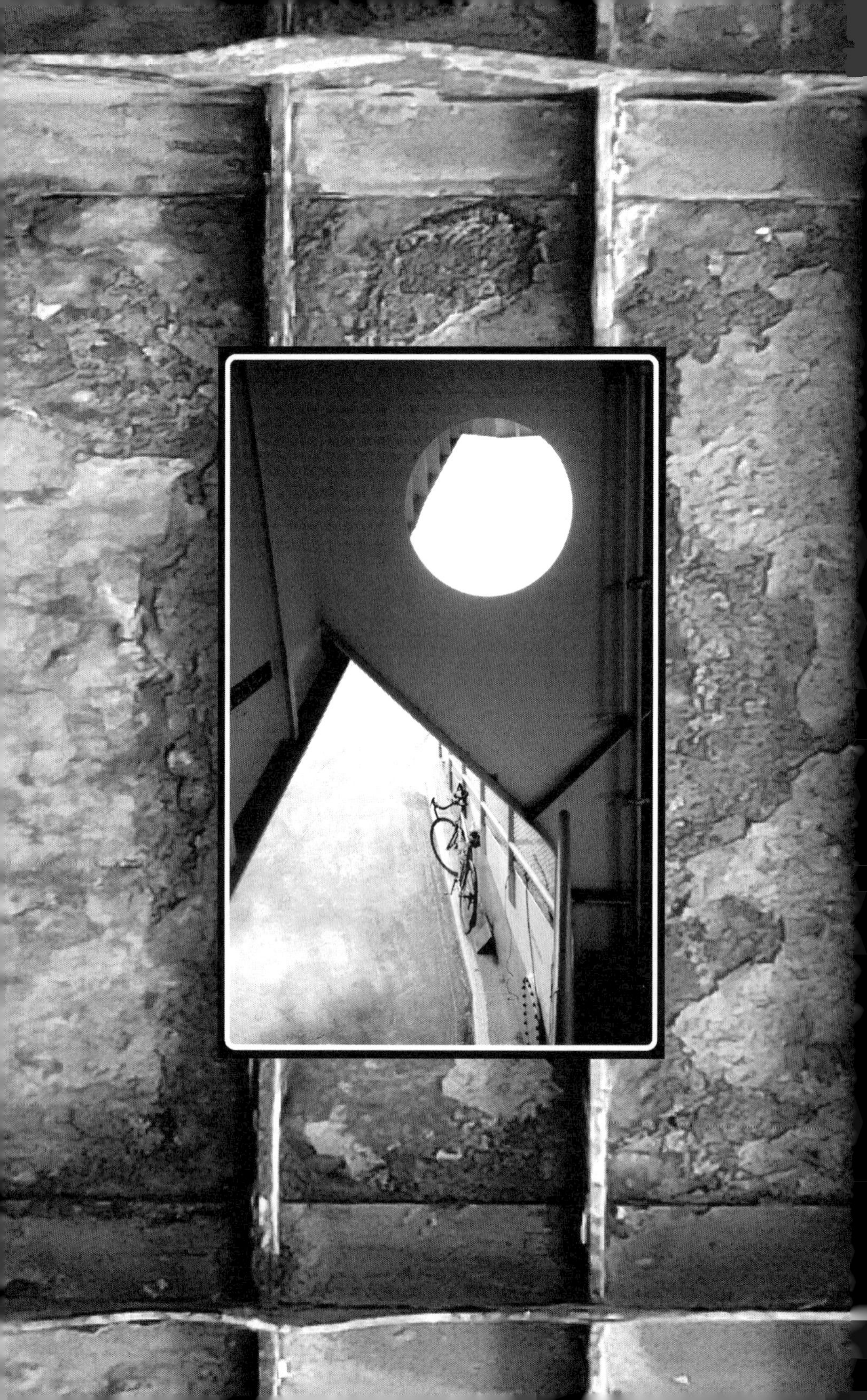

Chapter Twenty Nine

Thursday August 30th 21:35

After getting off of the radio with Dizhwar, Khoury Dhakâ offers up an uplifting dua to Allah. Once again, Allah has bestowed a shining opportunity upon him.

I now have the chance to demonstrate my dedication to the mission, the team, and The Faith. Khoury's thoughts are filled with pride at this and proceeds from his location on the outside viewing deck. He walks past the Zodiac davits and their busted open locks.

Seattle is Khoury's escape from his parents, as much as San Francisco had been a place of political asylum for him and his family from Serbia. Khoury is reminded of the similarities between 'Frisco and Seattle as he looks over the water back to the city. As he walks the exterior railings down to find Abia he thinks back. Since coming up from 'Frisco for the mission, Khoury has grown a particular fondness for both cities. *As they are both next to the water,* he confirms. *I had never even seen the ocean before flying over the Atlantic with my family as war* refugees.

Since he and his parents moved to San Francisco, Khoury had wandered about San Fran' looking for the right place to fit in. Weeks of searching rewarded him with a small tea shop. *There were people speaking my language, studying my faith openly and smiling.* Khoury remembered the scene all too well.

Khoury was caught up in the memory as he pushes through the exterior door into the heart of the ship. Back in San Francisco, he could remember when school was let out for the day. *Instead of heading home, I would go to the tea shop to study, listen and learn.*

Home was becoming a place for him to sneak into, grab whatever food he could and lock himself inside his bedroom. His parents weren't adjusting to America well. They would barely leave their condo for anything other than work, mosque or the grocery store. His parents just didn't seem to fit in and were not trying to. *Mother and father would stay at home; mother crocheting and father doing cross-words cocooned in their condo. Frustrations with their lives were just bottled up instead of being taken out on each other.* That was in stark contrast to the men at the tea shop. The people there were talking about Allah, their faith and government with such passion that Khoury was drawn to his own beliefs with a greater passion.

There, in that tea room, he was introduced to a grey-bearded man. Just a few months after Khoury had graduated high school; he was taking openly with Grey Hair about serving the faith in a greater capacity.

"I want to do something substantial with my life other than escaping parents and just going off to college." Khoury explained to Grey Hair as the man sat across the table from him listening intently.

Khoury had seen Grey Hair a few times at the tea room and was drawn by the man's serenity. Khoury saw the way some of the other aged men behaved around Grey Hair and he likewise felt the same kind of reverence. That was why Khoury decided to approach the older man.

They had a few conversations, Khoury holding onto every word that Grey Hair had said. At his very last game of chess with Grey Hair the man spoke up half-way through the game. "I think there is a way for you to serve."

Khoury couldn't believe his ears! "Really," he asked joyously. Khoury jotted down the information Grey Hair had given him. After loosing the chess game to Grey Hair, Khoury went home and packed up. The next day the young man got on the first Amtrak train to Seattle.

When Dizhwar and he had first met, Khoury knew from the look Dizhwar gave him, that he was not going to be invited in. He was not broken by it, just accepted it as another hurdle he had to overcome. He was fully prepared to travel back to 'Frisco, but was also going to give his best effort. He would try everything within himself to impress Dizhwar and the other men. Once he had given his best effort, then and only then would he travel back home.

Khoury walks into the passenger deck and then makes his way past the tied up hostages. Unfazed by their predicament, he gives a nod to the big Tarriq and the man smiles back. Khoury felt comfortable with most of his associates, but is close with Tarriq and Raphael. Khoury comes up to Raphael, who is sitting on a bench with his rifle across his lap.

Raphael sits up straighter as Khoury gets close. "What are you doing?" Raphael asks with genuine interest.

Khoury stops to talk, "I'm headed downstairs for a few minutes."

Faaiq chimes in from behind the both of them, "Thought you were supposed to be outside patrolling? Did you make a mistake?"

"Uh, I'm doing something for Dizhwar," Khoury replies as he turns to address Faaiq. "I've been ordered down to the car deck…" Faaiq comes to stand in front of Khoury, and as Khoury tries to pass by both of the men, Faaiq blocks his way.

Faaiq reaches out and grabs Khoury's arm. Grinning deviously as he asks, "Downstairs was for Abia…do me a favor and find out if Abia will be stopping by to patrol up here. See if she will leave us be, by keeping her dour self away from all of us? I would like to be elsewhere if she decides to appear!"

"Faaiq! Get back to your post!" the big voice of Tarriq booms within the passenger area.

Faaiq winces slightly at the command, but lets go of Khoury's arm and starts walking backwards in order to still look at Khoury. "Remember what I asked Khoury!" Faaiq points his finger at him and then turns back around to look where he is walking.

Raphael nods toward Tarriq and gets up off of the bench. Tarriq smiles back to Raphael, and as he stands, "Don't pay Faaiq any mind Khoury. He's just being his usual self…a blowhard," Raphael says it loud enough for only Khoury to hear. Khoury smiles neverously at Raphael's putdown of Faaiq, but understands what Raphael means and decides to ignore Faaiq's comments.

"I've got to hit the head!" Raphael shouts out to his other three conspirators on the passenger deck level. "Come on," leaning in to Khoury, "I will walk with you until the stairs."

Khoury and Raphael talk a bit about how things are going and how Khoury is not feeling particularly confidant. They talk about looking forward to their escape out of country and how they both are eager to travel.

"Don't let Faaiq get under your skin." Raphael finishes, reacting to the concern still written on Khoury's face. "You're doing good and all of us see your hard work, above all Dizhwar." Khoury nods his head in thanks and parts ways with Raphael at the stairs.

Khoury remembers back to exactly what Dizhwar's reservations had been. *I had been seen as too young, too inexperienced and with no vital talent. My youth was to be my undoing and I was forever trying to overcome that when it came to Dizhwar.* Khoury takes the first set of stairs two at a time. He circles the stairway taking the second flight down. *This was despite Grey Hair's recommendation...*

....But most of the entire team had taken to me, Khoury smiled at the situation. In the few days of testing and initial training they took him in and treated him with a sense of camaraderie that he rarely felt. Khoury also made quick friends with Driver, not knowing at first, that the man was second in charge. From his days playing in the volatile streets of Serbia to coming home into the middle of a remote relationship between his parents, Khoury stayed optimistic.

I knew it was my attitude that made it easy for the team to like me and I certainly did my best to keep up the effort. Khoury remembered hearing, after getting the surprise of being hired, that the majority of the members let Driver know that he should be accepted in. *All except Faaiq, Parvez and Jibril,* Khoury recalled. *Yet I also had it on good word that it was Driver and Tarriq that had convinced Dizhwar to let me stay.*

Smiling, Khoury finishes going down the second set of stairs and heads for the large fire door that opens to the car deck. Intent on finding the irrepressible Abia. Khoury is eager to do something for their team leader, for the team, and especially for Driver. *I just wished it was something more important than going to find her.*

Yet, Dizhwar and Driver had given me the chance to come on this mission, and for that, I am thankful. I showed them all my absolute best during the months of class work and the field training. I never let them down. There, up in the Cascade Mountains, I proved it to most of them.

Khoury has one last thought before opening the metal fire door, *The Cascades...just like the Dinarides where my childhood town was nestled in...*

He takes a deep breath and straightens his shoulders. Khoury Dhakâ steels his will and convinces himself that he is the *man* capable of the mission.

Chapter Thirty

Thursday August 30th 21:35

Is this a hijacking? If it is, can't I just wait here and let it go down? Why is it my responsibility? I could just grab a life raft 'cause I know where they are... and be gone. If it's not an attack then why bother?

Enough waiting!

Different parts of himself are arguing. James holds his head in his hands. *Do I even get involved?* The frustration within him and his own hesitation overcomes his reluctance to act. James decides. Having all kinds of things in his van, he grabs a big piece of tape off a roll of duct tape and places it over the mouth of his captive. Her eyes expand in alarm at the treatment and James just shrugs a response.

With the industrial grade tape nice and secure, he sits back down. The woman is furiously shifting from side to side as James places the semi-automatic rifle across his lap. She continues to squirm until he points it in her direction. It is only then, she instantly stops struggling.

With his finger off the trigger he balances the not-so-light AK on his knee, still pointing at the woman's throat. Guarding his restrained and gagged prisoner, James makes a call on his mobile with his other hand.

"This is 911, please state your name and the nature of your emergency."

"This is 911 is anyone there?"

James hesitates, but gives in. "My name is James Maly of Black Diamond Washington and I believe that I am currently in the middle of a terrorist attack." He provides the female 911 operator with the rest of his personal information and tells her that he is on the 21:05 ferry en route to Bremerton.
"Sir please repeat your details to me, slowly. You say, 'you think you're in the middle of a terrorist attack?"

James carefully explains the situation as he sees it. "Look Miss, I think there are terrorists on this boat. I am assuming that they have taken complete control of it, and that, except for me, these terrorists have rounded up all of the other people, someplace else. Probably upstairs."

The 911 operator performs her due diligence. She asks again for the pertinent facts, "Your name is James Aley? What is the purpose for your travel on this ship?"

James is about to respond to her questions, with incredulity. But thinking better of it, "I am traveling on the ferry for work, the company..."

Before James can finish 911 interrupts, "Are you in any immediate danger?"

Happy she at least feigns concern, James answers, "No." She asks him to please wait while she finishes imputing the information.

Regretting to have even called, James debates about just hanging up when her computer keys stop clicking.

The 911 operator comes back on with another man, a serious one.

With all of the activity going on that evening any "new" situation that involved the Salish Sea was to be escalated immediately to her supervisor. The female 911 operator, frazzled by the massive amount of evening activity, was doing her best to enter in the necessary data from the new call. This evening, she'd barely able to stay on top of things because they were happening so fast. Her supervisor transfers the call to ask more pointed questions.

"Sir, this is 911 escalations, what is your exact location on the ferry?"

James pulls back for a minute, he didn't know there was a second level to 911. *Well, I'll be,* he says to himself in amazement. He'd heard of second and third level call centers for tech support, but second level 911? "I'm sitting in my work van, in the center of the main auto deck of the *Wenatchee*. Me and my vehicle are about a third of the way back." James replies in a plain and unemotional way.

"Can you see any of the terrorists?" The new, male operator questions.

"No," incredulousness seeping into James's tone once more, "I am in my *van*."

Not fazed, the operator asks, "How long have you known about this situation?"

James answers as specifically as possible. "Maybe, ten to fifteen minutes."

"Why didn't you call 10 minutes ago, Sir?!?" was the next question that the stern male voice asked. Then, while James searched for an answer, "How do you...uhh...James Murphy, know there are terrorists on the *Wenatchee*?"

The detailed questions just kept coming and James can't answer all of them without telling the two people on the phone that he had personally captured a woman. That he had most likely illegally detained her, and worse yet, imprisoned her. James didn't want to tell, he wanted to hold that fact, that wild card in his hand until the very last moment. He wanted to make sure that he wouldn't get in trouble for kidnapping, unlawful imprisonment or some other such thing crazy thing.

So, James didn't answer the questions.

The line is silent for a few moments. The male operator comes back on. "Sir, are you there? Can you still hear me?"

"Yes, I can hear you. I am still listening." James gets another grilling from the male 911 operator, this time even more serious. The punishments for a false report is discussed and even arrest for 'taking up vital airtime of the emergency responders'.

James reasons that he should probably just start over. Come clean and just tell the truth. After all, "...the truth will set you free," right?

"First off, for the third time it's James Maly." James spells out his name again, then proceeds, "Let me start from the beginning."

"Alright," The male operator replies. This time the operator sounds incredulous. "Get to the bottom of this as fast as possible."

James relents, deciding to say everything. James lays it all out from the moment he left his house to the present. The tone of the male operator changes slightly; there is a higher level of concern in the once serious and robotic voice. James knows he is being believed. He is being trusted, the people on the other end of the phone were going to verify, but James sensed his honesty has finally been accepted.

"James, we need you to stay in your van, you should be reasonably safe until we get an emergency responder out there to check on things. We are currently very busy at the moment, the Seattle area seems to be under attack. But I promise you we will look into this. Is that clear?

The terrorist's radio crackles an interruption before James can respond. A quick set of beeps goes off and then nothing.

Another set of beeps, like someone is being paged.

"Abia. Abia! Dizhwar to Abia, are you there?" There is a pause from the radio caller and then a firm request comes over. James stares at his captive and watches the bound woman's reaction.

The male 911 operator's voice came through James's mobile phone "Is that their radio?"

"Yes sir. I captured a radio, a mobile phone, body armor and a rifle off of my prisoner."

"Abia! Answer the radio!" The commanding voice demands.

James looks down at his prisoner, places his own mobile against his chest. "Hello Abia," taking joy in watching his prisoner's frustrated look. The radio chirps out a different set of beeps.

"Go ahead for Khoury," a youthful voice speaks, clear and concise.

"Where are you?" The firm voice, the one with authority, responds.

Khoury responds, "Upper deck, patrolling."

"Have you seen Abia?" says Authority.

"Negative, Dizhwar."

Authority, now Dizhwar demands, "When was the last time you saw her?"

"We finished our search of the cars, headed to the passenger deck to check in with Jibril. Afterwards, we split off. I think she was heading to the lower car deck."

"Head down there and see what she's doing. Abia is not answering her radio."

"Certainly. I am breaking away from perimeter patrol. I will find Abia." With Khoury's response, the radio clicks off.

At the ending of the radio transmission, James once again puts his mobile to his ear. The male, 911 operator asks if James can repeat all of the names. James dutifully repeats the names as he carefully watches the look on his prisoner, Abia's face.

James knows that something is there from watching her face. *Something else bad is still brewing on the ship.* He gets the sense that this hijacking and absence of passengers is not the only thing that's going to go on.

If he only knew more information!

He feels the need to quietly go check things out throughout the boat. It is the only way. After dealing with the new visitor the radio has just warned him about, he will start from the bottom of the ship and work his way upward. *Forget about my safety*, James reflects, *there has to be more facts, and that requires action on my part.*

The 911 operator was saying something to James, but James was too deep in thought to hear it. "Look, I've got to go." James speaks into the phone, "I'm going to be getting some company as you heard."

"What! Wait you need to stay in your van until…"

"Call you back in a bit," and James ends the call with out waiting for a response.

James hurriedly slings the terrorist's rifle over his back, grabs his own pistol, Abia's radio, and a sandwich from his lunch box. James's mobile phone rings. Unknown number. He presses the red button that silences his ringing mobile phone. The electrician switches it to vibrate and stuffs it into his new vest's pocket.

Before closing the van's sliding door quietly, James looks to the woman with a sarcastic smile, "Don't you go anywhere Abia McBeal, I'll be right back."

James wolfs down the ham and cheese sandwich as he moves, hoping the food will keep his nervousness at bay. He furiously searches for a place to wait, to hide and to possibly set up his ambush.

For lack of a better place he settles on hiding in front of a '66 ford mustang with a view of both of the stairs.

Sit and wait, sit and wait...I sure do a lot of that.

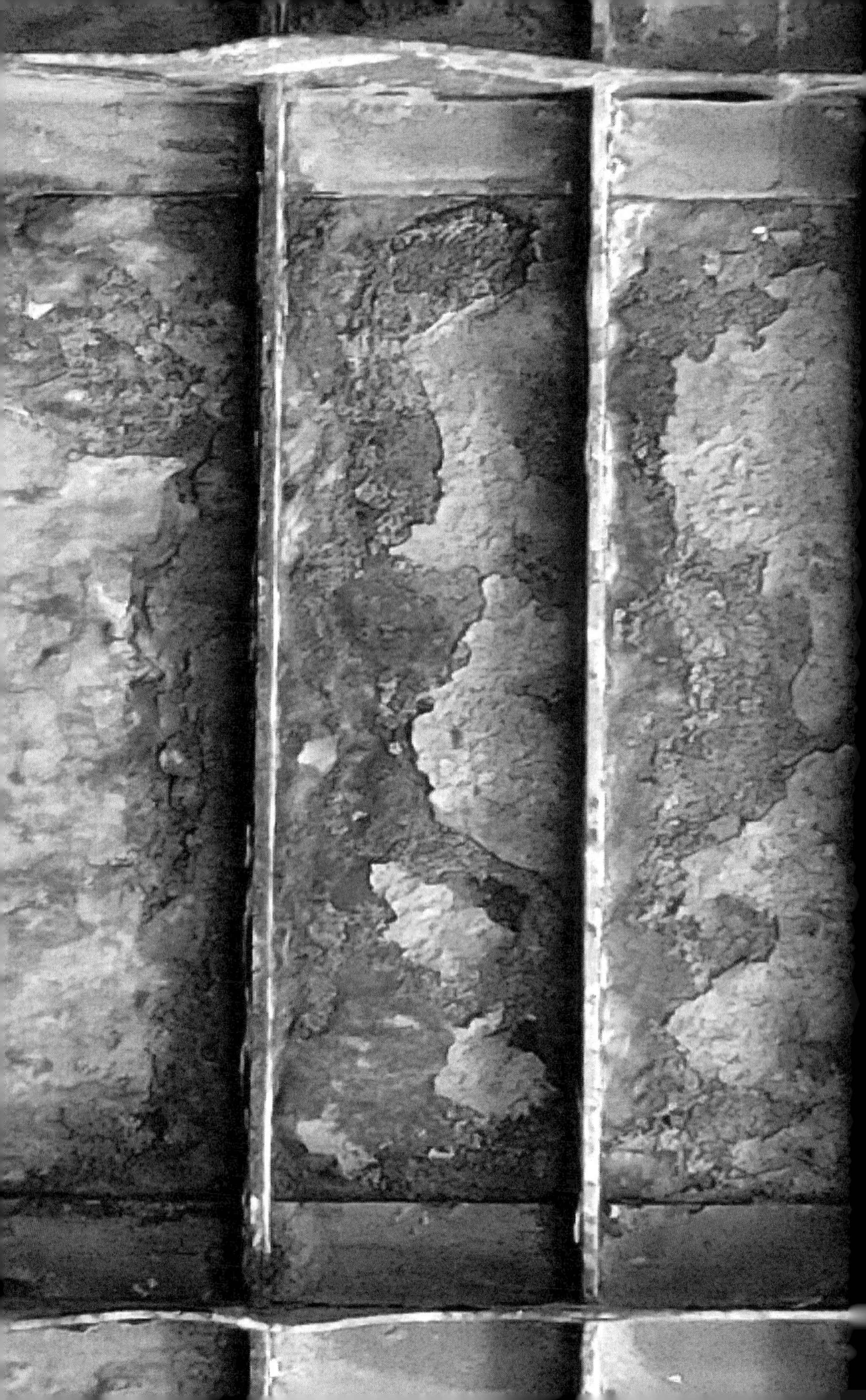

Chapter Thirty One

Thursday August 30th 21:35

What in heaven's name was I thinking? Do I even have my higher reasoning functioning? Or has it all turned to mud? Trevor Jacobs is so disappointed with himself.

I had walked right into it! He yells once more inside his skull. *I had strode right through the wisps of smoke and the damaged pilot house door with my stupid feet on autopilot.* Something inside of him screamed for him to: *Stop walking! Turn around immediately! This is all wrong!*

Yet, I kept going forward, Trevor ashamedly says. *It was like I saw the proverbial car coming and for no logical reason whatsoever I just kept walking out in front of it. What a stupid, idiotic nieve thing to do!!*

It was unexplainable to have not listened to the warning and to have marched right into the thick of the terrorists. *While they were making the pilot house crew go to their knees no less,* Trevor declared to his thoughtless brain. Trevor had been so focused, so single minded on getting the message to the Captain: *There are people with guns on board! I had spotted them opening their trunk.*

No one had seemed to hear his radio transmissions, so he ran up to the top to deliver the message in person. The big terrorist in the pilot house had turned around at the sound of Trevor's feet, with his eyes wide in surprise at seeing the Ship's Loadmaster. Then the gunman patiently, almost kindly, motioned with his rifle to get down next to the rest of the crew.

Trevor could have, should have, grabbed the barrel and yanked away the gun. *I should have given some sort of struggle!* Trevor hisses out his hot breath, heated by his own frustrations. It comes back into his face as fast as he has pushed it out. *I should have done something!* Instead, he obeyed the directions given to him and surrendered his freedom.

His heart was very heavy and he felt like such an idiot for not taking greater notice when he came into the room. Now, he feared, it was too late. *It's what you get when you are not paying attention*, he instructed himself while under the hood that keeps forcing his breath back into his mouth. Trevor is fermenting under the hood that covers his head and it adds to his self-defeatist attitude. *That's what happens when you are oblivious to the situation around you! You do it and you will get blindsided!!!*

With his hands restrained behind his back, and under the hot and stuffy hood, the lesson for Trevor does not escape him. The reality of getting blindsided was as real as the hood over his head. It was like he had done something terribly wrong and his punishment was to stand with his head in a corner.

No, dammit! The lesson does not escape me. Trevor confirms to himself.

The young man lowers his head, trying to lift the hood between his chest and chin. Trevor shifts the hood back and forth with his chin, but is still reduced to breathing recycled air. Trevor chokes on his own breath and he is finally successful at getting the hood up enough for fresh air.

In one moment in his short life, he is capable of loading a multimillion dollar ship with cars and people. In the next, he can't do a darn thing.

Trevor asks himself, *is this now my fight? Just struggling for a breath of fresh air?*

Trevor tries not to answer his own question, afraid of the reply.

Chapter Thirty Two

Thursday August 30th 21:40

James is on edge, listening for the sound of footsteps. He waits just a few cars away from his van, behind the old mustang. James fidgets with his rifle across his back because the sling and rifle have various latches and catches that kept poking into his side, neck and back. Not being used to slinging a rifle across his back, James does not intend to use the untested AK-74; he just doesn't want to leave the rifle with his captive. James trusts his I.M.I .45 cal Desert Eagle Pistol and his knife. He has used his Eagle extensively at the range; and his knife a lot at work. James is comfortable with these two tools, and they fit his needs perfectly on the ship.

James gets the rifle adjusted, and focuses on his position between the stairwells. Second guessing where he is currently hiding, he decides to move again. He hurries toward the center of the main auto deck. As he moves, he keeps to a crouch as much as possible. The auto deck has a stairway on either side at the front and the back. James stops in the center of the space, *probably in the very center of the ship,* he thinks. *This is a good place to wait for my visitor descending either stairs or elevator.*

James hunches down between two cars and waits. In between his breaths he strains to listen for the sounds of walking. James quickly drinks down most of the milk in his Thermos while listening. *Between the creaks of the boat, the ocean's waves, and the slight engine thrum, there might be too much noise to hear footsteps,* he worries. Purposely, he turns down Abia's radio to its lowest volume. He doesn't want the radio to give away his position.

James quickly glances over to where he hears the telltale sign of someone approaching. He holds his breath waiting to see a figure. The clatter was not footsteps, it's a false alarm, a seagull just landed hard on a nearby vehicle.

Throwing caution to the wind, James thumbs the transmit button on his recovered radio. He thumbs it just once to see if someone will speak back. James waits again, but is rewarded with nothing.

Wait! Was that an echo or the sound of footsteps? James strains again for the noise, but it keeps getting lost in all of the other sounds of the ship. *It is so hard in these ferries!* He complains to himself. *With that cavernous space in the front and rear of the ship open to the outside, the central garage area acted like a wind tunnel too.*

Well, if there was something, it's gone now? James silently asks himself. He nervously peaks around cars. As he looks first to his front, over the cars, then to his sides, and lastly to his back. James tracks his vision with his pistol. Still no Khoury.

James finds it odd, that just a few minutes ago he was filled with subtle terror. When he exited the van he had faced it, and now, with the terror abating, he is starting to get anxious. *Will he meet this Khoury character? Or will Khoury find him first?* James is acutely aware that Khoury is coming down, but James wonders, *what type of man is he?*

Silence and the false signs of movement are taxing on his awareness. Starting to wish that it will just be over already, James squats back down behind a car. He abandons his Thermos and starts to nervously play with his folding knife. Knife in his left hand, quickly opening and closing it, watching the steel blade flash in and out of the handle. He looks all around his surroundings, unconsciously now opening and closing the Spyderco blade. His right hand holding his pistol, waiting and waiting.

Jumping at the thud of a door closing high up in the ship, James searches from where it came from. *Behind? In front? From where?* The questions come fast to James.

Left! Feet on stairs getting... closer! James swiftly moves over to the left lower stairway door and looks to see which way the door will open. *Inward,* James confirms as he makes a last minute decision to holster his pistol with the hammer cocked, just in case he needs to make a fast draw. James decides to use his knife.

James the Electrician stands just to the right side of the door. Taking deep breaths, he tries to hold each one and let it out slowly. James waits just a minute and the footsteps come closer. The heavy ship door swings inward. The moment that James sees the feet pass through the threshold, he comes around the corner as fast as he can.

The terror once again flows through James's veins and he catches this new person totally off guard. Just like Abia, this young man is carrying a rifle too. Because the man is armed, James continues his forward momentum. He has no problem in pushing the barrel of the rifle up and away as James brings his right hand around to place the knife against the presumed terrorist's neck.

Khoury remembers all of his training. The youngest member of the hijackers is walking down the stairs, finger off of the trigger, carefully paying attention to his surroundings. He is keenly aware of his muzzle control. Khoury is sure that Abia is down here, somewhere. He feels that this is all just a game to her, and Khoury will once again have to be the subject of her humiliation.

Derision always came from her or Faaiq, never anyone else. Khoury assumes that Abia is trying to catch him off guard or worse yet, catch him not performing his duties correctly. She is always short-tempered with him. Pushing and shoving physically and verbally. *Maybe even Dizhwar knows about it and is part of the test?* Khoury is thinking all of this, when he steps through the door.

James's intention is to hold the knife at the throat of this new threat, get the young man to drop the rifle, like the woman, and capture another. He needs another captive, hopefully, one that will talk. *But the naive young man doesn't stop walking! The gunman didn't even see me*, James realizes too late. The gunman's attention is toward James's right, as the guy exits the door. James's knife is already too close and his blade hasn't had the time to turn flat; so the tip pierces. From the swing of James's hand and the forward movement of the terrorist, the sharp SpyderCo goes handle deep into the throat.

Both of the men stare at each other in disbelief at what's just happened. James's eyes are filled with the scene and his heart fills with instant regret. Khoury on the other hand can't grasp that his short life is now over. A vital artery has been opened and the knife only slows the flow. The young man drops the rifle that he had been carrying correctly.

The gunman grabs at the arm that is holding the knife. In his last show of strength, he does it with both of his hands. Khoury's grip tightens on the arm that holds the knife. Time is frozen as they both gaze into each others face. At first, just an uncomfortable silence falls over the pair, and then the young man tries to talk, but nothing comes out of his mouth except blood.

His hands are not fully responding to his intent. Khoury tries to speak again, and starts to feel lightheaded. As he sinks to his knees, the right hand that is holding the knife is covered in his frothy red blood and his own double handed grip. Khoury looks to his attacker's left hand as it still holds the barrel of his rifle. He lets the sling slide off of his shoulder as his attacker sinks to his own bended knees in front of him.

James watches Khoury starts to shake from the loss of blood. The color drains from the young terrorist's face. They both kneel in front of the other, each of their minds are filled with questions. The young man tries to speak one more time, but can't from the flow of blood into his throat. The words come out as red frothy bubbles. James watches wordlessly as the blood soaks into the front of Khoury's shirt.

James slowly withdraws his knife. He quietly whispers, "Hush," as the young man tries to speak again.

Amid his victim's blood bubbles, James lays a hand on the young man's shoulder. James tries to calm the gunman, it's all James can do. Khoury starts to slowly lean forward, the life ebbing out of him. James supports him by wrapping an arm around his shoulder and lets him gracefully fall face first to the deck.

Khoury Dhakâ, formally know as Rick Duqyakha, son of Marcia and Stanislav Duqyakha of San Francisco, California tries his best to grasp what is happening.

The last conscious thought that passes through the young man's blood deprived brain is just as much a statement as it is a plea. *...I'm certain that all of this is a mistake...*

WARNING

OPEN FLAMES OR SMOKING PROHIBITED ON CAR DECK OR IN VEHICLES

STOP

YOUR MOTOR
SET HAND BRAKES
DO NOT RELEASE BRAKES
UNTIL FERRY DOCKS
DO NOT START MOTOR
UNTIL DIRECTED BY CREW

M.V.
N

Chapter Thirty Three

Thursday August 30th 21:50

The woman shoots her driver spiteful glances from around her shoulder. *You convinced me to get on this stupid boat and now what are you going to do about it? Not talking so much now huh? Why don't you get up of your oversize butt and take these four on if you think you are such a great guy? Little use are you now when you've gotten a bit of an infection; of cowardice!*

Terra Freeland watches the man like an eagle swimming over salmon. She scrutinizes Brad as he keeps up his humble act and how he never looks up from his downcast posture. *What exactly was he looking at? His shoes? He's worthless! This entire week is such a cluster!!*

Her driver sits behind Terra by a few rows, and on opposite ends of the passenger deck benches.

They had become separated during the high-jacking. Terra was the first one of the two to confirm that they were in danger. She had felt guilty for leaving him alone in the car, so in a rare bit of compassion, she grabbed both of them coffee. She was headed back downstairs to give Brad his when she had seen some men pull out firearms from a trunk and then, *(what prepare them for use?)* Terra questioned. She had just got back to her car when everything seemed to enter the rabbit hole.

Men started shouting and passengers started screaming. There was a few sporadic gunshots. She didn't know how to use guns or what the guys were doing with them, but she had to do something. She pulled out her mobile and tried to dial 911 but her cell phone had no signal.

Interrupting her grand plan, "Are you seeing what I'm seeing?" Brad had sunk down low in his seat as he asked his passenger for confirmation of what he was baring witness to.

"Yes you dope!" Terra followed her driver's example and hid behind the drivers seat. She sat with her knees on the floorboard, peeking around the seat as the men with guns started shouting. "My phone has no signal! Do you have yours?"

"What..." her driver asked, lost in the moment.

"Your cell phone! Do you have it?!?" She asked forcefully.

"Yeah ugh," the man patted his black blazer looking for his phone. "Here it is!" The driver of her car pulled it out of his inside breast pocket and then looked over to Terra with surprise.

"What is it," she whispered. The terrorists were pulling people out of their cars now. At gunpoint they were forcing people into a group and they were working their way toward her car.

"Sorry, Ms. Freeland. My phone doesn't have any signal either. But don't worry I have a gun." Before she could respond her back door was flung open and she was pulled out by her long hair, screaming.

She screamed from the pain and in shock of the moment. Brad shouted something and then her driver crawled over the center console and out the front passenger door. He brandished a small pistol while running down the car ramp toward the back of the boat.

Almost like he was going to jump off the ship, Terra thought as she caught a glimpse of him while being yanked out of the car. Then she was on her knees, frisked, pockets emptied into a backpack and then gathered up with other passengers.

She was held at gunpoint at first by one man and then another joined him. A moment later a woman carrying a big rifle pushed Brad and two others toward the growing crowd. Terra's driver, Brad, had a big knot on his head that was just beginning to turn a darker tone and Terra suddenly had no pity for him. *Not an ounce...*

She shouted her thought, *You were running down the deck, you stupid fat man! You were just feet from freedom and you blew it!* Terra had hoped that Brad was going to make it, but now, she didn't care too much at all.

Just a few minutes later they were taken up, as a group, to the passenger deck's observation area.

They were told to get on their knees and place their hands behind their backs. Quickly and efficiently one of the gunman came along and placed plastic, zip tie handcuffs on everyone of them. They were then lifted into seats and had another tie run through their cuffs and the chair.

Terra sat and fumed, shooting everyone her most evil stare. *I can't freakin' believe this!*

I hate Seattle! I hate the Puget Sound! I hate the state of Washington!

...And I hate this stupid ship!

Chapter Thirty Four

Thursday August 30th 21:50

Dizhwar, Driver, Abdul, and Monifa are all armed with 9mm pistols like a few others in their group. They are further armed with heavier rifles than their other teammates. Dizhwar hadn't been satisfied with the AK-74 rifle's accuracy or penetrating power. *Such an important mission,* he observed. *All of our tools must function well and must be the best suited for the job.*

Even though it has become de rigueur for his brothers and sisters in the Middle East, Dizhwar wanted to pick the best possible weapons, *not the most available.* Dizhwar eventually chose a heavy hitting rifle that was based on the AR platform. The .308cal rifle would be perfect for the distinct possibility of repelling a boarding party.

The military version is the 7.62mm rifle, which is very similar, to the civilian .308cal. The rifles were pretty easy to find and purchase. What made it especially nice was the plentiful match-grade ammunition. Dizhwar had procured four of the rifles and he gave them out to the pilot house crews specifically. If his people needed to stop or dissuade any invaders, Dizhwar knew that the heavier caliber rifles would come in handy. All of the .308s are AR-10 models. Two of which were made by Smith and Wesson and the other two by DPMS. They all carried Leupold 4x20 variable riflescopes that had flip away night vision magnifiers. All of the 'special rifles' shared magazines and ammunition.

Allah forbid, one of them was to get killed during a boarding. But if they did at least the others in the pilot house teams could use the magazines and bullets interchangeably.

Dizhwar had also made sure, that other than the heavy .308s; his entire team had either the AK derivative, firing the 5.45x39 round, or a weapon that shot the 9mm round. He would have preferred to keep it down to just two types of cartridges, but there was a need for all of them to carry pistols. If there was a gun fight in the passenger area, ammunition needed to be shared there as well. Everyone on the passenger guard team had to be capable to give to one of their brothers or sisters in need. Especially, if there was a prolonged gunfight.

Hopefully, that was not going to be the case, Dizhwar offered his *dua* to Allah. Mostly all of the team members went to the AK style rifles in training. They picked them willingly, with pleased grins. Yet, two of his team hated the rifle. Dizhwar had understood their disgust of the gun because he shared it. *So I let them offer another single sugges-*

tion, that was it. The only caveat was that any other rifle had to shoot either 9mm, the 5.45x39 used in the AK or a .308. After much debate, the two men that wanted something different came up with the Uzi.

Dizhwar blanched at the suggestion of using the Uzi. These were the submachine guns that were made famous by the Israelis and he wanted nothing to do with his enemy's weapon. His two team members pointed out that they were now being made new in the United States, they used the same 9mm ammo that the team's pistols used, and they were cheaper than the AK's. So convinced, Dizhwar relented. His team had the right tools to complete the task.

Considering his missing people, Dizhwar keys the radio for Khoury and waits. No response. He keys it again. Still, silence.

"Khoury, have you found Abia?" Dizhwar speaks into the radio. The cell leader waits a few moments more and then radios again. "Khoury! Do You Copy?" Dizhwar starts to worry. It's abnormal for Khoury not to answer back right away.

Khoury, sounding odd, finally radios back. "Nothing around." As it comes over the speaker the voice seems odd to Dizhwar. Then the radio goes silent.

Dizhwar isn't satisfied with Khoury's answer. He is just about to call Khoury back, but gets another call. Abdul. "Go ahead for Dizhwar," he sounds back, slightly perturbed by the interruption. His concerns are on his missing men.

Abdul's name comes up as the radio chirps, "We've got company!"

"What!?! Say again!" Dizhwar can't believe his ears. He is staring out the front windows along their path and does not see a thing.

"There is a Seattle City fireboat behind us, coming our way from the downtown docks." Monifa radios in the details.

Dizhwar is perplexed. The terrorist team has planned for possible craft coming to rescue the passengers, but not this soon. The problem is simple; firemen they can handle: but if there is a SWAT team or police presence on the boat, then there's going to be a situation that could go bad. Really bad. They did not need that kind of attention from law enforcement while they are still on the ship. That will make their escape incredibly hard. *If the charges have not yet disabled the fireboat, then it should be responding to the cruise liner first, right?* Dizhwar was asking more questions, *it should have been going to the aid of the possible explosives on that closer ship, not a ferry taking its time across Elliot Bay?*

Dizhwar transmits "Who is on it? Have you determined that yet?" Dizhwar no longer shouts. His concern is clear.

Dizhwar mentally goes over the hijacking. Looking over a mental list of the major points. Did someone witness them taking the ferry? Is that why this fireboat is coming toward them? There isn't much time in-between Dizhwar's questions and an answer. Dizhwar almost asks again when his radio chirps.

"Negative on police, but it's hard to tell. No one's on deck. Everyone must be in the pilot house. Both Monifa and I have looked carefully. Also there is something else."

"What?"

"Nearest as we can tell, the charge to take out the fire big fireboat has not gone off yet. Are the charges on schedule?" Monifa adds.

"Three charges have gone off.' Dizhwar radios back, all business. "Jibril and Parvez have discussed the last explosive charge with me and we are waiting for the back-up fuse as the solution."

"Let us know what you want us to do." Abdul ends his transmission with a sense of assuredness. Born and raised in a farming community outside of Boise, he started becoming radicalized after college in his search for God and answers to life.

Trusting the tone that he hears in Abdul's voice, "Damn it!" Dizhwar swears and then apologizes to his god. He makes a quick decision that he hopes will stop the fireboat from getting too close. Dizhwar realizes that the jammers are not on when he hears the hails from the fireboat over the ships communications. "Abdul and Monifa, be ready at the rear," Dizhwar orders the pair and asks Driver to do the same there in the front. Dizhwar second guesses himself and comes up with a better plan. He orders Driver to take the gag and hood off of Captain Blair as he takes one last look at the encroaching fireboat.

Dizhwar counts to ten, maintaining his calm and presses the call button for Abdul.

"Go ahead for Abdul." Abdul replies back quickly, a little tension rising in his voice.

Dizhwar orders, "Don't get jumpy. You and Monifa keep your rifles out of site and await my instructions. Be careful!"

"Ready." Monifa responds this time. Monifa Bashandi el-Shazli came to the United States, from Egypt when she was three. Her entire family, uncles, aunts, cousins and grandparents all moved to Portland. From the first day that she could remember, she had always been a follower of Islam. When she turned eighteen she joined the United States Army, served her tour and got out the year prior to joining their group. Her last post was at Joint Base Lewis McCord. She started re-attending mosque with her entire family until her life changed when she became friends with the passionate Abdul.

Dizhwar is leaning out of the fore pilothouse, just catching a glimpse of the Seattle Fireboat as it draws ever closer to their Jumbo Mark II class ferry. Concern rising, Dizhwar radios his rear pilothouse operators again, "Monifa and Abdul, act normal. Pretend to be busy doing something, anything. No matter what don't let them see your rifles! Understand?"

"Understand." Monifa responds again, in her normal and confident tone.

Dizhwar hopes that their choice of the longer range and heavier caliber rifles will work against this possible threat. Dizhwar grabs the Captain of the ferry, cuts his bonds, takes the tape off of his mouth and pulls him close enough to smell his sweat.

Dizhwar speaks flatly and plainly, "Look here, Senior Officer Blair," in a voice that belied menace. "You will be responding to the hails from the approaching vessel. You will be polite, courteous, compliant, yet firm. Do you understand?"

The Captain Michael Blair nods, as tries to rub his mouth where the tape had been just moments before. Dizhwar bats the hand away, making the Captain flinch.

Still in the Captain's face, "If you say anything out of the ordinary or attempt to divulge any information, my friend over there will kill one of your crew with a nod of my head. And then you'll be next."

Dizhwar looks over at Driver and speaks to him in their shared Arabic "Use your silenced pistol on my nod. Clear?"

Driver looks at him curiously and asks "Which one of the crew?"

"You choose." Dizhwar whispers.

Driver withdraws his 9mm Beretta 92FS from his shoulder holster and from a side leg pocket removes the Beretta's silencer. The Captain gazes with growing dismay at the site of the pistol, and now with even more revulsion, as the silencer is screwed on. Driver pulls the only female in the bridge crew out of the group, and forces her down to her knees. Driver places the muzzle of the pistol against her head.

Dizhwar, seeing the look in the Captain's eyes, "Get the fireboat to go away. Get it to go away without raising any alarm."

Captain Michael Blair, a 15 year veteran of the Puget Sound Ferry Line, hails the approaching fire boat, *The Chief Seattle*. Dizhwar dons a bright crew vest and pretends to be a crew member. Dizhwar stands besides Cpt. Blair at the helm, slowly advancing the throttles of the ship. Michael starts to explain why they couldn't use the ships communications before.

"We've had intermittent electrical power losses in the pilothouses, but the problem has been locked down by our engineer," Captain Blair carefully explains to the fire boat.

"*Wenatchee*, we are coming up alongside to provide you escort back to the ferry terminal." The Captain of the Fireboat responds. "There's been a few incidents of suspicious activity tonight."

Dizhwar's radio chirps with a call. The screen on Dizhwar's radio reads "Jibril, engine room."

"Hold on, Jibril." Then Dizhwar nods to Cpt. Michael Blair to continue.

"Not necessary. Our engineer has located the source, wires rubbed raw, occasionally shorting out controls and comms. The Wenatchee is showing her age, but the old girl is running just fine. We don't need an escort, fireboat *Chief Seattle*."

Every time the nervous captain of the ferry is at a loss for words or explanation, Dizhwar, perfectly calm, whispers a word or phrase to help the senior officer along. In preparation for the high jacking Dizhwar read the emergency rescue manual put out by the United States Coast Guard as well as the *Wenatchee*'s design blueprints. He knows the vernacular and the terms down to the smallest detail.

"*Wenatchee*, we will render you aid by an escort to the ferry docks." The fireboat seems insistent upon its way. Even though the Chief Seattle is making the demand, the *Wenatchee* is four times the size of the *Chief Seattle*. *It might just come down to size*, Dizhwar wonders.

Dizhwar is a second from nodding his head to Driver, but he holds back. The fireboat is getting too close to the ferry, soon they will certainly see into the forward passenger lounge filled with too many passengers.

"The crew and engineer were able to repair the problem and are watching the situation carefully. Your escort is unnecessary." Captain Blair transmits back. His voice becoming more forceful from seeing the look in the eyes of the two gunman.

Advancing the throttles to three quarters power, Dizhwar reaches over to his rifle. The firearm remains down to his side but he pulls and releases the charging handle on his

AR-10 while it remains out of sight from the fire boat.

Another minute goes by with a tense silence filling the pilothouse. Cpt. Michael Blair looks to the gunman that is in charge and then to the one holding the pistol to his crewman. The two gunman watch Cpt Blair as he waits, holding the little speaker of the radio in his hand.

"Very well, *Wenatchee.*" The radio crackles to life. Cpt Blair breathes a sigh of relief as the radio continues. "We have a higher priority call at the cruise ship terminal. Are you sure your status is fixed?"

The fireboat inches ever closer. Dizhwar radios his men a warning "Passenger lounge, possible fireboat approach. Disperse into seats. Look inconspicuous. Clear?" The four men each radio a confirmation.

"Our status is okay, Chief Seattle, Thank you." Captain Blair speaks, wishing he had the wits to provide the firefighters some sort of subtle clue to the *Wenatchee's* real situation. He was never one to come up with a witty retort to make people laugh. He was not a glib man or a conniving person. He can think fast on his feet when it comes to ships, but not when it comes to conversations.

"Very well, *Wenatchee. Chief Seattle* out." With that, the fireboat radio man signed off.

Within the passenger deck, one of the gunmen, shouts "If any of you try to attract attention, you will be the first one to die!" He then folds the buttstock of his AK-74 and holds it down low. Keeping it out of the fireboats line of sight.

Dizhwar makes a slight course change, turning five degrees away from the intercept with the fireboat. He hopes that the course change will be imperceptible to the fireboat, but it just might give them the a few seconds more. Still pretending to be a crew member, he advances the speed to eighty percent.

"Do you copy?" Dizhwar looks at his radio and sees that it's Jibril once more.

"Go ahead for Dizhwar," he speaks quietly, turning down the volume of his radio as he does so.

"The engines that are online, almost full power; it's making it difficult for us." Jibril queries. The sound of the engines almost drowning out his voice.

"Yes, Understand. We have a visitor. You and Parvez need to get the job done fast. Clear?"

"Understood." The men in the engine room could die from the actions that Dizhwar is taking right now. Not only could the increased vibrations set off the explosives prematurely, but the increased heat and static electricity from the engines presents great danger. Dizhwar, thinking back to his classroom training thought about the what if's that they went over. The teachers and students would talk hypothetically about various circumstances and what the students should do when faced with such things. But now, it wasn't a theoretical or philosophical construct, Dizhwar knows this is life and death for himself and his team.

"...Dizhwar..." Driver, nodding his head, "The fireboat is leaving."

That brought Dizhwar out of his thoughts and back to present. "The way is clear. Praise Allah!" Dizhwar exclaims with a feeling that this mission was just pulled out of trouble and then tones his enthusiasm back a bit.

He keys in Abdul on the radio and orders the jammer to be turned back on. Dizhwar pulls back the ship's throttles to fifty percent to give his men in the engine room the time necessary to finish.

Awaiting confirmation from Abdul or Monifa, "On your knees," Dizhwar speaks forcing Captain Blair down by the shoulder.

Capt. Michael Blair, with worry plain on his face, thinks it's his end. He is hit with the notion that the last time he kissed his wife was two days ago and the last time he said "I love you" to his two full grown sons was months ago. The fireboat turned back and his use is now over. But, instead of a silenced 9mm bullet, he is zip tied, has tape placed once again over his mouth and a hood over his head. Capt. Blair is shoved back into the huddle, with the crew, by Driver.

"Jammer's back on." Monifa speaks quickly, then clicks off.

Dizhwar works through the various aspects of his team's mission. The timing, the plan, the possibility of interference from local, state, or national law enforcement. Dizhwar continues to work out everything that's transpired and heads outside turning on the second jammer that's closest to him. The responsibility of his dozen operators weighs heavy on his shoulders.

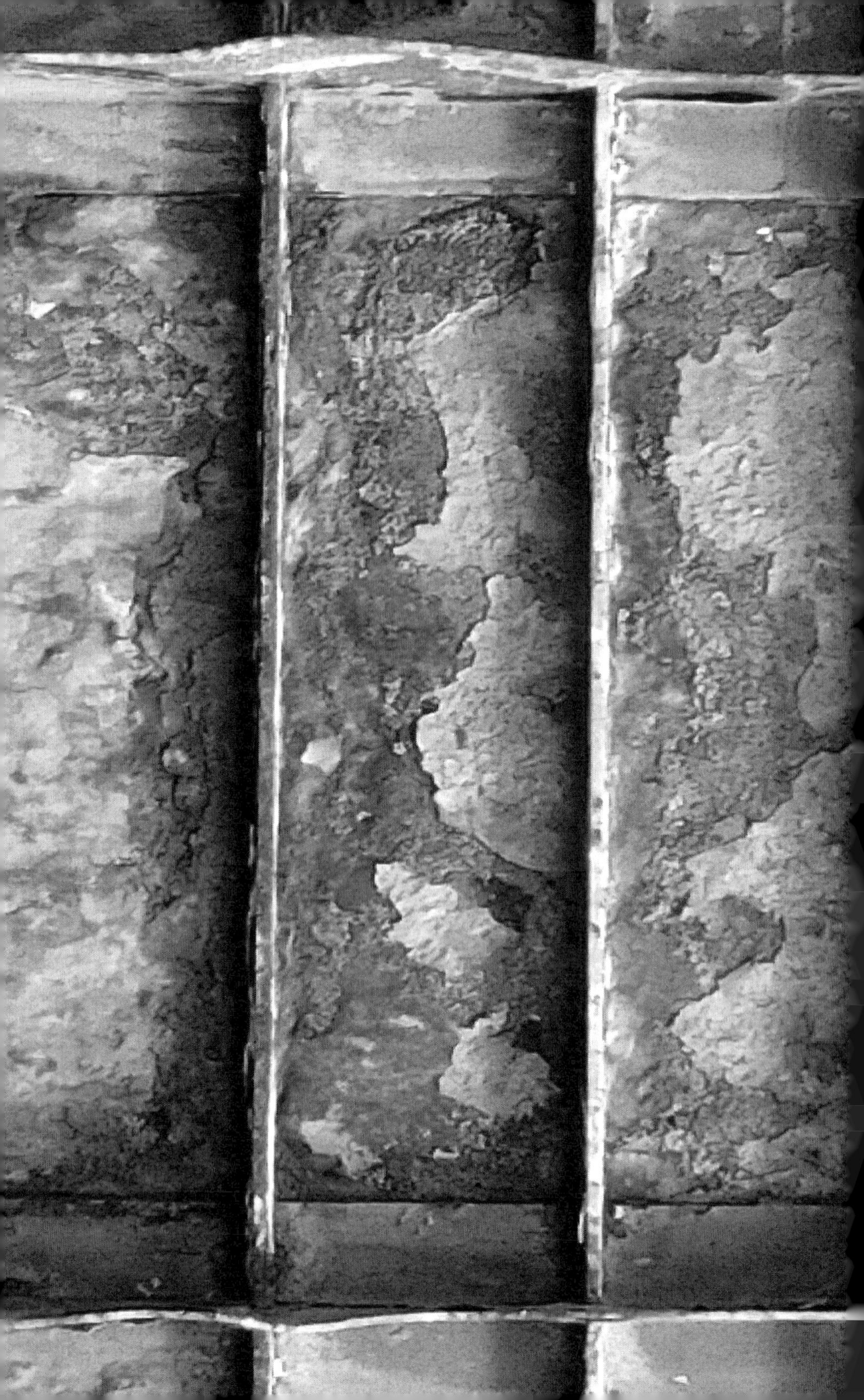

Chapter Thirty Five

Thursday August 30th 21:50

No matter what you believe about the afterlife, death is not something that one faces lightly. Regardless if it's Heaven, Hell, or even a great void that awaits you. Encountering it by himself, James is no different.

James Maly takes a few moments to work through the act he just took part of. He tries to rectify what he's done within his soul. He takes off the gunman's flannel over shirt and tears it in half. Still with a heavy heart, James wraps the neck of Khoury tightly to still the seeping blood flow. James uses the other half to mop up the pool of red at the base of the stairs.

James keeps seeing the knife slide so easily into the young man's neck. *What have I done?* James wonders.

Careful with the body, James Maly pulls the young man by the feet. James heads back to his van. *My intentions had been good. Yet I knew, implicitly, that I had every right to try and defend myself and those around me.* James curses to himself, hating his naivety. *What a quaint, almost forlorn notion I had, to capture my opponent rather than just kill him outright.*

As James drags the body, his mind is berating him. *Now your inexperience has paid you back with tremendous regret. With either act, both paths had led to this same awful conclusion.*

More than that, James begins to get concerned that at any moment, someone else will come to look for Abia or now, Khoury. James is almost to the van when his victim's bloodied radio chirps.

James ignores the radio for now, hurrying even quicker to make it to the safety of his van. His passage ends as he gets his victim right next to the E150's sliding door. The radio gives a second chirp, then a transmission comes over the radio "Khoury?"

Another pause, "Khoury are you there?" "Khoury did you find Abia?" James looks at the radio. Not knowing what to do, James racks his brain to come up with a response. He keeps seeing the blood bubbles and finds it hard to put together a thought.

"Khoury, respond!" again the transmission from that same commander's voice.

James asks himself, *was the commander's name Dizhwar?*

At a loss for words, James nervously keys the transmit button. He is momentary speechless for what to say, but stumbles out, "Nothing around." Then second guessing himself, he kills the transmission. Immediately regretting saying anything at all.

James searches the pockets of the dead man before lifting him into the van. James finds even less in Khoury's pockets than in Abia's. There's a knife, spare magazines for the rifle, a small Quran, and an armored vest with the attached radio.

James leaves the blood soaked shirt on top of his victim and tires to get the man into his van. It seems like James's strength was sapped. He gives up on lifting the body and proceeds to shove him under his van. Putting the dead man under there seems a bit disrespectful, but he has no where else to hide the body.

I could choose any one of the other cars, but that might not be a good idea. James, ever the electrician is still thinking like one. *The car alarms might go just off,* James worries. *And if a dead man doesn't bring down the wrath of the terrorists then a car alarm certainly will!*

Covering his tracks, James quickly goes back to the spot where he killed Khoury and makes sure to clean up any and all of the blood. The car decks aren't the cleanest things, so James takes comfort in wiping up anything that looks like blood. James walks backwards toward his van, his eyes trying to find any drop he's missed. Satisfied, James heads back to the perceived safety of his van.

James carefully open's the van door and climbs back into his van with Khoury's gear, leaving the bloody bullet-proof vest on the corpse. As he shuts the door, James feels the ferries engines throttle up and knows time has got to be running out.

The seriousness that he feels clearly comes through his new questions. Ripping the tape off of her mouth, and as Abia winces with the pain, James yells at the woman. "Alright, Abia, you need to tell me all of it! Right here, right now!!!"

James grabs her face, his fingers and thumb framing her face. He makes her look his way. "What's going on in this ship?!?" He spits it out, just inches from her face.

The pair are eye to eye. Abia still does not say a word. James grinds his teeth, his jaw muscles flexing. He waits, making sure he has her attention, then he puts the tape back onto her mouth.

The killing of another human being has affected him. *Dear God,* James prays, *I can't get the blood bubbles out of my mind!*

James once more rips the tape back off of Abia's mouth. James waits for her answers. Nothing.

With Abia's silence, his own seriousness and regret at taking a life; James slowly transforms into man full of frustrating anger. James gives Abia a few more moments to respond, his rage build further. In his fury, he begins to shake the woman hard and escalates to punching her.

Abia, easily weathers the un-aimed blows by taking it on her shoulders. *What's come over this guy?* She silently asks herself. She tries to grasp why he is so different. She caught a quick glimpse of his face when he came into the van and new whatever had happened out there wasn't good. She also notes the smell of something on her captor, but can't place the odor.

Smells like metal, copperish and yet, something else. Quickly looking him over for some hint, the woman notices the blood on her captor's hands and arms. For the first time, she becomes alarmed by her assailant.

In a last bit of frustration, James has an idea hit him. In a scene he'd seen on '24', James grabs his water bottle, yanks Abia to her back and sits on her chest. *I've had enough of this!* James yells it inside his brain, the sound echoing like a reminder among the blood bubbles.

Abia instantly focuses on her captor as his face changes. *Like he just put on a mask,* so caught up in his facial features that she has totally forgotten about answering *all of his questions.* She was just searching what was wrong with him and little did she know what he was capable of.

James pins her shoulders to the floor with his own knees, and he can see Abia wince from the pain of being thrown back. Their combined weight is placed fully on the woman's tied arms and hands.

"One more chance, Abia. That's it!" James sits there on Abia's chest and shoulders waiting. His eyes burrow into hers in a vengeful stare. "Forget it Abia! Time is up!"

James takes off the cap to his water bottle and pulls back Abia's head by the hair. With one hand wrapped up in hair, James's words disappear as the overworked electrician pours water with his other hand into the nose and mouth of Abia.

"You will tell me what's happening!" James shouts.

Gagging and sputtering, Abia resists the best that she can and James can see that. He pushes his point home, "I've had enough of this! I've already fought you and killed another of your teammates. No more nice guy… not about this…anymore!!"

She is choking on the flow of water. Drowning in her effort to breathe. Abia had been warned of this kind of thing before. Dizhwar had told them about this at the North Bend school, they had heard about it on the news too, but *she had never actually experienced it.*

Abia had been taught to resist all sorts of torture and told explicitly not to divulge any information, but this is totally different. She is drowning and everything within her screams…STOP!

Abia tries her best to buck and squirm, *but this heathen, this enemy, has me tied at the arms and legs.* Abia is tightly pinned, at the shoulders, too. Her concern at the blood and her captor's out of place rage had her apprehensive. But now, Abia is afraid for her life. The water continues slowly, seemingly never-ending, and her lungs start to burn from the lack of oxygen.

As more water flows in, she gags even more. She keeps snorting in water every time she tries to breathe, which only makes the burning sensation in her lungs worse. *A couple of seconds seem like minutes, and a minute seems like half an hour,* she tries to comfort herself. Nevertheless, it doesn't work.

"Ok!" Abia coughs out. Sputtering out more water, she tries to roll over to expel it out of her lungs. James stands up slightly, letting her lean to her side. Abia gags and coughs out the water from her nose and mouth, expelling the liquid from her lungs.

James stops the pouring as Abia forces out the water. He has only a little water left in the over-sized water bottle, so the torture would have had to stop anyway. James needed to grab the second water bottle anyway.

"Answer all of my questions!" James barks.

Between the coughing and spitting of water, "A minute!" she blurts out trying to buy herself some time.

James gets up and finishes off the small remainder of water left in his first bottle. He grabs his second bottle and rolls his captive back to her back, pinning her once more. Her eyes go wide as James forces her head back with the palm of his hand and pinches her nose. James shows her the second bottle of water. He unscrews the cap with his teeth and then hovers the bottle conspicuously over her wet face.

"This time you might drown," James says in a serious whisper. "Decide…" He hisses through clinched teeth.

The water starts to trickle out and the moment before it becomes a flood, Abia's resistance dissolves. Her face was ashen white, "Yes, yes, anything! No more water," Abia coughs out.

James starts with the basics: "Who are you? What are you doing on the boat? How many others are there? Who is your leader?"

"Abia ibn Abi Talib." Sputtering still, she finishes, "I'm part of twelve to take over ferry. Dizhwar is our leader."

James relaxes a little and asks about the details. "Why aren't the cell phones working? Where are the other's located?"

"Jammers are stopping the cell phones," Abia pauses still trying to cough up her forced baptism of water. She continues, "There's four of us on the passenger deck, two in each pilot house, and two more in the engine room."

Abia pauses to make sure she's answered all of the questions, but her captor leans in, as if the man was about to start pouring more from his water bottle.

"What are your guys going to do with the ferry? What's the objective?"

"Objective! Yes," Abia blurts out, as if just remembering the most important question. Abia looks into James's face and sees nothing but a hardened resolution. Weighing her options she finally just gives in.

Dejectedly, Abia shares, "Once close to the Bremerton ferry terminal, the team is to flee the ship with the on-board Zodiacs and then crash the ferry into the military base piers. We think that the impact will cause a big enough hole in the side of the ferry to sink it. It would ruin the naval harbor for a long time. Not only with the ship, but also the environmental impact. Lawyers circling for years before the port is opened again. Just like the Exxon *Valdez in Alaska*. Or the Italian *Costa Concordia*, the *Doña Paz* in the Philippines or the Korean *Sewol*."

James leans back, he can see the defeat in Abia's demeanor and knows, *I'm getting most of it. Truthful information, probably. I remember some of those ships names on the news. Still, she's still withholding something. It doesn't matter though,* he accepts. *I have more knowledge of what is happening on the ferry than before. .*

James considers the terrorists plan carefully. *Valdez, Costa Concordia and the Sewol...a whole lot of destruction. The Bremerton Navy Shipyard was what, four, maybe six hundred yards away from the ferry terminal? If these terrorists time it right, letting the au-*

thorities know there are innocent people on board, it could possibly prohibit the Navy from repelling the ferry until it's too late? James works through the logistics some more, *the Navy probably wouldn't even see the Zodiacs leave the ferry prior to impact. Not at night.*

James breathes out a sigh of weariness and worries at the awful plan. So ugly, so many people to die, so much destruction. He furiously tries to call 911 back on his mobile, but he has no signal. *The Jammers!* He hammers out a text message to his wife and hopes that it will eventually go through. *When I take out the jammers.*

James focuses back on his captive. "Abia, why are we underway again?"

Abia quickly answers, "I don't know. I have no idea why it's started up, then slows back down. Maybe, the men in the engine room thought they were done, but they are not?"

James has enough now to act. His text doesn't go anywhere either. "Undeliverable" is the message he gets back. He quickly copies and pastes the same informative text he sent to his wife and sends it out to his Boss and his coworker Nick. Afterward, he gets another confirmation of the same undeliverable message and he holsters his mobile phone.

James checks Abia's bonds and makes sure that they are secure. He re-tapes Abia's mouth and gives her a shrug for the cause. James checks his weapons' conditions, making sure they are all loaded, bullets in chambers and safeties off. James considers as he makes ready, *is it up to me to do something rather than rely on someone else?* He fills up his armor vest's pouches with magazines from both of the terrorists. James then exits his van once more. His van; his perilous refuge.

James keeps his head low and walks away hunched over toward his first goal. *Jammers or the engines? Clear the boat of bad guys or focus on just one goal? I have to try and clear the engine room of the terrorists and then stop the engines. I have to do this, I will do this...or die in trying.*

Every machine has a heart, James tells himself. *The heart of every machine is its engines...and this ferry is no different.* He ignores the jammers for now and decides on preventing the ship from being used as a temporary harbor blockade. He figures instinctively, *control the engines and you have control of the ferry. If I can figure out how to control them...*

Looking for the entrance to the engine room, he is cautious about stepping into the same kind of situation again. Resolution fills his mind, as James finds the door to the engine room and tests it to see if it will open. James peaks through, rifle tucked tight against his shoulder, elbows down, the AK's barrel pointing in the direction of his sight. He mimics History Channel shows he's watched about the military and various entry teams he's seen on the Military Channel.

The landing is clear just on the other side of the door, with a stairway leading down.

As he slowly and cautiously descends the stairs, James has thoughts of having to kill someone again. He doesn't want to, he shouldn't have to, *but who else is going to do something?* James demands of himself. *And if that something involves killing, then it's what must be done.*

He finds the conviction that he has to. James comes to terms with what the goal is.

As James walks downstairs, his epiphany is clear. *In order to stop wolves from preying on lambs, I need to be the sheepdog.*

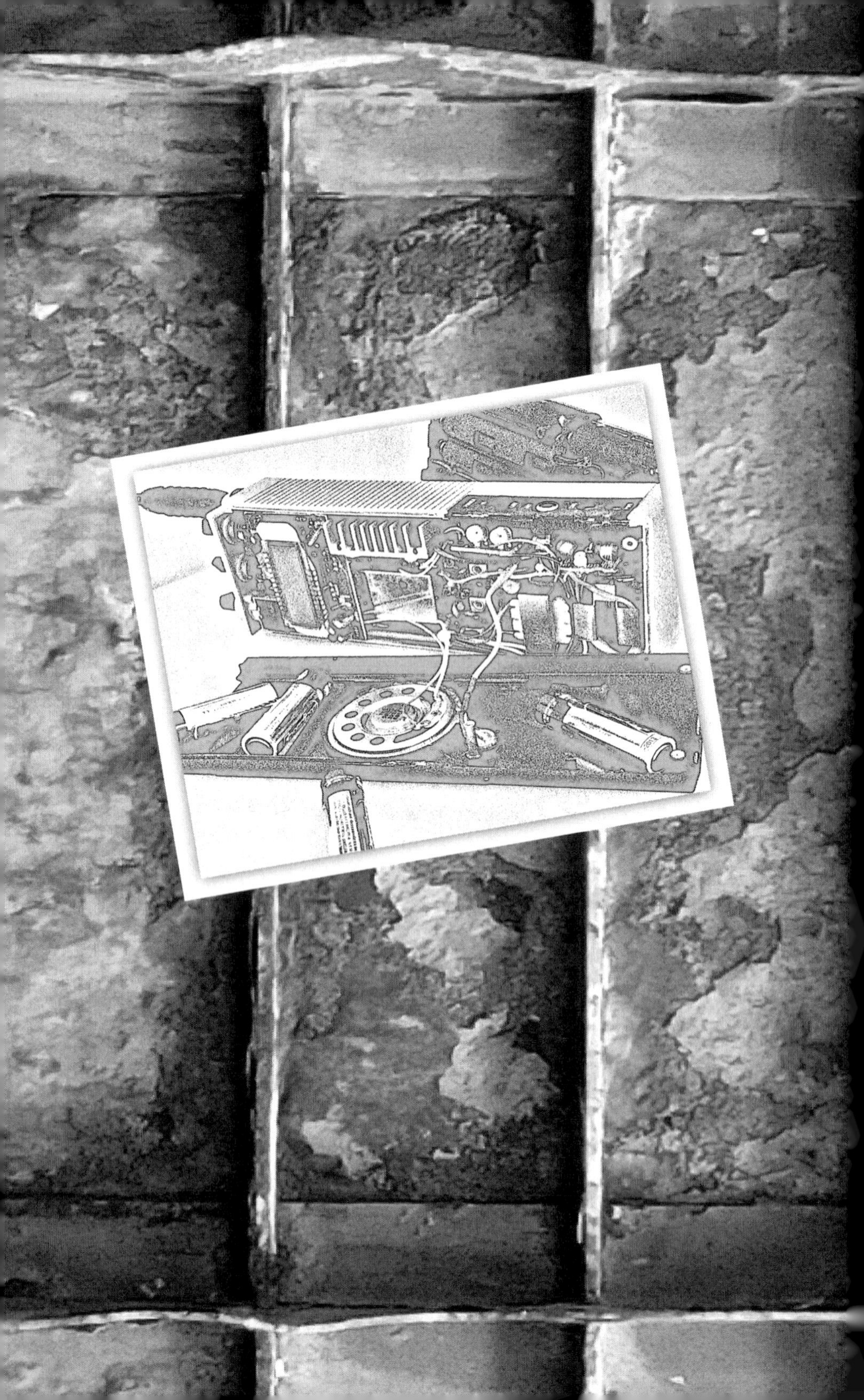

Chapter Thirty Six

Thursday August 30th 22:00

Foush! A pillar of frothy water comes out of the ocean. It was like an eruption from the blow hole of a whale. It pushes upward in a column of white just behind the fireboat. The SFD boat is finishing making its turn back toward Seattle. Dizhwar's countenance is first shock and then surprise at the display. His face turns toward a wide grin. Their way was true and Allah was making it so.

"The back of the fireboat just erupted in water!" Abdul exclaims over the radio. He has a great view of the water geyser from his position in the aft pilot house. Abdul continues his group channel broadcast, "It must have come out of the water six feet!"

Dizhwar looks on, as the fireboat slowly comes around to port, listing slightly, with no perceived wake. Dizhwar realizes it must have been the charges. The boat looked dead in the water.

Those timers were erratic or must have gotten water in them. Dizhwar considers, then he opens a group channel on the radio to confirm Abdul's news. "The fireboat has been disabled. Everyone at ease." Dizhwar broadcasts to the entire team. Driver comes out of the pilothouse at the noise and grins at the sight of the fireboat.

Dizhwar changes the radio settings on his comm's set for the two engine crew and clicks the radio.

"Go ahead for Jibril." Jibril responds.

A moment later Parvez does the same, "...Parvez."

After the responses come back Dizhwar queries "Engine room, are you almost finished? Do you need me to slow the ship?"

"Hold on," Jibril transmits, but he can barely be heard from the noise of the engine room. Jibril comes back on in a minute, obviously now outside of the engine room. "Yes. We need fourteen...fifteen more minutes to wire the controllers, but everything else is ready. We might be deaf and dehydrated, but we are working hard."

"Very well. When you finish, get out of there and head to the car deck. Then radio in. Understood?" Dizhwar walks back into the pilothouse and eases back on the throttles to fifty percent power.

"Understood," Jibril replies again. Parvez was just content to listen because he was still in the engine room. Jibril walks back through the engine room door and dives back into his work; absorbing all of his attention.

Dizhwar just shakes his head at those two. The pair were constantly answering for each other, yet it's nothing new. When Dizhwar had recruited them he had no idea that next to Driver, Jibril and Parvez, were the most vital members on the team.

Much to Dizhwar's surprise, he and Driver had hit it off with the two men. From the moment Parvez and Jibril met each other there was a clear and immediate bond. The two acted like they were siblings with each other. You could obviously see it in the training, schooling and especially during the long nights of mission planning. Jibril and Parvez would finishing one another's sentences. They would leapfrog from each other's thoughts and arrive at quicker conclusions, unmistakably appreciating the other's contributions.

Jibril and Parvez probably had the highest IQ's of the entire team, but were always humble about it. For their humility and patience, Dizhwar was thankful. The pair had everyone beat when it came to age and education as well. Dizhwar tried to remember while standing there on the bridge, *wasn't there seven college degrees between the two? And look how they use all of that education!*

Dizhwar relied upon the pair heavily to plan out this mission, not only because they instinctively new the various team member's strengths and weaknesses, but Jibril and Parvez had the uncanny abilities to think beyond the archetypes. Driver was always a quiet support during the planning stage, giving his opinion when asked, but not Jibril and Parvez. They equally loved pushing the younger team members' personalities, to see where they had weaknesses, and then they would kindly pull back and let them off of the hook.

The pair were sometimes quietly observant, sharing ideas with each other, but not always the team. Yet, what they considered and concluded upon was always brought forth with substantial argument and persuasive facts. They could see problems where he and Driver didn't. The pair were really good about bringing things to Dizhwar's attention that he had missed. Like the triple redundancy on the charges. A bit of over preparation, yes, but what would have happened if the charges hadn't blown? *I'm, thankful Allah, for bringing them to me and into the team.*

Their magnum opus was the entire distraction of the cruise ship bombing and the taking out the three municipal craft were solely Jibril's and Parvez's idea. Their concept was ingenious and now it finally yielded rewards, albeit a bit late.

The distractions in the north and south had to be draining away vital emergency resources. The cruise ship was having problems, the fireboat just confirmed that. And now, the last of the emergency craft within Elliot Bay was removed from operation. Too bad there wouldn't be any confirmation on the Ballard Lock charges.

May it be Allah's will, Dizhwar reflects, that those two explosives did their destructive work. Dizhwar walks back out onto the railing and stands next to Driver.

"Hopefully, we will be left alone now ." Driver throws his remark in.

"Yes, our team only needs forty-five minutes more to carry out the entire plan. We are half way through the op."

"Short, quick and to the point, that was why it's so brilliant." Driver leans on the railing next to Dizhwar and watches the SFD fireboat languish. "We have taken a ship and no one has noticed. We've created distractions, and will use this ship and be gone before anyone is the wiser."

Dizhwar nods his head at his friend's observations. "Sun Tzu, would be proud. Too bad he was not a believer of The Way."

Dizhwar and Driver are full of a sense of accomplishment. They and their team have performed admirably.

Yet with Dizhwar's overflowing happiness about the explosives going off, mostly according to plan, he momentarily forgets. Dizhwar's joy at his success has made him loose focus on his two team members that had gone MIA.

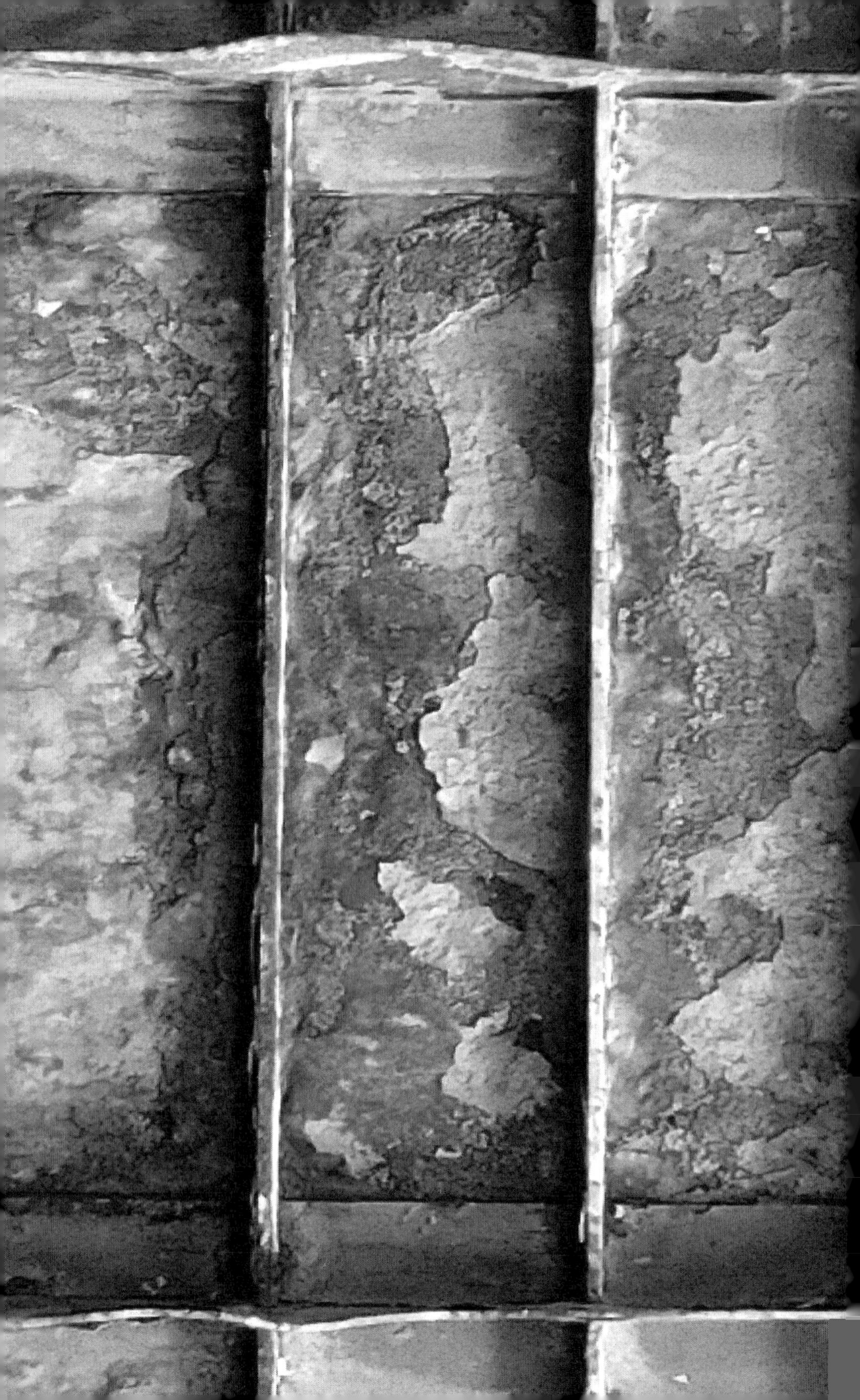

Chapter Thirty Seven

Thursday August 30th 22:02

Latisha still can't believe she had not reacted faster! Now she is tied to her chair with all of the rest of the passengers. A prisoner. She feels so humiliated, like she not only let herself down but those around her as well. *I should have stopped Tweaky! Curse it!* Latisha Reynolds offers a few profanities at her lack of success. *If I had just moved faster!*

Latisha had been trying to catch some peace, but it had been so hard on the brightly lit ferry and she kept sticking to those uncomfortable green vinyl seats. The ferry wasn't away from the dock for long, when all of the shouting had started. Just as she thought she might dose off there was someone shouting. Latisha had turned to see what in Satan's Fire all of the commotion was about. She was angry, she was tired and she wanted to take it out on whomever had disturbed her quiet rest.

Yet, when she turned and looked over her shoulder, Latisha couldn't see anything over the head of someone else; so she stood up. There in the back, right in front of the cafe, some pencil shaped man was shouting at all of the passengers. One of the crew was down on her knees with hands behind her back. Latisha could barely understand the man because he was nervously yelling so fast.

Latisha stood there amidst certain chaos, and found her anger changing to a slight grin at the humor of it all. Latisha knew she shouldn't be smiling, but this gunman reminded her of a tall Yosemite Sam. Even more so, this guy, was armed with a rifle. No, it was a submachine gun. It was hard sometimes to tell the difference, but she faintly recognized it. It was the type Israelis were famous for.

"What was the name of that thing?" She quietly whispered to herself. "An uni? A uzel? Uzi! That was it! Whoever heard of a terrorist armed with an Uzi? Wasn't that an oxymoron?" Her grin widens at the tragic comedy of the entire situation. She had such a rough day, such a down right horrible day that it was a bit cathartic to see others have their day ruined.

All around her people were ducking and running forward, moving toward the observation windows. But she was different, whether it was from her hard day or the things she had been experiencing this past couple of years; she had enough lemon juice squirted in her eyes. Latisha had walked *toward* the tweaky looking man with the gun.

What were those people going to do? She reasoned as she walked past more of them running out the front two doors. *That direction wasn't the way off of the boat, that was a dead end. They were as good as corralled sheep. You had to go through the armed man to get downstairs or upstairs!* She had grinned at her next thought...*I can take him.* Latisha worked through all of the chairs and people in a matter of seconds. Her senses were sharp despite just being woken up. With the adrenalin moving through her body her long week no longer mattered; her brain was on overdrive. Despite her diminutive size she could make up for it in her character and charisma. *Just a few more steps toward the gunman,* she urged herself. *While he is distracted, yelling at everyone else, then I will win.*

I'll rip that Uzi right out of his hands and shoot him with his own misplaced gun!

Her plan came to a screeching halt just out of arm's reach from the gunman.

The loud and nervous looking man, whom she called Tweaky, finally noticed her. In a blur of motion the gunman with the Uzi wasn't funny anymore. The barrel was pointed at her right eye socket. Latisha could see the light reflect off of the polished copper bullet at the bottom of the short barrel. Tweaky shouted at her, cursed at her, then demanded she get down on her knees next to the female crewman.

Latisha Reynolds didn't bend her knees to anyone but God. Not her boss, not her kids, not to circumstance, and defiantly not to this Tweaky Yosemite Sam. Yet, looking down the barrel of that *loaded* gun, faced with the fact that she could die; all of it changed. She wanted to see her husband and children again. She still had a hobby of canning to pursue. She wanted to become a grandmother.

She wanted to live.

Latisha obeyed the gunman and fell to her knees, putting her hands behind her head in the most humiliating act that she had ever been forced to do.

As her thoughts now linger on the initial siege, the chaos and the fear, she picks something to focus on as she now watches the four terrorists control the cabin. What she thought initially was a lone gunman, is in fact a choreographed take over. She gives her best effort to count all of the gunman's different faces. *An hour into it, I've seen nine so far.* Latisha is scrambling for any hope. From the entire time she and her fellow passengers have been tied up, she is trying to work out a glimmer of light in all of this shadow. The woman is grasping to be able to do something, anything to stop this hijacking. *If I can only get one more chance to take action.*

This time, she promises to herself, *I will jump at the opportunity.* "Please, God," she quietly whispers. Latisha Reynolds is not going to take this sitting on her hands.

Maybe she can help others get out of this alive as well.

Chapter Thirty Eight

Thursday August 30th 22:05

Parvez cuts the radio connection between himself, Dizhwar and Jibril. *I'm looking forward to getting out of this sauna,* Parvez thinks to himself. The stifling and painfully noisy engine room is unrelenting on his senses. *North Bend never prepared me for this.*

Either I'm going to go insane from claustrophobia, that I never knew I had, or one of these charges is going to go off.! Parvez quietly worries to himself. He watches Jibril come back into the engine room, give him a nod of acknowledgement and they both go about their work deep in their thoughts.

Jibril worries that he really didn't think all of this terrorist business through all of the way. If it wasn't for Parvez's friendship, Jibril would have left the group long ago. Forcing down his doubts, he focuses his thoughts back on the dangerous business before him. Every moment that goes by fills him with a little more fear, that in the next moment, one or both of them will be blown to smithereens. Jibril knows it's Parvez's fear too, he can see it in his friends eyes and in his careful movements. Static electricity coming off of the running engines, the ship through the water and the surrounding machinery is the constant threat. All they need is for one of those static charges to arc and set the entire explosive chain into motion. Even though he and Parvez are careful, grounding to whatever they can, with electro-static discharge wristbands, the danger of the situation is staring at him in the face.

Taking every caution, they still hurry as much as they can. Jibril is busy working on the final connections for the explosive charges to the receiver. Parvez walks off, up the length of the engine room, and out of sight. Parvez's final task is the stringing up of the receiver's antenna as he moves away from Jibril's position. Using sticky tabs to string the antenna along and to anchor it as he moves. Almost all of the explosives are wired to the receiver Jibril has in front of him; once the connections are completed, it will allow a remote detonation of the fuel tanks.

Of course, *after* the entire team leaves the ferry.

Jibril and Parvez have set all of the shaped charges along the metal bulkhead plates that run the length of the engine room. These plates separate the fuel tanks from the rest of the room. These bulkheads are dual-purpose in design: They act as a barrier from fire or flood in case of an accident, and add structural rigidity to the forces of torque present in the powerful engines. A fuel tank, even for diesel fuel, must be stable and rigid.

Every other one of the charges, on the fuel tank bulkheads, is loaded with something special. A kinetic energy penetrator (KEP). The KEP is molded within the homemade plastic explosive, all but ensuring tank puncture. Even if the tank charges don't cause the explosive reaction hoped for, there are the backups. Twelve incendiary charges are placed along the fuel lines that run from tanks, to metering valves, to the engines. These charges are set for a half second delay from the primary tank charges. The terrorists have planned; that the ship will become an inferno no matter what.

The KEPs, in their unusual metal cylinders, are something to behold. The penetrators are molded within the explosive. They are essentially, large machined needles made out of tungsten steel, hardened to a density far beyond the ships steel plates. The needles were made to Dizhwar's specifications and heat treated to an incredible hardness. The shop had been paid almost double its going rate to make the eighteen inch long narrow cones, no questions asked.

Tungsten, also known as wolfram, when literally translated into English means "heavy stone". Heavy stone indeed, the material is almost twice as dense as lead and usually is manufactured into armor piercing projectiles for the modern battlefield tank cannons. All the KEP's needed is a massive explosive push and a hole would be made where solid steel once was. The only reason the tungsten spears could punch through the steel is because the steel is far softer than the tungsten.

Physics, chemistry, engineering and the principals of electricity all coming together to sink a perfectly good ship.

Chapter Thirty Nine

Thursday August 30th 22:05

James sneaks his way down the stairs, watching his steps as he looks through the AK's sights. Making sure he doesn't end up tripping or worse: running across someone coming up the stairs. He stops for a moment hearing a door close below and waits to see if anyone is coming up the stairs. He counts to ten and then finishes making the two right turns to the bottom. Upon reaching the bottom, he faces yet another door. *The one that was just closed,* he tells himself. This one has a small window in it. The small window is as opaque as shower glass, but James can hear the distinctive sounds of the diesel engines on the other side. He can feel the vibration of the running engines under his feet and smells the machinery even with the door closed.

The noise coming from the engine room is loud. He could only imagine what the volume is with the door open. James searches his pockets for ear plugs and thanks Heaven that he has a pair. He usually had a few in a pocket or two because of his working around noisy construction equipment. The plugs are old and nasty-looking, but he isn't going to be eating them, just sticking them in his ears. James lets his rifle hang on the bandolier strap, rolls the ear plugs, placing one of them in each ear and waits for the silence.

James opens the door with the bright yellow and red lettering "No Admittance! Crew Only!" He brings his barrel around and through the doorway first, and can clearly see one man about halfway down the engine room. No one else. From Abia's information, James remembers that there should be two men down here setting up the engines to run from remote control. *How you can get such a large ship to run remotely?* James ponders it, but doesn't have a clue. *Regardless, I've got to stop them. Control the engines, control the ship,* he kept telling himself.

Everything takes on a muffled volume, as the ear plugs fully expand. James leaves his rifle to hang and withdraws his .45 from the holster on his hip.

The heat is staggering! James reactively thinks to himself, not used to it. He can only imagine what it would have been like in some of the older ships, much less one of those ancient coal-fired steam ships. James can't hear his own steps as he walks through the doorway and slowly closes the door behind him, leaving it unlatched.

The single terrorist he spotted is fifteen, maybe twenty yards away from him, just down the aisle between two of the big engines. The man is messing with some electrical wires.

James can see the gunman work. The man's rifle is pointing downward, hanging off of his right shoulder on its strap. James hopes that he can sneak close enough and capture him. He will not have any regrets if he has to kill the gunman, but he will still try to capture. *Regardless of my last failed attempt,* James tells himself, *I will at least give the guy a chance to surrender.*

As he walks slowly forward, James checks to make double sure that the safety on his pistol is off.

He is ready to shoot if threatened.

Chapter Forty

Thursday August 30th 22:08

Jibril is so absorbed by his task that he doesn't see the engine room door open or a man enter. He can't hear anything over the engine noise anyway, but he should have seen something when James Maly closes to within five yards. If he only was looking ten more degrees to his right.

Those ten degrees will cost him.

James creeps forward in a crouch, holding to his promise that he will still try to take the man alive. *...unless there is resistance, then I will show no mercy.*

Jibril is so caught up in his work that he perceives nothing. Until he gets the feeling he is being watched. In a split second, Jibril is aware of James's movement. *A figure is to my right, where no one should be.* As Jibril thinks it, he smiles as he glances over, thinking it's his best friend, Parvez. Yet, when he gazes into a stranger's face, there is total unfamiliarity. Instinctively, Jibril grabs the rifle hanging from his side. If there ever is one, this is clearly a case of you should think before you act.

Jibril's adversary, James, watches as Jibril brings his weapon to a near firing position.

James is left with only one choice: Live or die. This gunman in front of him has chosen to fight instead of surrender. James chooses to live and makes .45 caliber bullets spit out of his pistol a millisecond later.

Through the sights on his firearm, James, has a perfect sight picture of this target. James makes purposeful and regular pulls on the trigger. Letting the pistol buck and then come back to rest onto the gunman's shape. With that, a rhythm is established. The 185 grain critical defense bullets do their staggeringly ugly work. The horrible sight fills James's vision. The first round hits the gunman's forearm. The next round makes contact with the gunman's right elbow. The next two collide into Jibril's rifle butt and rifle receiver.

Those bullets that hit the rifle continue on. They go through Jibril's bicep muscle and shoulder. With continuing momentum, the rounds twist and arc to tear deep into Jibril's ribs and lungs. As they strike flesh, the bullets expand to three times there size, turning into star shaped mushrooms. The wound cavity, that the heavy .45cal rounds create, causes massive hemorrhaging like they are computer modeled to do.

James lets each consecutive shot climb upward on the gunman, away from center of mass. The last pair of rounds hit Jibril's neck and head.

James lifts his finger from the trigger. Just like that, the fight is all over. The five yard distance and the fact that the engine room was so noisy gave James the tactical advantage. The person that was once Jibril ibn Amirzade ibn Amir Khan dies in a fusillade of .45 caliber critical defense hollow points.

James watches his target go down and knows by the way his rounds impact, and the way his opponent crumples, the gunman isn't going to get back up. James's right hand is still on the pistol's grip with his finger hovering over the trigger. James waits for an inevitable explosion, cringing at the thought that maybe one or two of his rounds missed the target and maybe hit some fuel lines.

James knows enough about mechanics that engines needed fuel, *there's got to be fuel lines that I could have hit. Thankfully, if my bullets missed, they didn't start any other explosion.* He ejects the mostly spent magazine in a smooth and practiced action. As James does so, he kneels, making himself a smaller target while he reloads. James places the mostly spent mag in his pocket and then inserts a fresh one from his holster. James does the exchange quickly and at the perfect time.

Because of his total lack of familiarity with large marine vessels, the muddled pops that Parvez hears, he mistakes at first for backfires. Parvez makes his way back toward Jibril's position to check on his friend. The man is more concerned for his friend, than his own safety, and doesn't rationally work out the problem *before* he starts moving. Parvez is very uneasy that Jibril might have been injured somehow by the backfires and wants to make sure that Jibril, his closest teammate, is okay.

While winding his way back the fifteen yards to Jibril's location, the conclusion dawns on him that it couldn't be backfires. His intelligence and mechanical aptitude override his initial concern. As he walks, the more he thinks about it, the more he realizes that the exhaust routes up and away from the engine room.

"So what were the noises?" He asks himself out loud, his voice drowned out by the engines. He does this several times in a row, as is his habit, when he works out problems.

Parvez considers it might just be gunfire and he instinctively brings his rifle to a carry position with it's muzzle pointed downward. He is weaving through the engine room and watching out for the charges and wires he and his friend just placed.

Committing a slight error, just like his recently deceased friend, he does not have the weapon tucked up against his shoulder. If he was looking down the sights, in a shooting position, he might just have been able to defend himself. It wasn't a lack of training or inexperience on his part, he and the rest of his team were secure in their safety. All of the people were under guard upstairs and he wasn't expecting anything. So, any possible threat will have the drop on him for just a split second while he takes the time to raise his rifle to firing position. In combat with firearms, that's all it takes to loose.

As Parvez walks toward James, James is heading toward Parvez. James steps over the recently deceased man and takes a few paces past the body. James is just beginning a cautious and careful sweep down the engine room aisle. *Expecting* that one more man is down here somewhere. He is at the ready. As he rotates in his third searching arc, James sees a man walk into his sights carrying a rifle.

This time, James doesn't hesitate, he unquestioningly starts firing.

As the bullets hit the gunman, the man slowly rotates to face James. Whether unconsciously from the impact of the hollow point bullets or purposefully in order to fire on James, James doesn't know. All it succeeds in doing is making the man a bigger target. James stops firing when the terrorist falls to a sitting position. The gunman is never able to raise his rifle to fire.

Parvez doesn't even know what hit him. One moment he was walking around the corner, and the next he's seeing an unfamiliar face in the engine room. The very instant he sees the new face he's experiencing stabbing dagger like pain all over his body. Parvez is turned by the force that stabs him deeply, his ability to stand vanishes. While he tries in vain to control his own body, he is forced down hard onto the engine room floor. It's efforts at control are mostly pointless, he cannot do anything. He looses control of his bladder, as he also uncontrollably slumps forward.

The mortally wounded man is motionless. With a watchful eye, James walks up to this second engine room gunman. With his pistol in the man's face, and again with his left hand, James pulls the terrorist's rifle away by the barrel.

Parvez is still trying to grasp what has just happened. "Allah in heaven! Why have you abandoned me?" Parvez whispers as his vision starts to dim. His next question, now mute, because his voice doesn't seem to work, ...*what has just happened?* Before his vision goes completely black, Parvez sees a single worn and stained boot in front of him and then watches mutely without any ability to resist, as his rifle that he trained so hard with, is slowly slid from his grasp.

Vision fading, Parvez finds it hard to even think. Everything goes black.

Parvez ibn Saeed ibn Abd al-Aziz Habibu-llah, Commendable, Happy Servant of the Magnificent, beloved of God, dies sitting in his own urine and blood.

WATCH YOUR STEP
WATCH YOUR STEP
WATCH YOUR STEP
WATCH YOUR STEP

Chapter Forty One

Thursday August 30th 22:11

James Maly stops moving. He's unsettled by the confrontation and takes a few deep breaths to calm his rapidly beating heart. The entire fight took a few mere minutes. James confirms that the second man is dead while holstering his pistol and ejecting its magazine. *No way is he getting up from those wounds.* James pulls the remaining .45 cal rounds out of the magazine. One by one they end up in his hand, then he pushes the now empty magazine into his pocket. As he is doing this, James looks over the complex wires and controller box.

James the Electrician has enough wisdom to recognize explosives when he sees them. *One black box has all of the explosives connected to it, that is clear as glass,* James confirms. *Another metal box is connected to the first, with more wires attached to it.* James pulls out his first partially full magazine and reloads it with the leftover rounds from the second. He is so familiar with this process of loading rounds, he can do it blindfolded.

As he reloads, he scans the wires. *There are mysterious cylinders attached to the wires that have to be explosives. That is also clear, but what can I do? It explains the thin green rope Abia had,* James decides. Staring at the wiring, a saying from his childhood comes to mind; *do not touch what you don't comprehend.* James concludes to not touch anything and leaves it all behind. He has equal sense to know that the wiring for the explosives is out of his league.

James looks to a panel that has to be the engine controls and sees what looks like a new wire run from the engine controls to one of the black boxes. *I don't dare touch the engines controls, they might be wired in somehow.* James just shakes his head at his defeat and walks away.

Abia lied. No surprise there. She didn't say a thing about explosives. They weren't going to remote control the ferry into the aircraft carrier and leave it at that. Oh no! James begins to feel growing anger at the catastrophic plans the terrorists have. He makes his way back out of the noisy engine room. Back on the move once again, *the former plan is pointless, so much for controlling the engines.*

James finishes topping off his pistol rounds, giving him almost one full magazine, and reinserts it back into the pistol. James returns to the stairs and then up to the car deck. *I can't control the engines, so the only thing left is to take out the terrorists. In the spur of the moment, with my cell phones dead, I have to make my way up to a pilothouse, or die trying.*

Abia's radio, that James now carries, comes to life "Abia, do you copy?" James doesn't respond.

Just try and make your way to the pilothouse, is what he tells himself. James knows that time is running out. He has taken out four men out of twelve, *and soon the rest are going to realize it.* James has learned from all of the books, television shows, and war movies that he must keep the element of surprise. He is just a single sheepdog against eight more wolves, and the odds are still not in his favor. Especially if they gang up on him.

Dear God, keep them down to just a few in number... and unorganized.

Finishing his silent prayer he ascends back to the car deck. James checks up on Abia. She seems ok. Still tied up, still confined, still gagged.

Harmless, right where she should be. James begins to close his van door once more, *let her rot.* Khoury's radio chirps in James's van, it is the same voice that has just paged Abia.

The voice is starting to sound desperate now.

"Your boss is starting to loose control of this. He is starting to get worried," James remarks to Abia, smiling as he does so. He shuts the door quietly and then takes large and rapid strides to the door of the stairway. *This is the one that ends above me in the passenger area.* He strides past the place where just a short time ago he fought with Abia. The place where his entire night started becoming topsy-turvy.

James stops his climbing, halfway up the stairs. He says another quick prayer for protection. In the stairway, with doors closed on either end he feels a bit of safety, rather than being out in the open. Leaning his back on the cold steel wall, he swiftly goes over his weapons conditions. His pistol and recently acquired rifle are unlocked and loaded. Bullets in chambers, safeties off. After a deep breath and a good look out the window to appreciate the sea, James continues his climb. Accepting whatever is his fate.

Back in the noise and heat of the engine room, the radios of Jibril and Parvez crackle to life. "Do you copy," Dizhwar's voice is barely heard above the engine noise.

No one clicks back to respond.

Chapter Forty Two

Thursday August 30th 22:13

Trevor finally succeeds in getting some fresh air into his hot and stuffy hood. There for a bit, he convinced himself he was going to suffocate for sure. His coworkers must be feeling the same terror. Although he can now see the cabin light coming in from under the hood, he doesn't dare try to work the hood off any farther. Fear is a great motivator and he now fears retaliation from the hijackers.

As he stops his struggling with the hood, Mr. Trevor Jacobs tests the zip ties. He tries to see if he can break the ties behind his back. He tests the zip ties three times. Flexing all of his muscles in his arms and back, sadly, three times he is met with failure. The zip ties are just too strong. He lowers his head in shame feeling like things don't look all that good for him or his fellow crew members.

He wonders too; *what happened to my co-worker that had started the shift with me? Did he make it to the engine room? Or did he just find someplace to hunker down and hide? Did he get captured or worse yet, did they kill him?*

I'm sure that there are no other crew members that have been brought up after I joined the captives here in the pilothouse. Yet, Trevor tries to figure out, *from what I could remember, of those that were tied together in the bridge. It did not seem like it was everyone.*

The space up here in the bridge is cramped and if my friend was captured, Trevor hopes, *then he must have gotten placed with the rest of the passengers. There just has to be some crewmembers with the passengers.* James wishes it to be so, and tires to believe it.

Despite Trevor's assurances, *I am not too sure. Yet, I hope that my co-worker has just hidden himself somewhere and is safe.* His co-worker is a good guy. He has worked for the ferry system for a few years. *The man had a sister that worked on the ship, didn't he?* Trevor wonders. *They carpooled together didn't they? He had at least two or maybe it was three kids?*

Well, the hijackers spared the Captain when the fireboat had come. Trevor listened carefully to the entire exchange between the Captain and one of the hijackers. *Hopefully these gunmen are not the violent kind. Maybe they just want some prisoners released from Israeli custody or from Guantanamo Bay? Maybe they want guns or money for their brothers and sisters in some war torn Muslim country? Then the hijackers will be off? To disappear into the night and maybe end up a fantastic mystery just like D.B. Cooper?*

Trevor listened as he heard one of the crew members crying and was empathetic of their position. He couldn't do anything to reassure them, but sent some good thoughts their way. He said a quick prayer to a god he barely worshiped anymore and leaned his head down to suck in some of that fresh cool air.

Trevor once again tries to comfort himself. *If the way the gunman treated Captain Blair was any indicator, then things will probably work out alright.*

Hopefully. Trevor wishes. *Well, Maybe...*

Chapter Forty Three

Thursday August 30th 22:15

James walks up the final few yellow stairs with, "Watch your step!" stenciled on every other vertical riser. He makes it to the top and has an odd thought. *I wonder if my wife and children are safe and in bed yet? The things you think of when faced with the worst situations,* he confides in himself. James checks his phone and realizes he has gotten a text, no two, and a voicemail. James glances at his signal strength and sees, yet again, that it is still zero.

He asks in a hushed whisper, "But then, how did the texts and voicemail make it through?" Before he opens the door into the passenger area, James looks at the texts and sees they are from his wife.

Wendi Maly wrote in her first one, "Hey u! Just thinking of u. Don't work too hard!" The next was much more romantic "Hello my dear, I'm in bed and wishing u were nxt 2 me. Wke me when u get here? Gnight c u in a bit." James stands there a moment and contemplates her messages. His outbound texts from a few minutes ago, all of them, went through. *There must have been a reset or temporary shut off of the jammers,* James is relieved. *That'd explain why my outbound texts went through without any responses and my wife's inbound ones came in as well.*

James could remember back to easier times in his life. Times when he wasn't working so many hours, times when his peace wasn't so fleeting. After marriage to Wendi, his girlfriend of three years, they bought a house together and began the life of a married couple. Living every possible moment at each other's side with a shared wish that it would never end. They shared hobbies, interests, money, and would even car pool when it was possible. Wendi soon became pregnant with their first son and life began to change toward the complex. Soon three kids, financial pressure, in-law demands, house maintenance, and work issues all seemed to cause the bond between them to loosen. He really missed the times before, when he would get home, make them dinner; she would arrive from work and greet him with a big hug and kiss.

After the greeting, she would change her clothes; they would finish cooking the meal. Eating together and sharing their day, doing dishes together and figuring when their next shared day off was. They would watch a bit of news, shower together, and fall asleep in each other's arms. How could it of changed so much? Was this the natural progression of things? Was it because those moments were now gone, that they are so precious?

All of his life growing up on the beaches of southern California, he never thought he would get married. After all, there were lots of nice girls his age, and he had some fond memories of times past. He had every intention of being the perennial bachelor, but then he met her while he was shopping at a mall. His heart leapt. The first communications between them were sporadic, raindrop-like bits of contact. Later, the frequency of messages were a rainstorm and then a flood. They spent six months of learning to be the best of friends and then it spilled over into so much more.

After marriage and their first child's birth they decided to get away on a great adventure. They burned up James' three week vacation and set off on a colossal rode trip with child, truck and trailer. They ended up hitting all of the states west of the Rockies and fell in love with the Seattle area. Both sets of their parents were appalled at the possibility of their move. Their parents had reasoned that it wouldn't even happen. A few months later they had sold their house in California and purchased a bigger one in Black Diamond, Washington. They were much better off because of it.

Now, here I am trapped on a kamikaze ferry, looking back upon all of those moments. I'm blessed to have Wendi in my life, there was no doubt. James looked back at the texts and felt a little connection to her over the miles. *I did love her very much, her and the kids, regardless of the course that has been taken to get to this moment.*

With no cell signal, James didn't reply to Wendi's texts, but the warmth from them filled his heart. With a smile at the thought of being in a warm bed with his wife, he checks his voicemail.

And now the network won't connect and download the voicemail either. Oh well, it was probably just from the police demanding that I call back immediately.

"Well that isn't going to happen anytime soon" James says to himself and the empty stairway.

He's interrupted by another radio call.

"Abia! do you copy!" The demand was clear, the stress evident and Dizhwar's voice was convincingly worried. James waited and listened before proceeding further. "Abia, call back ASAP. Use ship phone if you have to."

James wants to use this opportunity to rattle and confuse their leader. He thinks carefully before coming up with the perfect thing to say, "They are all dead, Dizhwar. Soon we will take out your entire team."

"Who are you?!? Answer me!" Dizhwar demands. James gives him nothing. James tries to work out in his head if he should speak more or continue on upstairs. A call comes through again, "How dare you try to stop this. You will fail!"

James takes a deep breath and lets it out slowly. He offers back, in a cold and purposeful way, "I'm one who does not dare, more than I will perform."

James turns down the volume of the radio and opens the passenger room door. Thoughts of his wife and family and all of the things that he stands to loose hardens his resolve. It makes him that much more determined to make it back home.

The time has come to make things right. James figures it's time to kill or be killed in order to survive.

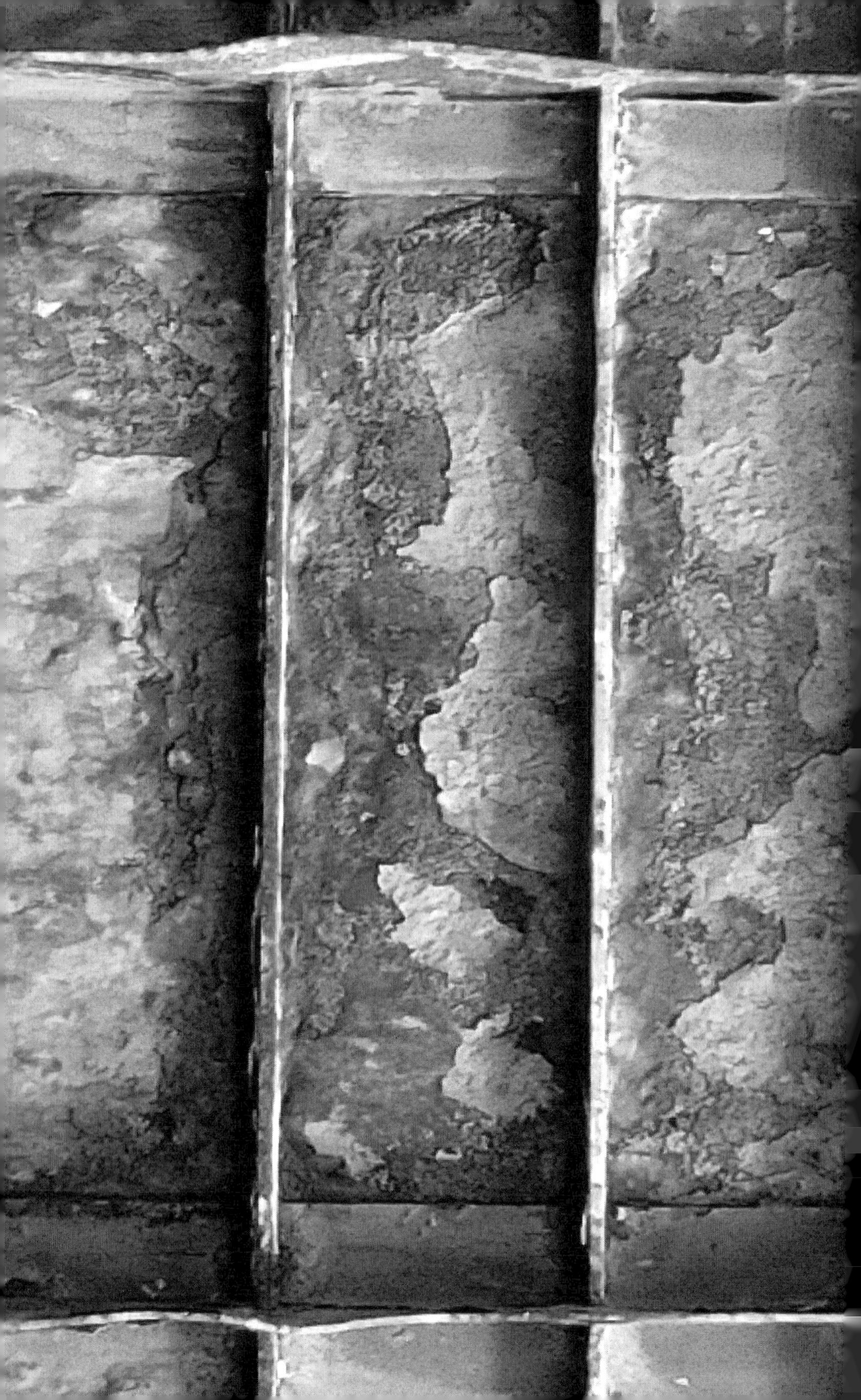

Chapter Forty Four

Thursday August 30th 22:15

Dizhwar Abdur Razzaq is feeling a bit better. The former threat of the fireboat and possible discovery is gone. The Cruise ship distraction, and most likely the others are working perfectly. And his team, well his people are performing flawlessly.

His team!

"Damn it!" he shouts to himself. His countenance changes slightly as he bows his head in yet another quick *dua* of forgiveness. *I cant believe I just remembered about Abia and Khoury. Come to think about it, I should have heard from Jibril and Parvez as well. It's been too long since either pair reported in.*

Dizhwar knew Jibril and Parvez should be on the car deck by now. He calls out to all four one at a time over the radio. Glancing at his watch and waiting one minute before calling out again. *Nothing. What in heaven's name is going on? I need them to call back.* "Talk to me, dammit!" Dizhwar shouts, this time without any apology to his god. Tactics and strategy run through his brain as he tries to grasp for a solution.

While working through his plans, Dizhwar walks out of the fore control house and onto the upper crew deck. "Are they missing or are they dead?" He asks the sky "Is there a SWAT team from the fire boat on board? Or is it something else?" Cussing aloud again, he knows he must decide something, anything. *This is your command, your responsibility,* he reminds himself. He apologizes to his god once more for his doubts and foul mouth. He kneels and silently asks for wisdom. Then gets back up and turns to look into the pilothouse; trying to work out the operation.

Climbing the stairs back into the pilot house he makes one more series of radio calls to the four missing: Abia, Khoury, Jibril and Parvez, asking them to call on the ship phone if their comms aren't working reliably.

Then, a voice comes over on Abia's channel. One that is definitely not Abia.

"They are all dead, Dizhwar. Soon we will take out your entire team."

Dizhwar stands there in stunned silence.

Dizhwar's anger overrides his shock, "Who are you? Answer me!" Dizhwar demands.

The leader of the highjackers waits for a reply. Silence is what he gets in return. Impatiently, he keys the transmit button again "How dare you try to stop this. You will fail!"

The answer comes back, cold, distant and heartless. "I'm one who does not dare more than I will perform."

Dizhwar hurriedly changes the channel and calls to his rear pilot house crew. He sets the frequency for the pair and clicks the transmit button.

"Go for Abdul."

"Go for Monifa." They both reply in quick succession.

"Are both of you absolutely sure that you did not see any splashes, anything unusual from that...*Chief Seattle*?"

They both respond that they are sure. The pair express that they didn't see anything unusual from the wounded fireboat.

"We watched the ship closely," Monifa explains, "there was nothing."

"I need both of you to head down to the engine room. Use extreme caution! Take rear stairs and go carefully. Guns at the ready, understand?"

"Affirmative," the pair communicate back.

Dizhwar continues to share his concerns with his two operators over the radio. He speaks to them about Abia's former radio and the transmissions from it, while Abdul and Monifa walk to the rear observation area. Dizhwar continues to supply his pair of cell members with as much knowledge as he has. All the while the pair head toward the rear stairs. Dizhwar explains his unease about a possible SWAT team or a previously unknown police officer on the boat. "Four of our team members are no longer transmitting," Dizhwar begins to conclude. Explaining, "...at the least, this *enemy* has Abia's radio and our cell has to assume the worse about her."

Dizhwar finishes with, "Use every caution," once more and clicks off.

Dizhwar radios the four men in the passenger cabin to check in. They all do. *Should he warn them too or leave them in the dark?* Dizhwar finds he's talking to himself again. If he warns them would the passengers over-hear? None of his team in the passenger area knows Arabic, so he will have to communicate to them in English. Maybe the passengers might panic? He couldn't afford that right now. He is grasping at straws. Dizhwar needs the men guarding the passengers focused on their job and he needs the passengers secured and afraid. Mostly, he must have the hostages fearful and left in the dark as to what is going on.

Dizhwar decides. *I wish everyone of my team knew Arabic, it would be so much simpler.* He sets his radio for Raphael, always the calm and cool one. Dizhwar choose him for that reason.

"Go ahead."

"Where are you?"

Raphael doesn't even hesitate like Khoury, "Passenger area, guarding."

"Step out."
Raphael raised his eyebrows at this, but does as he is told. The moment he was in the hallway between the stairs and the passenger area he calls in. "I am clear."

"Someone has Abia's radio and there are others not responding. Be on guard and warn the others, quietly. Understand?"

"Khoury? Is he..."

"Understand?!?" Dizhwar cuts him off.

"Yes, Dizhwar."

"Be vigilant, and be ready for anything." Dizhwar radios his warning and then clicks off.

Raphael works through many questions as he terminates the conversation. *Am I being let down by Dizhwar? By Dizhwar's plan? Seemingly...at every turn my his life it falls apart? First, the parents whom couldn't hold a promise. Moving all of the time from Turkey, to England and then to the GOD FORESAKEN United States. Parents always chasing some stupid dream...*

In just a few years, Raphael's mother and father filed for bankruptcy. Raphael couldn't take seeing his once proud parents subsisting off of food stamps and state housing. Raphael left them, all their troubles, and their guilty faces. One day he just walked away from both of them and never looked back.

He considers what has become of Dizhwar's promises; *are they just as empty as everyone else's in my life? Yet there is nothing else to be done? The ship is two thirds of the way across the Salish Sea and they all need more information before anyone can act further.* Raphael knows that if the explosives aren't set, *or didn't get set,* Dizhwar can't increase the speed of the ferry and order all of them to prepare to abandon ship. The explosives had to be finished *before* going into the terminal.

Raphael is sure that Dizhwar can't stop the ferry either, because it is within site of the Bremerton ferry docks and the farther away, Naval shipyard. *If the ferry slows or stops now, it would immediately raise suspicions.* Raphael reconsiders his previous doubt. *I am glad for this place on the team and I do wish Dizhwar all of the luck, but Allah please let this not be another dead end road!*

Dizhwar walks back into the pilot house as Driver begins the final turn to line up for the distant ferry dock. He reaches over and cuts the power to sixty percent as he makes a disgusted face to Driver.

Driver knows that with Dizhwar, sometimes not saying anything is best, but this time it seems different in some way. "Problems?"

Dizhwar glances at the imprisoned crew, then back at Driver and gives a quick, almost imperceptible nod of his head.

Driver steps toward his leader and friend. "What's going on?" he carefully asks in Arabic, trying not to prod too much, but still trying to get something out of Dizhwar.

Dizhwar shakes his head a few times and then nods his head towards the door leading out of the pilot house. The pair walk outside and Dizhwar leans against the railing.

Arabic flows from Dizhwar in a practiced and confidant tone. "I know there is someone on the boat, Driver, I just don't know who. I send Khoury and they turn up missing."

Driver doesn't say a word, just waits for his leader to finish.

"It is paramount for the wider goal. We must maintain control of this vessel until the very end. On one hand, I don't want to send more men and have them disappear. We can just stay where we are, and finish this. On the other hand, I want to overwhelm whomever is loose below so we can *all* get off of this ship."

Driver is in deep contemplation for a moment. Then he too leans against the railing, speaks back in Arabic as well. Driver, his voice aimed out to sea, "Four possibly missing? Abia and Khoury were each alone, correct?" Dizhwar nods his agreement

"Jibril and Parvez are or were in the noisy engine room. Those are all good odds for a sneaky assailant. That doesn't sound like a team to me. A group would have made a beeline straight up here. I think it is just one or two down there, not a group below decks."

Dizhwar nods in agreement again, but he doesn't say anything because Driver's logic is sound. He doesn't want to interput the man's train of thought. It's his turn to listen to his trusted friend analyze the situation. Driver waits for Dizhwar to work through his first observation, then follows it up, "I think it's clear that maintaining control of the ship and the passengers is paramount?"

Dizhwar again nods his head.

"...and you called out warnings to the passenger guards? Sending Abdul and Monifa down there with a caution as well?"

"Yes. Called to Raphael and he will pass the word." As Dizhwar speaks he turns to face his friend.

Driver returns the gaze, "We are so close to our objective. Monifa and Abdul are both good at what they do. Plus despite their arguments, they think like a *unit*. I think you are doing the right thing."

"Thank you, my friend." With that, Dizhwar pats Driver's shoulder and they both walk back into the pilothouse.

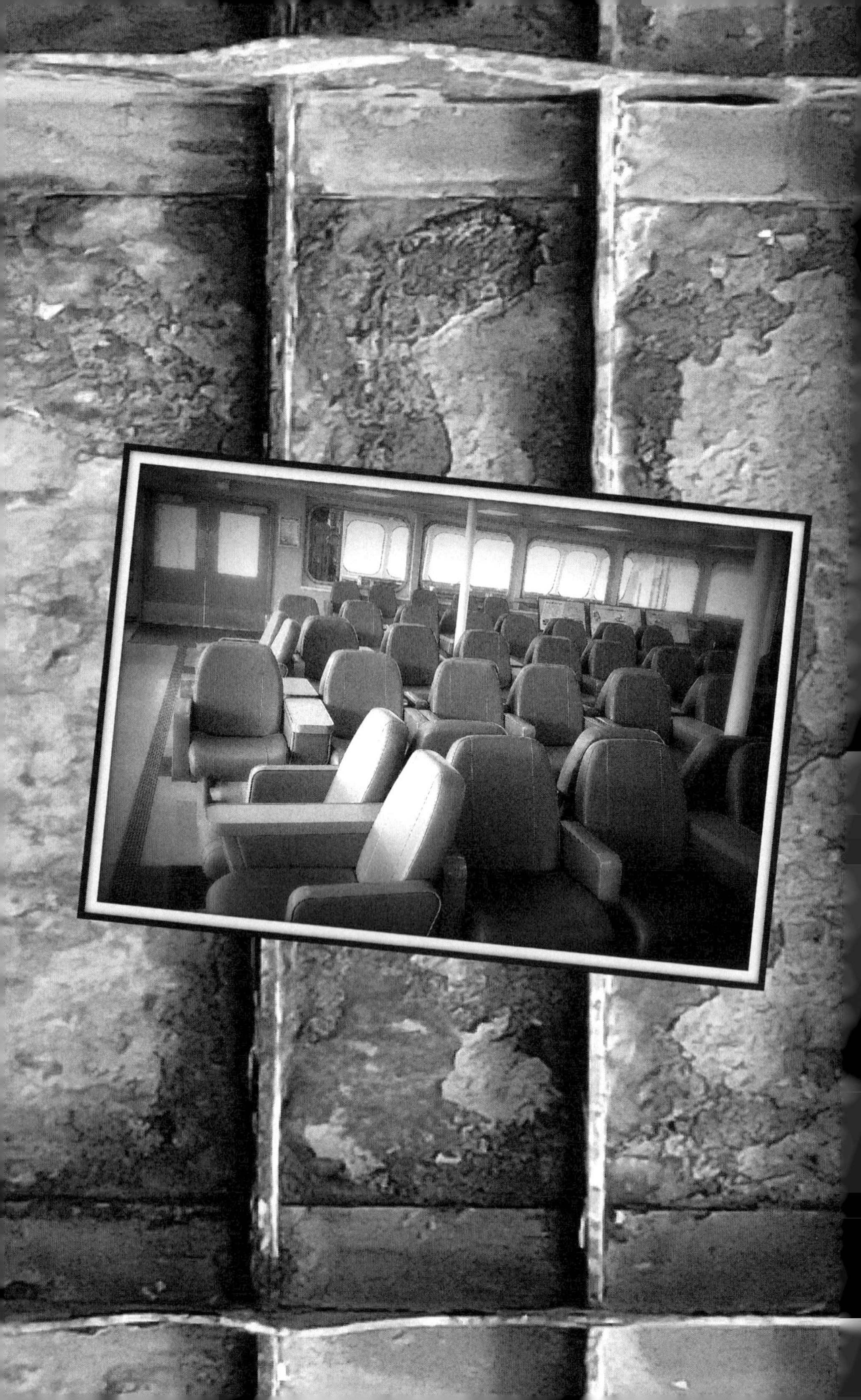

Chapter Forty Five

Thursday August 30th 22:19

After James's conversation with Dizhwar, he feels smugly pleased. *I know that I should have kept my mouth shut,* he tells himself. *I have never been good at coming up with quips at the spur of the moment, but I wanted to rattle Dizhwar as much as possible. Vague enough to leave more doubts within that evil man's little head than my words settled.*

James crouches down, *hopefully I will be successful at the rattling.* He walks forward slowly, trying to be aware of everything around him. He has a song lyric come to mind. "...He rides in force tonight and time will tell us all...side by side we await the night of the darkest hour of them all." He continues forward into the passenger area with the Led Zeppelin song on his thoughts.

James maneuvers his rifle's sights to the point in space where he looks. First he scans behind him toward the aft cabin area and then back to the passageways that lead to the fore passenger cabin. He turns his head and listens to crying, quiet and close, and muted whispers that he can't quite make out. James walks in a crouch to the rear passenger cabin not expecting to see anyone. He wanted to reconnoiter the entire passenger deck just in case. It's all clear behind him. He finishes his loop through the aft cabin, past the historical pictures of the northwest on the walls and walks to the threshold of the fore cabin.

James makes it to the edge of the main fore cabin, just shy of the entrance doorway. *I can't see any gunman, just passengers.* He remembers back what Abia had said, *there should be four of her conspirators here.* Pushing the rifle back, James slowly peeks his head around the corner.

There they all are, he confirms. He can see one armed man, maybe five feet away with his back to James. The passengers are all sitting down on the chairs, benches or on the floor. They were clustered to the front, by the observation area doors. All the passengers seem to be tied to things; ship furniture, each other, and hand rails.

This isn't going to be easy, he warns himself. Another terrorist walks into view, facing James. James quickly withdraws his head from around the corner. The gunman was a good thirty feet away, standing next to the doors that lead to the fore exterior observation deck. *Hopefully I wasn't seen,* he worries. James waits for some sort of response and approaching sounds with his AK ready. Yet, none come. James slowly pulls back from his point of scrutiny.

The stairway, from the car deck he had come up, ends in a "T" that leads to either side of the ferry. From those parallel hallways you can walk fore or aft on either side of the ship. James is currently on the port side. *Let's go over to the starboard side to see what things look like from there. A different vantage point, a different angle on some way to take these men on.* James take care to be quiet and unnoticed regardless of the time it takes.

Once there, James complains, *it is the same from this side as well.* Two different terrorists: one close and one far away. These passenger guards had to be relying on the two terrorists he already dealt with. It was the only way to explain why these four gunman are so focused on the passengers. *They are ignoring all of the other areas on this same level,* he acknowledges. *If you did not have to worry about other areas of the ship then it must have been, out of sight, out of mind?*

Well, James reflects, *at least I know where the terrorists will be.* The strategy of how to take these four comes to him as he takes in a few deep breaths. He tries to calm his heart, slow his breathing, but can't help wonder if this will be his last?

Muttering under his breath, James remarks to himself *the next step can't be as hard as it seems, right?*

Chapter Forty Six

Thursday August 30th 22:21

Latisha has been shooting all four of her captors the evil eye for most of the past hour. She has worked through her fear and is prayerful for the chance to do something and react faster this time. She keeps repeating the numbers and the physical descriptions she's assigned to the various gunmen.

"Number one is thin, gaunt face, scraggly beard down to his chest. About five seven with brown hair and acts like he is on speed. Number two is..." After reciting her list, her thoughts take her elsewhere. *If these fanatics get away with it somehow, I will at least be the one with an accurate description of all of them.* Latisha is doing her best to work through the shock and commit it all to memory. She has a sharp mind and trusts herself to keep all of the information straight despite the horrible place she is in. She fails to notice the man next to her lean in and whisper in her ear.

Whispering harshly, the man pleads. "Keep your voice down!" Latisha jumps away from his voice, as much as she can, being restrained. It catches her completely off guard.

"Just what are you thinking, scaring me like that!" Latisha demands. The man flinches at her whispered rebuke. Seeing that it's another passenger, Latisha calms herself.

"I'm sorry," the man looks downward at his feet in a penitent manner. "You're just drawing a lot of attention to yourself. The thin guy with the Uzi has been watching you like a hawk."

"That's cause he's afraid of me," she lowers her voice to finish, "and he should be. Yosemite Sam over there had a run in with me and I almost got the best of him. I was only a few feet from ripping his gun away and shooting him with it." The thought brings Latisha some joy. "Now, I have a special place in his heart." With that, she smiles a candy coated smile toward the gunman that she calls Yosemite Sam.

"You two! Stop talking!" Yosemite Sam yells at the pair of them. His real name is Faaiq and he hopes they will shut up and stop looking his way. He is already more nervous than what he should be and those two aren't making him feel any better. Dizhwar and his "easy mission." Faaiq just grinds his teeth about this whole thing. If he could make it downstairs, without being noticed, he'd grab a raft and be gone from the ship. Make his way to Seatac Airport and catch a flight out of Seattle before the warning went out.

Head back to Sacramento and continue the search for my real parents? Faaiq yearns.

Latisha lowered her head in a mock sign of submission. "See, what did I tell you?" she whispers. Trying to enjoy the little bit of power she has over one of her captors.

"Oh yeah, you made an impression on him. But you should avoid eye contact if possible or your just going to inflame the situation," The man responded with his head down as well. His chin hit his chest a little to soon due to a barrel chest and a thick neck. His head barely looked like it was lowered. "My name is Brad Hensley," Brad said in a breathy voice not used to whispering.

"Latisha Reynolds. I'd shake your hand sir, but I'm a little tied up at the moment." She tugged gently on her hands to demonstrate her confinement. They both forced out a quiet laugh to ease the tension they both felt. "If you don't mind, how do you know so much about what causes someone to get angrier? Are you a cop or a shrink or something?"

"Once a criminal profiler, now an executive driver." Brad stated plainly and succinctly. Latisha waited politely for more information and Brad, a little unnerved by the gunman, and a little unsure of himself under Latisha's gaze, chatted on. "I used to work for the Sheriff's Department, mostly Judicial Services. Fifteen years, I would help the judges, prosecutors and other law enforcement personnel evaluate those accused or convicted of crimes. But two years ago I quit. Started up my own business."

"Where were you when, you know, this hijacking started?" Latisha asked with a quick sideways glance to the closest gunman. Yosemite Sam was no where to be seen.

"I am ashamed to say it." Brad dug his chin deeper into his chest, almost as if he needed it to balance his large head. "I was bound for Port Orchard with a client.. I panicked in my front seat and I ran down the ramp, pistol in hand to jump off to swim to safety."

She tried to think up something that was conciliatory, but couldn't.

Brad continued, "One moment I was running toward the edge and the next I had a rifle butt smack me in the head. They took my sidearm and my mobile phone."

Latisha was still at a loss for words and tried to say something, "I was just goin' home myself. Don't beat yourself up, everyone..."

"YOU!!" The loud voice was right behind Latisha's head. She was hit hard in the back of it. Her jaw slammed down on her mouth as it made contact with her chest. She bit her tongue from the hard blow. Then there was another head right in between her and Brad's, talking in a tone filled with spite and aggravation.

"Look you two. I told the both of you to shut the hell up!" Latisha smelled a foul breath and an even fouler body odor coming off of the man. She turned away more in revulsion at the smell and in fear of his presence. "If there is so much as a peep from either one of you, I will cut out both of your tongues."

The man known as Faaiq stepped over their chairs right in between the both of them, pushing each of them apart as he climbed over. He had lived a pampered life in Florida with his adoptive parents. Mr. and Ms. Walker adopted the boy from an orphanage in Morocco when he was just four. The boy would never accept his parents changing his name to Samuel, so eventually they relented and let their son keep his first name. They proceeded to pay him every attention, being the only child, but Faaiq was never satisfied or easy to please.

When he was seventeen Faaiq left his adoptive family to find his "real family." In searching for his biological parents the young man followed the trail across the United States to Sacramento, California. While he continued his search in California's capital, he was introduced to a Grey Haired man at a Muslim outreach center.

Latisha did her best not to smile at the grimace that was painted all over the guy's face. He did look like Yosemite Sam even more so close up.

The man that looked like Yosemite Sam, but was known as Faaiq, gave his best angry look at the pair of them. "I mean it!" The bearded man stormed off to resume his position just a few yards away. Another hijacker with a stern look walked over to Faaiq and whispered something in his ear and then walked off.

Faaiq shook his head imperceptibly as Raphael walks away. *I don't need to put up with this, Raphael sticking his nose where it doesn't belong or stupid loud mouths.* Faaiq fumed, *I am better than her and all of these kafir.* Faaiq crossed his arms and once more his gaze bore down on the passengers. *Once this was over, I will find my family and finally have what I need.*

"Your right," Brad whispered through a bowed head and clinched teeth to Latisha. "...Yosemite Sam is afraid n' unstable. I've seen this kind of behavior before. But... I don't think it's because of you."

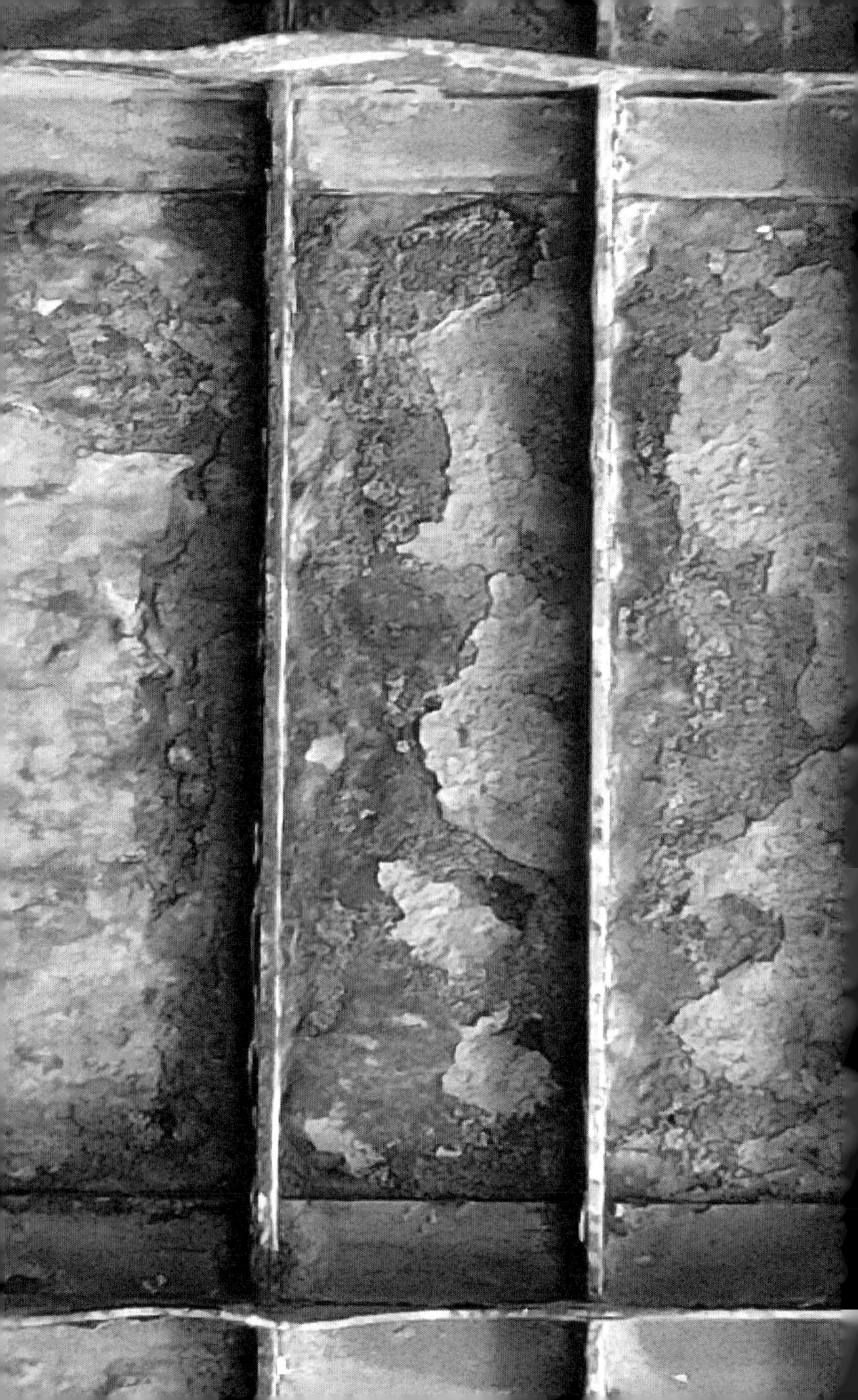

Chapter Forty Seven

Thursday August 30th 22:24

Fear falls over him. It feels as tangible as a cloak. James checks that his safety is off on his AK. He doesn't want to commit to the action that he decided on, so he's been waiting for minutes to find the courage to act. He nervously tells himself, *wait just one more moment before starting this next attack.* Yet, through his doubts and fear, James takes the step forward consigning his life to his plan. He enters from the starboard side hallway walking in a crouch.

Shoot, shoot, shoot, you fool! He yells inside of his head. His first shots from his rifle hit the man farthest away, directly in front of James. With his rifle braced against a doorjamb for stability, James keeps this farthest man in his sites. James works the trigger three more times, with measured pulls. He watches the gunman go down. One and a half seconds goes by since he started.

James clears the doorway to the fore cabin and brings the rifle around to his left.

"Faster! Faster! Faster!" His thoughts actually escape his lips as he engages the terrorist that he knows to be there. James does not even look through the sights, but just pulls the trigger with the barrel in the general direction of his target. This gunman is already turning James's way, ducking at the sounds of James's first burst of gunfire. The second man is raising his rifle at the same time he turns to face the stressed James.

This second man, Hakim Ali, starts to fire as James continues to walk toward him, firing point blank now. James sees his own 5.45x39mm bullets hit this terrorist in the chest and he walks the rounds up into the face and neck.

Hakim Ali, honorably discharged Iraqi army veteran, dies instantly. He had overstayed his tourist visa and joined the group shortly after Jibril and Parvez. Two seconds have now gone by.

The bullets from James's rifle barely have time to fully accelerate before slamming into flesh and bone of Hakim. Hakim's rifle stops firing before it's muzzle had been brought to bare on James.

Down! Down! Down for cover you slow poke! He screams at himself now, the adrenalin flowing through his veins. James falls to his knees besides the dead terrorist. James kneels behind the rear row of seats, practically on top of his recent victim. The blood and gore soak into James Carhartt pants at the knees. He sucks in a deep breath, preparing for his longest shot. *Clear across the passenger area, cross-corner to me.*

His third target, alerted by James's gunfire is ducking and firing wildly. The lanky Faaiq Walker doesn't care where or what he hits. He is panicked from the gunfire, not expecting to encounter anything like this. He had always been blusterous around others, but when he must take a stand alone, his cowardice is showing.

The thoughts fire rapidly through Faaiq's mind, *this was just a bunch of unarmed civilians. He and his team weren't supposed to be shot at! They were there to kill others, not to be killed themselves.* Faaiq's bullets smash into the ceiling and the bulkhead directly behind James. Before James can get a clear shot, Faaiq ducks for cover behind a bench on the port side, opposite James.

Faaiq is just trying to buy him some time so he can think too. Faaiq fires everywhere once more, trying to make whoever is shooting at him and his brother to duck. Faaiq hunkers down behind his seat and starts shaking in fear, forgetting all of his training. He realizes, too late, that he doesn't have the stomach for actually being shot at.

This isn't good, James worries. *I can't take the risk of hitting a passengers by shooting at the third man anymore.* Only eight seconds have gone by since he started firing.

Move! Move! Move! A snap decision comes to him like a spark from flint. Keeping his head low, James moves out the way he just came in. With quick precision he empties his rifle of the mostly empty magazine and replaces it with a new one. James retreats from the starboard side back to the port side, rifle up, walking in a crouch. He enters the port side hallway looking through the sights. As James comes around the hallway leading to the port passenger area, he can see all of the way forward to the front observation deck.

The fourth terrorist, the one he has yet to shoot at, is right there! James excitedly tells himself. The gunman is walking perpendicular to James, pointing his rifle to starboard.

Right where I used to be. James quickly kneels, steadies himself, elbow on knee and squeezes off one, two, three, four, five rounds, in measured succession. This fourth terrorist is still in his sights and James watches as the wounded man turns toward the source the injuries.

James watches the gunman collapse onto his own knees.

James Maly hesitates, not knowing if his target has had enough. *Will he stay down from my gunshots or does he still have some fight left in him?*

Chapter Forty Eight

Thursday August 30th 22:25

Raphael, the fourth gunman, looked toward the sounds, *I hope that is not gunfire.* He had just gotten off of the radio with Dizhwar and had barely warned Faaiq when the noises started. He had said a fast *dua* for Khoury that turned into a longer one, once he knew the noises were gunfire. Raphael hoped, *maybe it's one of my teammates just killing an escaping passenger. Like that one woman that would not shut up? Or the fat man sitting next to her? The one that was watching us all too carefully? All of my team believed that this ferry was ours.*

So secured and under our control, Raphael acknowledged.

Dizhwar and Driver had told us this was to be an easy and safe mission. A first chance to get their cell's feet wet. A way to strike at the kafir, the unbelievers. All of us were to get away scot-free.

Just like Faaiq, Raphael believed, *there was supposed to be no deaths, at least not on our parts.*

As Raphael turns toward the sound of gunfire, he sees the first one of his compatriots, Tarriq, being gunned down. The once strong and powerful Tarriq is reduced to a bloody heap on the floor in a split second. Raphael's senses are struck at the gory sight. *Tarriq didn't even get the chance to fire a single shot! The big man didn't have a chance to defend himself or even lift his rifle.* Raphael's thoughts are pulled from Tarriq when there is more gunfire from somewhere, and then Faaiq returns it. The confusion of real combat settles in and Raphael is almost overwhelmed by it.

Almost.

Raphael watches Faaiq blasting away wildly, without even aiming. Raphael doesn't take cover, he just stands at his post in almost total loss. His face and eyes flinching at the incredibly loud gunfire, Raphael isn't fearful. Not at all.

Then he snaps out of his inaction and begins to confidently walk forward in hopes of surprising the unknown attacker. Raphael brings his rifle to bear, looking down the sights and is ready to extract vengeance on the shooter. He first checks to see if Hakim is ok. Hakim was stationed to Raphael's immediate right, just around a vending area of the passenger cabin. Both he and Hakim were guarding the entrances to the fore passenger cabin from the rest of the ship.

Raphael turns a corner and is horrified to see Hakim sprawled out in a pool of spreading blood and brain matter.

Raphael is alarmed by the sight of death, *Hakim is barely recognizable! The yet unseen attacker, the one that I was warned about, has totally vanished.* His eyes start to burn from the gun smoke and he blinks away the irritation.

Raphael doubles back and tries to clear his thoughts. *There is so much noise in the cabin!* Many of the passengers are crying, screaming and praying. Raphael's life as a loner and surviving on the streets of various cities provides him with a vital skill. He can think on his feet. He swiftly turns to Faaiq, who has taken shelter behind one of the booth seats.

"Faaiq! Get up!" Raphael orders, taking control of the situation. Raphael's mind flashes back to his training and his mind runs through tactics.

Raphael glances back to his teammate and Faaiq doesn't move. "Follow me, Faaiq." Raphael pleads. Faaiq doesn't respond to Raphael.

"Work together on this!" Raphael begins to lay out his case, "We can kill this...kafir, if we just work as a team," Raphael tries to explain. All of the while visually searching the area for the attacker. Raphael's gun swings around in arcs following his eyes as he searches.

Convince Faaiq, Raphael's common sense pleads. *Two are better than one!* "Faaiq Walker!" Raphael yells this time, as he watches Faaiq reload his 9mm Uzi.

Had Faaiq even fired a shot? Raphael's bloodstream is pulsing with adrenaline and it is fogging his memory. Faaiq turns to Raphael, furiously shaking his head at Raphael's commands. Frustrated, with Faaiq's cowardice, and distracted from the threat that's now facing him at his blindside, Raphael turns toward the hallway that comes from amid-ships.

In that moment, Raphael is hit. The shock of immense pain shoots through his entire right side. He feels the tugs and pushes from his leg, all of the way to his shoulder.

The pain is debilitating. Raphael almost drops his rifle as he goes down hard onto his knees.

"My God..." he gasps out. "Faaiq..."

Raphael's right leg just stops working. It's so quick, Raphael has to go down to both knees to avoid collapsing forward onto his face. His left hand reaches out to stop himself from falling over forwards. He straightens at the waist, his right leg still refusing to obey. Questions and terrible pain flood his senses, overloading and shutting down his capability to respond.

Then a noise draws his attention toward his right.

There. Raphael sees the stranger with one of their rifles. "Khoury, did you loose your gun in a last mortal struggle?" Raphael asks no one.

So where did he come from? Raphael silently asks. Then it occurs on him, as he looks down the barrel of his own assailant's smoking weapon, "This dog has shot me?" He hisses it aloud and his voice is drowned out by the crying and the sobbing from the passengers.

Raphael looks at himself and tries to move his right arm that's holding his own rifle. Everything takes on a blurry, surreal look and feeling. Raphael's right arm moves so slowly, like its pulling on a heavy weight to large to budge quickly. Raphael struggles against the rubber-band like resistance that's stopping him to bring up his rifle for a response.

Then, he cannot. Raphael's entire right side just shuts down.

Through tremendous agony, Raphael is able to get his left arm to function. He uses his left to grab the rifle from his damaged right arm as it hangs useless. The terrorist is just able to bring up the rifle, to bear upon his assailant.

Raphael Webber works hard at a chance to pull the trigger.

DENVER VANCOUVER
SAN FRANCISCO
LOS ANGELES
CHICAGO
MEXICO CITY
SEIKO

Chapter Forty Nine

Thursday August 30th 22:28

James is still kneeling when he sees the gunman in his sights begin to go down. James can see that this individual, down on his knees, has an intense anger in his face. It radiates out toward James like a laser...*and if it was a beam of light, like on Star Wars it would have killed me.*

James watches to see what the terrorist will do next. James speculates, *will the wounded man surrender or will he continue to fight?*

James takes a breath and then two. He's strongly aware of his own life and his own death, as he sucks in another breath and releases it. James tries to reach out to the man that he shot, with a silent plea, *I hit you with at least seven rounds from my rifle, just go down!*

James watches for a half a minute as the terrorist struggles. James surveys the struggle, unmoving, as the gunman tries to bring up the rifle that he carries with his right arm. James can see the man is having trouble raising it. James just looks upon the man with a little pity, for it is James that had just dealt the wounds. The gunman arches his back in a bid to raise up his right arm once more, but the action is unsuccessful.

"Come on, I know you want to just lie down," James encourages the gunman through a whisper that comes through clinched teeth. James looks over his partially lowered rifle, "Lie down and die. Give up, already."

The gunman is clearly injured; James can see that *he doesn't have a prayer to survive.* James lowers his rifle, just a bit more, giving him a clear view over the receiver of the weapon. James looks to the wounded man, even slightly remorseful at the damage he has done. This fourth gunman struggles hard against his injuries. James is caught up in the struggle, like witnessing a tragic death of an animal that got hit by a car.

James eyes the man, and can see the blood seeping into his target's clothes now. Then James witnesses the most increbile thing as the bloodied man reaches over with his left hand to bring the rifle to bear.

James can't believe his eyes. "Dear, God!" He exclaims in total astonishment. James was only *slightly* remorseful.

In one fluid motion, James rapidly raises his own rifle. He takes a millisecond to glance through the sights. His AK booms as James squeezes the trigger one more time. The spent brass cartridge bangs off of the steel wall next to James coming to rest next to his feet in a smoking arc.

James's sights are hovering directly over the man's head as his AK's round zeroes in on its aim point. There is a quick puff of red and the terrorist falls onto his side.

Although James is affected by the carnage, he quickly compartmentalizes it. Grabbing the image that he just saw and mentally stuffing it down where the other images from this evening reside. He whispers a quick prayer and returns to his standing position. He slowly begins to walk forward. James remains slightly hunched over his rifle; kneeling slightly as he walks.

Three of the terrorists are permanently down, he believes. *Only one more to go in this area.*

James passes the doorway back into the passenger cabin. It hits him how much sound the passengers are making. His ears aren't ringing from the gunfire, because he absent-mindedly left his earplugs in his ears, but he can hear the cries and the pleas through his muted hearing.

Everyone must be scared for their lives because I am as well. But, I can't free anyone just yet, not until the last hostile is down. Not seeing anyone with a gun, James walks cautiously over next to the first bench, and scans the room. He makes two full scans of the entire passenger cabin and doesn't see the last terrorist that had ducked and run.

Where is the one that was spraying the bullets around, James wonders to himself.

"Where is he? Did he leave?" James demands out loud, to his rifle. James surveys the room again, this time, carefully. He can see the first and third man he shot still lying on the deck and he hopes the second one is still there too. Scrutinizing every corner, every place where someone could hide James is thorough, barrel following his line of sight. One of the passengers, a man in a business suit points with his eyes and then his head to James.

James diligently examines the cabin in the general direction of where the business suited man is pointing with nods. Soon others catch on and they are also pointing toward a specific corner.

James holds a breath, willing his eyes to see what he missed. *Wait a minute!*

Is that the gunman right there?!?

In the first aisle, next to the windows, last bench, straight in front of me? Is that a barrel pointing upwards? Just the very front of it?

James brings up his rifle, tucks it into his shoulder tight and slowly starts to rise from his squatting position next to the bench, every muscle in his legs flexing tightly. This slow rise up is a demonstration of James's will over his own body. Almost at a full stand, James is sure it's the barrel of a gun. He can see the hair at the top of the man's head. The gunman is hiding behind a bench.

James ignores the rest of the passengers now and focuses on the man's gun barrel, there against the fore bulkhead.

James has a decision to make, *shoot or not to shoot? For the moment I'm safe, no danger from what I believe is this final terrorist left alive in the room.*

James tries again to come up with a desperate plan. *If I walk around at an oblique angle to the gunman I will put the passengers in his sights. I can't get to the outside of the ship and come in through the observation deck; although that would be ideal. The only way to access the observation deck is to come down from the pilothouse.*

That might take too much time! James desperately tries to work up something, but is left wishing for some climbing gear and a rappelling rope.

Tick, tick, tick, time to make a decision.

Because time is running out.

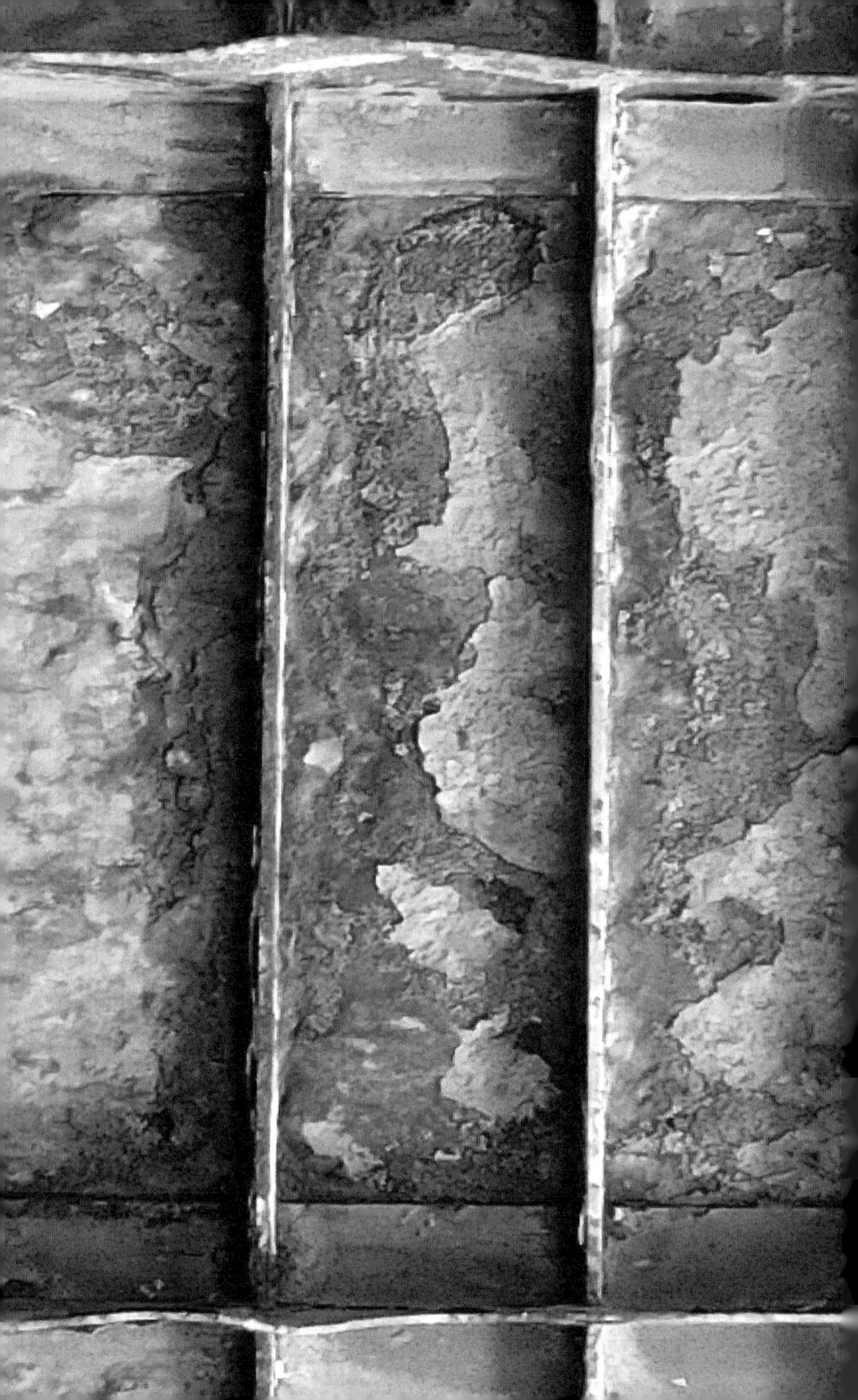

Chapter Fifty

Thursday August 30th 22:30

"You have got to be freaking kidding me! Whatda mean I can't take the yacht out?" Captain Ian gestures emphatically with his hands, pointing from the ship to the lock, "...the ship isn't a crime scene! It didn't get attacked! Isn't it obvious the lock is what got damaged!!"

Ian motions furiously, his hands flying about, trying to illustrate his point. He looks aghast from one police type to another and they all look at him with impassive faces. Ian Sandivick takes the three steps back into the gathered circle of officials. "Come on now! Throw me out a lifejacket here!" Ian smiles at his naval reference, but it is again lost on the gathered law enforcers.

The whole world is crazy and deaf! Captain Ian has been going round and round with whoever will listen. First it was the lock operator, *a guy named Oliver that didn't seem to want to listen to anything that I said.* He just took his magazines and off he went with some other law enforcers to one of the big buildings next to the lock. Then there was a local Seattle police officer and now it is a few different officers from a few different law enforcement agencies. Ian is trying to convince someone to let him get his ship out of that concrete berth, that they call a lock, with all due haste.

Captain Ian needs to fuel up the *Eternity* to have it ready for tomorrow's trip. *50,439 gallons of fuel didn't get transferred from shore to ship in a few minutes,* Ian acknowledges. *But now, the police are talking terrorism, bomb threats and freakin national security. Saying things like the Department of Justice and the Department of Homeland Security are going to get involved! For a stupid, fifty year old, neglected and damaged lock motor!!*

Captain Ian Sandivick stands there among them as they start talking about all kinds of other intertwined law enforcement agencies. One officer is talking on his radio to someone who is saying the FBI are on their way. Another is busy on the phone talking about calling up the national guard. *This is giving me a supreme headache,* Ian gripes.

Captain Ian, in no way, wants to make phone calls to his bosses. *Yet, it's looking more and more like that is what I'm going to be forced to do.*

I'll give it one more valiant effort, he convinces himself. Trying to get the five gathered law enforcers attention he thinks fast on his feet. "Can't you see the yacht has nothing to do with this?" He is pleading now, making one last bold attempt to get his precious ship out. "The locks pumps should be able to be turned back on and *Eternity* will be level with the ocean in just half a..."A dark grey van pulls up, interrupting Ian's pontification.

The van is marked with some King County logos on it, and as Ian watches, people get out and start putting on big thick armored suits. Ian looks to the nearest official in the group that he is talking to, someone from the Seattle Water Patrol. "What's the deal with the suits?"

"EOD." The Water Patrol Officer says dryly. "They have to inspect the area to make sure it's safe and then we bring in the dogs to discover if there's any other ordnance around that they couldn't find."

""EOD?"

The Seattle Water Patrol officer looks at Ian sideways, "Yeah. Explosive Ordinance Disposal? Bomb squad?"

"Ordinance...Bomb Squad?" Ian asks with a bit of perplexity over the words.

"You know your ship is not going to get out of there anytime soon," the Seattle Water Patrol officer informs Ian. "So why don't you just stop the speeches and go sit down with your crew? We will be with you shortly."

Ian tries to interject something else, but for once in his life he is out of words. Regardless, it's too late, the group that he was just talking at walks off to continue their police work. Ian overhears from the officer's radios that there is a bomb scare at the cruise ship terminal. That one turned into a *real* explosion and there were others as well, but they keep saying municipal boats. Ian tells himself, *too many municipal terminals around to know which other one got hit.*

Over the radios and from bits of conversation, Ian hears there are also some sort of problem up in the north *and* in the southern part of the Salish Sea. *Rescue operations are ongoing with the Coast Guard? Canada is involved too? What a friggin mess and I'm caught up in the middle of it?!? Add to that, there's a damaged fireboat out in the middle of Elliot Bay and the 'municipal boats' that are damaged?*

He asks to the sky, "What in God's name is going on?" That's because none of the officers are left nearby to hear him.

"Captain!" a voice behind him snaps him out of his thoughts.

He turns around to look upon his crewmember, the one that got his attention. "What?!?"

As he looks back toward his crew, the starting their slow and meticulous work.

"How long are we going to have to stay here?" the crewwoman to his left asks.

Before she can finish a crewman on Ian's right asks "And I got one too, sir. Are we gettin' paid for the time we're just sitting here? I can't afford to sit here for free."

"Captain, I asked the question first," the original crewwoman jumps back into the discussion while the other crew watch. Ian Sandivick raises both of his hands, fingers up as if he is going to make a point, while he answers both of them. He reconsiders and just shakes his head, burying his head into his worn and battered hands.

Ian Sandivick is going to have to make a phone call and he is going to have to do it now. This was to be the maiden voyage of the *Eternity*. Now, he is going to look like a novice, worse yet, a simple fisherman if he can't find a way out of this mess. Ian wasn't going to get tossed from this opportunity. Not when he just got his golden ticket. His wealthy employers' will not be able to take out their very expensive new toy.

Ian curses, *on its first cruise no less! The Kings are not going to be happy with me, but hopefully, it should be a short delay.* He resolves not to make matters worse by making that phone call.

He sits down heavily on the bench with the rest of his crew. *Treat them like Kings? How could you tell a King, no?*

Maybe this isn't such an easy job after all?

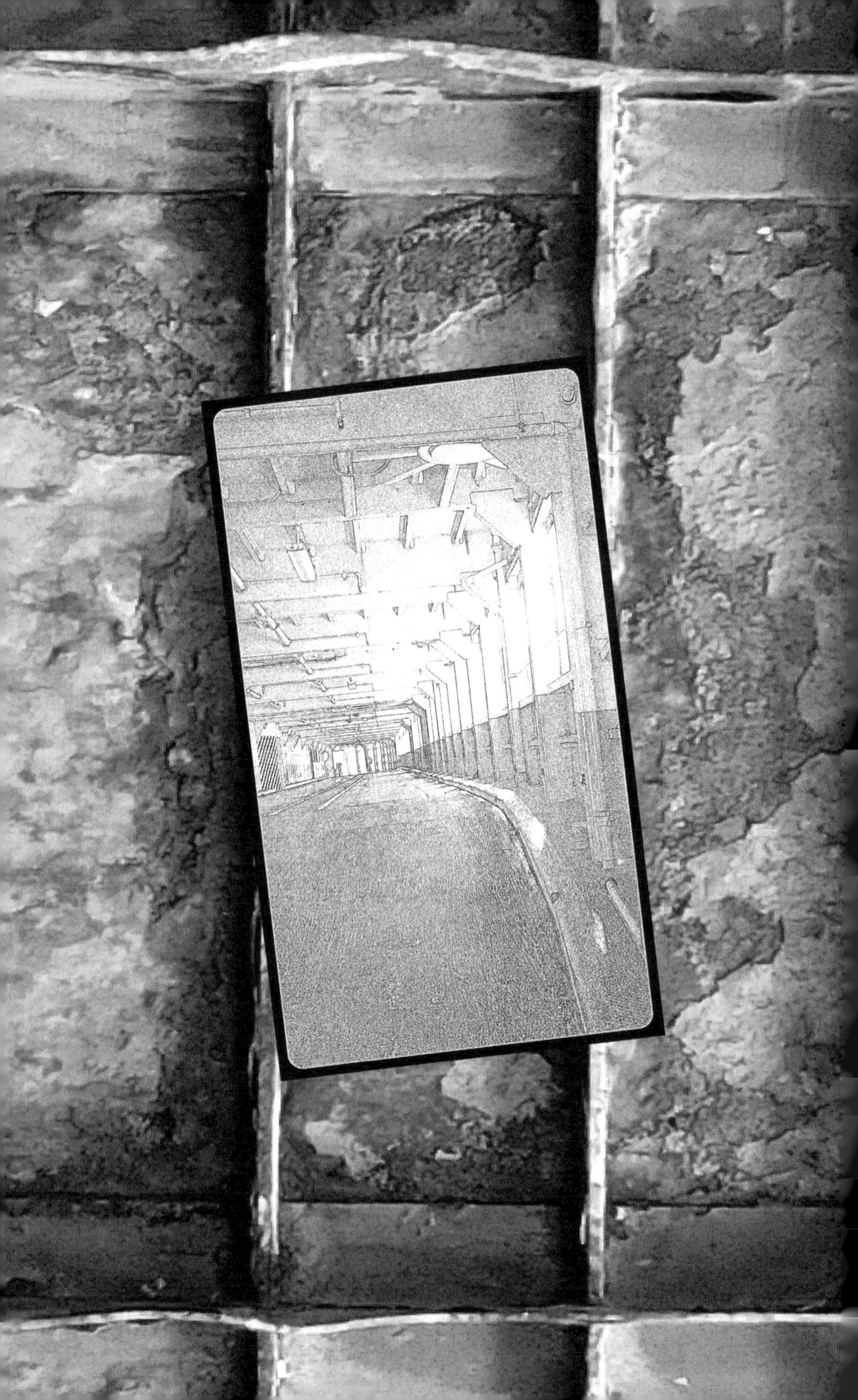

Chapter Fifty One

Thursday August 30th 22:30

Dizhwar Razzaq eagerly awaits Abdul and Monifa to check in. He drums his fingers on the ship bulkhead, eagerly waiting. In the first ten minutes the pair had already checked in twice, once upon getting to the observation deck, once down at the car deck. Any moment they should report that they are at the engine room.

As if he was some sort of fortune teller, Dizhwar gets a beep on his radio. His fingers stop their mindless drumming as he grabs his radio.

Not even looking he speaks "Go, ahead for Dizhwar."

"Dizhwar…" comes a timid and shaking voice over the radio. For a moment Dizhwar doesn't recognize it. He is momentarily confused because he was expecting to hear one voice and gets someone different. Dizhwar glances at the radio ID number, if it wasn't for that he wouldn't have been able to guess who the voice belonged to.

"Faaiq? Is that you?"

"D D D Dizhwar…. he's killed them. Killed them all! I, I, I, I, saw Raphael's head explode! Right, right before my eyes…" Faaiq rattles out his words in a shaking whisper. Like a tree during the fall winds that doesn't want to get rid of it's final leaves.

Dizhwar's blood runs cold, he speaks plainly with a steady cadence "Listen to me carefully, Faaiq. You need to tell me exactly what happened. Who, what, when, where. Remember your training?"

"Dizhwar I'm…. scared. I, I, I, I don't want to die. Th, th, th, this wasn't supposed to happen like this! We were…. all meant to get off of…"

"Faaiq!" Dizhwar cuts in. Temper rising as he tries one more time to control the situation. Softly he speaks, "Tell me what's happened."

That seemed to get through. Faaiq tells Dizhwar about the moments after the entire passenger guard had checked in, Dizhwar's warning that Raphael gave him, and the gun fire that had started. And now he, Faaiq, is the only one left.

How is this possible? Dizhwar asks of himself. He didn't hear any gunfire, is that likely? He is only two levels above the main passenger area. Had he been struck by his god temporarily deaf? The fighting started right after Dizhwar had walked back into the pilot house. Right after his warning to Raphael. Has Allah turned away from him? Was this Allah's plan for this task? Dizhwar's head is spinning from the questions as his radio chirps.

"Go ahead," he replies reflexively, his mind still caught up in Faaiq's news.

"Abdul and Monifa, checking in." For a moment Dizhwar can't even answer, he is still dumbfounded by his talk with Faaiq.

"Report." Dizhwar says back, in an exhalation of stress.

"We checked the engine room. Jibril and Parvez are dead. Looks like all of the explosives are intact and live... but we can't be sure. No sign of Abia or Khoury."

Dizhwar stunned, leans against the pilot house bulkhead for support. Allah's plan, all... wrecked? So many of his team are dead or missing? First, his team in the passenger cabin and now the engine room?

Dizhwar pulls back a second and asks himself a simple question: *What does he know for sure?*

"Dizhwar..." It was Faaiq's clearly panicked voice.

Snap out of it, you fool! Dizhwar's conscience barks.

His Gray Haired recruiter's voice echoes within him, "You must complete the mission at all costs." Dizhwar's voice is almost mechanical as he still recoils from the chaos that his plans have now descended into.

The radio chirps again "What is your next command?" Abdul queries.

"Dizhwar, don't we need to begin the abandon ship process?" adds Driver, speaking next to him.

Five? That's all that are left? Just five out of twelve? Dizhwar struggles to pull all of his disorganized thoughts together.

"Dizhwar...please tell me what to do. He, he....I think he must still be here..." Faaiq fades off into a whisper.

"Dizhwar, you need to command." Driver warns.

Monifa calling in this time "Dizhwar…"

"ENOUGH!" Dizhwar shouts into the radio, directed at all of them, himself and the situation.

"FAAIQ!" Dizhwar bellows. Checking his radio to make sure he is transmitting just to Faaiq. "You must kill the bastard and kill him now! That is an order! After doing so, YOU WILL meet up with your brothers at the starboard Zodiac and prepare it for immediate launch. DO YOU UNDERSTAND!?!" Dizhwar is back. Composed and once again in control.

There is a long silent pause while Dizhwar waits for Faaiq to acknowledge.

"Dizhwar." Do you copy?" Abdul asks again.

"One moment, Abdul!" Dizhwar shouts, making Abdul and Monifa cringe a bit down in the engine room.

There's a long passing of silence on Faaiq's part, Dizhwar has had enough. Loosing all patience with the cowardice of Faaiq, "FAAIQ!!!!" Dizhwar screams.
"Yes… Dizhwar, uuuunderstood. Meeting Abdul and Monifa after I… kill the intruder…" the meek voice of Faaiq trails off.

Dizhwar takes ten seconds to compose himself. Back in control, Dizhwar calls to Abdul and Monifa.

"Go ahead for Abdul."

"Make it to that Zodiac… plan B. Ready it to hit the sea. Be careful and alert! Faaiq's the only one else there. Enemies are trying to stop our plans. If you see anyone other than your teammates; shoot them! Understand?"

"Yes. What about Abia and Khoury?" Abdul asks.

"Forget them. We'll honor the fallen and their sacrifice once home. Allăhu Akbar."
With that Dizhwar clicks off.

Abdul doesn't respond, he is taken aback by Dizhwar's final words. He looks at Monifa with a perplexed look, "Dizhwar just used 'Allăhu Akbar' in his sign-off to me. This isn't good."

Monifa, agreeing, "No it isn't. He said he would never use that blessing. Come…" patting Abdul on the shoulder, Monifa starts back toward the engine room exit. She looks at her on again off again boy-friend, "…let's finish it and get off of this thing." She takes the lead, marching up the stairs two at a time with purpose.

Back in the pilot house, "Prepare for the final maneuver, remove the steering wheel and throttle bolts..," Dizhwar says to Driver.

While Driver works on the steering, Dizhwar pushes the throttle up, all of the way.

Chapter Fifty Two

Thursday August 30th 22:30

James Maly can hear the entire exchange between Faaiq and Dizhwar over Faaiq's loud radio. James feels the M/V *Wenatchee* lurch forward under her full power. He steadies himself on the balls of his feet keeping his rifle pointed at his target. A little bit of confidence seeps into James's heart as he gets comfortable with the new speed and runs through various thoughts.

The terrorist cell's leader is definitely called Dizhwar. It's the same voice that called out orders to Abia. It is the same commanding tone that I heard over the radio of the young terrorist, Khoury...and Dizhwar isn't happy, making James smile. James particularly enjoys being a thorn in the side of Dizhwar.

James holds back from shooting the man in the back of the head. This man called Faaiq will make his own life and death decision. The social stigma of shooting Faaiq in the back, even though he and his crew have forcibly taken control of others, outweighs James's better judgment. James will offer mercy first to Faaiq.

Try and see if Faaiq has it within himself to surrender, then if he doesn't, kill him. The overworked electrician moves backwards while facing Faaiq, keeping his rifle pointed at the gunman's position. James makes it to the first set of benches coming into the area. He conceals himself back behind the seat, kneeling so that his left elbow rests on the top of the seat back. James's rifle and thus his aim, now has a solid rest.

Ready, James shouts. "Faaiq! Throw away your rifle!" He listens for a moment and tries again. "Faaiq, throw away the gun and put up your hands!"

The top of Faaiq's head drops out of sight, but James can still see the barrel of Faaiq's submachine gun. It's pointed away from him, to James's right and up toward the ceiling. James can imagine Faaiq's position behind the seat cushion and places his rifle's sights right where he thinks Faaiq's body should be.

Faaiq is intimidated, he has to be. James knows.

And James is right. In all of his life Faaiq was never asked, or demanded to make a decision like this. *I don't want to die! I want out!* Faaiq whispers to himself, "But I'm not about to be labeled a coward, a betrayer of the Faith." *This wasn't supposed to go down like this!*

Dizhwar's angry words echo in Faaiq's brain like some empty cave. He is afraid of what he has been commanded to do. *But to just surrender? Is there any honor in that?* Faaiq wars with himself, *my stupid adopted parents didn't prepare me for this! My training didn't prepare me for this! Dizhwar didn't either!!*

Faaiq was alone; faced with life and dishonor, or death and some vague promise of eternal life. *This wasn't supposed to go down like this!* He keeps yelling in his head. The crushing pain on his heart, the anguish in his soul and the alarm of the moment snaps something within him.

James makes his last attempt, "Faaiq, you have five seconds before I come. Time to decide!" James tries to ratchet up the pressure on the doubting man. *Get him to surrender.*

"Allăhu Akbar!!!" James hears the shout above the din of the passengers. He realizes too late what his inaction and pushing gets the terrorist to do.

Faaiq leaps up, screaming the chant at the top of his lungs. Tears streaming down his face he begins to fire wildly into the passenger area.

My God! What have I done? James reels, his self-confidence crushed, as he sees Faaiq jump up.

Faaiq is screaming and James screams back. Faaiq starts his murderous rampage against the restrained hostages. Faaiq lets the stress take over and fires from the hip, squeezing the trigger of his Uzi in an un-aimed stream of bullets.

His 9mm rounds trace high at first, contacting the lights and then the fuse panel at the back of the passenger cabin. Faaiq screams out his rage and fear as he brings his submachine gun's barrel downward. The stream of fire tears into the restrained people as his first bullets still ricochet within the ship.

James, still screaming, watches the sight with complete disbelief. He track the terrorist with his rifle's sights through his own cries, waiting just briefly until he aligns his sights on the gunman. James fires a single, well aimed volley.

The overhead lights blink out and the entire passenger area goes quiet.

There's not even the voices of terrorists to break the silence.

Chapter Fifty Three

Thursday August 30th 22:30

The Grey Haired man has had his sleep schedule adjusted to Pacific Time for a week now. Despite his travels and moving through several different time zones he always tries to re-sync himself with his team in Seattle. The operation was important to them all. He wanted to be sharp and on his toes if something happened, *regardless if the Brigadier wants to make me a pariah, I'm involved with this thing to the end.*

Currently, the Grey Haired man has six mobile phones sitting in front of him. One is his and the other five are all throw-a-way PAYG phones. He has two laptops and one desktop PC all up and running. He is busy, furiously multi-tasking, but manages it well. One laptop is set to refresh on Al Jazeera continuously while the other is opened to his company's secure email program.

The two laptops are tossable just like the mobile phones and Grey Hair intends to get rid of them most of the electronic gear once he gets home. The PC on the other hand is his personal one and he has it opened to an automated stock trading program. His PC is the only device that is tied into the hotel's network. The two laptops are getting their internet from a stolen signal, masking their MAC address and buffering their data requests. He has his room's television split screened to Fox News and CNN looking for any new information.

Regardless of him being up, because it was 9:30 am Friday morning local time, and it's a hotel suite, Grey Hair has the volume low. *After all,* he confirms with himself, *I might be up, but my loved one's are sound asleep still.*

Grey Hair furiously checks all kinds of public data resources for any news about the activities in the Puget Sound. He got a little snippet about his OP a few minutes ago. Grey Hair watched a streaming video of a fire under the Tacoma Narrows Bridge. It was being generated from a local blogger that was on the scene. A Seattle based Fox affiliate, Q13, was also posting some delayed pictures from the blogger's video, but the local news hadn't started doing any live commentary.

There was nothing else that I could find, Grey Hair worries.

He was frustrated because there should have been more traffic on the web and the news about the multiple attacks that were going on. *Maybe it is too soon? Maybe all of the plans have not worked out?* He questioned the reality of what was happening on the ground, hoping for success. *It is always hard watching his spiders leave the Nest and enter the world. They must disappear, like they are trained to, but I always have concerns about them.* Grey Hair typed away some more on his laptop running different search engines that masked his MAC and IP addresses. *Particularly so, when an operation is in process, coming to fruition.*

One of his mobile phones vibrates for a second and then stops. Sitting at his hotel room's desk he glances over all of them quickly and grabs the one that made the motion. Its little red light giving away it's change of status. This is his second text for the morning.

The mobile phone reads, "At home. Sorry late. Bridge was busy. C u soon." It seemed a pair of spiders has finally returned. Grey Hair has them everywhere. He even had spiders in the United States, and he ran the numerous teams with an experienced and practiced air of efficiency. Finally, two more had checked in. these two "fishermen" had been very late in confirming their status. Grey Hair hadn't been too concerned, after all, the pilot had checked in just thirty minutes ago via a separate mobile phone text message. Yet, he still needed to know what was going on.

Nevertheless glad that these two operatives are safe, especially this pair, he mentally lets go of some of his concern. The "fishermen" have already approached the margin of their use once and this time was worse. They seem to have a lack of motivation and had a history, up until now, of responding to his requests days late. Grey Hair is concerned that they will take the stuff that he has taught them and proceed to drop off the radar. Never to return. That would make him disappointed and angry at the loss of time and money he and his company have put into them. Yet, they wouldn't stay hidden for long, and when they did creep out from whatever rock they'd been hiding under; squish! Treated just like the spiders that they really were.

Grey Hair had brought up his feelings about the pair and his concerns to the board. The two fishermen seemed to be waning in their dedication to the cause. During one of his many video conferences he confessed to the board and the C.O. that the two fisherman would either need to be retrained soon or be terminated. Several of the board objected vocally and wanted Grey Hair to make a personal visit to the two lovebirds and perform a slight attitude adjustment to the pair. But Grey Hair did not think that would work.

During his last visit, he saw the way that the woman held her own hands in her lap, along with the rest of her body language. *She was not into this kind of thing anymore,* Grey Hair clearly observed. *...and if I as much as hint to cause her any harm, her man would do the right thing and defend her. Pushing him off the reservation too. Whatever,* Grey Hair thought to himself. *The board will decide and I will act, that is what I do, without too many questions.*

Well, at least the two Canadians are consistently paying off. No complaints from them. They were both very happy to fight for the cause of the Islamists. This was their biggest mission yet, before they had mostly performed package deliveries and data pick-ups. But, it seemed they were destined for greater things, plus making some spare cash.

Another of his mobile phones vibrates. The older man grabs that cell phone and sees that the dummy email account that he had paired with it has a message. It's from the General and the Programmer. Grey Hair reads through the short message and pounds out a response on the phone's keyboard. There are board members that want an update as well. He is vague on purpose, but ends his message with two numbers. 75. That was Grey Hair's way of letting them know the percent chance of success.

Having enough and knowing that he just needs to give it more time, he decides to take off for a bit. He was starting to get sore just sitting there anyway. Grey Hair clears the desk of everything other than one laptop. He shuts down the other laptop and his personal PC while tossing the four phones into his luggage. After making sure they were each off, battery removed, of course.

Grey Hair looks in on his sleeping family just to make sure all is well. Peeking into the separate bedroom by cracking open one of the two double doors that leads into it. They are still sound asleep in the enormous California King bed. Grey Hair smiles to himself and quietly shuts the bedroom door. He leaves the hotel room just as quietly as he has done while looking in on his family. He makes sure that the room's door locks behind him and that the 'do not disturb' sign is firmly attached to the door handle. The man has some things to do before they wake up and he wants them to sleep for as long as possible.

He heads downstairs to go work out in the hotel's gym for thirty minutes. From there he intends to take a quick walk. The two phones were to contact the two couples in America, post operation. That was their entire use. Now it's time to throw away the two mobiles with their sim cards and batteries removed. *Might as well do it on my morning walk. Then, I will get back to the hotel and order up a big breakfast from the resort's five star restaurant. I had eaten there many times and was impressed with the food, its preparation and the staff. They were always willing to cook the unusual "off the menu" dish and every time I came, the staff gave top-notch service.*

Hopefully, I can make it back before my family awakes, he considers. *I will try and plan the timing to enter with the maître d' as the man delivers the morning meal for all of them. That should be a nice surprise.*

A hot breakfast in bed for the two most important people my life.

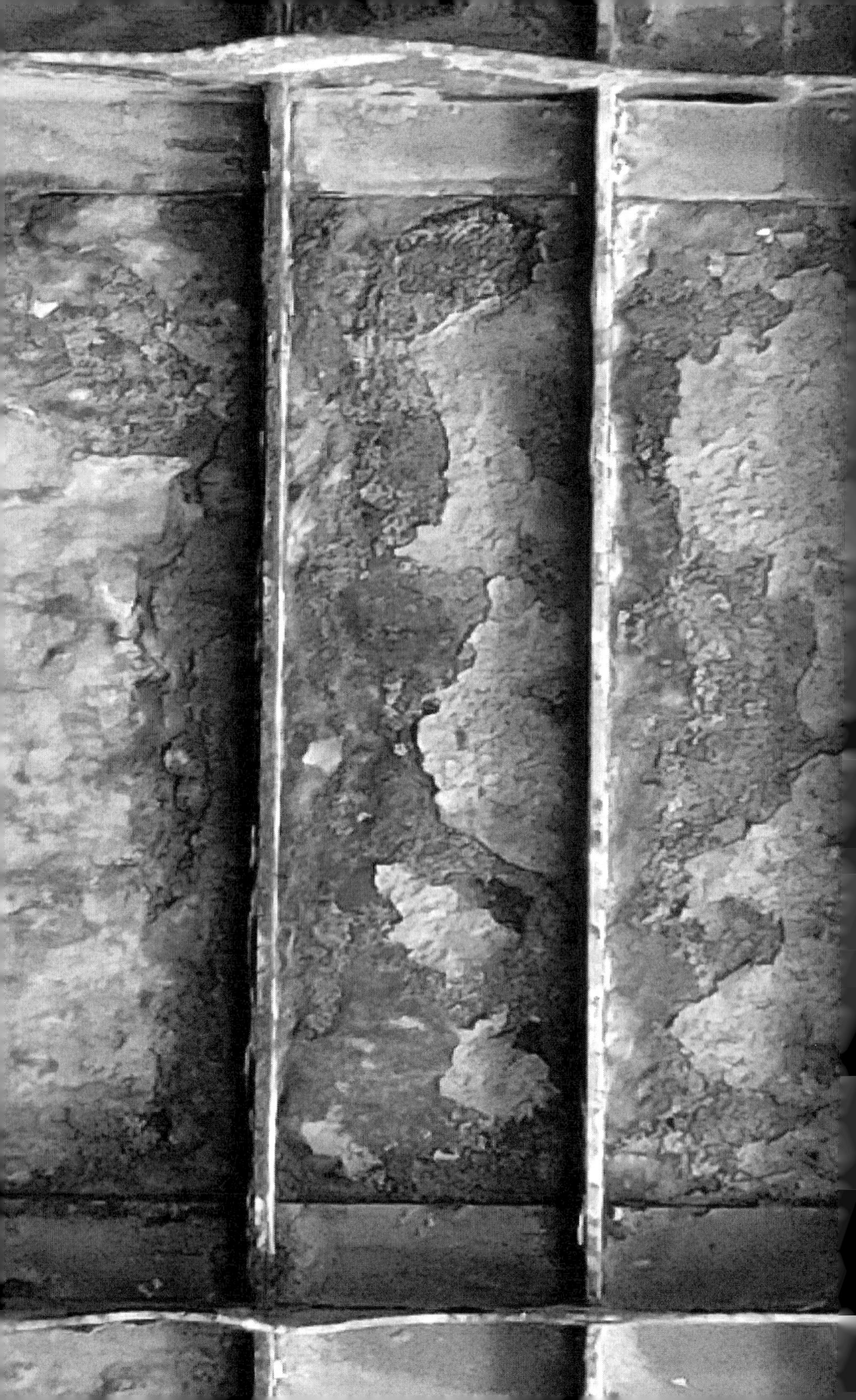

Chapter Fifty Four

Thursday August 30th 22:35

James hesitates in that moment of pitch black. He remains in that place of uncertainty and waiting; a feeling that complete darkness often gives. He lets out the half breath that he had held before he had pulled the trigger of his rifle. *Thankfully there are no monsters in this darkness*, his brain whispers. Then he asks, *where are the lights?* And just as if someone heard his prayer... the ships lights flicker on a split second later.

James attention is immediately drawn to movement. He watches as Faaiq finishing his sideways fall. The impact of James's 5.45x39 bullets performed their savage task; the bullets just took a few moments to produce an effect. To the deck Faaiq goes, right in front of his victims. The gunman was alive and screaming one instant, the other, silence. As if James himself turned off the lights, along with shutting down Faaiq.

The lights flicker off again, back on for a moment, and then die completely. James walks forward slowly, lingering until the emergency lights kick on. James has worked enough with electrical circuits, especially having to do with public areas, that he is confident that the ship is equipped with battery powered emergency lights these days. Sure enough, his self-assuredness is confirmed, they come on with a dim glow. James carefully stops at the side of Faaiq and kicks away the dead man's smaller sub-machine gun. The electrician moves toward the front of the passenger cabin with his back to the fore observation deck and making sure that the first three terrorists he shot are also still down. They are still dead; no miraculous resurrections. He quickly collects their guns and magazines and lays them in a pile in the front of the room.

I need to lead all of these people off of the boat as fast as possible, the thought hits him like a wave. *Forget about taking the bridge.* At first he struggles to not let the task completely overwhelm him. He asks himself the most obvious of questions, *How am I supposed to do this?*

He lets his rifle hang from its shoulder strap and yells at the top of his voice for silence. It is easier than he thought. All the passengers are already riveted to him and his fight with the terrorists; he quickly is given their rapt attention. He begins to cut them free, careful not to hurt anyone in the dim light. One by one he cuts their bonds, talking with a loud and clear voice.

"All of you please listen..." he begins without thinking through what he has to say. The first person he cuts loose, a business suited woman, comes unglued.

"What where you thinking!?!?" She gets up into James's face. James's eyes are drawn to her veins bulging in her neck, "You should of shot the terrorist while he was sitting there! You had the ability and the means! Yet...you didn't shoot!!!"

James was quiet, he didn't have a good response.

Terra Freeland continues her tirade, "Your... inactions... endangered all of the passengers! I don't want any help from a coward like you!" Not even waiting for a response from her rescuer, Terra rips a life vest from under her seat still yelling at the armed man. She raves about calling the police, her anger building as she talks. Terra takes notice of the pile of guns, and makes her way over to them. Terra doesn't know anything about firearms, but figures she will grab one just in case. *Just in case of what*, she doesn't know. *Everybody has a gun on this stupid ferry! I might as well have one too!!*

James watches the lady grab a pistol and disappear aft, heading toward the stairs. Unfazed James continues talking to the group, "I need your help." He explains, a bit uncomfortably at first. James makes eye contact with as many as he can, careful with his blade while cutting. James tries to catch every helpless gaze, every confused stare.

"Once I free you, I need all of you to help out each other and free everyone else. We also need to help the wounded." James keeps cutting away the unwounded passengers free from their zip ties with one of his captured knifes. Next, James cuts a couple free and they are more gracious than Business Suit. James hands Abia's and Khoury's knives to both of them and they began cutting people free as well.

James comes across the section that took Faaiq's gunfire. *God, almighty how many of them did Faaiq hit?* concern filling James's thoughts, interrupting his talk. He approaches one victim, clearly dead and stands at the center of Faaiq's gunfire. James pulls his mind away from the carnage and tries to keep things going. He has to save everyone that he can.

The emergency lights are almost up to their full eerie glow. "We need to stay together. For your safety, all of you that can, need to take a life vest located under the seats and put it on. After putting it on yourselves help those around you. We will try to bandage the wounded as best as possible, then we all have to get downstairs as a group. There we will all meet at the rear of the main cargo deck. Does everyone understand?"

Some of them understand, but James can see that others have different ideas. Still others are clearly unresponsive because of their injuries, slowly becoming worse.

In five minutes they have everybody free, even the wounded. In just a few minutes James has everyone with their life jackets on. It seems Faaiq's rage isn't as bad as James had feared. Seven of the passengers are found dead and another twenty are wounded from the gunshots. Five of the victims are going to have to be carried down to the car deck by volunteers, but thankfully the rest of the injured can walk.

James walks over to the first couple he freed and tries to give a rifle to each of them from his pile of guns.

"Sorry, we can't take your weapons," the male of the pair explains, extending out both of his hands. "My wife and I are Quaker pastors, but we will help out in any other way we can. Thank you for saving us."

"You are welcome. Thank you for your help," James replies. Thinking about the best way to hand out the weapons he begins to ask other newly released passengers. They decline, clearly fearful, but listen respectfully to his requests.

"Please may I have your attention once more? Everybody please," He pauses, waiting for all of faces to turn his way. "Does anyone have any firearms experience?" James shouts over the crowd. "Has anyone ever fired a gun before?" Only a scattered amount of almost two hundred people admit to having fired a gun before.

"Would any of you take a rifle and lead a group of freed passengers downstairs to the main car deck?" He is stunned and discouraged by the response with only getting two volunteers. James whispers, "Out of all of these people, just two?" A woman and a man walk toward him.

"James," he says extending a hand. "Thanks for volunteering," he speaks to the pair.

Just finishing shaking his hand, the woman speaks first, "Latisha Reynolds, my husband was a cop. Thanks for freeing me, well, all of us."

James hands her the small Uzi submachine gun from the pile and turns toward his male volunteer.

"Name's Brad Hensley," not extending his hand to James. "I'm of the same mindset as her," nodding his head toward Latisha. "I am in your debt."

James nods an acknowledgement to him. James quickly goes over the firearms operation and use. Brad and Latisha both nod their heads in understanding of James description. James sees this and asks if they know firearms well. The pair informs James that they each have firearms experience.

Assured at Latisha's and Brad's confidence, and ready to get the people to safety, James speaks up once more, encouragingly "Everyone, make your way downstairs. You will be led by these two with the guns. Please stay behind them as you head to the car deck."

James takes off his brown Carhartt jacket, getting too hot in it and tosses it on a seat-back.

Will they trust me to get them off of this boat? James asks himself. He nods and tries to look assured and confidant as people pass by.

Yet inside his chest, is full of anxiety and uncertainty. *How am I going to get all of these people into the water?*

Chapter Fifty Five
Thursday August 30th 22:35

Terminating the transmission with Faaiq, Dizhwar looks over to Driver, and quietly in Arabic, "Did you hear what I discussed with Abdul, Monifa, and Faaiq?"

Dizhwar nods his head toward the crew looking at Driver, "They need to be tied together my friend. Lets finish it together."

Driver had heard all of this end of the conversation, but was thankful for the question. "Yes, I got it all," Driver speaks as they head over to tie the crew all together. It takes them just a few minutes, Driver returns to his piloting, as Dizhwar walks out of the pilot house. Dizhwar attentively leans in to the sound of the two different bursts of gunfire. He proceeds partially down the pilot house steps, listening for what must be Faaiq's shots and hopefully Faaiq's successes. After the gunfire subsides, Dizhwar waits for his radio to chirp with a communication from Faaiq. He pulls it out of his pocket, waiting two, almost three minutes.

The call from Faaiq never comes.

Dizhwar has taken to cursing quite a bit lately and lets out a few more choice words. Another let down in a series of many. Well, it doesn't matter, he's already started a secondary plan.

No matter what, there should always be a plan B. Dizhwar learned from his school that every successful operation has alternative plans and if they were thorough, there would be an alternate plan C and D as well. The terrorist cell had practiced all four of them. Plan B was for all members alive to converge on the starboard Zodiac then disembark, regardless of where the boat was in transit. All Dizhwar had to do was give the order.

Dizhwar sets his radio for transmit all. He relays the call for plan B. "Go for Zodiac. Go for Zodiac." He waits thirty seconds and calls it out twice more to all radios, then pockets the device.

Once away, they will remote-detonate the charges and head to the waiting van, watching the ferry burn down to the hull. If they were picked up before reaching the getaway van, they were to pretend to be survivors using a cover story.

Plan C was to be used if Dizhwar went missing or was killed. If any single member was left alive during any unforeseen circumstance. Any available teammate were to call out on their radio twice in five minutes, then make their way to the engine room to set the default fifteen minute timers on the charges. Once done, they would jump off of the boat with a life preserver. If able to make it to the van, to do so, but if picked up by anyone, pretend to be a survivor and use the memorized story just like in their previous plan.

Dizhwar walks back up the stairs, into the pilot house and asks Driver in Arabic, "With the crew secured, is the final course set?"

"We are still on a full speed course with the terminal. We still have…" Driver looked at the ship GPS screen and then continued "uuugh…seven to... eight minutes before we should make our turn."

"That leaves us with fifteen before impact then?"

Driver concedes the point, "...that's about right,"

"Make the turn now Brother, and let's get off of this ship." Dizhwar's voice is heavy with weariness. "Too many have been lost today."

Driver nods his head. He shakes his head at the loss of it all as well. He swings the wheel slightly to port, visually aligning it with the ultimate destination. Once lined up, Driver slides the unbolted wheel from its collar. He shoots Dizhwar a hopeful smile and then removes the throttle from its linkage as well.

This act makes the ship impossible to steer now from the foreword location. Heading out of the pilothouse doors, Driver takes one last look at the course the ship is taking before tossing the ferry's wheel and throttle arm out into the Salish Sea. The pair hurriedly disable the rear pilothouse with the same actions.

After their final act to disable the ship the pair of conspirators steps out onto the gangway heading downstairs toward the observation deck landing. Armed with their rifles and pistols they make their way down to the Zodiacs.

Chapter Fifty Six

Thursday August 30th 22:40

Dashing down through the ship, Terra Freeland has one thing in mind, *Everyone for themselves!* She carelessly searches, *come on Terra! Where did you see those emergency life rafts?*

Never being on a ship before, she only took the ferry because it was supposed to be faster than driving around. "Stupid Brad," she curses as she heads up one hallway, it dead ends and she doubles back. Having just arrived in Seattle a little over a week ago from Atlanta, the first time she'd ever seen a ferry up-close was today. Terra wanders around a little on what she doesn't realize is the second largest double ended ferry in the world.

She rushes past a stairway heading down decides not to take it and then reconsiders, *nothing on this stupid thing looks familiar!* She thinks for a moment about just going back and hiding in the car. *But where is the stupid Lincoln? Yet I'd rather have the car than getting into the cold water*, but she thinks better of it. *I hate these stupid ships! Now even more so!! You've got to take care of yourself,* she convinces herself. *No matter what you are the only one that will.*

Terra Freeland plans her strategy like it was a real estate deal, *if I could get to that life raft they talked about on the first safety announcement, inflate it and jump into the water...it was on the car-deck.* She makes another turn finds stairs going up and heads back the way she came looking a second set of stairs going down. *How many levels was I up? Two? Three? I will be off this deathtrap and safe, I promise!*

Abdul and Monifa come up through the engine room, moving purposefully through the car deck. On their guard, they leave the car deck and climb the aft stairs, guns up, ready for any surprises. They know where they are going; for they've memorized the massive ship's layout. On the way up they run across a woman on the way down.

A woman in a business skirt, wearing a life vest around her neck.
Terra's business skirt makes a swish shish sound as she tries to quickly run by the pair of figures; only noticing them out of the corner of her eye. She hopes, *that two more armed people will just leave me be.* Not distinguishing between a friend or foe, she stops when the pair bark a demand for her to do so. *Just about the voice that I use when talking to subordinates,* she considers.

Abdul takes one look at the woman, knows business skirt girl isn't one of his team, and follows Dizhwar's orders to the letter.

Terra Freeland realizes too late that fate has come to stand right in front of her and knock at her door. Fight or flight, are you ready or ill prepared? Have you been discovered as a sheep or a sheepdog?

Terra tries to raise the pistol that is in her hand; in an awkward and ungainly kind of stance. She has never shot a pistol before, she has no clue whatsoever how to use one and is just mimicking the action she has seen in the movies and on television. She squeezes the trigger on a gun that has its safety engaged. The trigger pulls, the hammer clicks, but the safety on the pistol has rotated the firing pin out of the way. Safety features are really good...sometimes.

Abdul raises his rifle, with the safety off, and amid the clicking of Terra's pistol, he shoots her. Not once, but several times. Giving no grace, showing not an ounce of mercy.

"Subhaana Rabbi yal A'alaa (Oh Allah glory be to you, the most high)," Monifa recites the passage as her partner shoots Terra.

The business suited woman with the blond hair falls. She tries to control her muscles, yet she continues to slide over at an ungainly angle. Her body slowly remains in motion; sliding down the stairs on her own blood.

Terra watches the blood stain her high-end designer blouse. The white quickly turns to red from the multiple bullet wounds. Terra wills everything to stop, but can't seem to do anything about it. She is finally freed from the ship's confinement. Not to mention, her earthly one too.

Monifa and Abdul on their guard, they wait a minute to see if any other one will appear, but no one comes. The pair proceed on their way. They leave the body of the dead woman alone; still slowly sliding down the stairs. Just like a snail would leave an opaque trace of its passage, the body leaves a red stain in its wake.

Abdul and Monifa move like cats up to the rear observation deck. They exit the ship onto the outdoor walkway. The pair walk down the entire exterior starboard walkway of the ship, toward the waiting Zodiac berth. Their own path is guided by small path lights placed at the bottom of each post of the railing. In their adrenalin filled minds from the recent shootout, they don't notice that all of the lights are out on the decks. They run on autopilot toward their goal, focused on their task.

Inside the passenger deck, "Please, help each other out," James speaks again to the crowd. He tries to keep his voice low and encouraging, while his head is filled with more the violent images that he's been part of and his worries. *Will all of these people follow my lead? What happens if I have to stay behind? What then? Are there more terrorists coming?*

Concerns flood his mind, so much so that James fails to notice the two armed gunman moving on the exterior starboard gangway in the darkness. The passengers don't notice either, as they are all turned toward the stairs, focusing on the person directly in front of them, or their loved ones next to them.

Sometimes, there are monsters in the darkness that have to be confronted. Monsters that must be destroyed before they wreak any dreadful carnage on anyone or anything.

Whether you are defending complete strangers or the closest of relations; more often than not, shadowed wolves will only understand violence.

Even if they are only heading toward a starboard Zodiac davit.

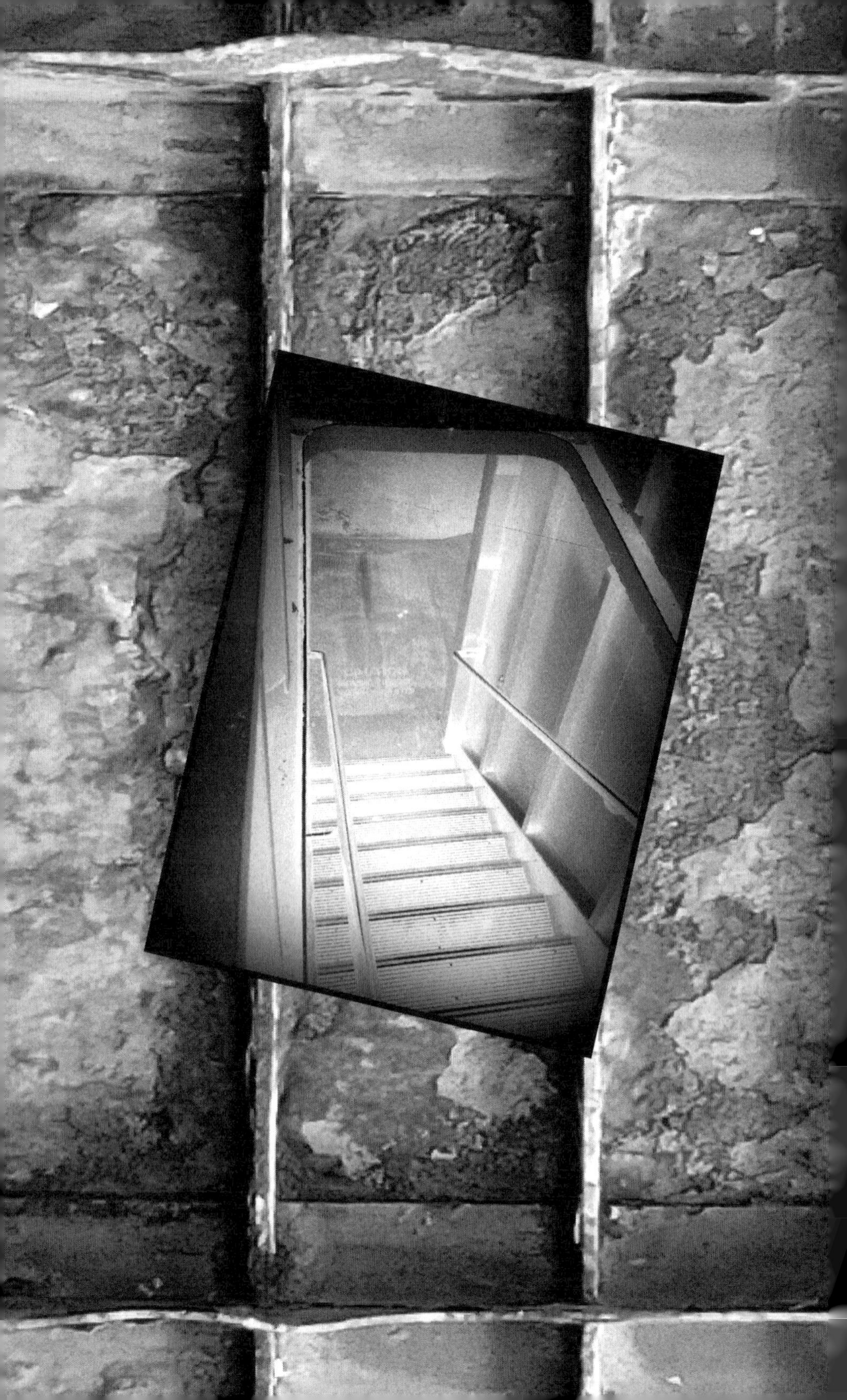

Chapter Fifty Seven

Thursday August 30th 22:45

The rigid inflatable boats are stored on either side of the ferry almost amidships. They are accessible by a locked gate on the exterior port or starboard passenger deck railings. Though intended as a quick response for a passenger overboard, they can also be used in an evacuation scenario with the ship's other emergency inflatable craft. Other than the Zodiacs, the shipboard emergency crafts have no engines, so the Zodiacs would serve as tow craft, pulling survivors in the emergency boats to safety.

Just in case the terrorists needed to abandon the ferry early on, the locks on the access doors to the davit and the Zodiacs were cut by Khoury. Both port and starboard doors, were cut by him in the first few minutes, of his patrol.

Monifa Bashandi el-Shazli makes her way quickly to the crane controls of the Zodiac and begins powering the controls on. Before she can successfully move the small craft, two safety pins have to be removed from the crane and its motorized pedestal base. "Abdul! Get the pins." She shouts over the davit crane motor. She raises the crane up to the appropriate height, but she cant swing it left to right, yet.

Abdul doesn't respond, he just stands at the railing looking into the ferry. She shrugs it off and comes around to do it herself. While she works on the firmly seated pins, Abdul is, at the least, supposed to be guarding her.

The fact is, Abdul doesn't even hear her request. He can't believe what he's seeing within the ship.

From his position, Abdul Muhammad can barely see into both the fore and aft passenger cabins, but he finally notices the lights are out. *Odd,* he wonders. Standing just feet from the windows, he looks in with his rifle up and ready. Vaguely, Abdul is able to make out people moving about. Abdul reconsiders his first assumption about the ships lights, there seems to be light coming from somewhere within. Then it hits him, *emergency lights...something has happened.*

"What do you think happened to the lights?" Abdul asks out loud hoping for a comment from his on-again off-again girlfriend.

When she doesn't respond he tries to fill her in. Still not noticing he's not keeping up on his duties, "The entire passenger deck was darker when we first came up. The passengers are no longer tied up." Abdul still doesn't get any ideas back from Monifa. He stares into the windows, and then another thought hits him... *the fore passenger cabin is looking empty?*

Abdul wonders out loud, "...it looks like only a quarter of the people remain. Are we moving the passengers down to the car deck?" Abdul watches as there seems to be two quick moving lines amidships going down the fore stairs.

"I don't know Abdul. Just help me!" Monifa replies urgently without even looking as to what Abdul is referring to. She is barely able to muster a comment because she's concentrating on freeing the boat davit and Zodiac.

This is our orders you foolish man! Yet pins are hard to remove with my small hands!!! "Abdul!" she whispers harshly as she strains at the resistance and finally pulls the first safety pin free.

The emergency lights, are now at almost full power, Abdul can see more clearly. *Is that a man at the end of the passenger line with a rifle? Another man that isn't one of his teammates?* Abdul shouts at Monifa "Look at this, will you?" and he furiously points at what he is witnessing. Getting the woman's attention, he points toward the inside of the boat, beyond the glass.

Monifa just pulled the last pin and is now standing slightly above the window line, readying the Zodiac. She stoops and leans her head over to see what Abdul is pointing at. The woman gazes at the empty passenger area quickly and then towards the unfamiliar man.

She looks back over at Abdul as she starts up the crane. "It's too late. Let 'em all go. They don't matter! We need to get off now, Abdul!!"

Abdul is furious at her, "No way!" he shouts back. The motion of the boat and the impact of the waves hitting the sea seems to make him all the more agitated. "That's him!! The one that has messed this all up. Don't you have a comment?"

She looks up quickly at him, tries to smile and it comes out as something else. "We have orders my friend. None of that in there matters anymore."

Ignoring her, "I'm going to kill this cowboy where he stands and get some payment for our brother's lives!!!"

Abdul steadies his aim, preparing to fire.

She maneuvers the crane out of its locked position to hover over the berthed Zodiac. While doing so, Monifa shouts at Abdul, "Do you want to spoil this right before we get off of here!?! We don't know how many of *them* are there! Let's just follow orders and get off of this wreck!"

It's his turn to ignore her. Abdul fires with his rifle, spider webbing the naval storm glass. With that line of questioning not working, Monifa tries a different tack. "We should let Dizhwar know!" She shouts from the ringing in her ears of the gunfire. "You know that, Abdul. Abdul!" Monifa watches Abdul's finger come off of the trigger and then Abdul turns his head slightly off center from his AR rifle's scope.

"Go ahead and call him. But I will keep sights on target until he says otherwise." Abdul turns back to looking down the scope, trying to keep the armed man in the brown jacket in his sights.

Monifa calls quickly, before she looses the chance.

"Go ahead for Dizhwar."

"Dizhwar, we believe we have the man that's caused the problems. He's next to the midships passenger cabin stairway, escorting passengers down stairs. Abdul has him in his sights!"

"What! Slow down, say again." Dizhwar quickly radios back.

She locks the cradle over the black craft and then repeats her statement, slower, and waits for a response.

"Is the Zodiac ready for departure? Remember priorities! Driver and I are en route. ETA five minutes. What's the description of the man." As Dizhwar speaks over the radio, Monifa can hear the sounds of feet walking on metal decking in the background.

Before replying to Dizhwar, she whispers to Abdul "Dizhwar and Driver are coming. Help me get this craft hooked to the davit for launch or we will both be in trouble."

There's still no movement from Abdul. Monifa Bashandi el-Shazli is adamant, "Now, Abdul!"

Abdul grunts an unclear curse under his breath, then lets his rifle hang from its shoulder strap. The pair proceed to secure the final ties from davit to Zodiac and finish the last of the launching procedures.

"Monifa?" Dizhwar queries again on the radio.

"Sorry! Yes, we are ready for launch. The man's a thirty something white male. Fit, short blond hair about six feet tall. He has a mustache. He's wearing brown pants, dark boots and black polo shirt with some sort of logo on his breast."

Halfway down to the starboard cradle, Dizhwar stops in his tracks and turns around to give an incredulous look at Driver. "Did you just hear Monifa? Is it possible? That electrician that went to McDonalds is the cause of all of this?"

Driver responds, "Well, besides the ice cream cone, he did look capable."

Chapter Fifty Eight

Thursday August 30th 22:45

    James Maly has almost everyone heading downstairs. There are about fifteen people still waiting in line to head to the perceived safety of the car deck. James has asked if one of the armed citizens would stay just at the bottom of the stairs while the other stood guard over the people gathered at the stern. James knew there were just a few more terrorist agents on board but, he hopes that they will remain out of his way. He can't see where the position of the ship is and tries looking outside into the darkness, but even from the emergency lit ship it's pointless. James reapplies his efforts on getting the people to the stern. Get all of these souls to safety.

With his concentration on the passengers and the immediate cabin area, he pays no attention to the two Zodiac berths just outside of the port and starboard passenger cabin windows.

He is so very lucky, blessed, or a little of both. James hears the noises that the davit and its winch make when they kick on and looks over in the general vicinity for the source. But he can't see anything within the ship.

Still hearing the noise, James focuses carefully, gazing out of the windows as well. And then he has the answer. A second, maybe only half a second goes by before he realizes that a lower half of one figure is visible and another figure is bringing up a rifle to bear down upon. James shouts, "Down the stairs, terrorists are back!" as he takes cover and raises his rifle to shoot.

James sees the window, yards from him, spider web. On past trips, he has sat by those windows and remembers seeing just how thick that glass is. The booms of the larger 7.62x56 rounds impacting the storm glass echo through the cabin. James uses this time to yell again, "Hurry up," at the passengers. He can't see any detailed person now beyond the windows, just shapes in cracked glass. James watches the two shapes momentarily converge on the starboard Zodiac. He waits patiently to take his shot.

Bracing his elbow on his knee, he let's out several aimed shots from his AK-74 and the gale-force storm glass absorbs the impacts of his 5.45x 39 rounds. The bullets splinter and spider web the storm glass even more. It seems like a few more rounds and it would give way. James moves again, this time walking backwards and slightly sideways to better protect the last of the fleeing passengers. Shouting again as he moves, he keeps his sights trained on the general location of the starboard Zodiac. James hears the booms of the much bigger rifle again. The observation deck glass can't take anymore punishment and it completely gives way in a cascade of shards and sound.

Abdul, on the outside gangway, just got his authorization to fire. Finally! He and Monifa have finally made the escape Zodiac ready for the last four of them. While he waits for Driver and Dizhwar, he can extract some vengeance. Abdul's vision is obscured too by the stupid glass. With his second set of rounds, he intends to break it. The gunman makes an educated guess where his opponent is and fires. The glass can't take anymore pounding, and collapses into a rain of shards onto the deck. The bullets would have caught James with several rounds after tearing through the glass. Fortunately though, the glass was too fractured to see through, so Abdul fired where James *used to be*.

James hears the rounds pass close by. He feels them pound into the bulkhead to his front and left because pieces of something sting his cheek and shoulder. He can perceive the cries of the people he's trying to defend behind him. The pressure, and the need to defend, focus his senses sharply. James reminds himself on *his sights and targets*. The first gunman, the one that's firing at him is a solid target. There's no shattered glass in the way now. James squeezes off several well aimed rounds. James watches the man jerk and blink his eyes in rhythm to the impacts. The terrorist begins to lower his rifle, then the gunman falls backwards off the railing. James steals a quick look at the stairwell to check and see if all of the passengers are gone. Thankfully, they are.

Monifa watches with horror as her long time friend goes over the railing. She rolls over onto her back, sheltered from sight from the man in the cabin. She tries to think about her task and her mission, but keeps thinking about Abdul. She wills herself to overcome her loss. She whispers something that might even be a lie, comforting herself, *"Abdul's wounds are superficial."*

She ejects her AR-10's magazine, more out of habit than anything, checks its level, reinserts the mag and pulls the bolt halfway out. She has a round in the chamber. She steels her will and prepares, *kill the one that must be the cause of everything that's gone wrong.*

James walks into the stairwell for partial cover, as more gunfire rips through the passenger area. He waits a moment and then trains the AK's sights looking for the new source. James doesn't see another gunman. Then, as quickly as the terrorist disappeared, the determined gunman pops up their head and rifle above the deck of the Zodiac to fire.

James and Monifa both fire at the same time.

James, emptying his magazine into his target and Monifa only capable to firing off a few shots that hit high. The rubber hulled escape craft and Monifa are punched with numerous bullets from James's AK. James doesn't have time to despair that he's just fired and probably killed a woman and retreats back to the shelter of the stairway. This time kneeling; he ejects the spent magazine, reloads and peeks around the corner. James can clearly see the woman's rifle dangling off of the front of the Zodiac. Hanging by its shoulder strap.

Was it all over? Was this the last gut-churning battle? James slowly stands, carefully watching the davit area for any more movement. A terrible weariness settles on his body as he turns back toward the fore passenger cabin to make one last check. He witnesses the destruction he was just part of. Bodies, blood, broken glass and scattered brass casings.

The brokenness that he beholds before him, closely parallels the emotions that he feels. It lies in such stark contrast to older, fonder memories of his own in this very cabin. James discards his memory of the time he and his wife had ridden clear up to Sequim, at the northern end of the Washington Peninsula.

He and his love had left at six in the evening, right after she got off of work. On a whim, they decided to take the ferry across to cut the journey shorter. Due to Seattle traffic and the ferry schedule, they missed two departures and had to wait for a third. They had a great conversation at Ivar's, literally waiting for their ship to come in. Once on the mostly deserted ferry, they had a beautiful time curled up against each other in this very cabin watching the final rays of sun set over the Olympic Mountains. It was easy pretending the ship was all theirs.

Little did they know that James had dropped his wallet out of his jacket pocket onto the green vinyl seat. The couple didn't find out about it, until they drove two more hours north and tried to check into his reserved hotel room. This time, Wendi hadn't brought any cash or credit cards, it was a company trip, she had only her driver's license and a few dollars to her name. They couldn't check into the hotel. The pair furiously tried to call the ferry terminal and the lost and found numbers, but just got the answering machines. They decided to drive all of the way back down to the terminal and see if they could find the wallet.

By the time they got back to the ferry terminal it was almost midnight, the gate employee explained that they could not gain entry until 4:30 the next morning. Also, by some accidental twist of fate, the very same ferry that they had come in on had a maintenance routine due, so no one else had ridden on it. The gate attendant said that the chance was very likely that the wallet was still there on the ferry.

Emboldened and with no where to go, James and his wife slept in the van until just before 4:30, when she drove him to the terminal. He stood and waited for the morning entry onto the ship with a group of early risers. Wendy waited in the running vehicle, trying to stay awake. The very moment the entry gate was opened, someone was calling out his name.

He turned to find the ship's purser calling out "James Maly, James Maly!"

James identified himself with his company badge, his only form of identification left. His wallet was returned safely to him. It seemed the gate employee, from the night before, left a note for the morning crew and the morning crew gave the ship a good search before letting on the passengers. They found the wallet and handed it over to the ships purser, who in turn heard that the very man was waiting for it at the passenger loading ramp.

The pair were elated, they wearily drove back to the hotel and checked in at six in the morning. They were barely able to make it due to their exhaustion. James remembered setting his alarm to go off in just one hour. He made the call by eight, was done by noon, and still got in another two hour nap with his special girl, before check out time at two.

What a precious memory.

The cold and musty sea smell brings him out of the reverie. The chilly and moist wind cuts through every layer of his clothes. James turns away from the carnage, pushes the memory away and proceeds out of the passenger area. He walks past the children's area with the puzzles on the table, right next to the too numerous recycling containers. Heading downstairs, he runs to join the rest of the passengers.

As he descends, a bit more hopeful from the memory, James shouts at the top of his lungs, "Coming down!"

Chapter Fifty Nine

Thursday August 30th 22:45

Dizhwar and Driver hear the gun battle underneath their feet. The brief staccato bursts of sound, the breaking glass, and more punctuated gunfire. They can do nothing about the battle at first, but make every effort to increase their pace, without running across a trap themselves. The pair of friends get down to the starboard Zodiac cradle just as James disappears down the stairway.

They don't realize it, but they miss him by seconds.

Dizhwar lets out a cry of sheer anger and frustration at the turn of events, stopping just shy of the last two stairs. Dizhwar gazes confused and furious at the carnage around him. Driver passes by his boss, finishes the last few steps, barrel downrange pointing at the interior stairwell. He sweeps the passenger cabins with his rifle, looking through the sights hoping to catch the killer of his teammates. It is too late, all Driver and Dizhwar see are bullet marks, bodies and broken glass. There isn't a soul alive on the interior deck.

"Clear!" Driver shouts, as Dizhwar comes down the last of the stairs himself, rifle ready. Dizhwar goes over to check on Monifa in the Zodiac, one look tells him that she is dead. Driver comes over to the railing and glances over it. They heard a splash amid the gunfire and Driver assumes that it was one of the two, since there is only one of theirs to be seen. "Monifa is gone," he looks over to Driver, watching his friend glance over the railing. Driver tries to catch a glimpse of Abdul, but Abdul is gone as well.

"This Zodiac is worthless," Dizhwar says to no one. "Were going downstairs to kill all of them, especially that Electrician!"

"No Dizhwar!" Driver exhorts. He pulls away from the railing, looking straight into Dizhwar's face. "We barely have enough time to get the other boat free before impact. Look!" Driver pleads, pointing up the length of the ship.

Dizhwar turns and sees the target looming.

There isn't going to be time for vengeance. Not if they want to save themselves.

"There might not even be time to get off of here before impact." Driver further tries to plead with his leader.

"We can get off in time." Dizhwar agrees, his thoughts still not fully on the moment.

Driver however is very much focused. He imagines the ferry, traveling at eighteen knots, coming to a complete stop in just a few meters. His racing experience has taught him a thing or two about speed and the forces involved. He mentally calculates the rate of closure. It's going to be to close.

Dizhwar is caught up thinking about all of those unsecured automobiles flying forward at the ships old speed. Oh, the terrible mess they will make! All those passengers and the electrician will be shredded.

Driver knows they must get off, now!

He grabs his boss by the arm and half pulls him forward, back into the passenger cabin and then across it to the port side Zodiac cradle.

Dizhwar, being led by Driver, is still caught up in his own ruthless thoughts. It would bring a sense of pleasure to Dizhwar to know that all of the passengers down below decks are caught unaware at impact. They will be scattered and thrown forward like bowling pins in the main car garage; all twisted and torn among the cars.

"What a glorious sight that would be." Dizhwar whispers aloud. A twisted smile growing on his face.

"Dizhwar, I need your help!" Driver demands, as he looks over his shoulder trying to operate the davit crane's controls. His own sense of self-preservation overriding any of terrorism.

"Maybe, the electrician will get caught up in it as well and suffer a horrible maiming? What do you think, Driver?"

Driver doesn't respond, just waves Dizhwar over to the safety pins. Dizhwar snaps out of his merciless revelry, he obliges the wishes of his friend. He pulls the pins and then climbs on to the Zodiac. It comes up from its moorings, dangling by the crane. Driver hits the cable deploy switch and quickly climbs on the small craft as it lowers into the sea.

"If Allah would only be so merciful to his servant," Dizhwar answers his own question.

Chapter Sixty

Thursday August 30th 22:45

The crew begin fighting for their lives just minutes after their captors leave. All eight of them are determined to free themselves and retake control of their precious ferry.

A very flexible twenty something, Trevor Matthews, has his hood half off moments after the two men head downstairs. Not sure if they are going to come back, but still holding to his promise to himself to do something, he does. Trevor is able to lean his head over far enough into the hands of one of his fellow crewmembers and through some form of miraculous communication is able to get them to understand. The other crewmember holds on to Trevor's hood while he pulls his head free of if. Once accomplished, he does the same for the tape on his face and is able to get it painfully removed from his mouth.

Now that Trevor's vision and speech are restored he lets his shipmates know he is going to free them. "We are all tied together in a loose circle with hands joined to each other's by zip ties." He explains trying to give them the picture he can now see. "We have tape placed over mouths and hoods placed over our heads. Does everybody understand that?"

Getting a bunch of hoods to nod their heads seems quite comical in the moment, but Trevor squelches the laugh. He has a second chance to redeem himself and now he will. To his limit. Taking full advantage of the opportunity, he first goes to work on the crewmember to his left. Using his teeth he lifts the hood and then removes the tape from this next crewmember. "You start to work that way," Trevor says, nodding with his head, "and I will work the opposite. Got it?"

When Trevor is finished, he turns to the person on his right and begins to work on them while the first crewmember he frees turns to the left and tries to free another. During that time, the first collision warnings sound in the pilot house. Various electronic warnings start to give out their notice and then the collision avoidance radar starts its series of alerts. Racing, the crew work against time, getting themselves free. A few minutes later, the crew hear klaxons from outside of the ship.

Leaning his head back, Trevor shouts above the alarms. "Captain, what are those new alarms?"

"Probably from the Navy Base. We must be close to one of their ships."
Soon, they are all free of the hoods and tape. They work out a way to get up from their

sitting positions and see their impending impact for the first time. Some stand in sheer shock, completely frozen with fear. Captain Michael O'Brian furiously glances at the controls and throttles. Not at all letting the moment get to him, he realizes he could no more steer the ship away from its intended course than stop it. The wheel and throttle were missing and they all could not make it to the aft pilot house in time.

"Everybody down against the bulkhead. Quickly!"

Jointly, they hurry to the better location against the fore pilothouse bulkhead. The sit back down together.

The Naval horns sounded like it was right on top of them.

"Brace for impact!" The Captain barks as the two massive ships collide.

Chapter Sixty One

Thursday August 30th 22:45

James comes down the stairs shouting and runs headlong into Latisha at the bottom of the landing. She had heard his calls and has her weapon pointed away as James came too fast down them. Latisha and James leave the stairwell together at a run. James knows he has to lie before she even asks a question.

"You're bleeding!" Latisha shouts and points at James's face. "Are all of the terrorists dead? Are there more of them coming?"

James needs to get all of them off of the ferry quickly. "I think so…" nodding his head as he runs. "There's more coming." James takes a few breaths and finishes "we need to get everyone into the water. Before…terrorists and before collision."

"Collision?" She breaths out in a rasp.

"Yes, the terrorists are going to run…." between his own breaths, James continues "…the ferry into an aircraft carrier!" James can see the immediate concern on her face, but keeps up the pace until they make it to the gathered throng of passengers.

Pausing to catch his breath, James blurts out "Please, may I have your attention," and wipes some of the blood from his right eye. "I need everyone to jump into the water now! There are more terrorists coming and we are about to run into an aircraft carrier."

Nobody moves.

The passengers just stand there gazing at him, their faces filled with questions. They stared at him and then back to the water in clear doubt and confusion that that was their only choice. James looks to his two fellow armed passengers and thankfully Latisha speaks up, "Its true. We need to all get to safety and the only way is to jump off." She points into the black water to illustrate her point. "You must save yourselves, now!"

Knowing that the passengers are going to need to be prodded in some way, a quick idea hits him. James turns toward the stairway in full view of the gathered group and leans forward as if listening for something. James yells back over his shoulder "Hurry, here they come!" and turns back to point his AK-74 toward the empty stairwell.

James squeezes off a short volley. The bullets pot-mark the steel and leave pinky-sized metal divots where they strike. People reach for their ears, others glance toward the end of the ship and the gaping maw of ocean. James walks away from the crowd, rifle pointed at the empty stairwell. James looks back toward the passengers and yells "Go! Hurry!"

Latisha follows James's lead. She starts to move with him, and then falls slightly back. James glances back again to see Brad pointing at the water, waving at the crowd to jump.

"Jump for your own sake! Everyone off of the boat and into the water now!" Brad's voice is booming in the car garage.

James sees that people have ducked instinctively from the gun fire, even though it was aimed in the opposite direction. Then, slowly he sees a few of them jump into the ocean.

Comforted, James looks back toward Latisha, motions for her to get down with his left hand and with his right hand, he squeezes off another few rounds. James looks back to see what is the result of his second prompt. *That seemed to do it,* he confirms. The crowd of passengers are moving en masse'. All of the passengers, with life jackets around their necks, begin their jumps into the water and to safety.

Latisha slowly creeps up to him and whispers "The terrorists aren't coming are they? That was all just an act? Wasn't it?"

James looks at her, lowered his head at the embarrassment of the lie and nods. "Sorry, I had to lie. I had to do something to get them off of the ship. They don't realize the impact is imminent."

She in turn nods her head in agreement. "I understand. You did ok. You know what? I had a crummy day. I've been dying to shoot this at something, since I got it. I'm going to let out some aggravation. So, if you don't mind…" Her voice trails off as she raises the Uzi and fires.

James letting out another rare grin this evening, "Be my guest."

She continues, empting the 9mm Uzi with a long burst at the stairwell, bullets ring out their impact. A few ricochet out of the confined area and she stops short of emptying her magazine. She lets out a devilish grin, "See you in the water." She sets the submachine gun onto the deck, kindly pats James's shoulder and runs. At the edge, she takes a flying leap off into the black.

James watches her go, then waves for Brad, the last one there, to go. He is clearly confused by the pair's gunfire and the concern is written on his face. He eventually bows his head, in understanding of the message, and takes his rifle with him, as he too follows the rest of the passengers into the sea.

James knows the collision is coming. It can happen at any second and his mind goes to the crew. *Where are the crew? Probably dead or tied up in the pilot house. It is too late for them and come to think of it, too late for Abia as well. The poor woman is still locked up in my van.*

James's thoughts are interrupted when hears a great, loud, ship horn that seems all around the ferry. At that moment, James realizes he hadn't gotten a life preserver for himself!

"Crap!" James cusses loudly and runs hard for the emergency evacuation lockers. He struggles to open the life preserver closet and then to separate one out of the tangled preservers. A ship's horn blares again, filling the ship with its sound. James considers it must be coming from the aircraft carrier. He finally separates out one of the jackets for himself.

A collision warning? James is just able to make it to the end of the cars, at the back of the ferry, before the wall of sound hits him like some Soundgarden concert. Metal grinding on metal echoes throughout the *Wenatchee*. James reaches the back of the last automobile, a moving truck, and hurriedly grasps the fabric handle used for pulling up the moving truck's large rear door. The impact fills his ears with a screeching crescendo.

Suddenly, everything starts moving forward and James holds on for dear life.

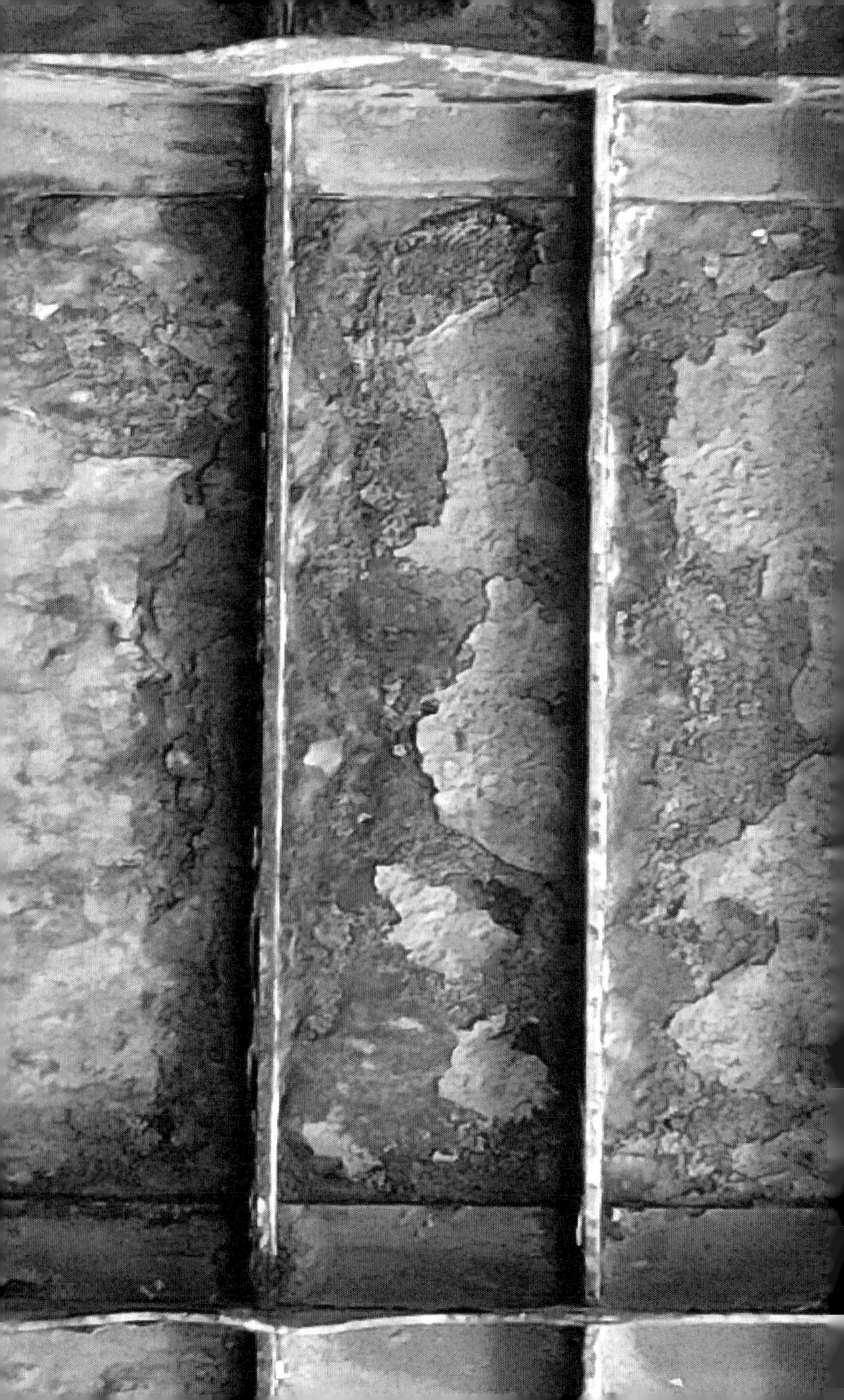

Chapter Sixty Two

Thursday August 30th 22:50

Horrible grinding, glass breaking and the sound an aluminum can makes when crushed fills James's entire being. His ears demand him to place his hands over them to muffle the noise, but he is too busy holding on for dear life. His ears are filled with tremendous pain, like a fire engine siren is going off next to his head. Every muscle in his back and arms tense with the strain of just holding on.

The truck that he tied his arm around just moments before, is sliding forward quickly. The moving truck impacts the car in front of it, then careens sideways. The multi-ton truck pushes one car and then another with its incredible mass. The laws of physics have their way, and the far heavier truck ends up pushing four cars forward, into the building pile of vehicles at the front.

The journey forward wasn't very rough. It is just the abrupt stop at the end.

As it stops his forward momentum, James slams his left shoulder, side, leg and head hard against the back of the truck's door. Powerless to slow his collision with the back of the moving truck, he does everything in his power to just hold on; and he wasn't prepared for the sudden stop.

Everything ceases moving just as quickly as it has begun. With his head doing loops and the immediate ache in his shoulder, tells him he has hit both especially hard. Blinking away the stars and tears, James pulls his left arm free from the fabric handle and misjudges the height of the bumper. Instantly, he falls to the deck. He tries to stand up, but can't stand from the dizziness. James tries unsuccessfully to stand again, but knowing he isn't going to be able to do it, collapses yet again.

You have to flee! His soul is screaming it at him.

Instead, James resolves to crawl.

It's the only thing he can physically do.

At first it's kind of an army man shuffle. Right arm forward, left leg. Left arm forward and then the right leg, repeat. He moves ever so slowly toward the aft of the boat. The fantail looms like some great goal line and all he has to do is get across it.

James can hear the creaking of metal as the two ships, now intertwined, shift from the pressure of the sea. His world is still spinning and the movement of the ship doesn't help. Alarm klaxons sound all over the ferry and also outside in the darkness. James collapses back onto the deck, too shaky to even crawl.

He lays there, his face on the cool metal, feeling such relief.

I can just lay here? Right? I don't need to get off of the boat. His mind almost disengages from his physical body as he partially blacks out. James raises his head off of the deck considering.

Maybe, just a bad nightmare? Yea that was it. James rolls onto his back, wincing with all of the pain.

Contentment washes over him, it gently tugs at him, like a child leading him by the hand; to give into the void. A black from which all things have come and all things must once again return.

An abyss that once again forces its way into his conciseness.

Chapter Sixty Three

Thursday August 30th 22:50

BOOM! The sound and shock reverberates through the ship like it was a hollow drum. The M/V *Wenatchee* hits the gigantic aircraft carrier with tremendous force. Tremors and a wall of sound travel throughout the ship. Dizhwar and Driver are tossed out of the dangling Zodiac by the force of impact. They had not gotten the small launch fully deployed into the water before the two ships collide. The two hijackers are ten feet off of the waterline, suspended in midair when they are thrown into the sea.

Dizhwar plunges his head out of the cold Sea and looks for Driver. He treads water, "Nassir," he shouts and spins in a quick circle searching. "Nassir!" Dizhwar cries our again, but his friend is nowhere to be seen. *He was right next to me just a moment ago,* Dizhwar questions.

Dizhwar turns once more completely around, looking for his ally. "Driver!!!" he screams it out and his ears strain at the silence. He hears the creaking and popping of the ships, the lapping of water, but the voice of his friend is not there. Dizhwar becomes incredibly livid, and it fuels in him a great energy. Giving up his search for Driver, Dizhwar swims to the shoreline. He does not take the shorter route, towards the Navy base, but instead toward the highway that runs beside the once tranquil bay.

My men and I had planned on so much, Dizhwar calculates as he swims. *The passengers being left on board, the crash and even our escape. There's a van waiting for us in the parking lot of a run down dance club next to the freeway. My entire team was supposed to be in it, drive down to Portland and then be gone, but now?* Dizhwar swims with powerful strokes toward the highway. As his hands start to numb, he goes through what was supposed to happen. *We were to take flights to Medan, Indonesia and Manila, Philippines. But everything has been spoiled! We were meant to fight again, take indirect routes to once again reunite in Yemen.*

"Now, no more!" Dizhwar yells out as he nears the shoreline. Swimming still with his fury, and despite the frigid water temperature, his strokes remain powerful all of the way. *No cost was too great, yes, but this wasn't supposed to happen like this!* He pulls up all of his determination, *all of those men gone, his whole team wrecked!! A bastard!!!* In his swim, Dizhwar starts thinking about what America means to him. Then his thoughts head to the electrician...*this vile, white, Christian, capitalist, snake, has spoiled it all!*

He pulls his cold and wet body up onto the rock causeway that's the foundation bed for the freeway. He shivers with the chill as he removes from his jacket pocket the coup de' grâce. Dizhwar inspects the small plastic box, his final act, and is further let down. The homemade case is battered, cracked and broken from the escape. Not only that, but it's filled with seawater. Dizhwar sets it gingerly in his lap and takes a deep breath. He gazes out over the inlet that leads to the ferry and Naval ship docks, hoping Driver will be there. Dizhwar looks back over the water one more time, "Maybe, by Allah's will, there still might be hope."

Dizhwar easily separates the broken case and removes the two 9V batteries that was its power source. It looks like the batteries have become dislodged from their cradle within the transmitter. Dizhwar individually sticks the batteries to his tongue to make sure that each is still charged. He gets the confirming buzz on his tongue from both. The terrorist cell leader blows out all of the water from the circuit board and wires.

He looks up at the ferry and aircraft carrier and can see military and civilian boats starting to congregate two hundred yards or so from the back of the ferry. He also hears a helicopter, or perhaps, multiple helicopters in the sky. They are coming closer and Dizhwar needs to hurry. In the darkness he can't see if there are rescuers moving onboard the ship, but it's no matter. He saw all of the life vests in the water right before the collision. All of his hostages, his glorious human torches, are all off of the ship.

"Maybe, Driver will be among the rescued? Maybe he can still catch that spoiler of an electrician on the ship?" With that thought, Dizhwar makes haste, continuing to blow and shake out the water from the black remote box.

Satisfied, Dizhwar replaces the batteries back into the holder and connectors, flips the half destroyed remote trigger back over and presses the button.

Nothing!

"DAMMMIT!!!" He shouts and presses it again and again.

Still no satisfying boom. No explosion greets his ears!

Desperate, he looks up into the inky black depths of the sky for some sort of help. Yet, the divine help that he once thought inspired him, does not come. For one final time, before Dizhwar tosses the remote into the harbor, he turns the remote trigger back over.

The frustration ebbs as he forces himself to reexamine the entire unit. "Breathe and have patience," Dizhwar ibn Muhammad ibn Abdur Razzaq, Strong Slave of the Provider tells himself, "...this is just another test from God. You must regain control of your emotions."

There!

Dizhwar notices one of the two wires going to the antenna has broken loose. *Every electrical circuit needed a + and a - for a circuit to function, that I knew well.* In desperation and haste, Dizhwar strips the single detached wire with his teeth. He wraps it around the antenna contact. Without turning the unit over, afraid the wire might come loose, Dizhwar presses the button again.

Does he hear something? A rushing of wind? Or is that his imagination?

Wishful thinking? Or do prayers get answered that fast?

FIRE
EXTINGUISHER

Chapter Sixty Four

Thursday August 30th 22:55

Except for some minor whiplash, the entire Wenatchee crew makes it through the collision nearly unscathed. For a few moments they stay in their sitting positions, exchanging ideas to get their bonds cut. Trevor again is the quickest, and once more he is there with the best ideas.

Explaining to the rest as fast as he can, "If I could just brace myself against all of you, I think I can use my feet and break the safety glass on the emergency fire ax." These are located all over the ship and there is one strategically placed right there in the pilot house. Trevor continues "I think I can pry it free with my feet and then we'll have a sharp edge to cut our ties." Plans are made and Trevor once again goes to his heroic work.

Determined not to fail, in a few minutes of kicking and prying Trevor is able to get the ax free and it falls to the floor with a triumphant clang. In just a few more moments they have all cut the zip ties, and await commands from their captain, Michael O'Brian.

Michael issues orders that are about saving and preserving the passengers and his ship. At this point, he doesn't know what has become of his passengers or the terrorist hijackers, but he will do his best to find out. He instructs his crew to spread out *carefully* to the other pilot house, observation deck, main car deck and engine rooms. He instructs them to be cautious, to refrain from undue heroics; but try and retake complete control of the vessel with the axes. This has the possibility to be a valiant action, but it can also be rather misplaced. That will be determined by time and circumstance.

On his way down to the car deck, Trevor looks at his mobile phone that he hid from the quick search of the terrorists. When the terrorists took control of the ship he figured that they would search everyone. With no other brilliant place to hide the phone he dropped it into his inner pocket on his safety-orange security vest. He took off the vest and held it limply in his hand; out and away from himself during the search. And by some act of fate, his gamble paid off, the terrorists *had* incompletely frisked him. Trevor looked quickly through his phone. He didn't have any unanswered messages as he checks it and moves. Heading down the stairs, he wanders, *why does my phone strangely still have no signal?*

Trevor and the entire crew don't know what James saw in the engine room. Little does Trevor know that his efforts and very possibly the crew's efforts, are likely in vain.

Captain Michael Blair makes furious mayday calls that are not heard. His transmissions are still being jammed. Trevor's Houdini like effort of escape could very well be wasted, unless he immediately evacuates the ferry.

Even though it is an anathema to loyal crews, as much as a U.S. Marine will never leave someone behind, it's plain and simple; the entire crew needs to leave their ship and save themselves. It is still the crew's best chance to live. Despite the reality of the hijacking around them, the group of dedicated and trusting civil servants feels the M/V Wenatchee is their second home. *It's hard to abandon your home without overwhelming cause,* is their universal feeling.

The trendy bike rider from Capitol Hill, the soon to be fly-fishing retiree, the pair of siblings from Kent and the Burien woman with the rocky marriage will all have their lives cut short if they don't leave. Maybe they just might run across James or some of the freed passengers before it's too late. Realize the danger they are in and flee?

On the other hand, Captain Blair, Trevor Matthews, and the entire crew might end up a human sacrifice on the altar of terrorism.

Tick, tick, tick. In just a few more minutes time will run out.

Chapter Sixty Five

Thursday August 30th 22:55

James Maly comes to. For a moment he doesn't have a clue where he is or how he got there.

"Thank you for taking Washington state ferries..." the automated voice begins as he lays there on his back and listens to sounds. The grating of the ship, the lapping of waves, and even the brash sound of cars rubbing up against each other.

The ferry is going through agonizing groans. A cars rolls off of the pile with the rise and fall of the waves and James flinches from the cacophonous sound. He is immediately hit with the pungent smell of gasoline. It almost overwhelms James, as he notices that he is drenched to the skin with fuel and water. He stares at the rainbow like mixture on his hand, the fuel moving in the water like a multi-colored snake.

The ship's PA announces, "All passengers must disembark the ship with walk on passengers leaving first via the first level car deck."

A sound comes to the attention of James from one of the cars within the tangled heap and it focuses his attention.

Someone is moving within the twisted mess of vehicles, James can confirm. Someone is struggling within the heap of cars. The automobiles are tossed around and piled up like a child's hastily gathered bunch of matchbox cars.

James lays there and wonders aloud "Who's in the car?" forgetting Abia because of his pounding head.

Once more his attention is drawn away from survival to comfort. He begins to get incredibly cold. James's senses start giving him contrary information. *Don't move you're hurt, get up there's going to be a fire! Flee the ship it's going to sink, save the person in the pile of cars! Give up, it's too late; you're to weak. Keep fighting, it's all you have!*

He rolls back to his stomach and wills himself to move again. James begins to smell a new odor, *Smoke!!* his clouded brain screams at him.

Move! move! move!

Time to get up!!! Continue your push forward. James strains, barely able to get himself up on all fours and he begins to crawl. He moves like a child, through herculean will

and focus; every movement a struggle. Yet, he finally gets to the end.
The edge of the car deck is at his fingertips. Dripping and shivering, James peers into the cold black sea.

Into a black mirror-like surface that reflects back his own distorted face.

"Please take a few moments to collect your belongings and proceed to the disembarking areas." Again, the automated ship address comes over the loud-speakers. "Drivers and passengers please return to your vehicles and await directions from the crew."

James sits down heavily from his crawl on the very edge. He drapes the dangling life vest over his head. Sitting there for just a moment, he takes a deep breath and tries to tie the lines that secure the vest.

He can't. His fingers wont obey.

"Hope you have enjoyed your passage on the Washington State Ferry System. Please come again."

James is nauseous, faint and completely disoriented. His hands won't work right. James can see them, but they refuse to follow his directions. And James clearly knows it.

James hears a sound behind him and then he watches his Thermos pass by and roll off of the stern of the boat. James commands his body to work but his brain is not issuing commands to his arms. His body is not obeying him fully.

He tries yet again to tie the lines and is partially victorious.

James gets his arms to fold across the vest and his chest. James notices the blood dripping unto the deck. He can see it's from his own head wound.

The blood mixes with the water, that mixes with the fuel. James glances forward at his path to the goal line and sees he paid for it with his own red smear. His blood trail leads all of the way back to the moving truck.

I'm dying...a voice speaks plainly. James doesn't recognize it as his. With one last thought, a last and final command from his brain, James utters a whispered prayer. His entreaty heads off to someone that had been talked to a lot this evening.

He fights no more.

James's body falls the five feet backwards into the icy cold sea.

Chapter Sixty Six

Thursday August 30th 23:00

Abia doesn't fare much better, even when James's van is built by Ford to be, "Ford tough".

The E150 is a sturdy work horse and the van retains its shape and integrity throughout the demolition derby in the main car deck. Abia wakes up from being knocked unconscious, finding herself lying on the windowless driver side of the van. It is now the floor because the van is on it's side.

She comes to, realizing what has just taken place.

Not having any idea how long she'd been knocked out and knowing what is yet to come, she begins to feel the pressure to get off of the ship. She tries to get her bonds cut by something, anything in the electricians van. Unfortunately, she doesn't look hard enough or try long enough to slice through James's plastic zip ties. There are plenty of things there that will cut through her bonds, but it will take time to find them. Every time she tries one thing that isn't an instant fix, she tries something else. When that also doesn't work quickly enough, she moves to something new.

Abia Al-Tikriti makes so much noise that she doesn't hear James make his slow journey across the main garage. If she did, maybe she could have gotten some help. And maybe not. But, when you know that the hooded figure is coming with the sickle, there are very few of us that don't panic. As the moments slip by, the woman begins to hyperventilate from her worry that the explosives are to detonate at any moment. She doesn't know that she has minutes to escape because her leader has not gotten off of the boat in time either.

Abia still has tape on her mouth. For her, it is quite impossible to breathe in enough air through the nose for her lungs to supply the required oxygen to her overexcited heart and mind. Mouth still taped shut, her blood pumping excitedly because of the confusion and stress. It overwhelms her. She can't get her hands free, she can't remove the tape, so the process of hyperventilation proceeds on for just a few short minutes.

Abia starts to get dizzy and then passes out.

She never hears the explosions that rip through the engine room, never sees the fire rush in to the main car deck igniting everything it touches. An intense heat builds up, melting tires, cracking out automotive windows and turning electrical wire into molten strings.

Abia Al-Tikriti never feels the fire come into the electrician's van, as the inferno turns all of the vehicles into raging bonfires. Because of her body's hyper-need for oxygen, she is still rapidly breathing in her unconscious state. She quickly, mercifully, asphyxiates from the smoke like she was running her car in a sealed garage.

Unlike the *Wenatchee*'s crew, that spend their last moments on earth in sheer terror of the fiery death; benevolently, quietly, the last terrorist on the ship meets her Maker.

Chapter Sixty Seven

Thursday August 30th 23:05

The flash is monstrous! The explosion blinds Dizhwar, in fact it lights up the whole bay like a bright search light and he hurriedly sits down upon the rock before he is pushed over by the blast wave. There is a brief moment of daylight and then darkness again as the wave hits him, not as hard as he expects.

Oh, you can even see the fires that start from the explosion! Dizhwar silently grins, a devilish grin, and tosses the remote trigger into the inlet. He turns away from his carnage and walks slowly to the nearby van.

Dizhwar is now sure, despite loosing his entire cell that the mission is a success. Ashan had everyone's attention now and Dizhwar ibn Tariq ibn Abdur Razzaq, Strong Slave of the Provider, is happy to carry out Allah's will. But Allah has demanded a heavy price for obedience. The United States will soon show respect to him and all of his brethren around the world. Or the Untied States will face more domestic attacks. Eventually, America will collapse upon its own selfish weight.

Dizhwar makes it to the van, unlocks the door with the hidden wheel well key and climbs inside. He starts up the van and cranks up the heater while he changes. He strips off his wet clothes and changes into fresh ones that were left inside for each of the twelve team members. Once in the dry clothes, Dizhwar drives the van southwest down State Route 16 to the town of Gig Harbor. There, he pulls into the big box hardware store that is right off of SR 16 off-ramp.

Parking his van a few aisles back from the front doors, Dizhwar pulls up his bag and removes the pay as you go phone. He turns it on, dials 411. "Yes, Taxi please. Gig Harbor Washington," he asks. The terrorist leader gets connected to the taxi company by the automated 411 system. "I need a taxi to this address." He feeds the taxi dispatcher the address of a 24-hour restaurant located just over the overpass. Once he gets confirmation, he disconnects.

After making his reservation, Dizhwar goes through all of his operator's bags, removing the preloaded debit cards and IDs and three more of the prepaid phones. Dizhwar is still fuming at the waste of all of these dead men. A long list of them has made such a sacrifice. Especially, Driver. He burns with an incredible need for vengeance against someone. Someone who turned this entire plan upside down. Dizhwar removes the battery from the first phone and tosses it on the pile of remaining items.

With anger and destruction on his mind, Dizhwar packs all of the items he grabbed from the other team member's bags. He tosses all of it in his carry on luggage bag suitable for the overhead bins of an airplane. Dizhwar makes a call to their former safe house on a second mobile phone. He waits till the answering machine kicks on there in Redmond, Washington. Not saying anything, he pounds in a series of numbers and then disconnects. The numbers are a simple beep code that start the 24 hour timer to ignite his rental house into flames. His team had made every effort to clean it thoroughly, but they could never be sure. Dizhwar had seen through many news reports about how the FBI and other investigative units will go through a residence with a fine tooth comb. The less left behind for them the better.

They had talked about a way to sanitize the residence within the cell's inner circle. Driver had come up with the solution of burning it to the ground. The house was wired with a few discreet plastic valves to open up the houses interior gas line. Just a spark from a carefully placed igniter in the kitchen will set off the inferno. In 24 hours the team's former residence would be fully engulfed before anyone can put it out. Dizhwar removes the battery from the phone he just used and tosses this second phone on the pile of remaining items in the van.

Satisfied, he locks the van from the inside, tosses in the keys and enables a switch located on the bottom of the dashboard. It blinks out a series of green pulses, slowly becoming faster. With one last glance around, he shuts the doors. Before walking away from the van, Dizhwar administers a final blow. He pulls a small fishing line that is taped under the right rear wheel well. The line is attached to a plug, it pops out and gasoline begins to pour from the nearly full gas tank. Dizhwar walks the ¼ mile to the entrance of the 24-hour restaurant with his two bags and waits for his taxi to arrive.

With only three minutes to spare before the van ignites, the taxi pulls up. Dizhwar gets into the taxi's back seat without waiting for the driver to come around and let him in. The taxi driver, just in the process of getting out, sees his customer climb in. The cabby hurriedly jumps back into the car a bit unraveled at his fare's independence.

"Where to?" The taxi driver asks, situating himself back into his seat and seatbelt.

"Tacoma. The Holiday Inn Express. The one right next to the Five and Sixteen freeways." Dizhwar orders. Dizhwar has no intention of staying at the hotel, but he intends to book a room there for a night, just the same.

So many things to do and not enough time to do it, Dizhwar considers as he glances at his watch. They leave the parking lot, getting on the freeway on-ramp. He glances back to see the satisfying orange glow from the van. As they proceeded up the southern on-ramp for SR 16, Dizhwar watches his van in the Lowe's parking lot burn. By the time they pass by at a distance, Dizhwar can clearly see the van fully engulfed. More flames to lay waste what has been worked hard for, in order to carry on the fight.

The cab pulls up to the Tacoma Holiday Inn and Dizhwar pays the toll in cash. Exiting the vehicle, carrying his two bags with him, he check in and walks up to his room. Careful not to leave any fingerprints, he works from his laptop without getting on the network, beginning his write up of an after action report for Ashan. After an hour, Dizhwar places a "do not disturb" sign on the door and walks to the next nearest hotel. He walks right into the lobby of the Travel Lodge that was just four blocks down the street. Pretending to be a guest, he asks the front desk agent if they could call him a taxi. Dizhwar patiently waits in the lobby until the it arrives.

"Where you wanna go?" This new taxi driver asks.

"SeaTac. The Red Roof Inn on International Boulevard."

Dizhwar once more remains silent and doesn't engage in any small talk. On arrival he checks into the Red Roof Inn for two nights. He makes hints he just got off the airplane and is thoroughly engaging to the receptionist. In an hour, he leaves his room once again, 'Do not Disturb' hanging conspicuously from the door handle.

Duplicating his previous actions, he exits the hotel through a side exit, avoiding the front lobby and walks to the fourth and final place. A Hilton just seven blocks up the street from the Red Roof. This particular Hilton has tennis courts, a pool and free shuttle service to the airport. Dizhwar knows that any and all pursuit needs to be thrown off of his trail and these are the ways he is trained to do just that.

At last, Dizhwar arrives and checks in. He enters his room, sets down his luggage and turns on the news. Using his last smart phone, he purchases round trip tickets to Portland for the morning, then removes the battery and disposes of it in the trash. Dizhwar gives it a second thought, reconsidering. *It will probably be better to leave the phone on a chair in the hotel lobby. With the hopes that someone will take it.* He reconsiders, removes the phone from the trash and sets it, without battery, on the dresser as a reminder for the morning.

Starting at 6am, there are flights leaving every half an hour from SeaTac airport to Portland and San Jose. Once in Portland, he will catch his previously booked flight, with a different passport, that will begin his circuitous route to Yemen for the personal debriefing.

Dizhwar cranks up the volume with the remote as he walks into the restroom. While relieving himself he listens to the initial reports of the ferry accident. Most of the passengers, maybe all, are being recovered by military and civilian watercraft

"How has this happened?" Dizhwar wonders as he flushes, washes his hands and strides back into the room with the bed and television. He sits on his bed watching the TV, opens his laptop and pulls up CNN, Fox News, and BBC news pages to see what they are reporting on. The reports on the television are not much on facts. He tunes to a local station and there is already a news crew filming wet and soggy passengers. They waddle out of all types of boats, up to arriving ambulances and fire trucks. Emergency personnel giving out blankets and minor first aid.

In the background the ferry burns. Dizhwar notices from the camera shot, *it looks like the aircraft carrier has fire crews on her decks soaking their ship and the ferry.* The once majestic ferry is just a shadow of its former self. The front and back of the poor *Wenatchee* are still fully engulfed, with the middle of the boat seeing only smoke.

I need to kill some time before my flight leaves, I might as well watch, wait and see? He makes himself comfortable on the bed and has another thought, *try and provide more intelligence to Ashan about the strike's effectiveness?*

"Here's to hoping that it will be valuable information." Dizhwar raises a small mini-bar bottle of tequila and drinks the whole thing in one pull. While surfing the news sites on his laptop, he catches a glimpse of something out of the corner of his eye on the television. Quickly he switches his focus to the TV and sees a man being carried to a stretcher with clothes that are vaguely recognizable.

Worn black boots, brown work pants, and an armored vest? That is impossible!! His stomach sinks as he witnesses the man! Dizhwar watches the electrician being loaded onto an ambulance. Pulling himself away from the news coverage, he furiously opens another web browser on his laptop.

Duck Duck Go Web Search:

Heading: Puget Sound Electricians

Subhead: 24 hour response for commercial customers.

All I need from the web site is to see the company logo, an Eagle holding electrical sparks in its talons. Dizhwar furiously scans through pages of search results. *Then I will have all of the company information necessary.*

Dizhwar takes a little bit of solace, *After that, vengeance is going to be child's play.*

Chapter Sixty Eight

Thursday August 30th 23:00

      Captain Ian Sandivick is a fine communicator and a quick talker. His sharp wit, improvisation, and acute attention to details have been traits he has always put to good use. After all, his talent to be glib is what landed him this yacht captain job in the first place.

Just a few minutes ago he called both of his bosses and gave them the bad news. Their yacht and the two king's vacations will not go off as planned. One of the pair was very understanding, almost conciliatory, especially when Ian shared about the circumstances. His other boss was not so reasonable and hung up the phone on him.

Ian is back on the bench, sitting there with his crew and waiting.

When things seem to die down with the law enforcement presence, Captain Ian of the pleasure yacht *Eternity,* overhears some of the police types talking. There are some of them conversing about examining the *inside* of the lock. It is being suggested, by some of the people with badges, that the situation would be better if the big yacht is out of the way. Some of those in charge want the corralled ship out of the lock. Especially since law enforcement has to inspect both locks, empty.

Some of the officers claim that they will not need to put divers at risk if the two channels are emptied of water. Jumping at the opportunity, Ian carefully worms his way into the conversation that is taking place within earshot.

"I could have my crew and I get the yacht out for you guys," Ian raises his eyebrows as he points to the *Eternity*. "We can park close by once we exit, for further evidence gathering of course."

"I think it is a good idea," one of the badged commanders, a women interjects.

  "My people don't know how to drive that." One of the other officer's in charge suggests to his peers. The man looks over the large yacht, "Plus the liability issues are enough to break any budget. "I think we get the Captain here to get his big toy out of the locks, we empty them and then inspect them at a distance."

Another lady from the BATFE agrees. "Well, correct me if I am wrong, but no one wants to wait until we have a crew to move it?"

Federal, state and local police types agree. Ian and his crew are allowed back on board, they are back in business.

Little do the officers know Capt. Ian has a different plan. The closest place to dock, just out of the Ballard Locks is where he needs to go anyway. That is the exact place where he needs to pick up his large amount of fuel for the vacation trip. He doesn't feel like telling the law officers anything more than what they need to know. After all, that was exactly how he had been treated for the past two hours!

As the clock turns eleven, he and his crew find themselves back on board the *Eternity*. They all wait while emergency power is used to open the lower door of lock two. In just a few minutes more they have *Eternity* fired up with her lines untied. As the ship slowly creeps out of lock two, Ian is thinking *got to find a way to get my bosses vacation back on schedule.*

Ian comes up with a few options as his stern clears the locks. Then there is a quick flash of light to his southwest. He looks at it quickly, as he and his ship are clear of the doors of the lock.

"Holy...what was that?!?" His port-side lookout calls over to him from the port side railing.

Ian doesn't say a word. "Boss, did you see that flash of light?"

"Yeah I did but just focus on your job. Stick to watching the yacht, will you?!?"

Moments pass and *Eternity* is finally in the channel that leads to Elliot Bay. Ian smiles with the realization, *nothing is in the way.* He considers his freedom for a moment and knows, especially in light of recent events, that the flash he just saw has every reason to be really bad.

A little faster a little faster, Ian urges the ship as he tells himself lies about the seriousness of the explosion he just saw. Ian creeps up the throttles, *That flash is meaningful. There must be more attacks going on tonight,* Capt. Ian knows it. Yet, he doesn't foresee what happens next.

"*Eternity*! *Eternity*, do you copy?" The radio's crackle goes through the cabin like an unwanted fly. Buzzing about, not escaping from the *Eternity's* control bridge. "*Eternity*, this is Seattle Harbor Patrol. Respond!"

In amazement, his stern-side lookout watches his Captain just ignore the radio and continue to steer the ship. Moments pass and the radio barks to life once more before the port-side lookout finally works up the nerve to ask, "Boss, are you going to answer that?"

Breathing out a sigh of frustration, Ian glowers once again at both of his lookouts. The pair sees the glare from their captain's face and they both quickly go back to watching their assigned areas.

Another voice comes over the radio, "*Eternity* this is the FBI respond to the hails or we will consider you hostile!"

"Yeah.....," Ian picks up the radio, talking to the cabin. "Go ahead," Ian speaks in an almost knowing monotone into the handset.

"*Eternity*, this is Seattle Harbor Patrol. We need the use of your ship to transport some of our units immediately to the Bremerton Naval Ship Yard."

Biting the inside of his cheek, Ian lets out "Of course you do..." before keying the microphone. "Alright there," Ian blurts out in a most unconvincing way. "We will slow to a stop and take you guys on right away."

Ian Sandivick tosses the microphone's handset carelessly onto the dashboard, shaking his head as he pulls the throttle to idle.

So much for his best laid plans.

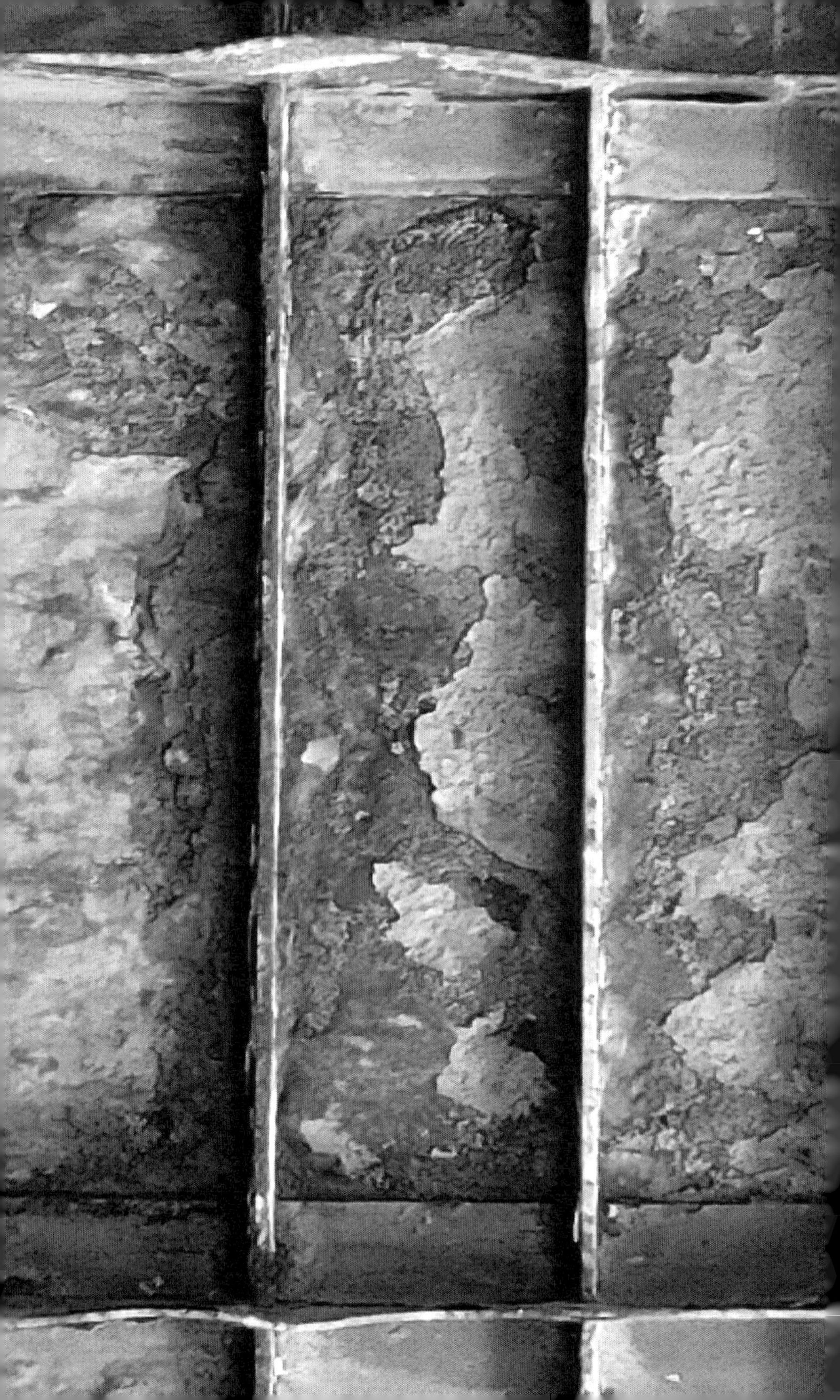

Chapter Sixty Nine

Friday August 31st 10:45

"...while today, Kuwaiti Ambassador to the United Nations stressed his country's dismay that its border teams face repeated attacks by Iraqi citizens hurling stones..." the news drones on in Arabic. Ibrahim Al-Duwaisan sits in his hotel room looking over the initial reports from Dizhwar. He has made it to Qatar to meet with a few investors and to finish his vacation with his wife and grandson.

"Grandpa. Grandpa! I want to swim!" The bare chested little boy in swim trunks and sandals calls from the porch. Grandson and grandfather can hear the cries of joy drift up into their room from the open sliding glass door. The warm breeze filters in their hotel room with its splendid view of the Persian Gulf and the massive courtyard swimming pool below.

Ibrahim springs from his chair and lifts up his five year old grandson from out on the porch, "Let's wait until your grandmother is ready. Here," handing the television remote to his grandson, "find something to watch while we wait." Ibrahim sets his greatest treasure down upon the bed. As he sits back down at the desk, he resumes the video feed from the throw-away laptop.

The man with the closely trimmed beard focuses his attention back to the presentation he is watching via the online meeting software. He is furiously keeping notes on a hotel pad of paper, as the slides of pictures and words flash across the screen. Ibrahim is also making sure that the company's relay software is up and functioning, as Dizhwar's presentation from Washington State is being retransmitted to a secure server in Malaysia for later review.

The bedroom door opens, and a graceful woman walks through the door, making eye contact with Ibrahim. She beams a radiant grin, "Did you finish your breakfast?" Distractedly Ibrahim answers, "Yes, my raven."

"Then, are you ready to go?"

"No." He was still in his sweats and running shirt from his morning exercise, but had removed his sweatshirt, shoes and socks. Ibrahim is still in decent health for his age. His doctor has told him as much during his yearly check-up. With the regular exercise and weight training he does his best to keep up his physique from his soldiering days. Ibrahim did what was right and this morning's breakfast was no different, other than some

Belgian waffles with his grandson. Just as long as he stays away from his pair of vices; the Cuban cigars and American whiskey he will be fine. "Why don't you two go down now and I will meet you in a few minutes. I still have some work to do."

In a fluid motion, Ibrahim's wife Alyaa, leans over his shoulder to see what he is working on.

"...stay tuned for more breaking news about the ferry accident in the United State's Seattle, Washington. Just after the break." The male newscaster smiles quickly into the camera and the screen changes to a commercial for a German automobile.

"Are these the results from the collision?" Alayaa whispers, her arms wrapped around her husbands neck and shoulders. She knows mostly everything that he does, with the exception being his enforcer tasks. She supports him furthering the cause in whatever way she can.

"Yes," he quietly responds back, leaning his chair back slightly to look at his wife and the television at the same time.

Keeping their voices low around their grandson Ibrahim continues, "It didn't go well. The news is just about to come on. What I know is, it seems a policeman or someone like that disrupted the trip. A lot of our men were lost. But we shouldn't be concerned, it's all too soon to tell." He turns and tenderly places an arm around her waist, "You should go before our grandson looses his patience and jumps into the pool from here." She smiles, kisses him just above his left eyebrow, "Make sure you hurry, he will miss you."

With the kiss still warm on his forehead, Ibrahim nods and offers a smile, as grandmother and grandson walk out the room's exterior door.

It's just in time. Ibrahim gets a blinking icon in the lower left corner of the software program's presentation page. At the same time Al-Jazeera comes back with its top news.

"There are initial reports coming in from America of a collision accident involving a Washington State ferry and an American Aircraft Carrier. Emergency personnel are on the scene recovering survivors. We are going live to a local Seattle affiliate for an update..."

He mutes the television, turning on the close-captioning. The blinking icon on Ibrahim's laptop is a request from someone else wanting to join the meeting. He already had the Brigadier General, the Programmer and the Mariner online with him, silently watching the forwarded information from *their asset* in country.

With a few keystrokes, Ibrahim quickly runs a secure transfer file protocol (SFTP) check on the request. Just to make sure that it's genuine. Always on his guard to hackers and other hostile intelligence agencies. Once he gets the SFTP confirmation, he proceeds through an in-house authorization process. Their proprietary software busily works away. In another minute, after all the verification procedures check out, Ibrahim accepts the request.

Hmm, I wonder who else on the board is joining? He considers. The SFTP icon next to the chat box is a reminder that their presentation is encrypted and secure. Including any chat messages.

Directly next to the blinking icon, a digital identifier pops up. "C.O. has joined the meeting!"

Surprised, Ibrahim types into the chat window "Hello C.O.."

"Hello, Grey Hair. What in Allah's Name has happened? Things go well?"

Nothing like his boss to get directly to the point. "No, they didn't. I was just explaining to others: He is getting to us the preliminary info now. News is showing up on CNN, Fox and Al-Jazeera. Full report will happen when he's out."

"K." The C.O. types. "Their courage is being seen by the world. Will continue to watch presentation from my side."

"Wanted you to know, successful at the Orient meetings. Have good news." Ibrahim types, trying to take the sting out of the loss of their men in the States. "Had great success with three meetings. Met dozen businessmen. All agree to support."

"Good." The C.O. replies. "You have a few more meets?"

"Yes. This evening and then home."
The chat message came back fast. "Do we know if all survived?"

Ibrahim hesitates not knowing what to type. "Unknown, but there were many losses," is all he can come up with. Ibrahim's concern for Nassir Al-Din aka "Driver" is intense. Ibrahim knows that the C.O. and the entire Shura Council at Ashan had concerns with Dizhwar's anger management. His passions could get the best of him. Ibrahim had seen, first hand, the man's anger fly away during the initial recruiting meeting. Ibrahim had heard it come up a few more times during training. This was why the C.O. reluctantly activated his grandson, to help keep Dizhwar focused and in control.

Nassir al Din had quickly become the son that the C.O. never had. Ibrahim knew that the C.O. was uneasy about sending his grandson in the first place and now he was missing. Ibrahim would have been worried too, if he had only just met his grandson a few years ago. So much time to make up, so many precious memories had already passed unrealized. Nassir didn't have a clue that his grandfather was the head of an international terrorist organization, nor did Dizhwar. It was a closely guarded secret. In fact, only the seven Board members, Ibrahim a member himself, knew the identities of the others.

"Our man is sure he made it into the water with him. They are closer than brothers. Our man searched. Possibly separated. We should hear from both soon." Ibrahim types, trying to keep it hopeful. "Driver knows about meeting as well. We might get a log on request."

"Thank you, Grey Hair." There was a pause, and then the blinking cursor typed out "The Higher Order shall reign." The chat curser went out as the C.O. killed the chat feature from his end. Ibrahim could see however that the C.O. remained logged into the presentation.

Grey Hair, a nickname he carried since he turned prematurely grey at twenty eight, finishes watching Dizhwar's preliminary presentation report and the top news from the TV. The web conference video is slow, but is accurately displaying Dizhwar's report. Within the presentation are screen captures from many media outlets. Their courage was indeed seen by all. As soon as Dizhwar finishes sending all of his information, the man logs off.

Ibrahim strokes his grey beard which has become his calling card. He sits patiently and waits. The Programmer, the Mariner and lastly the General, all log out without a word. Ibrahim delays going to the pool a little longer. He fires off a text to his wife letting her know that he will be down in just a few *more* minutes. The C.O. still has to log out of the group before Ibrahim can shut down the conference link. Tolerantly, Ibrahim watches, as the C.O. remains logged in. The C.O.'s cursor blinking away like a heartbeat.

Ibrahim will stay for as long as it takes. He is sure his boss waits for news of a grandson, as Ibrahim listens to the cries of joy from his own at the pool.

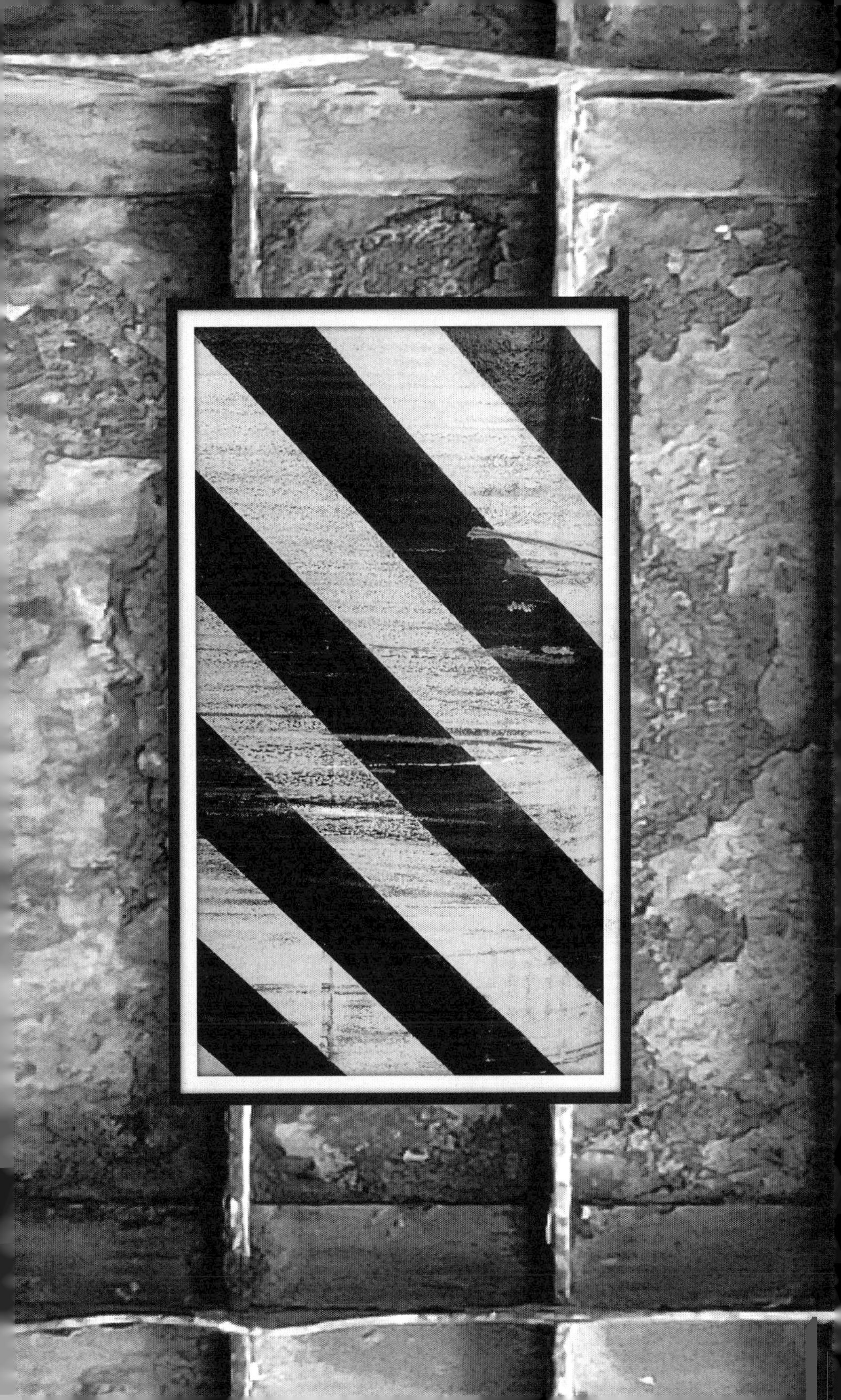

MUSTANG
SUITS INSIDE

ABANDON SHIP
GEAR INSIDE

Afterward;
Or so it seems...

Saturday September 1st 4:06 am

James's dream is suffocating him. Which is odd. He could never remember his dreams. If he ever did, they were always the nightmares.

This dream is approaching the nightmare label, James considers as it is filled with too much water and not enough air.

With freezing cold salt water trying to pour down his mouth and nose, James gags at the fluid every time he comes up for a breath. *No, it's definitely not a dream. It's a cold and dark nightmare,* James confirms. To make matters worse is a periodic threat of terrorist men trying to kill him. They reveal themselves whenever he sticks his head out of the vast inky black sea. James tries his best, to aim and then shoot with his own pistol, at the men with guns. They rise out of the water as he does. The terrorists quickly fire at him, then the gunman sink quickly down into the black. No matter what the gunmen's actions are too fast and James's gun doesn't seem to ever want to work properly.

Every time he tries to actually fire his pistol it's jammed with ice. Somehow, he's able to clear the ice from the semi-auto pistol's slide, reload, aim and then, there's ice again. James is trying his best in one instant to tread water, and then in the next moment struggling to make his pistol function. The difficulty to maintain balance between keeping his head above the waves and trying to shoot the terrorists is draining him.

James is loosing his battle to live.

Just as he sinks under, James watches one of the gunmen emerge out of the water, Khoury he thinks, and about the same moment James notices that there's more light to see by.

"Fantastic!" James congratulates himself, he won't have to rely so much on the night sights affixed to the Israeli Arms pistol. Then, what he thinks is Khoury, sinks beneath the water and is gone. He doesn't even fire a shot. Afterward the area Khoury is in takes on a peculiar light.

The illumination isn't coming from the sky. *It's coming from... where?* James asks himself.

He looks around, *the faint glow seems to be coming from the inky black ocean? Does the light have warmth even?* James can feel it in his toes every time his feet run across the radiance. Like sticking his feet in the warm sand after being in the cold ocean. James has no idea why it's coming from the depths. James is also not about to dive in after it.

The cold isn't that bad, he tells himself. *I've been colder before in Colorado when it was zero degrees during that install.*

Furthermore, James has questions. For once since appearing within this ocean nightmare he's actually able to think without being distracted by terrorists.

Where is Khoury? Where's Abia? What happened to the ship? Where are the terrorists going after they sink?

He looks down into the depths of the salty water for any more threats; for any gunman. That's when he first notices bubbles start to rise from among the rays of light. The moment they reach the surface the entire ocean turns to thick blood. The bubbles pop, and every time one pops, James hears a single clear voice. The first two bubbles that burst he doesn't recognize the voices at all.

"What in heaven's name…?" James speaks to the vastness around him…and nothing echoes back.

Another bubble pops and he hears a familiar female voice "…You are also loved by me…" His wife? *This just doesn't make any sense.*

A bubble pops out of the water to his right "Daddy, can you hear…" This time it's his youngest daughter.

Another, faster now "…The moments that we share will always be cherished in my heart…" His wife again and now the light is all around him. The warmth pushes aside all of the cold. It also seems to push away any possibility of the gunman as well. The evil men are still coming up and then sinking back into blood that was just water, but they were doing so farther and farther away from him. Soon they are completely out of sight.

James tosses aside the pistol and the bubbles start coming up even faster, from all around him. The voices of his children, his wife, friends and family; he is totally overwhelmed. James starts to cry because he is so alone and all of these voices seem to be just memories, of what he had and what he knew. Then the light's intensity becomes so powerful that he can't look directly at it anymore. The voices and the light somehow merge, and they rise to a disharmony of indiscernible noise.

Out of the din, James can hear a simple, regular, digital beep. James searches for it within his mind and holds onto that with his entire consciousness. The moment that he finally succeeds in grasping the sound, the sea of blood rushes up around him like the world no longer experienced gravity, except for himself. The unclear noises cease, and he is lying in a bed with white sheets.

Surrounded by equipment, *A hospital bed*, James assures himself.

"Good morning, my dear," the soft, silky voice of his wife is close. So close he can feel her breath on his cheek and in his eye lashes. He smells her familiar and appealing scent. Breathing it in deeply, he drinks her in.

Wendi Maly comes closer, "I've missed you so very much my love. I'm glad to have you back." As she speaks, her warm hand gently slides down his muscular arm toward his own hand.

James winces at the pain in his entire body, that is brought to light by her contact, but he's soothed by her touch. Wendi carefully tucks her hand between the tubes and wires; grasping his. James looks up from his pillow at the old scar on her left hand. It is a scar that is so similar to his own scar and he smiles. He can feel her petite fingers intertwined with his and her touch brings him peace. James relaxes, letting his head sink into the chemical smelling pillow once more.

After her soft words are spoken, James closes his eyes and holds onto her hand. He doesn't let go of it, or her words. In his mind, her words are like precious diamonds. Now that she is close, everything, all of it, is better now.

-The End-

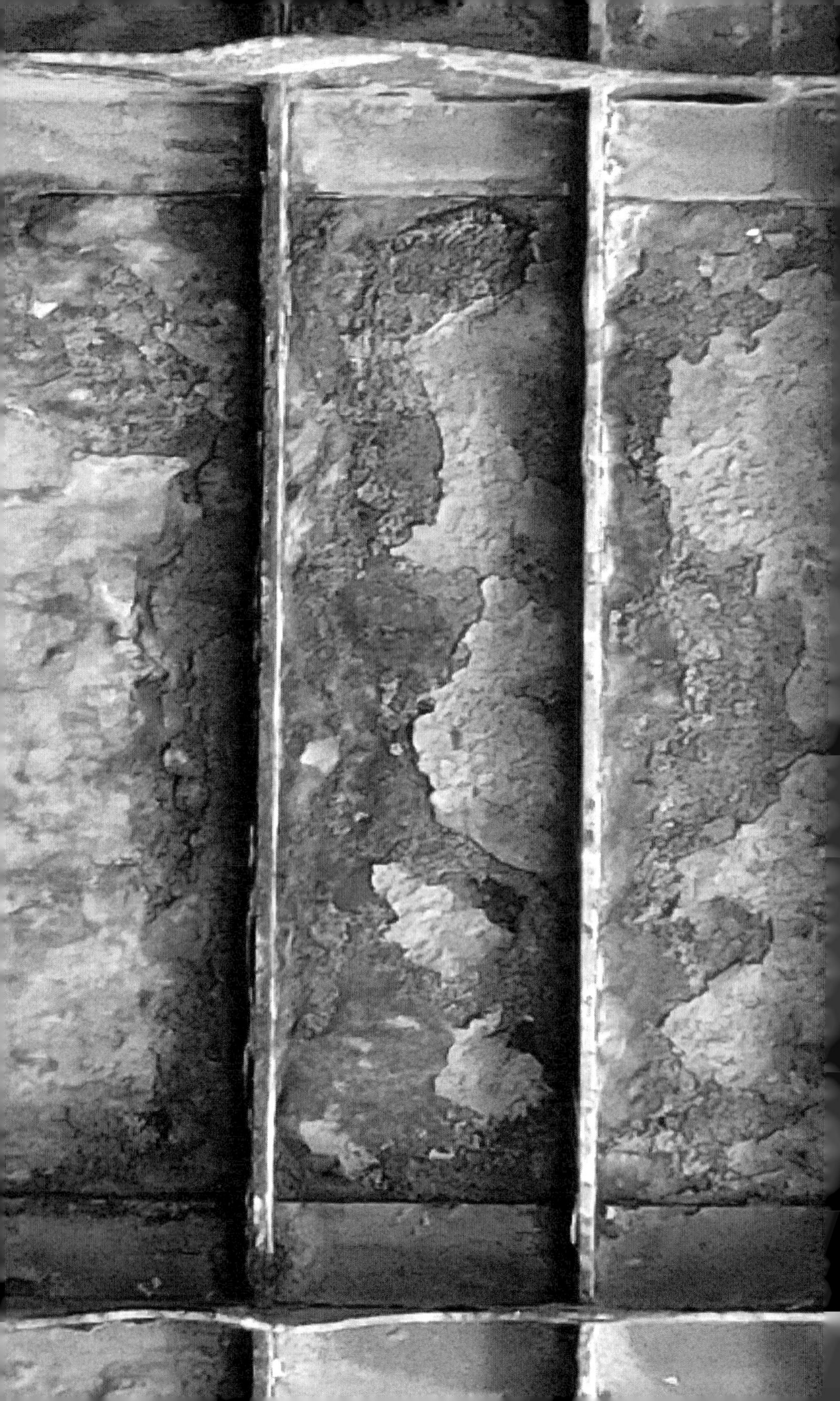

Appendix A: What the Law says-

לֹא תִרְצָח Lo tirṣaḥ

"Thou shall not kill," usually translated as, "...you shall not break, to dash to pieces, to kill, slay, murder..."

The sixth Commandment, עשרת הדברים from (Asereth ha-D' bharîm) 'the ten matters' in the book of Exodus, the Torah

"A well regulated Militia, being necessary to the security of a free State, the right of the people to keep and bear Arms, shall not be infringed."

The Second Amendment to the Constitution of the United States. Ratified Dec 15th 1791

"...Homicide shall not be justifiable, under this statue, if the slayer knows or should know, that he or she could avoid the necessity of using said force with complete safety by retreating."

Washington State House Bill 1012 -2013 Regular session (not passed)

"Homicide is justifiable when committed either:

(1) In the lawful defense of the slayer, or his or her husband, wife, parent, child, brother, sister or any other person in his or her presence or company, when there is reasonable ground to apprehend a design on the part of the person slain to commit a felony or to do some great personal injury to the slayer or any such person, and there is imminent danger of such being accomplished; or

(2) In the actual resistance of an attempt to commit a felony upon the slayer, in his or her presence, or upon or in a dwelling or other place of abode, in which he or she is ."

Washington State Law RCW 9A.16.050

Appendix B: Terms

Tsavo River *(Akamba):* Tasvo means 'slaughter' in the language of the Akamba. Tsavo was continually crossed by caravans of Arab slavers and their captives, until the British put an end to it. The Tsavo river is located in the south west part of Kenya, just at the foot of Mt. Kilimanjaro. This was the infamous site for the Tsavo Man-eaters incident of 1898. Approximately 135 railroad workers fell to the pair of lions until they were shot and killed. The great movie "The Ghost and the Darkness" is based on the tale.

Quran: (Arabic, القرآن *kor-AHN also* spelled Qur'an or Koran) literally meaning "the recitation", is the central religious text of Islam, or canon. Muslims believe it to be a revelation from God. Muslims believe that the Quran was verbally revealed from God, to Muhammad, through the angel Gabriel. The first copy was written around 661AD.

The Holy Bible: *(Greek,* τὰ βιβλία, tà biblía) is a word meaning the books. "The Bible" from English or French pronunciation of the Greek, is a collection of texts, letters and books sacred in Judaism, Christianity and Islam. There is no single "Bible" and many Bibles with varying contents exist. Judaism references the "Old Testament" called the Tanakh, as their canon. The Tanakh was finally gathered and affirmed from various authors around 300AD. Christians and Muslims reference both the "Old Testament" and the "New Testament," with both Testaments being used as the canon for Christians.

Ashan: (Arabic, عشان Ah-SHAhN) is word meaning the "Nest". It is the fictional spin-off spy/covert/overt operations organization founded by the CO of White Sands Engineering. Unbeknownst to Nasir al Din his grandfather is the reason for him to go to America.

Boyevaya Mashina Pekhoty (BMP)-3: (Russian) Translated into "infantry combat vehicle," it is a capable and well-rounded armored personal carrier based on the BMP1 and the BMP2.The vehicle can fire on the move, it has a wide array of weapons and can double as a capable light or scout tank. Originally designed and manufactured by the Russians, the BMP-3's are now being exported all over the world with the United Arab Emirates its largest user.

Boyevaya Mashina (BM) grad -21: (Russian) Meaning "combat vehicle, hail." It is sometimes called a Katyusha Rocket Launcher, a name given to it because of the rockets it fires. It was first built and fielded in WWII as rocket artillery. The more modernized version is based on a 1960's re-design. It fires up to 40 unguided 122mm 9ft long rockets, which can reach up to 20 miles, in a single salvo. They infamously are used by various terrorist groups all around the middle east to shell Israel and each other. Russia sells these all over the world; with them and Vietnam being the largest operators.

Sajjasa: (Arabic, الاضطراب sā-JA-sā) Literally means, "to cause unrest".

Zenitnaya Samokhodnaya Ustanovka ZSU-23-4M4: (Russian) Literally translated into "Anti-Aircraft Self Propelled Mount." Meaning "23" is the bore diameter in millimeters of the gun barrels and 4 is the number of guns. It was originally designed by the Russians in the 1960's, but now the designs are widely sold. Still considered "extremely dangerous" by NATO that, in the time of war, standing orders are to destroy it on site even if doing so requires the pilot to abandon his/her mission. The "M4" is the latest version with Syria, Egypt and Algeria being the largest users.

RQ-3A "Dark Star" stealth drone: It is a real 'Unmanned Arial Vehicle' (UAV) that was manufactured around 1995. It incorporated stealth technology like the B-2, and has been allegedly retired. I don't know its capabilities, because it's capabilities are still classified. I simply thought the UAV sounded cool, so I used specifications from what I know of other, more "public" UAV/drone specs.

Fairchild/Republic A-10 Thunderbolt II: Called the "Warthog" is an American ground attack/close air support aircraft. Designed and built in the early 1970's it became famous for its firepower, pilot armor protection and it's capability to take tremendous amounts of punishment and still remain airborne. The entire airframe was designed around its 30mm cannon, which remains the heaviest gun ever to be mounted to an aircraft. For the past forty years the A-10 has remained the deadliest fixed-wing tank killer aircraft designed by any nation.

Sukhoi Su-25K: (Russian) **K**omercheskiy called "**Frogfoot**" by NATO, is a single-seat, twin-engine jet aircraft developed in the Soviet Union to provide close air support for their ground forces, like the American A-10. The first prototype made its maiden flight on 22 February 1975. The aircraft went into production in 1978 at Tbilisi in the Soviet Republic of Georgia as a response to the American A-10. The majority are used by Russia, with Ukraine and North Korea being other large operators.

Ṣalāt: (Arabic, صلاة ṣalāh) is an Arabic word whose basic meaning is "bowing, homage, worship, prayer," but the *Ṣalāt* is more formal and ritualistic, being practiced five times a day, than the spontaneous *dua*.

Dua: (Arabic, دُعَاء duʿāʾ) is a word for non-ritualistic "reaching out or calling out" that can be practiced by Muslims at any time of the day. It can include *Salat* but is not limited to just the ritual prayer.

Shura: (Arabic, شورى *shūrā*) meaning "consultation." It can take form in a *Council,* or an elected or appointed group, or from a superior to a subordinate.

Nasi Goreng: (Indonesian) is a dish of fried rice. Can be spiced with *kecap manis* (sweet soy sauce), shallots, garlic, tamarind and chili powder. It usually accompanies other ingredients, like chicken, eggs and shrimp.

Imam: (Arabic, إمام *imam*) meaning "leader". It is most commonly used in the context of a head of a mosque or worship leader.

En Partibus Infidelium: (A Latin Proverb) meaning "in the land of the unbelievers" or "in the regions of the infidels".

Muslim Brotherhood: Is a transnational organization that started as a religious organization by Hassan al-Banna in Egypt in 1928. Although it maintained a high profile, over time it became gradually more militant in objectives and activism. It is considered a terrorist organization by many nations, but still maintains strong political power as a party and a contributor to candidates in various middle eastern nations.

al-Qaeda: (Arabic, القاعدة al-ky-də) meaning "the base" is a global militant Islamist organization. Founded by Osama bin Laden and Abdullah Azzam around 1988, it operates a stateless army following the strict Wahhabi interpretation of sharia law. Labeled a terrorist organization by the U.N. and N.A.T.O., it attacks military and civilian targets it considers *kafir*, in a struggle towards a Muslim Caliphate. It has been directly tied to the attacks on September 11th, 1998 U.S. Embassy bombing and the 2002 Bali bombings.

Wahhabi: (Arabic, وهابية, *Wahhābiyyah*) is an "ultra-conservative" or "orthodox" sect or form of Islam named after a Muhammad ibn Abd al-Wahhab. He was an eighteenth century Imam and scholar that started a fundamentalist movement that bears his name.

Emergency Position Indicating Radio Beacon (EPIRB): Is a tracking transmitter which aids in the rescue of people in distress. Mostly used on aircraft and boats, it sends out a radio beacon signal that's monitored worldwide. The location of the distress is detected by non-geostationary satellites and relayed to the nearest emergency response units.

Ḥalāl: (Arabic: حلال *ḥalāl*) meaning "permissible." The term can not only be applied to *food* and *drink,* but all manners of daily life of a Muslim.

En cauda venenum: (A Latín Proverb) meaning "the poison is in the tail". Can be used instead of the phrase "the worst is yet to come," or "save the worst for last."

Krav Maga: (Hebrew: קְרָב מַגָּע kʁav ma'ga) Meaning "contact combat" is a self-defense system developed for the military in Israel that consists of a wide combination of techniques sourced from boxing, kick-boxing, grappling and realistic fighting; combined with Thai, Chinese, and Japanese martial arts.

Sun Tzu: (Chinese, 孫子 *SOON-zuh*) Was a Chinese philosopher, military general, and strategist. Traditional accounts place him as a minister to King Helü of Wu. It is believed that Sun Tzu wrote the Art of War during his service to King Helü around 544–496 BC. His writing is full of Taoist influenced strategies, with Daoist rhetorical components. It is a foundational book on the strategies and psychology of warfare and is studied by many militaries around the world. The *Art of War* is one of the worlds oldest written works. Along with Homer's *Iliad* and *Odyssey,* the Sumerian *Epic of Gilgamesh* and parts of the *Tanakh* (namely the *Pentateuch,* often referred to as the five books of Moses).

Kafir: *(Arabic,* كافر *kāfir)* Loosely meaning "unbeliever," "disbeliever," or "infidel," it is a provocative slur used in a Islamic doctrinal insult or derision.

Valdez, Costa Concordi, Doña Paz or the Sewol: Are all modern steel ships that have met untimely ends in infamous ways; and all within the last forty years. They did so with all of the advantages of modern ship construction: redundant control systems, double hulls, watertight bulkheads, radar, sonar, diesel electric engines, modern life vests and lifeboats. The sinking of these ships had tremendous costs in lives, and/or financial, environmental, social, shipping and commercial aspects.

Magnum Opus: (Latin) meaning "great work".

Allăhu Akbar: *(Arabic,* الله أكبر 'ælə‚hu 'ak‚ba:) usually translated as "God is [the] greatest," or "God is great". It is used in various contexts by Muslims, being a common Islamic Arabic expression. It is used as an informal expression of faith, as a way to express joy or victory, to declare firm defiance or strength, in formal prayer, and in the call for prayer (adhān).

Zodiac: (boat): Is a term or generic name for rigid-hulled inflatable boats first introduced in 1967 by Tony and Edward Lee-Elliott of Flatacraft. It is used in a variety of military and civilian tasks in numerous countries.

Uzi: (Hebrew, עוזי UZI) A distinctive family of Israeli, blowback operated, sub-machine guns. They were invented by IDF Major Uziel Gal in the late 1940s. Introduced to the public under full production in 1954. A number of countries still use it today.

Davit: A small crane, usually mounted to a ship, for hoisting or lowering small boats, anchors, cargo or lifeboats.

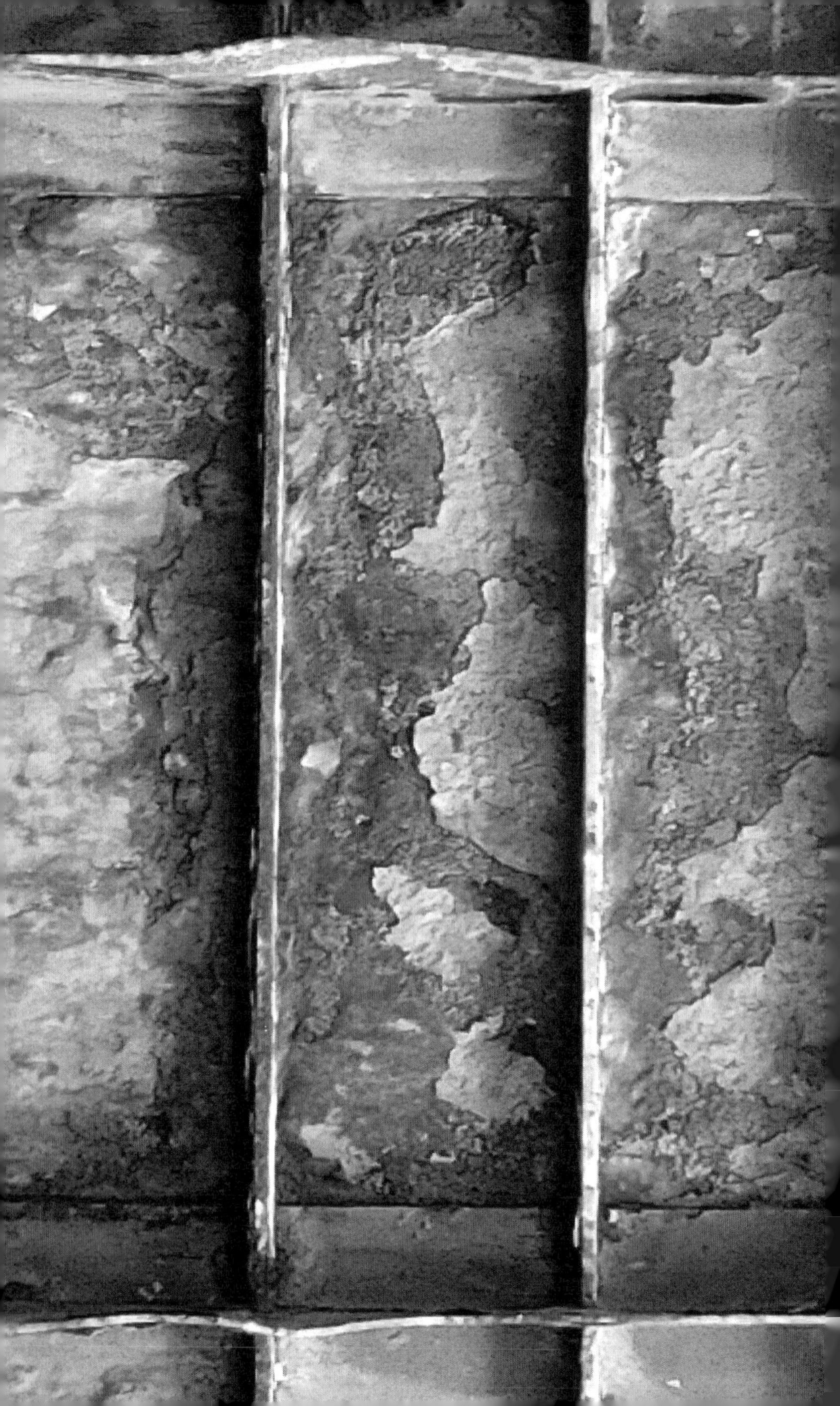

Postscript

> "The only thing necessary for the triumph of evil is for good men to do nothing."
>
> --Sir Edmund Burke

In the concern over international and domestic terrorism, disquiet for weakening liberties and the graphic mass shootings all over our country; this story idea started to develop.

Over the past few years we, as a country, have asked ourselves collectively, why? We have, collectively, faced horrific and terrible instances of depraved human evil, domestically and abroad. These instances beg for us to take action, right?

In light of this inhuman violence, how are we supposed to react?

Where and how should our measures take place? At the city and county level? At the state or national level? Or there, in the moment; at the point of fruition, within the hands of an appropriately trained and armed citizen?

Do we need to do something about the mentally ill, the guns, or both? Or neither? Why would a citizen give away their rights, and their liberties, in order for more security? Are regular citizens expected to rely *solely* on the brave people in uniform for their personal safety?

In this day and age, can or should, the regular citizen be empowered to take action on their own behalf? Regardless of what the local, state, or federal law lays out?

Be they evil men, or insane ones, must they be stopped by any means, no matter what the action? If so, what is the cost to our liberties and our freedoms? Benjamin Franklin wrote "Those who desire to give up freedom in order to gain security will not have, nor do they deserve, either one." Isn't this still true?

More and more, our culture relies upon, an ever growing federal, state and county bureaucracies to keep us safe. These civil services feed us, house us, give us loans and schools us. Where is America's vaunted individualism in all of that?

We stopped teaching in the schools and in church that there are consequences for your choices, both good and bad. We raise children to no longer act selflessly, with great courage always, obeying a higher law. We keep them away from experiencing defeat and loss; insulating them within a reality that is far different from the one they will soon face. We demonstrate to them, from the moment that they can walk; risk is not without pain, freedom is free and all they need to do is just rely on the government.

What about heroism? And the celebration of heroism? I am not talking about the "be a hero plant a tree" or the "be a hero don't drink and drive" types. Now, both of those actions are beneficial, sure, but hero status?

I know this still happens in some places, but what happened to the wide encouragement we would give our children to say thank you to soldiers, police, and emergency responders while those people are in uniform, these heroes? Especially, when we see them on the street? Or are there no more true heroes'? No one left to rise up and take a stand to protect their fellow citizens and possibly pay the highest price?

I believe, that this is still a world, that if it was without heroes, it would be no safe place at all.

What ever happened to the Golden Rule? Isn't what John wrote two millennia ago still true: "No one shows greater love, than when they lay down their life for their friends?"

It was this author's goal to describe a possible scenario where wolves, sheep and dogs, people of all types, have to deal with these concepts. The 'everymen' that try to live by the Golden Rule and the wolves that do not. Some that operate in a violent world, filled with hate, and some that live in a world where the hopes is, that everyone will act peaceably.

Where does the average citizen fail? Where would he or she succeed? Would Jayne or John Q. Public take the ultimate step or would the aforementioned citizen never take a stand?

Should a citizen kill in their own or in someone else's defense? Can they do so justifiably? In the moment, can't a citizen toss aside rights for a greater goal? Don't evil doers forfeit all rights when they act with their heinous *intent*? Is there a line drawn when it comes to protect the sanctity of innocent human life or is there any line left at all?

Has our citizenry been so limited by their government, so completely hamstrung by the numerous laws and restrictions that he or she no longer feels free to act in their own defense? Much less their countrymen's defense?

The main character functions within this new, tighter defined freedom and liberty. And yet still tries to act in a selfless way in order to protect those around him. The questions I asked before writing, as I watched the pundits and politicians talk about what they were going to do to stop gun violence, limit our rights and catch the plethora of evildoers, are numerous. But the answers fell under a simple concept:

There must be Freedom and Liberty for all, this can not be understated. This must happen without many restrictions. The freedom and liberty for all must be supported by a precious and strong originalist view of the Constitution.

Our Constitution is underlined by a society that believes in the Ten Commandments. I believe that those Commandments and the Constitution have been given to us by a Higher Moral Authority in order for all of us to live better, happier, more complete lives.

Whether you believe in God or not, upon those two written works all discussions should begin anew. There are creeping stones of liberalism, progressivism and secularism, that I believe will crush all freedom and independence. So many fear, I among them, that *this trinity* will be what eventually undermines the very foundations that our country has been built upon.

Let's just get back to the basics...please.

Blessings...

– TJ –

04/06/2012

09/1/2014

Please join me on Facebook @:
facebook.com/scarredreport

On the web@
www.tjscar.com

On Twitter @
tjscar@ **scarredreport**

Or Email: **tj@tjscar.com**